TO THE VICTOR

Jeffrey Stevenson

FIRST EIKON EDICO EDITION, 2019

ACKNOWLEDGMENTS
Scripture quotations are taken from the Holy Bible, New International Version®, NIV®. Copyright © 1973, 1978, 1984, 2011 by Biblica, Inc.™ Used by permission of Zondervan. All rights reserved worldwide.

Book & cover design by:
Eikon Edico Publishing
916 3rd Street
Clovis, CA 93612
www.eikonedi.co

Cover Art by Ryan Hite

First Printing: 2019
ISBN 978-1-672-85514-3

For Heidi - who has way more faith, patience and creativity than me. If not for you, I'd have given up long ago.

For John - Trajan's courage pales in comparison to yours.

For Ellie - Your grace and tenacity will serve as inspiration for countless tales to come.

For Izzy - If I'm ever at an impasse (writing or otherwise), your snuggles and joy for life help me find my way again.

If I were to name everyone who has offered help, insight, correction, support, (good) distraction, and creativity along this journey, the book would easily double in size (something my publisher would be less than pleased to see). However, I'd be remiss if I didn't offer a heartfelt, but simple THANKS to Michael, Alex, Ben, Bic, John and Mark. The Inklings have nothing on you.

"Now get up and go into the city, and you will be told what you must do."
~Acts 9:6~

Prologue

Our survival is dependent on the sacrifice of singular men and women, gifted in the art of death. Unwavering in their dedication to protect their citizens from the torture of truewar. Their violence gives us peace. And we give them glory in the highest. Our worship gives them the strength to stand in hell and fight back the demons of our past.

These words were written by our Ruling Ancestors hundreds of years ago and we still hold dearly to them. I repeat them silently as I follow my Mentor, Tori Motodada, through a corridor of perfectly white marble. Today I will embrace my mandate and become my nation's General.

We stop in front of two gold-plated doors, ten meters tall. The left door is inlaid with a platinum eagle, clutching a spear. The door on the right holds a mirror image of the eagle, but this one is shredding a viper between its talons. These are the symbols of my nation and behind them is the great hall where my Ruler, Demetrius, awaits to bestow my honor upon me.

Tori turns to me, inspecting the drape of my ceremonial robe. On my belt is the sword of my predecessor. A token of my victory, which I will present to Demetrius as a sign of my allegiance. Tori adjusts the hilt slightly, then rubs away the smudge left by his hand.

"You will be a great General, Trajan," he says. His voice is barely a whisper, but I can hear the pride behind it. He has been by my side for the last decade. Teaching, inspiring, nurturing and disciplining. My skill is his. What character I possess has been infused by him.

"We will serve Celsus proudly, and she will honor us," I say. He flinches slightly at the name of my nation. I often forget he is not a native Celcean. He was the General of another nation, which fell when my predecessor defeated him in Battle. "Thank you for your lessons, Moto-San. This ceremony honors you as much as it does me."

He straightens to full height, still a head shorter than me, and we lock eyes, "This is the beginning of the race, not the end. Now is not the time for sentimentality."

I nod while suppressing a smile. This is why Tori is the perfect Mentor. No matter how accomplished I become, he is quick to provide a sobering perspective.

There is a low rumble as the doors begin to swing open. Tori moves to my right and takes a step behind me. As the doors part, we are met with ear-splitting applause. The great hall is the crown jewel of Celcean political power. Two thousand square meters covered by a dome of shimmering amethyst, the great hall highlights the wealth and innovation of the world's most prosperous nation. The polished granite floors reflect the pure light of hovering chandeliers, and the sculptures that cover the walls depict the feats of our nation, from ancient times through the lost years, and as we rose once more from the ashes of failed civilizations.

Seated on a silver throne at the center of the hall is Demetrius. The father of Celsus. My Ruler. I will be his right arm for the rest of my life, or until a more powerful General takes my place. I have dreamt of this moment since I was five years old when I was chosen to begin my training, but as I stand at the threshold, my legs feel wooden.

The hall is stuffed with the Celcean elite, all of them basking in the honor of my young achievement. A swirling cloud of insect-sized drones hovers above the crowd. Each one programmed to capture this moment from every angle so their owners can broadcast their own unique perspective of the event. Every second I hesitate, hundreds of thousands of minuscule cameras zoom in, inspecting each breath I take, hoping to capture the slight curl of my lip or a tiny bead of sweat so their subscribers can feel as if they too are here. I feel a gentle hand rest on my shoulder. Tori offering his subtle encouragement. The anxiety immediately fades, and I take my first step toward Demetrius and my future.

Demetrius stands as I kneel before him. The rest of the audience in the great hall follows my lead and, for the first time since entering, there is silence. My ears, however, continue to ring with the echoes of the adoration.

"Rise, Trajan, and greet your emperor," Demetrius bellows. I stand, causing him to strain his neck upward to keep eye contact. "Your physique is a blessing. Perfect in every way. All around the world, the Generals of dishonorable Rulers must be numbering their days." The audience roars their approval as he raises his hands, inviting them to admire me. The second he drops his hands, the hall quiets again.

"This day, we celebrate the fulfillment of the will of our Ruling Ancestors." His voice carries easily throughout the hall, magnified by the acoustics of the room as well as the hovering minidrones, capturing every breath and movement in their perfectly tuned mechanisms. "Yours, my young champion, is a mantle which was set before you long ago, when humanity once again crawled out of the mire of chaos and hatred, following the bravery and sacrifice of the Twelve Ancestors."

Above us, the domed ceiling comes alive with the images of the Ruling Ancestors. Each one of them scarred and broken by the horrors of the lost years from which they rescued us. Each one of them clothed in the robes of kings, seated on golden thrones, watching over the new world they forged. Awe-filled silence settles over the hall as we gaze at our Ancestors, reflecting on the terrible life we would be living if they hadn't paved a truer way for us.

"These ceremonies are so very valuable," Demetrius says, breaking our revelry, "they give us the opportunity to reflect on the path which led us to where we stand. They show us the shoulders of the giants on which we stand, and the burdens of the tormentors we must carry in our shame."

The cloud of drones contracts and expands as they jockey for the best angle to record our Ruler's words. It has been close to a decade since Celsus last christened a new General and, given my age and skill, it will be at least that long until this occasion is repeated.

Demetrius gestures to the sculptures imbedded in the walls. "Celsus has always been a great nation. In ancient times, our borders grew as we followed the ideals of our twin founders. Weaned by wolves, they pursued the betterment of humanity with the animalistic aggression of their surrogates. And in spite of the gifts they lavished on the world, they eventually fell prey to the temptation of truewar, building the strongest army the world had ever known. And, in their jealousy, other Rulers grew their own militaries. First to oppose, then to conquer." His eyes have not left the violent sculptures which surround us.

I remain silent, paying tribute to the might of our Ancient Founders with mixed emotions. Their violence begat even worse brutality, but without it, the world would have never known the blessings of our greatest minds.

"Eventually," Demetrius says, resting his gaze back on me, "the world could no longer sustain the ease in which politicians sent their citizens into truewar. Sadly, truewar became so common that entire industries arose with the sole focus of making devices to annihilate as many people as efficiently as possible. While people became more adept at killing each other, our morality faded and with it, our society. Murder and barbarism became the catalyst of our demise."

In the audience, people dab tears from their eyes, mourning the devastation caused by the pride and greed of the world which existed before ours. Even the cloud of drones looks subdued.

"We need not dwell upon the global chaos that ensued. Through calamity, mankind was sent back to our earliest years. Before philosophy and mathematics and kindness. We reaped the evil that we had allowed to take such deep root in our societies. It seemed as if we had devolved into something less than even the wolves who had weaned us.

"When all seemed lost, the Ruling Ancestors stepped out of the mist and began to choke back what would have ended us. Yes, they were brutal, but one does not change the course of a river by blowing on it. As if sent by the gods, they were the first to embrace necessary violence in order to provide peace. Brick by brick, they built a wall strong enough to bend the waters toward a gentler slope. They were the first Generals. It is their lineage you inherit here, young Trajan.

"You are cut from their cloth. Uniquely equipped for life-sustaining violence. We honor you. And in so doing, we honor the Ancestors." His last sentence is drowned out by the roar of the audience. They cheer for Demetrius. They cheer for our way of life, enabled by our Ancestors. And they cheer for me. Demetrius closes his eyes and turns his gaze to the sky beyond our dome.

As the applause begins to subside, I draw the sword at my hip and turn the tip toward myself as I offer the hilt to Demetrius. "Please accept this humble gift as a token of my allegiance to you," I say.

He grasps the handle and thrusts the blade into me. It pierces the flesh just above my abdomen, but stops before it reaches muscle or bone. The audience gasps, straining to see my reaction. My face remains stone. He pulls the blade back and wipes the blood on his sleeve. "I bestow upon you the first of many wounds you will suffer as our protector. Each will bring you glory. May their scars weave a tapestry of wealth and prosperity for the citizens you live to protect."

The roar returns, sweeping away any remaining pain in my stomach. I bow, feeling my blood seep into the fabric of my robe, then turn to the audience. My charges, each one of them. If I could, I would embrace every person here and swear an oath to protect them. Instead, I bow, first to the crowd on my right. Then to those on my left. The applause grows louder as the seconds pass. Finally, as if carried by the love of the citizens around me, I march once again down the corridor. Each step leading me toward my future and the glory it will bring.

Chapter 1

I notice very little before a Battle. Not like the first time I stood in the cold prep room, waiting for the armorers to fit me with the best gear our nation had to offer. I saw everything more crisply than I ever had. But that was four Battles ago. Now, the sterility of my room, the cold, grey concrete that surrounds me merely serves as an annoyance. In fact, precisely two things interest me. Both are the cadence of breathing. Mine and Tori's.

My breath is slow, more controlled than any other time. Even though I feel the adrenaline thick and tingling in my veins, my breath simply grinds on. In and out like a metronome. I try to remember when this started-maybe in my second or third Battle? Regardless, even when I'm exerting myself, dodging weapons or grappling with someone twice my size, my breathing never changes. I should count myself lucky, but being so calm makes me wonder if I've lost something important.

Tori's breathing, on the other hand, makes him sound as if he had been running for days. His face is stone as always, but he can't stop his chest from rising and falling. "Don't underestimate him. He's small, but he's fast. You can count on the fact that when he strikes, it will be accurate and debilitating," Tori says. He pauses after each phrase, waiting for the next breath.

His anxiety calms me. Other than occasional anger over a poor training session, he shows little emotion even though he has become my surrogate father. To see his concern proves I am more than a student and he is more than a trainer.

When I was discovered, I was young. No one knows exactly how young, but I showed promise. Both physically and in my willingness to win no matter the cost. I don't have much recollection of my parents. I'm told they were part of the elite class and counted it a privilege that their son demonstrated qualities that would help our nation. This is easy for me to believe. Ever since then, my version of family has been people dedicated to ensuring our nation remains the most dominant and influential on earth.

"You've prepared me well, Moto-San," I say.

The Armorers work quickly on my uniform, racing to finalize their last-minute alterations before for my audience with Demetrius.

I'm taken to a room under the Temple of the Twelve where it's just Tori and me. The walls are covered in mirrors and cameras. I can see myself from every angle, as can the spectators awaiting my contest. It's the first time they can see me and, from the roar above, I can tell they are impressed. I hear a crack behind me, and I instantly drop into a crouch, sweeping my left leg behind me at knee level.

Tori swings a titanium rod at me, the arc of it passing where my head would have been. My foot catches him off balance and his knee buckles. If we were really sparring, I would have never caught him so easily. But my training for this Battle ended weeks ago and this is merely a sprinkle of salt on the tongues of the Crowd. They respond accordingly, enjoying the action, not realizing how rudimentary the exercise really is.

"The suit feels good," I say. It's true. Even though every inch of me is covered in some of the most impenetrable armor known to man, it feels light and unendingly malleable on my body. I glance in the mirror and see a warrior staring back. I feel as if I could balance this entire structure on my back.

"Don't count on the suit. Your opponent will expect you to be well protected. He'll seek to gain the advantage in some other way." Tori takes the hand I've extended to him and I pull him to his feet. "Take a moment to review your problem-solving techniques. My guess is he'll come at you quickly, but the true victory will be a mental one."

These are all things we've discussed before, but Tori likes to remind me of our strategy, as any good Mentor would. He's right, or course. Until the Battle actually starts, we have no idea what the engagement will be. We only have past contests to review. It's a fail-safe rule the Ruling Ancestors implemented. Since I've been General, my nation has never been challenged, so I've gone into every contest guessing at the Battle I'm about to fight.

The Ruling Ancestors survived and guided us through the darkest time in the planet's history. This is the mantra we're all taught from the time we can talk. Our entire life revolves around the few simple rules they set for us. They changed our planet after everything else failed. After nations rose and fell. After we vainly attempted to unite all people under one banner. After corporations tried to play the part of the government. Mankind eventually got so desperate, society devolved into total chaos. These were the worst years of all. No rule. City-states and anarchy. Morality was decided through brutality. Much of the technology humans had developed was lost. Eventually, after countless generations, the Ruling Ancestors rose up and united to form the structure in which we now live. Their vision was simple: Peace Through Equality. They divided the world into twenty-four nations, each the exact size of the other. Each with one Ruler who could decide on the system of government for their nation. Each with the mandate to rule humbly. Seeking the betterment of their citizens over anything else.

Before they could give us peace, the Ancestors violently wrenched the world from the clutches of the madmen who had seized it. They emerged victorious, but scarred. Warriors at heart, yet weary of death, they spent the rest of their lives setting up the world government which guides us today. Most importantly, they gave us the Battle. Once a year, if a Ruler chooses, he may pit his General against the General of another. The challenged nation decides the rules of the contest. If the aggressing nation wins, it gains control of the other. If it loses, the challenged nation takes control. Giving such an advantage to the challenged nation has proven a perfect deterrent for would-be tyrants.

Order sprung from chaos. The rules ensured a previously unknown equilibrium. It wasn't about big armies or better technology anymore. It was one General against another. It took years for a nation to challenge another. When it finally happened, the Battle became an instant phenomenon. Now, every year, citizens from all over the world travel to The Temple of the Twelve in the South Pole, the only neutral ground on the planet, to witness the Battle.

Tori walks around me in a slow circle. I watch as the cameras in the room do the same, mimicking Tori's scrutiny. Right now, every set of eyes on Earth are fixed on me, wondering what the challenge will be. Wondering if I'm up to the task yet again.

His voice is low and his breathing seems to have calmed as he begins the chant he's recited before every one of my matches. "One man, a nation on his shoulders. Another man, everything to lose. To the victor be the glory. To the victor, immortality."

He repeats himself over and over, his voice rising with each finished verse. After the third time, I don't just hear his voice, I hear the Crowd above me chanting as well. I wonder what the battlefloor in the middle of the Temple looks like. I wonder what it would be like to witness one of these Battles simply as a spectator, not scrutinizing a potential opponent, or evaluating what technique I'd use if it was me doing Battle.

The chanting comes to an abrupt stop as my guide enters the room. The guides are always beautiful and exotic. This one looks like she's from one of the water nations. Her hair is as golden as the sun and her skin is deep brown, contrasted by the aqua gown which flows loosely around her body. I wonder briefly if the Crowd stopped its chanting because of her beauty or because her presence signals the impending Battle.

Tori bows deeply to her, as is his tradition, and turns to me. "To the

4

victor, Trajan. You are that victor." He rests his hands on my shoulders and gives me a jolting shove. It's almost enough to make me step back in order to gain my balance, but I tighten my core as hard as possible, not wanting him, or the Crowd, to think I'm off my guard. He smiles, content with my focus. "Enjoy your conversation."

Chapter 2

My guide practically glides down the corridor that leads to Demetrius. She doesn't say anything to me, but I catch her glancing at me from time to time. It has always irritated me, the use of such distracting women. The pageantry of their dress and the elegance of their demeanor seem an affront to the actual brutality of the Battles. In all likelihood, in just a matter of minutes, a man will die at the hands of another.

We round a corner and I see the door that leads to my Ruler's chambers. Light streams through the seams of the frame and I imagine Demetrius, regally dressed with his attendants fulfilling his every need. He's a good Ruler. His people are wealthy, healthy and well respected in the world. We're one of the few nations whose citizens can travel from country to country without having to pay transfer fees or worry about being taken advantage of.

But there's an unmistakable edge to him. As the Ruler of the most prosperous nation on earth, he feels a deep responsibility to protect all citizens. Not just Celceans. The fact that I'm entering my fifth Battle is unprecedented, and proof of his willingness to risk everything if it means rescuing people of other nations from a misguided Ruler.

Just before we arrive at his door, my guide stops and turns to me. "This life you live, it is a good one, yes?" she asks. Her accent is alluring, and the tone of her voice is tinged with the sound of wind on sails.

I'm taken off guard for a moment. It's not unusual for a guide to whisper encouragement, even bestow a motivating kiss. But this question, just before Battle, is strange.

"I couldn't imagine another," I say. This guide is different than any previous. Her gaze is less differential than the silent guides I've had in the past. Most are happy to be seen with a General. She, however, seems ready to sit down with me and discuss philosophy. Any other time, the prospect of such a conversation with a beautiful woman would be welcome, but now I find myself irritated by the distraction. I turn and step toward the door, even though tradition calls for her to announce my arrival.

She puts a hand on my armor laden arm and dips her head. I imagine how callused her hands must be, constantly tying ropes and mending fishing nets, and I wish I could feel the grittiness on my skin.

"My apologies. One moment, please," she says and steps past me to the door. I wait while she knocks and is summoned.

I hear her voice as she gives the customary greeting to Demetrius and then I hear my title, Trajan, General of Celsus, humble servant to Demetrius. The first time I heard that title, I was a fifteen-year-old, wide eyed and terrified General. That Battle was the bloodiest I've ever experienced. The General I faced was well past his prime. He'd given up on strategy and simply came at me hoping to intimidate and overpower me. Our fight lasted for hours and they had to drag me from the battlefloor. They determined the winner by checking our pulse. Mine was barely there. His wasn't.

"General!" Demetrius bellows. My guide bows deeply and backs out of the room. Once she's cleared the door, she turns toward me and places her hand on my face. The hands I'd imagined as calloused are soft and smooth. I briefly consider returning the gesture, but I resist and chide myself for my continued mental lapses.

I quickly enter Demetrius's quarters and drop to a knee. "My lord," I say.

A minidrone hovers silently in the middle of the room, waiting to capture a meaningful gesture or a fumbled word.

"Rise, my champion. Let the world look on your splendor. The pride of Celsus." He crosses the room, arms open wide and embraces me. He's a smaller man than me, but his embrace makes me feel tiny and frail. I wrap my arms around him as well and we stand silently for a few seconds. I wait for Demetrius to back away before releasing my grasp.

He backs to an arm's length and appraises me. "Good. I spared no expense on your armor. Although, the General you're fighting is known more for his agility than his brutality."

"I'm grateful for your provision, as always, Highness," I say quietly. These moments of staged intimacy have always made me uncomfortable, but I see the need for us to show the world our love and trust for one another.

In the corner of my eye, I see movement. Usually, that wouldn't be startling. Demetrius is constantly surrounded by countless servants, each focused on a singular responsibility. But this movement is of someone much larger than a typical servant, so I break from our routine and turn toward it.

Fidgeting with a plate of sweetbreads and grapes is Castor, my protege. Demetrius is speaking again, but I can't hear him. I'm focused on Castor, trying to figure out what's going on. These audiences are supposed to be between Ruler and champion only. No Tori. No political staff or advisors. Certainly not the General heir apparent. They got their audience last night at the feast.

"My lord," I say, without looking from Castor, "may I ask why we're not alone?" As I say this, I can almost feel the gasp of the audience, hanging on our every word. I can also feel both Demetrius and Castor tense. Castor finally meets my gaze, eyes confident, stance proud, but I can see the artery in his throat throbbing. Even though he's only a couple of years my junior, Castor is very young. His only fighting experience coming from training or Mid-Year exhibition matches with other friendly nations.

"He's here, General, because I've asked him to be here," Demetrius says. "After all, he'll be standing where you are, someday soon."

"With respect, Highness, don't put me in the ground too soon," I bow, trying to soften the slight. Demetrius is a gracious Ruler, but he is not used to being questioned, especially in front of an audience. My adrenaline, it seems, has taken over even my tongue.

He laughs a hearty and long laugh and puts a slice of pear in his mouth. "My dear Trajan, your hubris, it's what makes you such a great General. Every time you set foot on the Temple floor, you're utterly convinced of your victory. But know this, my boy, no matter how much confidence you have, age will always best you," he says.

Age. With all the medical technology we have available to us, I could fight, and win, well into my sixties. I've seen nations with Generals as old as that, who are far less advanced as we. There's no point, however, pushing this conversation any further. My opponent is watching this, and I don't want him to have any more leverage than he already does.

I bow my head and say, "Thank you, Highness. Of course, you're right. I'm merely happy to be able to serve you and my nation today in Battle. Castor is certainly a fitting heir, if you deem him so." I hear the crowd cheer and I see Demetrius relax his shoulders. "Come, Castor, let us learn from our father," I say.

Castor, who has been silently waiting for us to acknowledge him, walks tentatively over. He's in perfect shape and stands slightly taller than me, which means he also towers over just about everyone he encounters. I wear my hair shaved closely, a lesson I learned in my third Battle. Even though I've advised him against it, his hair flows in waves to his shoulders. There isn't a scar on his body. Any wounds he received in training have been minor enough for our physicians to repair in their entirety. My skin is another story, riddled with reminders from fallen Generals. Tori calls me a walking tribute to the dead.

Demetrius sits and beckons us to do the same. As is tradition, his speech begins with a brief history of Celsus. He goes back so far that the story is more fairy-tale than history. With sadness he talks about how this empire, he calls it Rome, fell because of apathy and lack of discipline. Then the years of marginalization, when Rome was called Italy and it held no more power or influence than any other average nation. Then the abolishment of nations. Then hell on earth.

I look at Castor. He's wide-eyed, soaking in every word. When Demetrius is sad, Castor is near tears. When he's excited, Castor literally trembles with energy. I'm not unfazed by the speech. Once Demetrius speaks of the Ruling Elders and how they had to unite in a tenuous truce to oppose a warlord who had grown too powerful and ruthless, even though I know the story, I silently root for their victory because I know it will lead to the forming of the peaceful nations.

"We repeat our history often because it serves to remind us of how, even now, our nature fights to wrestle us back to savagery. This is why I wield you as my General so aggressively, Trajan." His eyes lock on me with a withering focus. "We risk everything today in the hopes of saving a few. Always remember, no matter how privileged we become, we will never be more important than those who need us. Defend us. But more importantly, defend those who are trapped under the Comumbran Ruler. Liberate them so they can finally understand the true blessings of our Ruling Ancestors."

"I only pray, my lord, that my defense of our nation will make you proud," I say. This isn't for the cameras, although I can hear the Crowd roar at my words.

"Of course, you do, Trajan. Your humility powers you. But know this, if you are to fall, the Comumbran Ruler has declared to lay waste to our cities as punishment for challenging him." Demetrius pauses, letting this news settle on me. For the first time in years, I feel my breath and pulse quicken. It makes the Battle I'm about to enter more real, more desperate than ever.

While this declaration is not against the rules, it's the most aggressive thing I've ever heard of. Usually, a challenged nation is happy to take over the governance of the aggressing nation in name only, leaving most of the customs and infrastructure intact. It's easier to govern that way. But the Comumbran Ruler has chosen to make a statement. If I lose, millions of people would be displaced by the vengeance of an offended tyrant.

The next thing I hear is the familiar tone, telling me to make my way to the battlefloor. It's one note, long and somber. Renewed adrenaline flows through my body and everything vanishes. The fear of losing my home, of letting Demetrius and my nation down, or not walking out of the Temple snaps out of existence. There are only two things left. My opponent and me.

My guide reappears and bows deeply, apologizing for the inevitable interruption. She doesn't say anything else, just looks at me and motions for me to follow her. I nod and rise in front of Demetrius.

"Our fate rests on your mighty shoulders, Trajan," Demetrius says.

"Kill him quickly. I don't want you too tired in training tomorrow," Castor says.

Chapter 3

The beauty of my guide does nothing to distract me this time. I think of nothing but my training and try to predict what the Battle will be. The Comumbran General, Hestor, is small but fast. There's nothing that says we must actually fight. Our Battle could be a chess match. It could be a race to solve a puzzle the fastest. It could even be a test of combat skills, like archery or marksmanship. Hestor already knows and he's been refining his skill for this specific Battle since Demetrius announced the challenge, while I've been honing skills that could be applied broadly.

My guide glides to a stop in front of an enormous iron door. I'll lose the cameras that have been following me once I walk through this door. Tori will be there and we'll have five minutes, no more, no less, to finalize our strategy. Then the platform will rise, and I'll be in the middle of the Temple. No speeches or politics or conjecture. Just me trying to survive.

The door shutters and rises with an ear-shredding shriek. I look to my guide, who stands motionless in front of me, hands clasped at her waist. The air here is cool, which makes me think the battlefloor is exposed to the Antarctic elements, and I can see goosebumps travel up and down her bare arms. I have the urge to warm her with an embrace. I wonder how the Crowd would react if I did. Maybe Hestor would let his guard down if he thought I wasn't completely focused.

Tori stands in the middle of the plain room, hands at his sides, eyes closed. Unlike earlier, he is the picture of serenity. As soon as I'm in the room, the door drops with a violent clang. The last thing I see is my guide turning to hurry back to a warmer viewing room.

"Any idea what's out there?" I ask. I can feel my pulse calming. There's nothing else I can do. No more training, no edge to be gained. All I can do now is wait and let my instincts take over.

"Uncertainty. A General who believes his motives are as just as yours. The love of the Crowd." He walks around me, performing a final check for anything the armorers may have missed.

"Try as I might, I fail to see how any General could fight for a Ruler who vows to hurt innocent citizens. It's in direct opposition to the Ancestors," I say.

He stops in front of me. Satisfied with what he's seen. "A poisonous berry does not blame its deadly nature on the plant which nourished it. Hestor fights for the only way of life he has ever known. If he reacted any other way, I would be astounded."

I look up at the giant clock. Second after second falls away, driving me closer to blood and pain. Less than one minute until the roar of the Crowd and the fury and the punishment.

"Let the Battle decide who is right, my son. Win. Win decisively." He's yelling now, as the solid stone wall begins to swing open. The icy air and the lust-filled roar of the Crowd eclipse anything else he has to say.

As I walk through the opening, everything falls away. This is what I'm made for. This is all I know. I'm home.

Chapter 4

Since I'm the aggressor, I'm introduced first. A one hundred meter wide display plays highlights of my past victories for the Crowd. I can't see it, but I can hear the reaction of the citizens as they watch my most brutal moments. My first victory when I won despite suffering a broken elbow and shattered jaw. The third Battle against the biggest General I've ever faced. His weapon of choice, a club which injected poison upon contact. Last year's Battle when the rules dictated I had to fight blindfolded. Out of respect, the Crowd quieted to a whisper so I could hear the crunch of my opponent's feet, the expansion of his lungs.

I look over the battlefloor. A barren ice field, as flat as a frozen pond with only a few snow drifts here and there. If it stays like this, I'll have an advantage regardless of the rules of engagement. But it won't. I know that somewhere, hidden under the drifts or invisibly suspended above me, are modifications which will change the playing floor mid-Battle. Each one of these modifications will have been designed to give my opponent a distinct advantage over me.

The cheering settles to an anticipatory rumble as they wait for Hestor to emerge. He's younger than I am and I know surprisingly little of him. He's refrained from participating in many of the Mid-Year exhibitions. The only time I've seen him in action was in a foot race which required him to change course mid-stride. Demetrius and Tori are right, he was one of the quickest people I'd ever seen move. But that couldn't be the only reason he's been chosen as his nation's General and I wish I could see his highlights as he enters the battlefloor.

I see the wall open across the battlefloor and I hear the Crowd's reaction. Instead of the usual cheers, I hear taunts and jeers. Even though not all are Celceans, they root for me. Their adoration sustains and invigorates me. Demetrius says their love is proof of my virtue. Tori tells me they are fickle and love me because I make the world predictable. Either way, they have aligned themselves behind me and I will not let them down. I stand straight and salute toward my opponent, giving him his due respect.

When my opponent's face emerges from shadow, the Crowd and I both gasp. This is not Hestor. Instead, I see one of the largest men I've ever seen. His skin is tight leather across his body and his arms are at least as thick as my legs. This man must have been genetically engineered. Compared to him, I may as well be a child. In an unprecedented turn, a screen rises in front of me.

I can tell I'm watching the same video as the rest of the Crowd. In it, this hulk is shown chopping a tree down with one swing, lifting a huge piece of farm equipment over his head. Then he's shown in a sparring ring, Hestor opposite him. Hestor juts and spins, throwing well-placed fists, elbows and knees. My opponent doesn't flinch. Rather, when Hestor fails to escape fast enough, I watch as he's seized by the neck, lifted high in the air and driven into the mat. I don't need to watch any more to know Hestor's neck was broken and his skull smashed.

I look toward my opponent. He's not looking at me as I would have expected. Instead, he looks like a child in an amusement park, spinning and gawking at his surroundings.

I've fought men bigger than me before so I wait, knowing the rules of this match will put an even more lethal spin on this surprise. I don't wait long. Within seconds, I hear the Crowd fall silent as their knowlinks begin to pull as much information about the Comumbran General and my past Battles as they can. Certain facts have been seeded by our respective nations while others are pulled from as many data archives as possible.

My opponent and I don't have our knowlinks in, so the Temple screen serves as our informant. At the same time, twenty broadcast drones enter the battlefloor. These are much larger than the thousands of personal recording drones which hover above their owners in the Crowd. Rather, these are equipped with hundreds of microphones and cameras. All of them specifically designed so each strike and pain filled scream are captured from as many angles as possible.

It's coming from the hovering stage that Braddock, the Temple's play by play man, uses to give commentary on the Battle. From it, he will announce the rules and analyze the fight for the Crowd. His stage is also equipped with hundreds of microphones and cameras–all of it specifically designed to enhance the brutality of our Battle.

I look at my opponent again. He still hasn't looked at me and is crouched, sifting the dry snow through his enormous, gloved hands. For the first time, I begin to evaluate his dress. He's covered in fur. Thick pelts of what look to be bearskin. His pants are made of the same material. The only exposed skin is his face, which looks oddly childlike.

The screen shows a live feed of me with my name and Battle statistics below. *Trajan, General of Celsus. Servant to Demetrius and victor of four Battles. Undefeated in sixteen mid-year and exhibition Battles. Fastest victory; twenty-three seconds.* Even though the Crowd is immersed in their knowlinks, they roar their approval.

After the cheers die down, my opponent's face appears. *Seth. Freshman General of Comumbra. Former farmer. One win: defeated Hestor in seven seconds by crushing his skull to earn the right to defend his nation.* The text fades away, but Seth's face remains. He peers into the camera and says, "Trajan will die here today. And as he dies, so will the spread of the Celcean virus." The Crowd cheers, but not nearly as fervently as it did when I was announced.

Across from me, Seth stands to full height and scans the Crowd. He turns his back to me as he spins and, if I hadn't seen his human face just moments before, I could easily believe I was in an arena with a Grizzly. I now have a better idea of what I'm dealing with. My skill, obviously, is greater, but he's driven by emotion and zeal. Two things that can take an ordinary man and make him untouchable.

The Rules, flashes on the screen.

The only thing I hear is the gusting wind pushing ice and snow across the battlefloor. This is where I'll find out if any of my training for the last year was relevant. I had trained to face Hestor. Looking at Seth, I wish I'd spent the last year building more mass.

The Ruling Ancestors set a few simple principles for the Battles. The first principle requires each General to abide by the same set of rules. The second principle states that the nation being challenged can choose any contest they want. The third is that no matter what happens in the Temple, no nation can challenge the outcome of the Battle.

The Comumbran Emperor has stipulated the following requirements. Rule one. No armor allowed.

I immediately begin to strip the lightweight suit from my body. When I'm done taking it off, all I have on is a thin pair of cotton underpants. The Arctic air instantaneously attacks my skin. Seth opens the fur coat he's wearing to reveal no armor underneath. He quickly wraps it across his chest. This is the first disadvantage designed for me. The Comumbrans have primitive technology compared to us and they found a way to make our arrogance a liability.

Rule two. Each General can use any and all of the ten weapons in front of them.

Five perfect and deadly weapons rise in front of each of us. My breathing is already labored, and I can feel the dexterity in my hands begin to fail. If the rules go on for too long, I won't even be able to hold these weapons. I begin to jump in place and contract my arms back and forth. If I don't keep my blood moving, I'll be frozen before the Battle begins.

One handicap exists. The Crowd cheers, excited to see what twist awaits us. *One weapon will be taken from each General for every Battle they have fought.*

Just like that, I'm down to one weapon. I'm not worried. Even with one weapon I should be able to make quick work of a farmer. I watch as each weapon sequentially disappears back under the Battlefloor. I'm left with a knife. The blade is barely ten centimeters long.

The last man standing will be declared the victor.

With this, the Crowd ignites. I can hear horns blowing and people screaming. Right now, in the seedier places, people are betting on whether or not they think I can survive these odds. They're stacked against me, which means a lot of desperate people are wagering on Seth. Hoping he kills me and, with my death, they will live a more comfortable life.

"We salute you, Generals. Your sacrifice will save millions." This is the yearly benediction, spoken with the thick accent of the Ancestors through every earpiece and broadcast screen. Seth and I hear it reverberate across the battlefloor from the speakers of all twenty drones. The last syllable signals the start of the Battle.

I move for the knife immediately and, within seconds, have made up much of the space between Seth and me. By the time I'm halfway across the floor, he has only managed to pick up the most powerful of his five weapons. A gun that uses magnetism to propel dense metal objects as fast as the speed of sound. If he gets me in his sights, I'm dead. There's no way I can dodge something like that. Even if he misses me, but comes close, the momentum of the object could easily break a bone and rip the skin from my body.

Knives have always been a specialty of mine and this one is weighted well. When I'm about seven meters from Seth, I let it loose, aiming for his right eye. He's just gotten the gun shouldered when the knife finds its mark. He cries out, drops the gun and spins from me. The cheering of the Crowd surges higher than I imagined possible. I get to the gun and consider using it, but the rules were explicit. Since I've already used the knife, I can't use anything else. Doing so would be cause for disqualification. Instead, I pick it up and smash it in two.

I can feel my movement slowing as all the blood in my body rushes to protect my core. If this Battle lasts too long, I'll be incapacitated by hypothermia. My fingers already feel as if they're moving through sand.

Seth gets up and turns toward me. I expect to see his right eye socket empty, or at least bloodied and swollen. Instead, I see a small nick under his eye and a tiny stream of blood on his cheek. Not the damage I was hoping for. We pause, sizing each other up now that we're closer. He's easily three heads taller than me and his features are chiseled from granite. With hypothermia setting in, a wrestling match would end badly for me. He doesn't appear too interested in hand to hand combat either. Instead, he looks quickly around at his weapons.

Poison mist, a spear with its own propulsion system, an electrified net and the same type of knife that I used.

Before he can react, I take the spear and throw it across the battlefloor. As soon as it leaves my hand, the propulsion system kicks in, rocketing it into the stone wall. Neither of us will have the time or the strength to remove it.

Seth has the poison mist pointed directly at me when I turn toward him again. Just as he's about to spray it, a gust of wind hits us both. Snow and ice fragments pelt him in the face which gives me the opening I need.

I duck and roll so that when I get to my feet, I'm too close for him to use the spray on me. I grab his wrist and yank it down while simultaneously bringing my knee up to his elbow. His breaking arm sounds like a tree ripping in half. The Crowd must be going nuts, but I can't hear it anymore. It's just the two of us and we're close to the end now.

His arm should be dangling at his side. Instead, I watch as he winces then begins to flex it back and forth. The wince becomes a vicious smile.

Immediately, I realize what's going on. I know why he's so big and why there was only a scratch on his face from my knife. He's been altered. Bodmods are common for laborers. Usually performed at the insistence of their owners to make them stronger, more resilient and to help them heal faster. If I had to guess, he's had his blood cells synthetically bonded with carbon, meaning his cuts will clot much faster because of the thickness. In addition, his skeleton has likely been reinforced with a composite metal that reconnects to itself if the bone fails. This changes my Battle completely.

Generals have never officially ventured into enhancements like this, preferring tradition and honor over making Battles yearly spectacles of science. Apparently, Comumbra thought differently.

I realize I've dwelt on this too long when Seth brings his enormous fist down, shattering my nose. I black out while I fall, but the ice on my torso jolts me back to life just as he drops the electrified net on me.

It feels as if I've gone from freezing to roasting. My muscles seize and, no matter how hard I try, I can't move my arms to remove the net. He turns from me and I watch as he deliberates over the poison and the knife. His inexperience shows when he comes toward me with the knife. If he had chosen the poison, the Battle would be over in seconds.

He's also showing his naiveté by waiting so long. Weapons like the net are only designed to remain charged for a brief amount of time. I can already feel the current dying as he walks toward me, flaunting the knife.

Another second and the net's charge is gone. I roll just as he throws the knife toward me. His aim is true. If I hadn't moved, the knife would have pierced my heart. Instead, it lodges in my shoulder. A painful wound, but nothing that would keep me from fighting.

Once I'm on my feet, I feel better than before the net seized me. Instinct takes over and I attack before he has time to charge. I sweep his legs and he goes down in a heap of fur and enormous limbs. Without hesitating, I stomp on his ankle and I feel it break. Working my way up his body, I break as many joints as I can find until I'm at his jaw. Finally, I focus my entire body weight on my knee and connect where the jaw meets the skull.

I know none of these breaks will remain. In fact, I'm sure he's healed most of them already, but I need a little time. I also need to intimidate him a little. Even though he's not broken, he felt every one of those breaks and I want him to think twice about that pain. I pull Seth's knife from my shoulder and, just as Seth rises from the ground, I find my blood-covered knife in a snowdrift.

Against everything Tori has taught me, I toss his knife at his feet and motion for him to take it. I've evened the playing field and I want everyone to know that a common laborer, even one with a bodmod, is no match for me. The Crowd screams and the battlefloor rumbles as I beckon him forward. I'm giving them the show they were hoping for.

In spite of the adrenaline in my system, I'm moving slower every second. The wind gusts are Seth's closest ally, at this point. He knows he's outmatched and has backed away from my reach. All he has to do is avoid me and the cold will do the rest.

My stupidity infuriates me. When Demetrius revealed the armor, I was nervous about using it as my protection from the elements, but I didn't want to offend him. Now, as I stand here, my body systematically shutting down, it's obvious to me that, if I lose, I'll lose because I was too timid to ask for a coat. Instead of being a warrior, I tried to please my Ruler.

The hum of one of the bigger drones interrupts my thoughts and I can feel the exhaust heat of its engines. I've never thought of using drones as a tool in a Battle, but I've never been in this situation before. Seth stands a few meters from me, obviously waiting for me to attack. It's a smart move, which makes me even angrier.

The drone is easily ten feet above me. Well out of reach even if my blood wasn't turning to slush. I'll have to figure out a way to lure it as close as possible. Blood. The cameras are drawn by it more powerfully than sharks. I've seen them come to within centimeters of a fight in pursuit of perfectly captured spilling blood.

I lift my tiny knife and cut a deep gash across my chest. The pain is tolerable, but I play to the Crowd and it works. The roaring becomes a gasp, then silence as I fall to my knees. The ice below me begins to melt, then pool red as it mixes with my blood. I hear the drone repositioning closer for a better view, so I lower my shoulder, masking the diagonal slice in my flesh.

As it maneuvers closer, I see Seth charging. His face is contorted into a snarl. The blade of his knife flashes every time he pumps his arm. It's a bull rush, meant to overpower and submit me. For an instant, I think about abandoning my plan and take my chances with Seth. But I'm at too much of a disadvantage. My entire body is numb and I'm moving much too slowly. If I stay, Seth will kill me within seconds.

If there's anyone in this stadium who knows what I'm up to, it's Tori and I'm sure he's measuring the distance with me. If I've calculated the speed correctly, the drone will become close enough less than a second before Seth reaches me. My crouch subtly turns from that of an injured man to that of a coiled spring. I try to focus all of my strength to my legs and force my breathing higher, hoping to oxygenate my blood as much as possible. The Crowd is on their feet, screaming. Half warning me of Seth, the other half anticipating my death.

The heat of the engines pour over me and I know it's time. With as much energy as I can muster, I explode, using equal parts technique and power to lift myself off the ground.

Silence. No Crowd, no engines, no charging opponent. It feels as if I'm the only thing in the world that's moving. I open my eyes and see snowflakes paused in midair as I rise above them. The drone gets closer and closer, but I immediately realize I haven't gotten enough lift to reach the top. I hear Seth roar below me and I feel a dull impact on my leg, but nothing else. Maybe he lunged for me and missed. Right now, I don't care. I swing my miniature knife and sink it into the soft metal side of the drone. The blade easily penetrates it and holds.

The impact triggers the drone's impact protocol, causing it to immediately lift higher. I'm not directly in the exhaust of the engines, but they're putting off enough heat to begin warming me. The drone climbs higher and higher until we're at least two hundred meters above the battlefloor. Even though I didn't think it was possible, the air up here is colder than before, but the engines are doing what I expected them to. With every minute that passes, I can feel my joints loosening and strength returning. I see Seth on the giant screen. He's staring straight up, yelling with his arms outstretched. Below me, I'm sure the Crowd is going nuts, cursing me for what they perceive to be my cowardice. But I'm not done with this Battle. I'm just taking a moment to regroup.

The first thing that comes to mind is the knife that's lodged in the side of the drone. I'm sure the thin metal is close to its breaking point. In fact, now that I'm up here, I'm shocked it's strong enough to hold my weight, and I don't want to tempt fate any more than I already have.

Even though my strength is returning, I'm still extremely weak. It takes everything in me to pull myself up high enough to get a grip on the top of the drone and lift my body up. The machine is coated with some sort of rubberized surface to ensure it's not damaged too badly in the event of a collision. In spite of having no walls, the temperature is warm and comfortable. Once I'm fully on the drone, I roll to my back and take a couple of deep breaths. The heat washes over my body and for a serene moment, I forget what's below me.

In a control room, somewhere deep in the Temple, a group of engineers work to override the drone's programming. It's a matter of seconds until it plummets me back to the battlefloor and Seth's waiting arms. I need to take full advantage of this time.

As my body warms up, I begin to feel the pain of my wounds. Worse yet, I notice an enormous gash across my Achilles. A parting gift from Seth as the drone lifted me. Blood flows freely from the wound, coating the top of the drone and spilling over the side toward the battlefloor. I remember feeling the impact of the blow but had no idea the wound was this bad. Further proof of just how debilitated from the cold my body had become.

I cut a long, thin strip of the rubbery surface from the drone. It's pliable enough to serve nicely as a compression bandage over my Achilles, stopping the bleeding momentarily. Still, I'll have to fight one legged if I want to have any chance of not severing the tendon the rest of the way. As I secure the last knot, I feel the drone drop beneath me. The engineers are in control and, given the speed of my descent, they want me back on the battlefloor immediately.

As the drone drops, I stand, testing my bandage and the strength of my wound. The bandage holds, but the tendon is weak enough that I may as well be one legged. Another drone maneuvers next to me and I immediately hear the Crowd come to life beneath me. I can see the lens of the second drone zoom in on my bandage, then move to my blood-soaked platform. Along with the Crowd, Seth now knows my vulnerability.

I know he'll be ready, placing himself directly beneath the drone so he can attack me as soon as I climb down. Something I don't plan on doing. When I'm about twenty meters from the ground, I pick out a snow drift that looks deep enough to break my fall and far enough to allow me to gather myself before he gets there. The drone's progress is steady enough for me to feel comfortable about my jump.

Just as I'm about to jump, the drone tilts, first left, then right, sending me plummeting. The drift on which I had planned on landing is no longer an option. Instead, I rocket directly toward Seth. He's as surprised as me. Less than a second later, I crash into him. His body crumbles under me, but the impact is equally as painful for me. I roll off him and stumble into a defensive stance.

"I'd hoped for more from you, General," he says as he lunges for me. His gloves are packed with snow, which means he's been searching through the battlefloor, trying to find his other weapons. From the looks of it, I don't think he found any of them.

His attack is the same as it has been, fast and without nuance. I kneel and, using his momentum against him, send him flying over me. My leg cries out in pain, but I push it back. Nursing the injury will only get me killed faster. No sense preserving a tendon if the rest of the body is dead.

Seth looms hesitantly in front of me. Most likely, his trainers had assured him I wouldn't last this long, given how they structured the rules. There's no way they could have predicted me hi-jacking a drone. If he knew how vulnerable I really am, this Battle would already be over.

The Crowd begins to chant. At first, I can't understand what they're saying. The wind is too strong. But they grow stronger as more and more of them join in the chorus. One simple phrase repeated over and over. End it.

End it. End it. I'd like to think they're talking to me. Encouraging me to overcome my injuries and walk away the victor of my sixth Battle. But the truth is probably that they don't care who wins, as long as the ending is brutal and decisive.

I look around the battlefloor, taking stock of anything that I could use to my advantage. The sparseness of the landscape seems to match the odds in my favor. Ice, snow drifts and pools of blood. My blood. The difference between Seth and me couldn't be more polarized. If he wins, he'll be an instant legend. The underdog farmer who defeated one of the most dominant Generals in modern history. He's well on his way. Warm and unharmed while I hobble around, freezing to death.

Somewhere above me, Demetrius sits, praying for my victory and for his nation. Castor, I'm sure, sits by his side, lamenting the fact he's not down here. Convinced I'm past my prime and, if he were here, the Battle would already be over, and Seth would be nothing more than a lump of flesh in a pool.

Blood. It keeps coming back to blood. The Crowd's thirst for it. My loss of it. Carbon bodmods swimming through Seth's. It's about blood.

The chant of the Crowd has grown impatient during this stalemate. Another gust of wind rips across the battlefloor as I push myself forward. I can't feel the pain in my Achilles anymore, but I can tell there's no strength in my leg either. My advance isn't as fast as I'd like, but it still takes Seth off guard.

His knife is in his right hand and he slices toward me with a wide, mistimed arc. I easily avoid it and thrust my knife up quickly, piercing his thick fur coat and digging deep into the underside of his forearm. As soon as I yank the knife away from him, I know my aim was true. A burst of deep, red blood spills out. I've hit an artery. Within seconds, the wound will clot, but there won't be as much blood left in his body. The one thing his bodmod can't do is replenish lost blood. It will take some time, but all I have to do is continue to open as many deep and vicious wounds as possible. Each time, Seth will grow weaker. As long as I can keep from getting hit with a lucky shot or freezing to death, I'll walk away victorious.

Seth doesn't react much, confident in the knowledge that he'll heal in a moment. Instead, he grabs my neck with his left hand and begins to squeeze. My vision immediately begins to blur as his powerful grip cuts off the oxygen to my brain. I stab up, catching him under the biceps. I torque the blade so it tears as much flesh as possible. It slices tendon and muscle and veins before I feel the blade nick bone.

He drops me seconds before I black out and stumbles back. I can tell the cut in his right arm has sealed already, but his left hangs limp, thick red blood flowing in rivulets off his fingers. The ground below us is red slush, which makes my footing even shakier than before.

My right leg is completely useless. I'm pretty sure the last lunge completely ripped apart what was left of my tendon. I watch as the blood stops dripping from Seth's fingers. It looks like someone simply walked up and turned off a faucet.

I can tell my strategy is working. His coloring is a little paler than it had been and I see a bead of sweat just under his hairline. The faster the blood loss, the more impact it will have. If I drain him too slowly, his heart will be able to keep up easier, so I know I need to force the action. I figure a few more well-placed slices will be enough to make him pass out.

He's either going into shock, or his blood loss has made his jacket too heavy. Regardless, he takes it off and throws it to the ground. I'm stunned at his naiveté. One of the circling drones drops down to capture the coat and all the gruesome details.

"Do you know why I volunteered to fight you?" Seth yells. The wind and roar of the Crowd makes his scream as difficult to hear as a whisper. Preferring to conserve all of my energy for the rest of the Battle, I don't respond.

While my first two strikes were on the mark, I still need to focus. The worst thing I can do is underestimate my opponent. The footage of him slamming Hestor to the ground plays through my mind as I plan my next move.

He lumbers toward me, flailing his arms wildly so that I lose sight of which hand holds his knife. I stumble back, trying to move at an angle, but the uselessness of my leg makes that impossible. Instead, I shuffle a few times before he's on top of me.

The pain of his blade passing through my ribcage is white-hot. I drop to the ground and thrust a kick at his knee, which connects. He tumbles over me and I'm able to twist just enough so I'm not his landing pad. The fall rips his knife out of his hand, but pushes it deeper into my chest, puncturing one of my lungs.

I roll as fast as I can, pushing the pain from my mind. In less than a second, I'm on top of him and have sliced through the nerve cluster in his armpit. He howls and scrambles mindlessly. His strength astounds me. Even with the blood loss, he's easily twice as powerful as I am. I know it's now or never. My blade flies in precise and efficient paths. From his underarm to his jugular, then a gash across his brow so blood will impair his vision while I reposition myself.

I'm sticky with his blood as I slide beside him and bury the knife in his inner thigh. The blade remains razor sharp as I pull it toward me, barely feeling any resistance as it severs one of the largest arteries in his body. My breathing is labored and I know I can't keep this pace much longer. I'll need to rest in order to let my one good lung catch up.

Seth still flails, but I can tell he's quickly losing strength. His throat has already healed and his brow has just a skiff of frozen blood. I'm dizzy from lack of oxygen and, no matter how hard I inhale, I don't feel myself recovering. I try to slow my breathing and heart rate through sheer force of will. After a few seconds, I can feel the effect. My breathing slows and my vision begins to focus as well.

The body of my opponent lies still next to me, his gently raising chest the only sign of life. I scoot toward him, clutching my knife tightly. He's either been weakened to the point of exhaustion, or he's baiting me. Either way, my action will be the same. Decapitation. It's the only thing I can think of that will cause enough loss of blood to end the Battle with certainty. With a blade this small, the thought borders on lunacy, but it seems the sole option I have.

As I raise the blade, I glance at his leg. It's still gushing blood. He should have healed by now, which means his blood has finally thinned. If I just sit here, he'll slip from consciousness and die peacefully.

His eyes flutter open and he takes a quick, deep breath. "Do you know why I volunteered?" His voice is barely audible above the chanting Crowd. *End it. End it.*

I lower my knife and cradle his head in my hand. "Why?" I ask. None of my Battles have ended like this. I'm known for decisive and brutal end games. But his desperation to explain himself has me intrigued.

"To prove to the world that you can be hurt. And if you can be hurt, we can stop you from conquering us all," he whispers.

Conquering. Such a different word than liberate. I know the Crowd can't hear what he's saying, but I'm sure one of the drone's microphones is picking it up.

"But you'd be free under our rule."

"Says the Pawn of Demetrius. I'd take slavery in Comumbra over freedom in Celsus." His eyes begin to dilate.

I look up to the enormous screen, expecting to see a close up of Seth, or an aerial view of the two of us. Instead, I see a small, pale woman holding what is obviously Seth's child. The features are almost identical. Both of them weep as they stare down at us while the Crowd around them screams, *End it. End it.*

The shot changes to the booth where Demetrius and Castor have been watching the Battle. Demetrius stands, his eyes huge with the anticipation of Seth's death. Castor, on the other hand is laughing, lazily popping grapes in his mouth and joining the chant when his mouth isn't too full.

I'm not surprised by what Seth says. Slaves don't realize their master is their enemy, but the image of Seth's child is too much for me. I gently lay his head back on the ground and raise my knife. The chanting wavers and becomes a wave of cheers and screams. Instead of bringing it down on his neck, I slice at his thick pants. Within seconds, I've revealed the open wound in his leg as it seeps precious blood. The Crowd quiets, unsure of what I'm about to do. I cut off the pants and slice them into thin ribbons. My fingers have stiffened from the cold again, which makes me work as quickly as I can. Once I have a few makeshift bandages, I shove them on top of the gash and tie the rest of the strips tightly, securing the bandages and creating a tourniquet. It takes all my strength, but I'm confident I've stopped the bleeding enough to be sure the physicians can save Seth.

I stand on my one wobbly leg and turn to the closest drone. "By the rules set by the Comumbran Emperor, I'm the last man standing. No fathers need die here today." My voice is clear and loud. Much stronger than it should be. It takes me a moment to realize the Crowd is silent.

The screen above the battlefloor switches away from me, back to Seth's family, where the child and mother are hugging, weeping different tears than they had been just moments before. When the Crowd sees the image, they erupt, throwing pre-bought flowers onto the battlefloor.

Chapter 5

When I wake, I have no idea how long I've been unconscious. There are vague and fleeting memories of stumbling out of the Temple, collapsing on a cement floor, hospital beds, needles, shouting, nightmares and unending pain. I always have nightmares after a Battle. Mostly, I dream of my past opponents banding together to torture and kill me.

I lie in a white bed in the center of a white room. There are tubes connected by syringes in my body, leading to machines that sit somewhere out of my view. Everything in this room is sterile. A barely audible tune plays. It's the same tune I hear every time I'm here. The healingsong. At some point over the eons it was discovered that physical environment was as important to our healing as all of the medications and surgeries. And this song, always played at a level which is just out of tangible grasp, proved to offer the best atmosphere.

There were a few other Battles scheduled this year, so I'm sure I'm not the only General in one of these rooms. I think of Seth and hope he's resting comfortably and that he's been able to see his wife and son.

"About time, General." I immediately recognize Tori's voice. He always stands sentry over me while I recover. It's been his voice which greets me every time I come to. "I was beginning to wonder if you had finally succumbed." He's not in the room, but I know he's close.

The familiar ache of recovery radiates through my body. Our physicians are the best in the world, but they are still limited by the weakness of human physiology. No matter how sophisticated the medicine, they cannot eliminate the pain of healing or the decay of wounded flesh. With considerable effort, I pull the blankets off myself, and I see what looks like the body of a person who has been tortured and killed.

This process always fascinates me. In just a few weeks, I will be on my feet with healed, although deeply scarred, flesh. Looking at my body this time, however, it appears the process will take longer. My frostbitten skin is covered in blackened blisters, some peeling in patches. The cuts I sustained, while skillfully sutured, will leave angry scars and I can tell my Achilles will take a considerable amount of specialized therapy.

The wall to my right forms a seam and reveals a door as Tori walks through. As soon as he's in the room, the door disappears and all I can see is the glaring white wall once again. Tori stands straight, his hands clasped behind his back. The only way he ever stands.

"You are uniquely grotesque this time around," he says.

"Yes. It's as if the Comumbrans had inside information about my armor. They framed the rules masterfully."

"A lesson which will remind you through pain. And will remind me through shame."

"Feel no shame, Mentor. We both agreed to the attire," I say.

He moves across the room to stand at my side. "We have let you rest longer than normal. Demetrius grows impatient and the citizens are concerned. They yearn to see their champion."

He does this often. Rather than disagree with me, he will change the subject to more pressing matters. Most of the time, my stubborn competitiveness resists, but this is a debate neither of us will win. We're both complicit in our oversight yet would never blame the other.

"I can dress in robes to hide the frostbite," I say. While our citizens love to watch me fight, they cannot abide the ramifications.

"The flesh on your face has not fared any better than the rest of you," Tori says.

"Then I will address the younger Generals and inspect the Ceremonial Guard first. They should see the toll a Battle takes. It will be good to remove the romance. Have the drones programmed to only film me from behind and we can release the footage to the citizens. It will satiate them until I am well enough to greet them in person."

"Navigating public opinion has become as natural to you as the Battle," Tori says.

While this is meant as a compliment, the comment stings. I have no interest in public discourse. It is merely another responsibility of being General. My heart will always be drawn to the battlefloor and the protection of my citizens. Demetrius is the politician and I'm happy for that.

"What of Seth?" It is my turn to change the subject.

He is silent for longer than I would like. "Dead." He turns and looks around the barren room, searching for a nonexistent distraction.

"Dead," I repeat, struggling to understand how it is possible. His blood loss, while significant, should have been an easy repair for Celcean physicians.

As if reading my mind, Tori says, "The loss of blood proved too much for him. He faded hours ago. I'm told that healing a bodmod is much more complicated than healing an unaltered body."

This news hurts worse than my unhealed wounds. I think of Seth's wife and child, the relief I saw on their faces when I spared him. Imagining their grief makes my pain seem like the scraped knee of a child.

"When you spared him, you won the Crowd in a way I have never seen. Most Generals are revered for their violence. And yet, almost all of the replays from your Battle have focused on your mercy."

"And yet, it appears even my mercy brings death," I say. This is an odd sensation. Mourning the death of a man who would have celebrated mine. But I cannot erase the image of his terrified family. No matter how justified my Battle, to them, I am the monster who took her husband and his father.

Tori is silent, allowing me a moment of introspection. He is perceptive and gracious to a degree I could never achieve.

"And Comumbra?" I say, changing the topic again.

"Awaiting their liberator."

There are a few more minutes of idle conversation, but Tori can tell I am too distracted to solve any more problems. No matter how hard I try to stay in the moment, I find my mind pulled back to those last seconds on the battlefloor with Seth.

Chapter 6

"To see you on your feet is to see the sunrise over the ocean," Demetrius says, his voice booming through powerful speakers as he embraces me.

The burnt skin under my robes screams as it cracks and oozes under his clutch. It takes every bit of my will to keep my knees from buckling under the pain. We stand, elevated on a stage in front of the Ceremonial Guard as they await my address. He grasps my shoulders and holds me at arm's length as he appraises my appearance.

"Your might astounds me, General. Not only did you fight a bodmod General, but you bested the weather itself. Is there no end to your supremacy?" This is Demetrius at his finest. Drones recording every facial expression and a hoard of zealots hanging on every word. He is so passionate, the pain of his touch fades as I bask in his pleasure. He turns to the guard, and steps back. "I present your General. The Lion of Celsus, Protector of the Innocent, Liberator of the Oppressed and Judge of Tyrants."

The men standing in perfect formation below us erupt into applause. Demetrius places his mouth against my ear and says, "Bathe in their adoration, General. Their worship not only sustains you, but it lifts Celsus above the clouds."

I close my eyes and allow the cheers to wash over me in waves. After a few seconds I raise my hands, immediately silencing the army.

There is no need for me to raise my voice as I address the army before me. The drones project my words in perfect acoustics and the men in formation stand at silent attention. "Soldiers. Brothers. Protectors. Servants. I stand here, my body weakened from Battle, but strengthened by the honor I see in you. I look at you and I see the beating heart of our great nation." In spite of their orders to remain at attention, they break into applause. While much smaller in number, the noise of their cheers rivals the intensity I feel when on the battlefloor. "Our Ancestors valued sacrifice. They modeled the very notion of it when they put their own lives on the altar in order to save this world from truewar after truewar.

"But our heritage runs deeper. To a time of violence and destruction where our forefathers built mighty armies in order to preserve their way of life. It is their blood which flows through our veins. And it is their tradition to which you paid tribute when you became guardians and Generals. You train in the ways of war in order to better understand the great gift of peace bestowed upon us by our Ancestors."

To Demetrius, I say, "My lord. Soon you will welcome a broken and oppressed nation into your embrace. I pray they will flourish under your mercy." I turn back to the soldiers and Generals, "As our father embraces his new fold, you must remain ever vigilant. There are those in this world who would throw our peaceful way of life to the side and plunge us back into the chaos which tore the soul from this world. We stand as gatekeepers, incapable of striking first, but with the fortitude to ensure that when we are called upon, we will land the final blow. You are the finest this world has to offer and it is my honor to call myself one of yours."

The roar of the army shakes the podium on which Demetrius and I stand. He leans in close, wrapping his arms around me again, "These men would cut their own flesh from their skin if you asked. Come, let us walk amongst them."

The field is broken into two groups. The smaller of the two is comprised of junior Generals, known as Hopefuls. Ranging from early teens into their twenties, they are the finest Battle specimens in all of Celsus. Each one of them with the sole focus of someday taking my place as General.

The larger group is the Ceremonial Guard. Every physically able Celcean male is able to volunteer to be a Guardian, but the invitation process is so rigorous, only one in every fifty actually make it through. For those with the strength to pass, they are a Guardian for life. Most of their time is spent training or helping improve the quality of life throughout the Celcean expanse of nations. If there is ever civil unrest, usually in a newly absorbed nation, these are the men to help calm the tensions.

Castor meets Demetrius and me as we approach the Hopefuls. I have not seen him since my pre-Battle audience. Given my recuperating wounds, the physical difference between the two of us is even more pronounced. His skin is as flawless as ever while I look like a leper. He quickly salutes me by raising his right fist to his left shoulder, then turns to Demetrius and kneels before him. "Your servants await you, my lord," he says.

Demetrius motions for him to rise and says, "Today is to honor the courage of your General, child. Not win points with your Ruler."

Castor stands and says, "Of course," then to me, says, "General. If I could take your wounds upon myself, I would. The Hopefuls learned much from your narrow victory." He says this as if reading a script.

I nod, unwilling to react to neither his attempted insult nor lack of emotion. "Back in line, Castor. I wish to inspect all of my subordinates."

His face flushes red, but he restrains himself. Demetrius and I wait while he inserts himself at the front of the formation.

"He is impetuous and brazen, but don't alienate him," Demetrius says, "you will not always be our General and there is no other Hopeful with even a fraction of the ability he has. What he lacks in maturity he makes up for in unbridled obedience to Celsus."

"You see obedience, Highness. I see covetousness. There are Hopefuls who may not have the genetics of Castor, but far surpass him in will and respect."

"Will I value. Respect only counts outside of the Temple. And a General is most valuable inside its walls."

Even though I've been General for a decade, I can still remember standing in formation as my predecessor passed by, bored and uninterested in the pageantry. The memory causes me to pause at each Hopeful and give them enough attention to ensure they remain inspired.

After chatting with a few Hopefuls, I can tell Demetrius is growing impatient. But these are my proteges to mold. I want them to know me, and I want them to see my wounds up close. To touch my broken skin and understand the fruition of true sacrifice.

We end with Castor, standing at a loose attention, his hair cascading over his shoulders. "They look good," I say, "a little undernourished for my liking. Have the nutritionist increase their protein portions for breakfast and lunch. As well as their water intake."

Castor doesn't break his stance, but gives a barely perceptible nod.

I can feel Demetrius evaluating our interaction. For better or worse, Castor has been deemed my heir and until another rises to realistically challenge him, he will hold a place of preference with our Ruler.

"Dismissed," I say.

The Hopefuls and the Guard begin making their way off the field when Demetrius calls Castor's name and beckons him over. Once Castor has joined us, Demetrius says to me, "We leave for Comumbra in the morning. I wish to dine with you both tonight."

Castor's lip curls into a slight, yet defiant, smile.

I bow without hesitation, acknowledging the gently spoken order.

We are seated at the royal table. It is one solid slab of white oak, large enough to hold an entire nation's delegation, sanded and lacquered so precisely, it feels as if we eat on glass. The meal is elegant and richly spiced. Most of the meat tastes of exotic places and the loaves of bread are still warm as we break them apart.

"Eat your fill, Generals," Demetrius says, "we will not receive food like this in Comumbra."

Castor grins like a child at being called a General. I make a mental note to remind him of his place once my body has completely healed. While the food is delicious, my body is at its breaking point. I have overtaxed myself today and I can tell I will pay the price in pain tomorrow. Before leaving this morning, Tori warned me against this very thing. Which means I will receive no sympathy from him when I return to my quarters. Rather than give in to the agony, I remain.

"What are we to expect in Comumbra?" I ask as a fresh platter of sizzling meat is placed on the table.

"They are very confused, sadly," Demetrius says.

"Then they are fools," Castor says quickly.

"One cannot blame a pig for salivating over slop when that is the only meal it has been served," Demetrius says, as if correcting a small child.

"And how is their confusion represented?" I ask.

The first two nations we liberated greeted us as such. But the last two greeted us with more resentment than gratitude. It wasn't until Demetrius began improving their cities with Celcean tech that they finally embraced their new Ruler.

"They are more resistant than ever, sadly."

"Allow me to go before you, then," Castor says, "I'll lead a squadron of the Guard with me to ensure your safe entry, Highness."

"March an army into a nation to seize control? Are you so dense as to not understand the implications of such an action?" I say, my voice slightly raised. Partly due to Castor's stupidity and partly because my wounds have removed my ability to tolerate such an attitude.

"Trajan is right. I would never send an army to seize control," he then looks at me, "but Castor is not far off either. We will be taking a unit from the Guard."

The news immediately turns my stomach. A General entering a newly won nation is one of the most sacred ceremonies in this world. To pervert it by using an army as backup is borderline blasphemy. It calls into question the validity of the entire Battle structure. It questions my victory and it weakens the will of the Ancestors.

"I can see by your reaction that you disagree, General." I've rarely heard such a cold tone from Demetrius.

"I do not disagree because I do not possess the information at your disposal. But I am disturbed by the implication of traveling to a liberated nation with an army," I say. This news combined with my weakened state makes the room feel as if it is attached to a cloud on a windy day.

"These are the decisions you must get used to, Trajan. A General is a dull knife. Good only for inflicting wounds. As your tenure grows to an end, your edge will need to sharpen into that of a scalpel so you can operate with more precision," Demetrius says.

"With respect. If a General is a dull knife, an army is a rock. Good only for crushing and splitting. How will we appear to our new countrymen? How will the world react? Are the Comumbrans truly that defiant?"

Demetrius sighs and places his fork over-gently on the table. "Things are rarely as simple as they appear." He waves the servants out of the room. "You, for instance. For a decade, you have been the most brutal General in history. Just the thought of you on the battlefloor of the Temple has been enough to keep certain nations in line. But then you Battle a bodmod. An utter abomination to the Battle. And you spare him." He stares at me with an intensity I have only seen on the faces of my opponents in the Temple.

Castor grunts his agreement. "It would have been so easy for you to slit his throat. Win and leave no doubt. Clean, violent and decisive endgame. Those are your words, General." He spits the last word.

I look from Demetrius to Castor. While staring at this confused and arrogant child, I say, "You were asked here by our Ruler. But do not forget your place. Neither should you mistake my mercy toward the Comumbran as a weakness to be exploited. You speak like that to me again and your days on this earth are over." I take a deep breath and turn to my Ruler. "Sire. If my actions on the battlefloor displeased you, I offer my deepest apologies. The rules did not dictate death and I thought it would reflect on your compassion as a Ruler if I showed restraint against an untested, glorified farmer." I could say more about seeing Seth's wife and child, but given his questioning, I remain quiet. The last thing I want is him questioning my focus on the battlefloor.

Castor looks like a caged animal. He wouldn't take well to such a reproach if we were in private. To be chastised in front of his Ruler is almost more than he can stand.

Demetrius is silent as he considers the two of us. Finally, he says, "You are correct. Your actions did reflect on me. The Comumbrans have begun protests. Some of them have turned to looting. But that is to be expected. I am more concerned by the emboldened narrative by other Rulers. They saw what you did as an act of defiance against me. As we speak, there is talk of sanctions against us."

"Animals," Castor says.

"Can you blame a lion for seeing a lame calf and not pouncing?" Demetrius says.

To hear that my actions have caused Demetrius to come under scrutiny by other, opportunistic and jealous Rulers is as bad as being accused of treason.

"Do you really think another nation would try to oppose our entry to Comumbra?" I ask.

Demetrius looks suddenly old and weary. "It is a fear I harbor deep inside. It pains me more than you know, but we need to take control of this situation. I am an increasingly easy target. Especially when there is cause to question the commitment of my General."

"My lord," I say, "these other Rulers do nothing more than poke at a hornet's nest. I pray their rhetoric hasn't permeated your opinion of me." I feel a panic rise in me that I have never felt. When I face an opponent on the battlefloor, the path to victory is straightforward. But to think Demetrius has lost faith in me is like being asked to jump from a ledge while surrounded by darkness.

"No. But we can leave no question with the other nations. And we can leave no question as to our ability to protect ourselves if the opposition becomes too pronounced."

"Of course. Your wisdom is sound." Even as I say this, I feel the weariness of my wounds taking over. More than that, there is something buried deep in my mind. I can feel it, still shapeless, but gaining strength. The feeling is the same as when I fight blindfolded and have lost bearing on my opponent. There is more which should be said but I am unable to manifest it.

We finish our meal on lighter fare. Demetrius and Castor discuss mundane matters of the army and the upcoming trip. Both anticipate the exotic foods and sights we will encounter. My exhaustion finally overtakes my will and I allow myself to sit back and drift from topic to topic until they have eaten their fill.

Demetrius sends for two of the Royal Guard to escort me back to my quarters. Tori is already asleep when I return and I am happy for the ability to sink straight into bed.

Chapter 7

Travel in our world is difficult. When the Ancestors first established order, they tried to build a single passageway around the planet which crossed every nation at the equator. But the initiative proved too difficult. The technology wasn't the difficult part. Some nations have more resources and ability than others. The less fortunate nations could not keep up with the demands of such a project and the wealthier nations were not willing to freely give their resources when they didn't see a logical return.

Some of us still use the remnant of the passage where we can. But Comumbra is an agricultural nation. All of their advancements are focused on refining and expanding their ability to produce and export fruits, vegetables and grains. They leave the transport of their goods up to the nations which purchase them.

Luckily, Demetrius has invested deeply in transportation, which makes our trip to Comumbra tolerable. We must pass through two independent nations, both of them allies, in order to reach the Comumbran border.

We travel in landskimmers. They use highly sensitive magnets mounted on the bottom of the ships to find and repel against the naturally occurring magnetism in the rocks and minerals in the soil. While the magnets are sensitive, we can't fly more than twenty meters above the ground or we'll lose connection. Each landskimmer is equipped with a laser sharpened blade mounted across the front in the off chance we come across a tree which hasn't already been trimmed during a previous trip. Using the magnets allows us to expend a very small amount of energy to thrust the enormous landskimmers. The one drawback to them, however, is their inability to skim over large bodies of water. At that point we have to either rely on the seafaring vessels of water nations, or as a last resort due to the amount of scarce fuel reserves, increase engine thrust and turn the landskimmers into slow moving air ships.

Our caravan sets out early in the morning. The personal skimmer of Demetrius goes first, followed by a ship dedicated to the politicians selected to bring Celcean culture to Comumbra. My skimmer, which I share with Tori, Castor and a handful of promising Hopefuls, is next. We're followed by three more vessels. One specifically outfitted to continue my rehab and the training of the Hopefuls, one bearing gifts for the Comumbran politicians and a final skimmer carrying an entire squad of the Ceremonial Guard.

Progress is slow, but unrelenting. Each landskimmer has a rotating team of pilots which allow us to travel around the clock. To stave off boredom, Tori and I train. The only other break in the monotony are the meals. Our skimmers are able to link for a short amount of time, which allows us to move from one machine to the next. I dine with the Hopefuls at breakfast, with Tori for lunch and with Demetrius, in his skimmer, for dinner.

On the third day, I stand at the front of my skimmer, watching as we creep over a particularly dense forest. Flocks of birds vacate trees as we get closer and, on the ground beneath us, scores of wildlife run in every direction, trying to escape the enormous and silent machines above them. We are one day beyond the Celcean border. Two more days and we will cross borders again. Three days later and we'll finally reach Comumbra. Demetrius is unsure of what awaits us there. Either a mob of protesters or a gathering of grateful citizens. Either way, I must be ready to greet them.

I'm so lost in thought, evaluating all of the possibilities in my head, I don't hear the door open behind me.

"I don't understand why we don't rule these people," Castor says, his voice louder than it should be.

It takes me a moment to bring myself back from my thoughts, but when I do, I arrive irritated by his attitude. "These people are our allies. They're ruled by a just king. There is no need, nor is there justification." I say this without looking away from the treetops below us.

"Yet they contribute nothing to the world. All they do is sit between us and our conquered lands. They're an unnecessary nuisance."

"Power does not give you privilege. Our world has already experienced enough devastation because of greed made to look like well-meaning convenience."

"I remember the first time I saw you fight in person. I had just been chosen to train as a General. Maybe fifteen years old. You were already a legend to me. But that first time? You were preparing for your third Battle. You were so brutal. Your sparring partner didn't put up enough of a fight for your liking. You broke him so quickly, then you berated his Mentor for how weak he was." His voice had a dream quality about it. As if talking about an interaction with a holy man. "But now I spar against you and you take it easy on me. Focusing as much on my development than on your preparation. And hearing you talk now, I wonder where that General of my youth went."

My body is almost completely healed from my Battle against Seth. I stretch my shoulders, feeling the new flesh tighten against the muscle underneath. "You'd rather I destroy you quickly? Give you no room to learn? A General must consider much more than the simple physicality of the fight. And he must be humble enough to realize that he serves the citizens. They are not a prize to be won." His single-mindedness reminds me of an

44

infant, focused only its next meal, or the rattle just out of its reach.

"The days of you destroying me easily, or at all, are long since passed." He's taken a few steps closer to me. I can also hear the increased labor of his breath.

Our skimmer approaches a tree which is taller than our path and slowly slices the top. There is no noise and we feel no opposition. I wonder what devastation it will wreak as it crashes to the forest floor.

"Do you think I'm that easily provoked? Or do you truly believe a couple of ill-placed and juvenile statements will goad me down your path?" If I keep pressing, I'll actually push him into the first move. While I'm not intimidated by him, I think about how disappointed Tori and Demetrius would be. "Go, child. Save your energy for the exhibitions in a few days."

Castor studies me for a few moments and I realize he is closer to tipping over the edge than I thought. I feel a sudden surge of adrenaline as I instinctively prepare for what may come next. True to Tori's training, there is no external sign of the building violence inside. I finally turn to face him, falling naturally into a fighting stance. His chest heaves, unable to mask his emotion.

As is true with every power structure, there is always tension between a General and the top Hopeful. But our Ancestors were clear to limit this dynamic by strictly forbidding outbursts like this. Rather, any Hopeful can challenge the General by petitioning his Ruler. In all honesty, I'm surprised Castor has not already tried this. Demetrius has likely held him back due to my popularity with the Crowd. Even if Castor were to best me here and now, it would disqualify him from ever taking the mantle of General. I wait calmly for him to reconcile his desire for unbridled aggression with his desperation for even greater glory in the future.

The door to our observation deck opens behind us. "General, I have prepared your attire for your dinner with Demetrius. I've done the same for you, Castor." The voice belongs to one of the countless servants on the skimmer. Her voice is lovely and I can see the aggression drain from Castor.

"Thank you," I say, without taking my eyes from Castor. "We will begin preparing immediately."

The servant bows, her gown rustling gently against the ground as she leaves.

Castor smiles at me and inhales deeply. "I'll see you tonight. And I look forward to the time when you can join us in training once again. Your students and I eagerly await your tutelage."

I stay behind for a few more minutes, watching the landscape change beneath me as the skimmer presses relentlessly forward.

"Castor is unsettled," Demetrius says.

We are a day away from Comumbra. Castor has been avoiding me.

"It seems he is constantly upset as of late," I say. "Trips like these take their toll on everyone. He would be well served to remember he is not the only one."

It is late. Demetrius dismissed all of the politicians after dinner but asked me to stay. He sips a dessert wine from an ornate glass. "Yes, these trips certainly make the body weary. But I do not think it is the journey which causes his displeasure," he says.

I clench my jaw as the realization for my private audience reveals itself. After our argument, Castor ran to Demetrius. A spoiled brother tattling. I remain silent, waiting to hear what Demetrius has to say.

"To lead is a delicate thing. Your motives are constantly in question, and there are times when a heavy hand is necessary. But there are also times when a gentle touch is better. To know the difference is to know wisdom," he says.

"I am fortunate to be able to learn from your examples. I have seen you demonstrate this principle. It seems I am still better suited for the battlefloor, rather than as a Mentor."

"Nonsense," he says. "I see you teach the younger Hopefuls. You lead them naturally. And your tempered response to me right now shows you have restraint. Maddeningly so. But you seem incapable of, or unwilling to, practice such patience with Castor."

My blood boils. It is one thing for Castor to act arrogantly toward me. It is another for him to try to turn my Ruler against me. Against every instinct screaming inside of me, I say, "There is no person in this world who I hold in higher regard than you, my king. But I fear you are being manipulated." As the words leave my mouth, I can hear Tori's disappointed rebuke. Demetrius is a gracious leader who has always encouraged me to speak my mind, but this feels different.

He sits forward and places his glass on the table with exaggerated gentleness. "We finally come to it. Tell me, how have I been duped?"

I consider changing course, but I know this would only anger Demetrius even more. He values honesty, even if it challenges him. There is nothing left to do but push through and trust his temperance. "When I became General, I vowed to do two things. Serve you and uphold the values of the Ancestors. To serve you is easy. You are consistent and fair. Your decisions are focused on the betterment of our people. To uphold the values of the Ancestors requires me to constantly view myself as a servant. I serve you. I serve the Hopefuls. I serve our people. This is what sustains me on the battlefloor.

"Castor, however, seeks only glory. Every action has the goal of bringing him a higher status. He's talented, and his physique is unmatched, but he does not fight in service of the people. He fights so the people will be compelled to serve him. I see him and I see evidence of the warlords who opposed the Ancestors."

Demetrius studies me as I speak. If this is what a rival Ruler feels when Celsus meets to negotiate terms of trade, it is no wonder we are the most powerful nation. He is every bit as intimidating a politician as I am a General.

"And yet, a General is asked to do one thing. Win. As decisively and quickly as possible. The two aspects of Castor which you so quickly passed over. His talent and his physique. Those are the two most important qualifications any General must possess."

I stand and gaze out the window of our skimmer. We have progressed beyond the giant forest and pass over an uneven and rocky terrain. "If that is true, why am I on this trip with you? Is my presence not helpful now? We are not on a journey to the Temple, rather we go to welcome an abused and misguided people."

"You are here because the Ancestors demand it. And because you are beloved. But make no mistake, my son. You are beloved because you are victorious. There would be no Trajan without the victories. You would simply be a statistic referenced by historians." He stands and joins me. "But what you say has merit. You have grown into more than just a General. I value your counsel. The world values your character. It is that character which will make the Comumbran transition possible. But when I found you as a child, I was not drawn to your love of the Ancestors and their rules. I was drawn to your brutality. Your willingness to win at any cost. Your single-minded focus on dominance. Could I not be describing Castor as well?"

When I was a Hopeful and would train with an older or more skilled opponent, there were times in which my haste or inexperience was easily used against me. I would end up in an awkward and painful position with the rest of the Hopefuls stifling laughter. Those moments were filled with rage and disgust in myself. Not for losing, but for allowing my weakness to be exposed so publicly. Standing here, listening to Demetrius gives me the same feeling. "Indeed, you could. However, it has been my hope that you have grown to value me for more than my victories. Even a primate learns and gains wisdom as he matures. You speak as if I am merely a weapon to be wielded. With respect, if that is true, I am no better than an individual manifestation of the armies of old."

He places his hands behind his back and inhales deeply. "The last thing I need is another advisor. There is a reason the Ancestors mandated a Ruler to guide a General and not the other way around. If you desire to become a politician, then we can promote Castor now."

I have never known Demetrius to react this way to me. As we stand here, one day from the Comumbran border, I realize I have taxed him too much. He deals with the second guessing of his advisors and world politicians enough. The last thing he needs is the whining of a General with an overdeveloped view of himself. "Please accept my apology, Highness. You have my full trust and admiration. If there is oversight needed, it certainly does not need to come from me. When we cross into Comumbra, I pray you will have full confidence in my support as well as my dedication to serve." His posture softens and, for a split second, I see a weary man next to me.

"I am surrounded by so many schemers throughout my day, I sometimes forget who is a true ally. I value you far beyond your ability to win in the Temple. I value you for the same reasons the Crowd loves you so much. Your purity of heart is inspiring. It will bring Celsus great fortune.

"I only ask that you don't make the mistake so many great men make. Please don't see your abilities as commonplace. Castor is your equal in many things. Virtue is not one of them. But even a wild animal can be brought into submission and bring great value to its master."

It is clear from his tone that our conversation is over. I bow and allow myself to feel his embrace before I leave. As I make my way back to my landskimmer, the pressures of our trip feel like hundreds of boulders on my back. How much more, I wonder, do the pressures weigh so heavily on Demetrius to the point where he accepts the service of a caged and murderous predator.

Chapter 8

The Comumbran border looms before us. Tori and I stand at the front of our skimmer, which has taken the lead position in our caravan. The tradition of the Ancestors demands the victorious General be the first to set foot on his new nation's soil. It is the only time I precede Demetrius.

We are still a kilometer from the border, but there is no mistaking the dividing line. It is as if we approach a stronghold from before the pre-chaos years. A wall made out of huge logs extends as far along the border as I can see, each at least fifteen meters around and thirty meters tall. The tops of each have been sharpened into spikes as if they were designed to stave off dragons.

"They are more isolated than I had imagined," I say.

Tori is dressed in the ceremonial armor of Celsus, as am I. The heavy metal breastplate and stiff leather buckles cause him to move in a stilted and overly purposeful fashion. A complete contrast to his usual demeanor. "Walls rarely serve a single purpose," he says.

"Our Ancestors gave us a world which lacks the need for such restraints. Whether these walls were meant to keep invaders out, or to keep citizens in, is of no consequence."

He fiddles with the shirt under his armor, trying to smooth out a wrinkle which is likely beginning to chafe his skin. "If this wall had been built by King Mansa, I would agree with you."

"If not him, then who?" I ask. Our skimmers continue their unrelenting march toward the wall. As we draw closer, I can see where we will be entering Comumbra. A tiny gateway, just big enough to fit a horse drawn cart.

"I have spent too much time filling your head with techniques for killing and not enough on the struggles of the Ancestors. You revere them, but clearly do not understand them."

It is as if he has reached up and slapped me. I say nothing, even though I boil at the rebuke.

"Calm, Trajan. I mean you no disrespect. If anything, the fault is with me. I have focused on the world which they gave us, yet I have neglected to highlight their struggle before it was theirs to give."

I turn to him, silently prompting him to continue.

"Our historians paint a very different story about the Ancestors and the chaotic world which they reshaped. When they began their campaign, the world had mostly stabilized. Powerful military leaders protected their populace, but often pulled additional war-making resources from the citizens as they saw fit. Truewars were common among the strongest leaders, while most of the world was free to build a sustainable way of life. It wasn't until one of the Twelve lost his son in a war that things started to change."

"A world where truewar is commonplace, even if only for the most powerful, does not sound like a stable place," I say. He is right, however. The way we speak of the Pre-Ancestor era is of utter mayhem.

"True. But some would say the same about Celcean Battles. There are nations who have Generals in ceremony only, content to live their lives in peaceful harmony.

"This wall," he nods toward the border, "is the remnant of the Stronghold of the Twelve. When they began their campaign, they became the targets of every Ruler on the planet. They were seen as terrorists. And if they would have failed, history would have remembered their efforts as a

51

quashed rebellion, nothing more.

"To the Rulers they opposed, their campaign was blasphemous in its audacity. In such, they sought to break the Twelve by eliminating their families and countrymen. The Ancestors hid their people behind the wall which we approach. You look at it and see a tool of a nefarious Ruler. I see a monument to twelve people who refused to submit to complacency."

"Which makes King Mansa's treatment of the Comumbrans even more starling. It takes a dark kind of jaded pride to oppress a populace in the shade of a wall which brought the first breath of true freedom to the world," I say.

"I am quite eager to see the evidence of his tyranny," Tori whispers.

Two hundred meters from the wall, our landskimmers come to a smooth stop. There is an immediate flurry of activity as our aides prepare the ceremonial order. Within fifteen minutes, we are fully assembled in front of our skimmers.

I stand at the front of the delegation as the ceremonial and functional tip of the Celcean spear. Behind on my left is Tori. To his right is Demetrius. Castor and the politicians fan out from there, a mist of personal minidrones humming above them. Each programmed to capture and broadcast this moment across the globe. Behind them are the servants and cartloads of gifts, clothing and food. Finally, broken into strict regiments is the Celcean Guard. Given what Tori just told me about the origin of this fortification, their presence seems even more offensive.

The sun is high overhead and there are no clouds to soften the rays. Ten minutes pass. Then thirty. At forty-five minutes, I turn to a red-faced and sweating Demetrius. "Are we expected? Might we need to send a scout to announce our presence?"

"Mansa has been well advised of our progress. This feeble demonstration is yet another example of his defiance." His voice quivers.

I turn back and search the wall for any signs of a sentry watching us.

"Five more minutes," Castor says, loud enough to be heard by almost every recording drone, "and I'm taking the guard through that door."

I spin and push past both my Ruler and Mentor. "Do not open your mouth again, infant. I will not have my place as General usurped by an impatient and entitled subordinate." My voice is low, but I'm sure the closest drones have captured my reprimand.

Tori places his hand on my shoulder, "General, maybe King Mansa is awaiting your approach. You are, after all, his conqueror. For him to open his gates before your command would deny the might of your victory."

He is right. This is the first nation I have liberated which has had an armament through which we must pass. The letter of the ceremonial law affords the victorious General every ruling right as soon as the Battle is complete. We have been waiting for an invitation when none was necessary.

I immediately begin marching toward the gate with the entirety of the Celcean delegation following behind. As I draw closer, I can see a sliver of daylight through the small door. Without hesitating, I push it aside and step for the first time into the newest Celcean territory.

It takes my eyes a few seconds to adjust to the shadow on this side of the wall, but once I do, I see a meager assembly of what I assume to be the Comumbran greeting delegation. Given the size of the opening, there will be a significant bottleneck as the fullness of the Celcean party tries to enter behind me. I check to ensure Demetrius and Tori are with me and proceed forward once they are through. I'll let Castor wrangle the politicians, servants and his precious Guard.

The land on this side of the wall is as barren as the other side. There are a few juniper shrubs here and there, and a smattering of dry wild grass, but other than that, the ground is covered with a tan dust.

A short and round man steps toward me and bows.

"Welcome, General. Behold the spoils of your victory," he says as he sweeps his hand over the arid ground. "Curtis, Agricultural Tsar, at your service."

I nod to him, "I am honored by your presence. Where is King Mansa? I am eager to finalize the will of the Ancestors."

Curtis bows again, this time even lower, "Detained unavoidably." He says this more to the ground than to me.

Demetrius takes a careful step forward, sure not to step in front of me. Until the defeated Ruler has officially submitted to the General's victory, the Battle has not been settled. At this point, Demetrius is my guest, nothing more. "Detained?"

"There is an outbreak of sickness in a nearby village and he has gone to oversee the treatment," Curtis says.

"More games and lies," Demetrius says. Three beads of sweat combine under his earlobe and drop onto the leather strap across his shoulder.

I share his irritation. This ceremony, while small and symbolic compared to the finality of a Battle, is vital to ensure the populace of the defeated nation accepts the transition. For King Mansa to boycott our entrance, regardless of the reason, calls the validity of my victory into question.

The buzz of the minidrones behind me grows louder as more and more Celcean delegates pass through the tiny entrance. The only other noise I hear behind me is the heavy pacing of Castor as he struggles to restrain himself.

Tori brushes my shoulder and I tilt my head to hear is whisper. "Perhaps the outbreak can be contained with the help of our physicians."

If only I could have seen him fight in his prime. What he lacks in size, he more than overcomes with strategy and precision.

"Clearly King Mansa is a caring Ruler to put his citizens before the joining of our two nations. You will find, however, that Demetrius is equally benevolent." I turn to the group of politicians bunched against the ancient wall. After a few seconds I find the chief physician and beckon him forward.

Pleased to be included in such a unique situation, he scurries forward, his robes brushing a tiny wake behind him.

I turn to Curtis and say, "May I present Marcus, Chief Physician of

Celsus. We offer his, and his team's, services to help with the outbreak."

"The stories of your kindness and temperance have been under exaggerated. King Mansa will surely welcome you with open arms," Curtis says. He turns to one of his assistants and whispers something. The assistant immediately begins running to the west. "The colony is twenty kilometers away. We have arranged transportation, but are not prepared for the size of your delegation. I fear we only have room for you and your advisors. Your army will need to march behind or wait here." The last sentence may as well have been delivered with a dagger.

Our transportation is slightly more sophisticated than the horse-drawn carriages which used to sustain primitive humans. We sit on elevated platforms without any covering to shield us from the sun as they are propelled three meters above the ground by enormous and deafening spinning blades.

I am in the lead vessel with Demetrius, Tori, and Curtis, which kicks up a blinding cloud of dust behind us. The only distraction from both the heat and the noise is the humor I find in imagining our politicians as they try to shield their eyes and cover their noses through the deluge of discomfort.

In spite of the outdated technology, we make surprising time. In less than two hours, I see a faint silhouette of a farming village on the horizon. A few minutes later, we are surrounded by perfect rows of lush, green plants. We come to a stop outside of a long, rectangular, mostly log building on the outskirts of the village.

"This is where the overflow of your delegation can stay the night," Curtis says, obviously referring to the guard. "We can walk the rest of the way; our infirmary is less than a kilometer away and I'd prefer to keep the displaced dust to a minimum." We lower ourselves from the platforms and begin walking before the rest of the advisors have stopped. "They will be shown to their quarters so they can rest before the feast tonight."

Demetrius pauses a moment to give a few parting commands to his head servant. Once he catches up, he says, "I was beginning to wonder if Mansa was going to feed us at all."

Curtis points to the fields on our left, "These are barley," then to his right, "alfalfa over there. Comumbran crop rotation is unparalleled, my only hope-" he cuts himself off before continuing.

"We are eager to become your students," Tori says, replying to the unspoken complaint.

"Yes, and imagine how much more efficiently we will be able to trade with the rest of the nations when I improve your infrastructure and technology," Demetrius says, as if consoling a scared child. "The joining of our nations will provide a great boon to this recovering world."

The infirmary is small and dark. I've barely crossed the threshold before my nose begins stinging with the acidic smell of vomit, followed by the pungent weight of sweat. We pause, mainly to let our eyes adjust, but there's a slight hesitation to proceed too far until we have a better understanding of the outbreak.

Marcus clears his throat, "General, with your permission, I would like to proceed. But I advise you and Demetrius to wait here."

I nod, then realizing he likely can't see me, I say, "Of course. Please ask King Mansa to make his way here. When he is able, obviously."

He bows and asks Curtis to take him to his Comumbran counterpart.

Children in Celsus are immunized against most illness starting at infancy. Every year, we are given boosters and any new inoculations that are deemed necessary. Because of this, sickness is virtually eradicated within our borders. Standing in this room, facing a potentially foreign disease brings as much fear as facing an unknown General in the Temple.

"My lord," I say to Demetrius, "perhaps you should wait outside until Marcus has identified the sickness."

"Nonsense. This is just another ploy by Mansa to make me look weak and oblivious." His voice is low, but his anger has made him short of breath. "He is not as altruistic, nor as backward as he is presenting. What they lack in technology, they make up for in political power. When you control the grain and produce for the majority of the world the way Mansa has been, you have the ability to control how other Rulers bend to your will. Our every movement is being scrutinized, not only by the Comumbrans, but by the Rulers of our allies and enemies alike."

I remain silent, unsure of how to respond. This is a rare mood for Demetrius. He is usually much more temperate and even. Then again, I cannot remember a time when he has been so openly challenged by the political maneuvering we have seen from Mansa today.

As my eyes adjust, I see a much different scene than my imagination had created. There is a level of sophistication in this building which was masked by the meager exterior. We stand on a landing, overlooking three levels, each with perfectly sectioned rooms. The bottom level, almost completely obscured by darkness, looks to be the heart. Physicians, assistants and other staff mill about, carrying trays of liquid, syringes, monitors and other unrecognizable equipment. To our left is a lift system which allows the staff to quickly adjust their level and location, depending on which patient needs their attention.

One of the lifts drops to the bottom where an elderly and chubby man is talking to Marcus. When the lift comes to a stop, he enters and immediately begins rising to our level.

"Mansa," Demetrius says.

He steps from the platform and makes his way, limping slightly, toward us. He does not look our way until he is within an arm's reach.

"My conquerors," He says, his voice deep and strong. A startling contrast to his physical appearance.

"King Mansa," I say as I dip my head in respect.

"Just Mansa, now that you're here." He continues to scan the floor below us.

"It appears our visit is untimely," I say. "Perhaps we should retire until this outbreak has been treated." I am at a loss. Every other time I have met with a conquered Ruler, it has been in a ceremonial hall, filled with dignitaries and elites.

He turns his attention back to me, his eyes strained with confusion and what looks to be amusement. "Yes. Great idea," he laughs, "we will likely have this contained in about a decade. Let's revisit this little charade then." His voice echoes across the thirty-meter-deep void.

I imagine Demetrius behind me, regal, powerful. I have never seen, nor would I have ever imagined, anyone treating his presence with so much disrespect. A surge of adrenaline propels me a step forward, "We come here, respectful and with clear hearts, under the Law of the Twelve and you choose to throw a tantrum? Disrespect toward me, I can abide. But act with contempt toward my king or the Twelve again and I will give you a taste of what Seth felt on the battlefloor, old man."

He straightens his aged back and broadens his shoulders as he inspects me. Even though his body is frail and stands almost two heads shorter than me, I feel myself shrinking under his consideration. He stretches his neck so he can see past me. "General Motodada," he says to Tori, "I see your fire in him." He steps back and says to me, "Peace, lad. You have defeated my General, and in so doing, you have dethroned me. At my age, I find it overly luxurious to act falsely for the sake of ceremony. If other defeated Rulers have appeared happy about their demise it is only because of their youthful pride. Your victory I acknowledge, as do I submit to the Will of the Twelve. But him," he gestures to Demetrius, "I do not, nor will I ever, call my Ruler."

"If it comes to that," Demetrius says.

The rules of the Twelve allow for an honorable death of the conquered Ruler, if they so choose. In my lifetime, however, I have never witnessed it. Rather, it has become the standard expectation that the previous Ruler is accepted into the political circle of the new king. Not only do the rules allow for death, they call for the General to be the executioner. While he is my king, I do not appreciate how willing Demetrius is to volunteer me. Killing a trained General is one thing. Taking the head of an old man is another entirely.

"I have no doubt," Mansa says to Demetrius.

There is a prolonged silence as we all struggle with how to move past this stalemate of wills. If we were in the Temple or on the battlefloor, there would be no struggle for me. And if this confrontation had taken place in public, in front of cameras and drones and advisors, they would no doubt smile and politely insult each other in an effort to win public opinion. But Mansa has chosen the perfect venue to cause as much discomfort as possible. The last gasp of a dying man.

After what seems like hours, Tori says, "Is their suffering severe?"

This seems to snap Mansa out of his stubborn defiance. His body relaxes and I can see his age take control of his body once again. "Just a virus. Seems to spread in waves. It burns hot and fast. Most of these people will be up and running, if a bit slowly, tomorrow. The bigger problem is the harvest. We're well behind schedule."

"Creating problems for me to solve?" Demetrius says.

I turn to him, surprised by my sudden irritation. Since I have become General, I have studied his demeanor and self-control. I have sat in countless meetings and watched innumerable speeches where he has been insulted, questioned and degraded. And every time, he has been able to turn the tide through wit and humility. Ever since we came into view of the Comumbran Wall, however, he has been overly irritated and aggressive. It is odd. More so, it borders on turning this transition into riots and even more suffering for the citizens. "My lord," I say, "the journey today has been long. You would warm my heart if you would go rest. Allow me to take this burden." This is the closest I have ever come to disrespecting him. I immediately feel my stomach turn. The faster we have appointed a governor and are headed back to Celsus, the better.

If he is offended by my suggestion, he does not react. "You are my champion in the Temple and now you honor me with your service. If only every Ruler had a General such as you." He kisses me on both cheeks and turns to go. Over his shoulder, he says to Mansa, "Curtis will accompany me, I trust."

After he has left the building, and Curtis has scurried after him, Mansa says to Tori, "How you have served him for so long, I will never know."

"Sire," Tori says, "you are speaking about my Ruler. If you respect me as you claim, please refrain from disrespecting him."

"Of course." Mansa says. "Come, there is much work."

We work well into the night, refiling water, administering pills and changing sweat-soaked sheets. Tori and I work silently. Seeing his gentle touch and perfectly chosen words throughout the night restores my calm. As we approach exhaustion, Mansa beckons us to a small room on the bottom floor.

"Thank you," he says. Then, to me, "accept my apologies, Trajan. In my anger toward your Ruler, I did not treat you with the respect I should have.

"Your victory feast will be tomorrow. As we speak, my most reliable servants prepare your table. Before then, however, would you accompany me on a short journey tomorrow? There is a place I would like you to see."

As has been true since waiting outside the wall, his request borders on audacity. The rules do not prevent a private audience between General and conquered Ruler, but if not handled delicately, such a meeting could be interpreted as conspiratorial.

For the second time today, I feel as if I straddle two pieces of soil as they retreat from each other. "I am flattered by your invitation. When I meet with my king tomorrow, I will seek his guidance."

"Of course. I will await your decision." He motions for the lift to be lowered. "You have been as gentle with your patients today as you are a savage in the Temple. Demetrius is lucky to have you."

Tori and I step onto the lift and are immediately swept to the exit. There is a small vessel waiting to take us to our quarters. As we skim across the dusty road, Tori silently watches the perfectly lined rows of barley. Just before we stop in front of our quarters, he puts his arm around me. Something he has done only one other time. "Mansa is right. Demetrius is lucky. As am I. Go with Mansa tomorrow. I will inform Demetrius and help him prepare for the feast."

"Comumbra used to be called the heart of the world," Mansa says.

We have been riding his royal vessel for close to an hour. Unlike the machines that carried us from the wall yesterday, this one is enclosed, operates at a higher altitude and provides comfortable seating. He still has not told me where we are headed.

"I was surprised to see how desolate the border is. Whenever I have imagined your nation, it has been overflowing with rivers and lush vegetation," I say.

"As is true with most good things in our world, it was the Twelve who first saw the potential. During the chaos, everyone avoided this region, assuming it was unlivable. But they found evidence of an enormous underground aquifer. It was only a matter of time until they found a way to use it to make the vast open spaces fertile." He sits rigidly in his plush seat, scanning the horizon restlessly.

"I have learned more about the Twelve in the last few days than in my previous two decades."

"History is rarely interested in nuance. Broad strokes are easier to see from a distance."

This is a much different Mansa than I saw yesterday. Whether he has resigned himself to the inevitable, or he was grandstanding yesterday, I do not know. Either way, if this continues, our trip will be much more pleasant than I anticipated.

"When the warstates heard about the newly discovered resources, they redoubled their resistance to the Twelve and their rebellion. Even the wall through which you passed yesterday wasn't enough to keep the marauders out." His voice trails off as his eyes glaze over, memory taking over any agenda he may have had in telling me the rest of the story.

"Moto-San told me the Twelve sequestered their families in Comumbra during the worst of the upheaval," I say, trying to regain his attention.

"Moto-San," he says. "An oddly caring way for a General to refer to his Mentor. Has he told you of his life before?"

He is right. Tori and I are closer than any other General and Mentor I have ever seen. And yet, he rarely speaks of his life before his defeat. Our Battle archives are used primarily for training purposes, rather than historical lessons, which means the footage focuses on technique and strategy. It is rare, if not impossible, to see an entirely unedited fight. From what I have seen, Tori was a proficient General, nothing more.

"Is our destination near?"

"Just beyond that line of trees." The trees are still a few kilometers away and rise above the perfectly tended rows of agriculture. "There is a canyon which was cut into the limestone millennia ago."

"And what, if you don't mind, awaits us in the canyon?"

He sighs, showing the same exhaustion I saw in him last night. "If I am to turn my nation over to you, it is my desire that you know the fullness of what you receive. Demetrius, I'm sure, sees our resources as a way of strengthening his stranglehold on the rest of the nations, but there is much more to Comumbra. It is my duty as caretaker for my Ancestors to ensure the knowledge is passed along."

We ride in silence over the final distance. The trees grow higher as we draw closer until we're forced to increase our altitude abruptly. After we clear the trees, the ground beneath us immediately drops. We follow suit, spiraling into the canyon. It is deep with jagged walls curving across the land. Almost obscured by shadow, a stream flows along the bottom.

We fly between the walls, following the curves and avoiding the occasional outcropping.

"I can remember the first time I saw this," Mansa says. "My father brought me here. As had his father and his father before him. You may be the first foreigner to see these walls since the Twelve stumbled into them so many years ago."

There is a beauty here which I have never known. The severity of the walls combined with the stillness of the canyon floor stand in direct opposition to each other. "Beautiful," is all I can muster.

Silence settles over us as we weave through the canyon, both of us lulled into a trance by the gentle rocking of the vessel. After traveling at least ten kilometers, I'm snapped back into consciousness as we begin a rapid deceleration. As we slow, we also drop deeper into the canyon.

Our ship falls below the shadow of the eastern canyon wall. Before my eyes can adjust, I feel our landing thrusters engage. We settle on the canyon floor with a gentle thud. Mansa stands and hands me a container of water. "Even though it's much cooler down here, the humidity is high. I'd hate for Demetrius to accuse me of trying to injure his General."

My feet sink a few centimeters into the damp sand as we depart. The humidity hits me ten paces from the ship, but I say nothing as I quicken my pace to keep up with Mansa. After a kilometer, we come to the end of walkable ground. He stops and takes a long drag of water. "I used to be able to make this trek at a sprint. It seems I have indulged a little too much in the comforts of old age." He sets his bottle down and strips to his undergarments.

I follow suit, my curiosity growing with each minute. "Tori will be happy to know I didn't miss a workout today," I say.

"The current is strongest on the left, but it's not as deep. If you find yourself fading, you try to stand or swim over to the right side and use the wall while you rest." He doesn't check to see if I'm ready before he wades into the water.

What looked like a stream from the air, feels like a river once I'm in it. There is a strong current under the surface which catches me almost immediately. Tori, ever the prudent Mentor, has incorporated water training into our regiment for years. I quickly find my rhythm and easily settle behind Mansa. For his part, he swims without any apparent difficulty, once again defying his physical appearance.

We stay mostly in the middle of the stream, skirting the left side in order to take advantage of the stronger current. I lose track of how far downstream we swim, but with each rounded curve in the canyon, I start to tally how far we'll have to travel against the water if we want to return to our transport. Just before I begin to pull even with Mansa to ask him about our return trip, the canyon opens up, allowing the river to expand into a basin. My protests fade in amazement as I look across the pool.

Carved directly into the far canyon wall are entrances to what I can only assume is a vast system of caves. These entrances, however, are not mere holes in the cliff. Rather, they are surrounded by delicately carved decorations, columns, mythical sentinels and ancient writing.

"Welcome to the Stronghold of the Twelve," Mansa yells as he begins to swim even faster toward the openings.

The water temperature grows colder as we make our way across the pool, which tells me this part of the canyon is much deeper than the rest. Mansa has opened a significant lead on me, but I don't care. I take my time, pausing every few strokes to soak in the scene around me.

Now that I'm in the middle of the tiny lake, I can see new openings on the rest of the walls as well. Each one surrounded by unique and extravagant carvings. The canyon walls tower over us, at least fifty meters higher than when we landed. Every breath and movement echoes off them. Whoever made this place would have used them as a natural alarm system.

I finally reach the far side where Mansa stands, dripping from head to toe and smiling with more delight than I thought possible.

"I never had a son to bring here. As I watch you, I can finally understand how much fun my father must have had when I saw this place for the first time. The mighty Trajan has been reduced to a schoolboy, filled with awe and wonder." He points to a small outcropping as my path for exiting the water.

"I never knew ancient people were capable of such beauty," I say, "everything I have heard of them is filled with murder and hatred."

He turns and points to an opening halfway up the cliff. "That one is my favorite. You can't see it from here, but there are intricate vipers carved around the entire frame. Each one devouring the one in front of it."

We make our way into the closest opening and are immediately presented with a flight of crudely carved steps. Mansa hands me a torch, then lights it from the one he carries. The steps curve up and to the left, quickly leading us away from any remnant of the sunlight. We are both silent as we climb, the air growing cooler and more humid with every step.

"We don't know if the builders took advantage of a pre-existing network of caves, or if they just turned this part of the land into a human sized ant colony. Either way, the system is vast. There are still tunnels which have yet to be fully mapped." Even though he whispers, his voice seems too loud, as if he may wake some supernatural guard if he continues talking.

A few more paces and the steps level out. The light from our torches only reach a few meters in diameter, but I can tell just from the feeling of the air that we have entered a much larger room. Mansa stops, glances at me and yells at the top of his voice. The volume makes me jump and I'm about to express my displeasure when his voice echoes back to us. From the direction and time it took to reach us, I can tell this room is massive.

"We brought in as many spotlights as we could when I first became Ruler. I wanted to get a perfect picture of this room so I could recreate it back in my palace. We made it halfway through before we gave up. The room is too big. And every centimeter is covered with murals or carvings. It would have taken hundreds of artists decades to replicate it."

We move to the nearest wall and begin inspecting it. He's right, I cannot find a flat or untouched surface anywhere. At first, the carvings and images seem completely random, like an ancient form of graffiti. But after a few minutes, I can tell I am reading some sort of story. "Have you been able to interpret what these mean?" I ask.

"Some," he says, utterly distracted by another section of wall.

"Does everyone in Comumbra know of this place?"

"Most know it exists. Few know how to get here."

I lose track of time as we separate, each of us following a different path of art. I follow a thread which seems to tell a story of three people in opposition to a king who are forced to flee as their families are tortured and killed. One particularly graphic and realistic mural shows the rebels as they return to their homes, only to find the dead bodies of their children scattered across the ground. The next scene, this one carved with jagged chisel marks, shows the three rebels standing in front of a castle, engulfed in flames. "Do you know the story behind this?" I ask.

Mansa slowly makes his way to me, then takes a few moments to pour over the scenes I've been studying. "It's amazing. The evil we're capable of." He studies the scene for a few more minutes, then says, "This is what started it all. The three rebels are the first of the Twelve."

"Tori told me the Twelve hid their families behind the Comumbran Wall."

"The other nine did. These three, however, were the first to oppose the warlords who oversaw the most powerful of the warstates."

"And the warlords responded like this?" The closer I get to the scene of the execution, the more graphic details I see. The more I see, the more I realize how corrupt this world had become.

"Yes. They did what they thought necessary to preserve their way of life."

I spin toward Mansa, shocked by his ability to empathize with the butchers who opposed the Twelve. "You make it sound as if they were justified."

"Their world had stabilized. Sure, the balance was tenuous, and when truewars happened, they were devastating. But the warlords saw themselves as responsible for achieving more peace than the world had seen in centuries. They saw the Twelve as rebels. Terrorists even. And they were willing to defend their way of life with as much tenacity as they could muster."

"Anyone who would go to such terrible extremes to maintain their way of life is either delusional, cowardly or evil."

"If you look at history with such tinted glasses, you will learn nothing. The warlords thought they were preserving an unprecedented world peace. Are you any different? Would you not take any measure necessary to maintain the system you represent?"

"You twist facts, Mansa," I say, realizing now why he brought me here. This is his final mission. To undermine my confidence in Demetrius.

"I do not question your integrity. In fact, the more I know you, the more impressed I am with your heart."

"But you seek to erode my allegiance."

"To what end? My time is over. At most, I hope to paint a more colorful picture of the world for you."

"Very altruistic."

He laughs. "You are indeed a lion. Ready to strike at the slightest indication of opposition."

"And you, it seems, are equally willing to fight on as many fronts as possible."

"Peace, General. I brought you here to show you the crown jewel of Comumbra, not to poison you against Demetrius," he says. The tiredness has returned to his voice.

I take a deep breath, as well as a step back, "Of course. Here we stand, in a perfectly preserved museum and all I can do is debate political ideologies. Perhaps I have spent too much time with the Celcean political elite."

"I must confess, however, I did invite you here under a false pretense," he says.

I remain quiet, unwilling to be baited again. The fact remains that I have defeated him and these are just his versions of a death rattle.

"Knowledge of this place needs to continue, that much is true. But I ask one simple thing. Call it a last wish." He beckons me deeper into the vast chamber.

I follow, although at a much slower pace, sure to use as many senses as possible to detect what else may be in here, suddenly aware of my vulnerability. We cross the room, which turns out to be close to seventy meters wide, and come to an opening so small, I have to lie on my stomach and pull myself through with my forearms. Once through, I'm only able to lift myself to a crouch.

"This is the start of what is known simply as the Corridor," he says. "Another fifteen meters and it opens into a seemingly unending labyrinth. Most of the pathways have not been successfully mapped. There is one I wish to show you. It is where the Twelve hid their families while they led their campaign for change."

We wind through the tunnels, sometimes traversing through cracks no bigger than the space from my chest to back. Mansa is much faster than me and it occurs to me that, if he wanted, he could easily abandon me in here, leaving me to stumble around in the dark until exhaustion and dehydration finally consumed me. In contrast to my fears, he pauses often, pointing out subtle spots in the rocks, encouraging me to commit them to memory so I may find my way in the future.

By the time we emerge from the Corridor, I am drenched in sweat and covered in a fine, talc-like dust. Mansa stands in front of me, silent and reverent.

"Every time I visit this room, I am overcome by the commitment of the Twelve. Their foresight as well. Midway through their campaign, the remaining warlords breached the Comumbran Wall. A traitor against the Twelve then gave them directions to the Stronghold. It seemed all was lost. But as the armies of the warlords searched the openings and tunnels, they never found this room. This is where the families of the Twelve hid. Silently they prayed for deliverance." He crouches down and runs his hands through the dust. "After weeks of searching. Growing disoriented and weaker, they emerged, only to find themselves surrounded and at a tactical disadvantage. The Twelve and their warriors slaughtered them. The bones of the defeated forces still rest at the bottom of the lake we swam through.

"When the Twelve finally retrieved their families from this room, they looked up," he raises his torch, "to see this inscription."

Five meters above us a sentence is roughly engraved in the limestone.
We will die as rebels before we live as slaves

There are tears in his eyes as he watches me. Standing here, knowing I stand on the very ground which the Twelve once stood, I am overcome as well.

"My family has kept meticulous records of our genealogy, Trajan. And it is with pure conviction that I tell you: the words you read were inscribed by my direct ancestor. This place is not just a historical landmark for me. It is a direct link to my past."

He runs his hands along the wall underneath the inscription. "My last wish is for Demetrius to never learn of this place."

To know of such a place as this and not reveal it to my Ruler would border on treason.

"You know not what you ask," I say, quietly.

"I do. I know it is a burden not only heavy, but divisive. And I will not try to justify it. I have made my request. But know this. I could have kept blissfully silent and allowed this place to fade into obscurity. Instead, I chose to trust you, confident in the knowledge that you are uniquely able to carry such a millstone."

He does not push for an answer, nor do I offer one. We make our way back. Retracing the same path we had just traveled. Again, he pauses often to help me commit the route to memory.

When we emerge into the light again, it is many minutes before I can see. The story of the ambush by the Twelve becomes even more real. We climb a slight path to the top of the cliff's edge where Mansa's ship waits for us.

As we travel back, our path is straight. Mansa naps beside me, the activity of the day taking its toll on his aged body. There is a weariness in me deeper than I have known. I wholly understand his request, and I also know I have no obligation to uphold it. Possibly overcome by the emotion of what I have seen, I find myself rehearsing alternate explanations for how we spent our time today. As I see the village approaching once again, I realize I have resigned myself to keeping Mansa's secret. Let Demetrius have Comumbra and the power which comes with it. Let him take credit for liberating a backward nation. Those things he covets more than symbols of the past. This small thing I will keep for myself after I gift him another nation.

Chapter 9

The Comumbran Palace looks to have grown out of the rocks on which it sits. The walls jut up at irregular angles and there are gaps between the unevenly cut slabs of granite which make up the majority of the structure. The inside, however, is ornately decorated and outfitted with as much, if not more, technology than exists in Celsus. As we walk through the corridor toward Mansa's ceremonial hall I'm reminded of the Stronghold of the Twelve in the subtle carvings and columns which are placed under windows, across door frames and embedded in the floors.

"Demetrius is pleased by Mansa's change of attitude," Tori says.

As it was when I first became General of Celsus, it is just the two of us. The rest of the Comumbran and Celcean ruling class wait in the hall behind the enormous wooden doors. I consider telling Tori about my visit to the Stronghold yesterday, but I refrain, not wanting to burden him with my secret as well.

"Mansa struggles with losing a nation. I doubt I would be any different, were I him," I say. As we walk, I feel more like a mortician, inspecting the personal effects of a corpse, than I do a liberator.

The doors shudder, letting out a deep growl as they swing forward. Through the crack, the golden light of Mansa's hall pours through. The audience inside reacts to my presence. Cheers from the Celceans, silence from the Comumbrans. Seconds later, minidrones flood the space above us, giving eyes to the rest of the world.

Tori puts his mouth against my ear, "Behold. The spoils of your blood."

The hall looks to have been pulled directly from antiquity. As soon as we step across the threshold, all technology is gone. Candles, torches and oil-fed chandeliers give a dim, yellow hue to the lacquered wooden beams across the ceiling. The floor bends and creaks with every step we take. I look up to see the swarm of the minidrones. Their juxtaposition with the environment is enough to make me feel as if they are the pre-cursing mist of a dragon.

Mansa sits on a wrought iron throne at the end of the great hall, wearing a simple, jewel-less crown. Next to him, Demetrius stands, wearing a fully synthetic purple robe, shimmering with its own embedded light source.

I stop, ten meters from the throne and wait for the crowd to calm. Mansa stands and raises his hands. The little noise coming from the Comumbrans immediately quiets, but the Celceans continue to cheer. After a few moments, I lift my hands. The hall falls silent before my arms are fully above my head.

I step forward and say, "King Mansa. Under the authority of the Twelve Liberators, having defeated your General in the Temple, I claim Comumbra for my Ruler. Demetrius, The Liberator of the Oppressed and Advocate for the Weak."

Mansa remains seated for longer than he should. His calm and welcoming demeanor from yesterday has been replaced by a smoldering rage. Finally, he stands, the minidrones move closer to him in a chaotic and synchronized vapor. "I acknowledge the defeat of my General, and with it, your invasion of Comumbra. In so doing, I recognize your authority as General. Your power having been handed to you from the mandate of the

Twelve. You are free to do as you wish with Comumbra, but I implore you, refrain from giving control to Demetrius. He is a conqueror, not a liberator. And his advocacy extends only as far as his waistline."

The Celcean side of the room gasps, then erupts in shouts of anger. For his part, Demetrius remains impassive, waiting for the scene to play out. Until I formally give him a physical token of control, he is merely a bystander. While subtle insults from the defeated king are common, Mansa's explicit refusal to recognize Demetrius is nothing short of outright defiance. Above us, the minidrones soak up and broadcast every delicious second.

Again, I raise my hands and again the Celceans fall silent. "As has been true with every defeated Ruler, I extend to you an invitation to join my king's inner circle of advisors in order to secure a peaceful and joyous transition for our two nations." Ever since the Twelve set their rules, this has been an unwritten agreement to ensure innocent citizens are not caught up in a violent rebellion.

Mansa steps down from his platform and removes the tiny crown, a single ring of gold, from his head. He extends it toward me. "I love my citizens and I love this nation. The Twelve started their campaign from these very walls. It is because of this love, and my commitment to continue their defiant pursuit of virtue, that I decline your invitation."

I almost drop the crown. To my knowledge, no Ruler has ever declined. I look to Demetrius, then to Tori. Both of them wide eyed and slightly more pale.

"Rather, young General, I invoke an older, bloodier Rule which our Ancestors gave. I choose death. Here and now. By the hands of your paper king." From the Comumbran side of the hall, a man approaches, holding an enormous double-bladed axe.

As the minidrones capture every sight and sound of this strange scene, I am increasingly aware of the need for me to respond, but try as I may, I come up empty.

Tori steps to my side and leans as close as he can. I drop my shoulder so I can hear his whispered advice. "This is a matter of kings and politicians now. Your role is at an end."

It is not in my nature to defer, but I am grateful for the counsel. I turn my gaze from Mansa to Demetrius. "My lord," I say, "I present you the Comumbran Crown. May your wisdom and kindness grow to be as vast as your empire." I hand him the crown and bow deeply.

He takes the crown and places it gently on his head, testing the slight weight. "I am honored by your love and loyalty. Celsus, and the world, breathe a breath of gratitude because of your dedication to what is right." Rather than launch into a traditional speech about acceptance and the strength of merging two nations, he turns to Mansa. "King, I beg you to reconsider. If not for yourself and your stubborn pride, for your citizens. Let us not welcome a weak and struggling population under the stain of your angry blood." There are tears in his eyes as he says this. My heart breaks for him. Even in defeat, Mansa seeks to undermine and usurp the rightful victory of my king.

Rather than responding, Mansa nods to the axe-bearer, then kneels, presenting the back of his neck to Demetrius.

This scene may as well be ripped directly from the pages of an outdated history book. Things like this should not happen anymore. The anger I feel is like nothing I have known and I'm overwhelmed with embarrassment for how easily I was manipulated by Mansa yesterday. Demetrius takes the axe with shaking hands. Tears stream from his wide, terrified eyes. He breathes in as he raises the axe to his shoulders, then above his head. The axe pauses at its pinnacle and Demetrius takes his gaze from Mansa and looks at me. I could live a thousand lifetimes and never want to see such a look of confusion and fear coming from my Ruler.

"Stop," I yell.

Demetrius pauses, the axe head wavering in the air.

"Highness," I say as the minidrones swirl around Demetrius, Mansa and me. "I am your champion. Bred and trained in the art of death so you can rule in peace. Mansa has requested death. That is his selfish right. But let it end there. The Twelve have given me the burden of brutality and I gladly accept it."

He slowly brings the axe down, then hands it to me. "Your greatness, it seems, lives in your ability to simultaneously kill and nurture. I will not easily forget this act of kindness," he says.

I take the axe. Its weight is perfect and the blade has been recently sharpened. It is a beautiful weapon. Light from the candelabras next to Mansa's throne reflect from the mirror-perfect finish on the head, leaving a glare in my vision. I clear my mind and let my training take over. This is the only life I have taken outside of the Temple and as my back flexes, starting the downward arc of the blow, I pray it is my last.

Tori and I sit quietly on our landskimmer. Two days have passed since Mansa's death. Our caravan is smaller as we head back, having left the entire squadron of the guard behind to secure a peaceful transition. My hands still feel stained from Mansa's execution. I absently rub the palms on my thighs as we creep across a meadow of grass, speckled with wildflowers.

"The world's opinion of your decision is one thing. More importantly, you must reconcile your actions within your own heart," Tori says.

I nod but remain silent. Guilt is an emotion I am unfamiliar with, yet this trip has polluted me with it. The secret of the Stronghold, which in spite of myself I have chosen to keep, and Mansa's death both fall outside of my introspective abilities.

"Mansa put you in a terrible position. As did Demetrius."

"What should I have done? Let my king be made to look like a blood hungry bully?"

"I am loyal to you, Trajan. If given the chance of leaving Celsus I would remain in the nation which dethroned my king, simply so I might have another day with you. But that loyalty does not mean I cannot find fault with Demetrius when it is appropriate."

"The whole thing makes me feel like a child. Mansa crafted a winless scenario. For Comumbrans and for us. And he took the easy way out. We are left to wrestle with the implications," I say.

"Battles in the Temple are much cleaner than Battles between Rulers."

Demetrius rounds the corner, "Truer words have never been spoken, Mentor," he says.

Tori and I stand awkwardly, unprepared for his visit. I have not seen him since leaving the Comumbran palace.

"All news from our new ruling governor in Comumbra is positive. There is a small pocket of resistance, but things have not progressed beyond rhetoric. The gifts and upgrades for the citizens are providing suitable lubrication," Demetrius says.

"Let us hope the peace sustains," I say.

We all sit as a servant serves us a gently brewed tea.

After a few minutes of contemplation, Demetrius says, "We are not going straight back to Celsus."

"Where to, then?" I say.

"Try as I might, I find my hatred for Mansa growing with each passing day." He stands and places his cup, still full, on his seat. "He wasn't the first to choose death. Tori's Ruler, in fact, opted to end his own life after your predecessor won."

Tori does not take his eyes from the horizon. I, on the other hand, am shocked. As close as we are, Tori rarely speaks of his life before serving as my Mentor. This news sheds new light on his opinion of Mansa's execution.

"At least he had the honor to take his own life in a private ceremony," Demetrius says.

I continue to watch Tori. To anyone else he would appear impassive. But I notice the subtle clenching of skin at the corners of his eyes. Pain and anger bubbling just beneath the surface.

"But Mansa took his final opportunity to shove a spear in my heart."

"I find myself unable to think of anything else," I say.

"I have not thanked you, my son," he says. "You saw my torment and acted with selflessness."

I am unused to compliments and I'm about to respond with awkward gratitude, but Demetrius continues.

"Unfortunately, you did exactly what Mansa wanted as well."

It's as if the air has been vacuumed from the room.

"There was no winning that scene. But when you took the axe from me, Mansa's demonstration accomplished its goal. The Rulers who want to see me dethroned have already begun to use it as an example of how I lack the strength to finish what I have started. They're even saying I hide behind your strength in order to gain more power." He shakes his head. "Can you imagine? The leader of the most prosperous nation on earth is now being portrayed as a sniveling weakling who exploits the might of his loyal General."

I have no words. Happily, Demetrius does not appear interested in a response. He turns to leave and rests his hand on my shoulder. "It is for this reason we must divert our trip home. There is an opportunistic Ruler of one of the water nations who seems to be leading the derogatory conversation. I'd like to meet her face to face and I'd like you to be there."

"Of course," I say, "whatever is necessary."

"Whatever is necessary," he repeats, "let us hope it doesn't come to that."

After he leaves, the air feels even heavier than before he visited.

Tori breathes a deep breath. "Come. You have been overly concerned with politics and the petty arguments of arrogant Rulers. It's time we got back to more pure things." He pauses at the door, "Meet me in the training room in five minutes."

He's right. Let the politicians scheme. All of it leads inevitably to the Temple. My realm. And my preparations are long overdue.

Chapter 10

The Aegeans are as surprised by our visit as I am. We wait for a transport to pick us up from one of their beaches for two days. When it finally arrives, it is the middle of the night and they give us less than an hour to board. Demetrius is gracious and inquisitive while he carefully chooses who should join us on the trip.

Once on the transport, we are stacked six to a room. Each of us given a rolled-up pad and a scratchy blanket for the night. In the morning, we are greeted with stale bread and warm water, freshly filtered from the sea. While the salt has been removed, the overwhelming taste of fish and seaweed remain.

After a week of this, we finally dock with one of their floating colonies. As we depart from the transport, we are greeted by a lovely older woman. Her grey hair is long, secured to the top of her head with a simple strand of leather. She is tall and thin. Her loose and flowing gown makes her appear even more wispy.

"Demetrius," she says without bowing, "if you had contacted me, I would have prepared a proper delegation and transport. As it was, I could only dispatch one of my maintenance vessels. Unfortunately, they run a small crew and subsist on the most meager of rations. Surely not meant for a king of your stature." Her green eyes glow against the dark brown hue of her skin. Although she smiles as she speaks, it is clear she is uncomfortable with our presence.

Demetrius nods. "My visit is as much of a surprise to me as it is you, my queen. But after the events in Comumbra, it seemed best to change our plans." His voice is even and cool. A stark contrast to the lilting tone of the Aegean Queen.

She turns to me and smiles. "I think we might need to add some stabilizers under us. You may be the single largest human I have ever seen."

I bow and mutter my thanks. I am unused to Rulers addressing me with such informality.

She laughs and says to Demetrius, "If I had never seen him fight, I would be tempted to call him adorable." To me, she says, "My name is Marcail. I oversee this simple nation. Welcome to Aegea, Trajan. I am very happy to meet you."

I smile and say, "It is my pleasure, Highness. Your nation reflects the beauty of its Ruler."

Marcail laughs and turns. "Come gentlemen. You must be weary from the travel. Allow me to offer remedy." She walks quickly across the colony. I find myself having to walk faster than my normal gait in order to keep up.

The colony is nothing more than floating pods stuck together. Each pod has random structures built into the base platform. None of them more than five meters high, all of them a basic sea sky grey. On a foggy day, it would be impossible to tell sky from structure.

Marcail stops in front of a long but short building and says to me, "This will be yours while you are here. If you don't mind, we will have your Mentor stay with you as well. I apologize in advance for the size. We obviously didn't anticipate your enormity."

"This is more than generous, my lady," I say. "Tori and I will be quite comfortable."

She nods quickly and turns to the rest of the delegation, motioning for them to follow her. I watch as she stops at the next structure. From her gestures, Demetrius and Castor will be bunking together.

"She is both charming and vexing," Tori says.

"I wonder how Demetrius feels about that arrangement."

"I would plan on welcoming Castor into our quarters tonight," he says with as much amusement as I have ever heard from him.

"We will save an especially comfortable space for him on the floor," I say.

Tori wakes me just before dawn. The second I feel his hand on my shoulder, I can feel the benefit of the first solid night of sleep I've had since leaving Celsus over a month ago. He nods to the floor where Castor sleeps. Even in slumber he is sloppy. His limbs are at strange angles and his breathing is loud and uneven. I dress quickly and meet Tori outside without interrupting Castor.

"Our training platform awaits," Tori says.

Because of my popularity, I travel throughout the vast expanse of the Celcean territories. In order to remain Battle ready, Demetrius poured the very best technology at his disposal to create a mobile training facility for me. It is as much home to me as any other place.

As we step into the temporary structure, I feel my muscles relax and my mind quiet. This place lacks nothing. Weapons line the walls and there are countless corners for specialized focus. Databases loaded with game theory and advanced problem solving and puzzles wait for us to unlock their knowledge.

"Castor will not sleep much longer, nor will the other trainees," Tori says.

We start our stretching routines. It's silent, save for the whisper of the sea wind. As I move from one position to the next, I focus on my breathing. Forcing myself to maintain a steady pace, no matter how I contort my body. It isn't long until I lose awareness of the room around me. It's as if I'm looking inside myself, taking inventory of the way my joints and muscles respond to and guide my movements. My mind is simultaneously empty and determined. I feel powerful again.

Time passes without me noticing. It isn't until I hear laughter and metal banging against metal that I open my eyes. The trainees are gathered off to one side. Most of them watch me, some of them have formed a line, mimicking my movements. Castor is swinging a staff around his head, jabbing it toward another, smaller trainee from time to time. The boy dodges unsteadily and looks around for something to ward off the attacks.

I look for Tori and find him against the far wall, watching Castor with disdain. "Enough," I say. My voice carries easily, bouncing off the synthetic material of the training facility. Castor immediately lowers the spear, looking like a child caught with a mouthful of sweets. I motion for the trainees to assemble in front of me. Once they are in formation, I begin stretching again. All but Castor immediately follow my lead.

Rather than acquiescing, Castor moves off to the side and noisily begins to rearrange pegs on the climbing wall. After a couple of minutes, I invite Tori to lead the trainees.

"Above prep-work?" I say.

He continues to change the wall configuration. "Routine is a crutch. I prefer spontaneity."

"And the rest of the trainees?"

He laughs, "Who do you think has been training these boys while you've been playing politician?"

"I owe them an apology, then," I say.

Castor is powerful with impeccable fighting instincts. But what he possesses in talent, he lacks in control and maturity. I know that if I push this much more, I will goad him into an altercation and I feel the familiar tingle of adrenaline as it mixes with my blood.

He turns, a predatory smile stretching his lips across his teeth. "I crave the moment when someone finally exploits your weaknesses."

"Funny thing about cravings," I say, "most come from a physical deficiency. The rest are driven by a weakness in character."

The door to our facility opens and a small man wearing the robes of the Aegean elite enters. Everyone stops and turns to me. Our training sessions are closely controlled, even in Celsus. Given that we are in a foreign nation, this interruption is not just out of place, it is borderline insulting. The Aegean looks around, pausing to make eye contact with both Castor and me before crossing the padded floor.

"General," he says to me. "My name is William. I am Queen Marcail's son. When she saw your facility being assembled, she requested I train alongside you today. Demetrius granted it." His voice is strong and his stride purposeful. In a room of brutes, he looks like a sprite. Even the youngest trainee is twice his size.

"Looks like sparing is out of the question," Castor says. This causes most of the trainees to laugh.

"Enough," I say. The room immediately silences, with the exception of Castor. He makes sure to laugh longer than the rest. "We would be honored, Prince. What would you like to start with?"

"It's your facility. I'm your student today," he says.

"We've been starting with combat. One on one. It's proving quite beneficial, isn't it, lads?" Castor says.

"That's good, Castor. But like the General Prince, you are my student today as well," I say while still looking at William. "You've not yet taken my place, unless I've forgotten in my old age."

"What would you suggest, in your considerable wisdom, then?" his voice drips sarcasm.

"Tactics," I say.

The students line the walls and one of the younger boys punches a series of commands into a console on the far wall. There's a brief vibration as a set of obstacles form in the center of the room.

I turn to William, who is visibly impressed, and say, "The floor is made up of millions of different moveable pieces. We can create innumerable configurations from them." He nods his head and begins to study the obstacles.

"Castor, choose two students and join me. William, join us as well," I say. We convene at the start of the newly formed course.

The obstacles take on true shape, looking as if they've been in the room from the inception of the training facility. The final stages of the transformation happen when their color changes, giving the appearance of old wood, rusted metal and fraying rope. The initial obstacle is a wall, four meters high that spans almost the entire width of the room.

"The goal is simple," I say. "Get from one side to the next as fast as possible." I gesture to the wall. "Feel free to inspect the course, but bear in mind, once you begin, it will change its form and its violence at random." Castor is already smiling.

Castor, William and the two trainees walk along the side of the obstacles, inspecting barrier after barrier. The two youngsters talk quietly. They're young enough to be more concerned with impressing their Mentors than competing against one another. William walks at the back of the group, glancing occasionally at the course, but spends more time watching Castor. For his part, Castor pours over the barriers as if they contain some secret message waiting to be unlocked.

When they've finished their appraisal, they reconvene at the beginning.

"The first one done, wins. Simply push the deactivation switch on the other side of the last obstacle and you'll stop the exercise. You will all enter the course together. There are no other rules," I say.

The rest of the students have taken vantage points that offer the best view of the course and its ensuing bloodletting. The nervous energy makes me feel more at home than I can remember.

Castor bounces gently on the balls of his feet, working out the inefficient energy. The younger trainees do the same. This is likely the closest they will ever get to a true Battle. I glance at Tori who has faded to the back, allowing me to take command.

"Any questions?" I ask.

Castor says nothing, still eyeing the course. The young men quickly shake their heads.

William takes a deep breath, "Good luck, gentlemen," he says.

"Luck is a thing Rulers hope for after their Generals die," Castor says.

"Begin," I say it quietly, yet my voice booms. Castor moves before I've finished the second syllable. His first attempt of lowering his shoulder and slamming into the wall is a failure, but he's undeterred. Next, he launches himself, catching the top ledge with his fingertips. He gracefully pulls himself to the top, three meters above the rest of the course. The Hopefuls work together, one offering to hoist the other to the top. William has yet to move.

Castor stands, readying himself to jump from the wall and over an icy patch on the other side. Before he's able to jump, the wall crumbles. At first it appears as if it has just dispersed into mist, but the particles quickly build on each other to form a one meter wide strip of spikes. Castor tries his best to control his fall, but his left ankle is impaled on one of the spikes.

The spectators gasp, each of them imagining the pain that must be burning through his leg. He doesn't make a sound. Rather, he pulls his leg up, allowing the spike to pass back through. The icy surface where he's laying begins to melt, no doubt opening some other terrible consequence for the participants.

William watches the two young men as they carefully, yet quickly navigate through the spikes and across the ice. Just as they reach the other side, the ice bursts into steam, leaving a boiling pool of liquid where it had been. He seems amused by how hard his opponents try. Every few seconds he glances at the spectators who have begun to chant Castor's name.

Castor's leg bleeds freely, making the floor beneath him slick. He and the other two trainees stand in front of a constantly morphing gelatinous pool. Other than the motion, nothing about it seems intimidating. The chanting of Castor's name increases. I flash back to the Temple and my Battle with Seth.

After a couple of moments, Castor reaches down to the smallest trainee, whispers something in his ear, then with an ease that astounds even me, hefts the child into the pool. As soon as the child makes contact, the substance erupts. At first it appears to be flames, but it's just the gel reflecting the light from the room. Instead, a net burst from under the pool, tightens and lifts him high above the course. The substance immediately hardens and Castor vaults over it, heading to the final obstacle.

William finally begins to move toward the course. Instead of beginning at the spikes, he veers left, toward the narrow path they walked down before the start of the competition. His gait is confident, but not rushed. As he passes the different obstacles, he looks at the spectators who have fallen silent.

Castor doesn't see William. The final obstacle, a field which alternates from electricity to flame to aluminum darts and back, cycles in front of him. He's so focused on learning the timing of it that he misses when William taps the other Hopeful on the shoulder and beckons him to follow.

Within seconds, William and the child reach the deactivation button. Just as they press it, Castor throws himself into the field. His timing is off and flame rains down on him before the challenge ends. The heat forces him to the ground and I can see his blistered flesh as the course reshapes itself back into solid floor.

Regardless of my competition with Castor, he's my student. I'm responsible for him and Demetrius has declared him my successor. I rush toward him, taking stock of the smell of burnt flesh and spattering of blood on the floor. The rest of the Hopefuls tend to the younger two. Neither of them are significantly hurt.

William reaches him before I do and has begun to wrap the ankle in his own shirt. I nod to one of the older students. He moves to the control panel. To William, I say, "Back away."

He looks at me with confusion but complies. As soon as he's out of the way, the Hopeful at the control panel presses a button, causing a medicinal mist to fall over Castor. He immediately falls unconscious as the mixture begins to heal him. Castor's bleeding stops and the smell of sizzled flesh vanishes.

"I'm glad you stopped it when you did," I say to William.

He nods, trying to find the right words, "Why would you let your own countrymen go through that? What lesson is worth such suffering?"

The rest of the Hopefuls have gathered around us, awaiting my response. I like what I have seen of him so far, but his weakness and idealism seem dangerous. Especially now, in front of such a young audience.

"What would you have me do? Castor is powerful, but the lesson was in tactics, not agility. He made a mistake. A mistake that would have cost him and Celsus dearly on the battlefloor. Some singed flesh and a minor scar are an acceptable price to pay for that lesson." This is meant more for my students than for William.

He shakes his head and bows slightly. "Thank you for the lesson, General. I learned much more than I thought I would." He nods to the group and makes his way out of the facility.

I say a few more words to the students, but I don't want to make a bigger scene than I already have. Moto-San always ensured training should be harder than the real thing and I've benefited from that philosophy. Under my tutelage, these kids will too. This scene of pain and injury should be more common than not, as long as it assures strong, intelligent and dominant Generals. Castor has obviously forgotten this.

Chapter 11

Castor lies comfortably in his healing room. It's been almost twenty-four hours since he was caught in the flames and he only looks as if he has a bad sunburn. Our physicians and the remedies they provide never cease to amaze.

He lazily glances at me, then back to the ceiling. "I checked that scenario. It was programmed to be impassable. And I was one obstacle away from beating it. Say what you want, but a little pain is worth that."

There is no nuance to the way he sees the world, but I'm not angered by what he says. Instead, I'm grateful for Tori. There were times in my life I teetered on the verge of this type of thinking. It's easy, being as powerful and talented as we are. But every time he saw the initial buds of hubris in me, he would cut me. Or break a bone. Or gouge an eye. He'd immediately remind me of how weak I really am. If he were here, I'd bow to him with a renewed respect.

"You see adversaries when you should see allies. You seek to conquer what needs no liberator. You are a gluttonous victor and if you don't control your appetite, you will burst from you own ill-gotten spoils," I say. I look straight at him as I speak, yet, either out of cowardice or disrespect, he refuses to make eye contact or respond.

The feast is extravagant. We have been in Aegea a week and it is clear Marcail has been preparing for this night from the moment she heard we were on her distant beach. Demetrius and I are seated with a mixture of a few top Celcean counselors and a few young members of the Aegean aristocracy. Marcail and William sit next to us, likely in an attempt to buffer us from the inevitable politics. Castor is nearby, fully recovered and loudly entertaining a group of Aegean women. Tori is at a small table in the back. I find myself envying his placement.

Our meal is being held on a covered floating platform which has been detached from the larger colony, giving us the sense of being adrift and alone in this vast sea. The breeze off the ocean is refreshing and adds flavor to the cuisine. Gentle music wanders from one table to the next.

"Tell me, General," Queen Marcail says, "how are you recovering from your Battle?"

"Our physicians are unparalleled, which Trajan has taken advantage of more times than he can count," Demetrius says. He lounges against a pile of plush pillows. So far back, a servant has been brought to shuffle food from the table to his plate every few minutes.

"I have no doubt of that, Highness, but there is more to recovery than the body healing," Marcail says. It's a gentle rebuke, but a rebuke nonetheless.

"After a Battle like the last one, it's difficult to focus on anything but physical recovery," I say. With how quiet the room is, I feel as if everyone at the party can hear me. Castor has quieted and sits straighter, clearly interested in my conversation.

"Shame. Our physicians would never dream of treating just the body. Maybe you would benefit from a consultation while you're here," she says. William sits rigidly at her side. I haven't seen him since our training session and he seems disinterested in holding a conversation with me.

"Careful, my lady," Demetrius says, "my physicians may take offense." His tone is light and he smiles as he says this, but I can tell he is becoming irritated. His pride in our medical abilities, rightly so, is boundless. Every time we have absorbed a new nation, our health care has made the biggest difference in improving their quality of life.

"With respect, but I doubt if my queen worries too much about offending any healer, regardless of the nation they serve," William says. It's the first thing he's said since we were seated and, if anyone wasn't already listening to our conversation, they are now.

Demetrius laughs loudly, a couple of short bursts from his lungs. "So refreshing, your lack of political hesitancy. From one Ruler to a future Ruler, however, I'd advise you to care more about what any physician feels. One never knows when one may end up at their mercy."

"True," Queen Marcail says as she raises her cup, "but let us hope we live lives fulfilling enough that when we're faced with our end, we welcome it, rather than run from it. An unfulfilled life strives endlessly for opportunity to redeem itself."

I raise my cup, along with the rest of the room, all of us apparently under Marcail's spell.

The conversation turns to politics and policy, the queen serving as gracious host by asking Demetrius about his philosophy of rule. He speaks freely, happy to share his experience. I eat sparingly, distracted by the alien setting.

The clothing style of the Aegeans matches the environment they call home and the room seems to ebb and flow, just like the waves supporting us. It's easy to pick out the people from Celsus, our linens contrasting brightly against the gentle coloring of the Aegean clothes. We look out of place in this soft room, like scabs on the back of a wounded slave. I'm not sure how long I'm lost in this thought, but a gentle hand on my shoulder rouses me.

"Would you like dessert?" The voice is accented and soothing. I turn to decline and I'm met by the same vibrant green eyes which escorted me through the Temple halls before my Battle with Seth. For a moment, I'm convinced I've conjured her. But her image doesn't waver, no matter how intently I stare. As I hold her gaze, her expression becomes uncomfortable. "General?" she asks again, while lifting a platter of perfectly iced pastries.

I finally find my voice and say, "Forgive me, no."

For the first time since I turned around, she breaks my gaze and bows slightly. As she begins to move away, I reach out, "Excuse me," I say. "Do I know you?" I immediately feel foolish for the question.

I see brief laughter in her eyes. She glances to her arm, where my grasp lingers, and says, "I think I'd be doing something much different than offering dessert if I had the ability to answer that question."

I release her arm and immediately miss the softness of it against my skin. "Of course," I say. "If I may, what is your name?" There's no reason for me to ask her name, just as there's no reason for me to be talking to a servant.

She smiles. "My name is Fiona, Trajan. I'm glad you survived your Battle." She walks quickly away, pausing briefly to exchange a whisper with William. I don't take my eyes from her until she's left the party.

"Fiona is quite beautiful, is she not?" Marcail says.

"She certainly leaves an impression. Did you know she was my escort for my last Battle?"

"I did know," is all she says before she is interrupted by Castor as he sits next to William. Even Demetrius is surprised by his presence.

"This guy," he says, pointing to William and slurring his words, "is quite the schemer." His voice is loud, which makes it difficult to know who he addresses.

Marcail laughs and touches William's arm, "Schemer. I've heard you described many ways, but that is a new one."

Demetrius has stopped eating and watches the exchange with what looks like a mixture of amusement and irritation. For the second time on this trip, I find myself irritated at his attitude. Any other time, and he would have stepped in before Castor had the chance to offend.

"Is that how intellect is regarded in Celsus? As the byproduct of an overly manipulative mind?" William says.

"Please do not misinterpret my student," I say, attempting to keep my tone light. "Castor likes to appear like a brute, and clearly he plays the part convincingly, but I have never seen a more calculating mind."

The rest of the table quietly laugh at what they perceive to be my good-natured joke.

Castor scowls and heaps the plate in front of him with flaky pastries and bite sized cakes, unsure of how to respond.

I reach across the table and slide Castor's plate away, dumping the remaining desserts back onto the service platter. "Queen Marcail is overly generous, but I would be a poor commander if I allowed you to indulge in gluttony." This would instigate Castor if he were sober. In his intoxicated state, I may as well have slapped him.

"Why so conservative?" Demetrius asks, as he sits fully upright. "You train so hard; you can eat what you like. I smell the stink of Tori's outdated methods." He motions encouragement for Castor to eat as much as he would like.

"He's never steered me wrong," I say.

"Says the man still in recovery," Castor laughs, emboldened by the support from Demetrius. The rest of the people at the table, with the exception of Marcail, laugh politely.

"Says the most dominant General in history," I say without laughing. The table quiets. A few of the guests shift in their seats. Others are so focused on the food that they chuckle as if I'd just confessed to liking kittens.

"Your dedication to your craft, Trajan, is quite impressive. It takes a strong will to be of such a single mind," Marcail says, clearly trying to cut the tension.

She has provided me the perfect opportunity to diffuse the conversation. I know I should take it, aware that I have already overstepped by showing the schism between Castor and myself. But I am tired of Castor's unrelenting challenges and even more upset at my Ruler's willingness to entertain such a lazy and prideful contender. I turn to the woman next to me, her name is Savay, and say, "Tell me, what's your favorite Battle?" She was clearly chosen for our table because of her full blonde hair and flawless skin. Castor has been paying a lot of attention to her, glancing over after complimenting the food or making a witty remark.

"There are so many," she says. Her voice is soft and her brown eyes widen at my attention. "I have to admit, I don't understand the subtleties of combat and the brutality disturbs me," she looks at her plate. The members of the table have to strain to hear her over the festivities. "But this last one. Against the giant. I couldn't breathe. And when you let him live, it stopped my heart." She almost whispers the last part.

Castor watches her every move the way a tiger would consider a wounded rabbit. It's obvious he's displeased with her perspective.

"You flatter me," I say, "but clearly you're just being kind. Your favorite Battle doesn't have to be one of mine. Nor does it have to be my latest. What about young Castor? He's a lion in Battle." I reach over and smack his shoulder. To others it looks like a brotherly gesture, but the power I put behind it causes him to spill the drink he's holding. "Careful, brother. People may start to think you're overindulging."

The rest of the guests, including Savay, laugh along with me. Castor clenches his teeth but restrains himself just barely. He says nothing and brushes the liquid from his shirt.

Savay, still smiling, says, "No flattery, General. The mercy you showed. It was the first time I can remember a Battle that was about something other than winning. It saddened me to learn the giant expired." The table grows quiet in obedient and disingenuous respect.

"I'm touched, my lady," I turn to Castor, "do you share our beautiful companion's opinion?" To everyone else at the table, this seems like lazy and inconsequential conversation. If Tori were here, he'd see what I'm doing and find a way to get me away from the table. I purposely refrain from glancing in his direction.

"With respect, darling," Castor says, without taking his eyes off of me, "I'd have taken the giant's head."

Turning my attention back to Savay, I say, "Would that have made the Battle more memorable for you?" I ask.

She simply shakes her head, either embarrassed or overwhelmed.

I look around the table, pausing my gaze on Marcail, "My apologies for the crassness of my young student. A warrior's tongue isn't always as well trained as his body."

An older man, I think he was introduced as a man of law, says, "An untrained tongue is merely a symptom of a lazy mind, General." As he says this, his face flushes a shade of red. This is probably the most confrontational he's ever been and I can see the conversation he's having with himself. Already plotting his early exit from the feast.

"Any shortcoming of Castor is my failing as his superior." I can feel the anger radiating from Castor. His temper, the thing that makes him such a formidable successor, makes him such easy prey outside of the Temple.

"Careful, General. Using words like superior to compare yourself to me won't keep you healthy for very long," Castor says.

"You go too far. I'll forgive you that one misstep because our gracious hosts have put me in such a good temper. But charming table mates and delicious food will only stay my hand temporarily." My voice is low and even. It feels good, the subtlety of this confrontation. The ease with which I brought it about.

"And who is to say I desire that?" he stands quickly, rattling the table, which draws the attention of the entire feast. Demetrius begins to stand, realizing this squabble has gotten out of hand, but he is too late, "Trajan, General of Celsus, I challenge you for your title." His voice is confident and clear in spite of the rapid rise and fall of his chest.

The room is silent. Savay and the rest of the members of our table look like scolded school children.

Within moments, I hear the voice of Demetrius, "I want to thank our gracious hosts. This stop has provided us a way of resting our overtaxed bodies. Apparently, some are wearier than others. For that I apologize. Please accept our gratitude and allow our leave. We eagerly anticipate our next encounter." Perfect political words from a perfect politician.

The delegates from Celsus rise simultaneously and politely, all smiles and compliments. Castor has already left the dining hall.

Chapter 12

Demetrius is waiting for me when I get back to my quarters. Tori is nowhere in sight. Castor sits on the floor, head bowed.

"Let us get the obvious out of the way. Castor will have his chance. Since he chose to challenge you in front of another nation, it will be at the Mid-Year exhibition. Instead of using that time for the political benefit of Celsus, we will spend it settling a selfish vendetta." He has perfect control over his voice, as if he is reading a pre-written speech. "Castor, leave us."

There is no hesitation from Castor. He doesn't look at me and I don't look at him.

Once the door has shut, Demetrius turns to me. "Why do you test me?"

The words sting as deeply as anything I have experienced before.

"A General who can't control his subordinates is not a General who deserves to lead. You allowed a stupid and impetuous child to disrespect you in public. That offense is no more his than is a monkey a murderer if he stabs someone with a knife. The responsibility lies with the person who gave the monkey the knife." He stands above me, a father chiding a child, his gaze harder than I've ever seen.

"Of course. Forgive me," I say.

"Forgiveness will not hold these jackals at bay."

His voice is as soft as the breeze outside, but his words feel like a hurricane.

"Marcail's is the strongest voice in the growing choir calling for our downfall. And tonight your arrogance put a megaphone to her lips."

"A squabble between two men would hold no justification for her to challenge us in Battle," I say, confused by his logic.

"A Ruler who cannot control his Generals may not be able to justly rule over the entirety of his nation."

"Anyone who would believe that is already looking for a reason."

"Precisely," he says.

"Let her challenge me. I covet a Battle in which I dictate the rules of engagement."

"You confuse yourself. A snake does not choose the sky as its battleground."

His implication hangs heavy in the air. "What shall we do?"

"A solution will present itself. Of that, I am sure. But I am wearied by this. More wearied than I can say." He sits on one of the soft cushions, cupping his forehead in his hands. "Do you find her charming? Marcail?"

The question takes me off guard. "She is not like other Rulers," I say.

"Indeed," he says, "and you find that enjoyable, do you not?" His words roll across the floor.

"It makes no difference. She is not my Ruler."

"She charms everyone." He pauses and shakes his head. "There have been growing rumors. Poverty. Abuse. Our allies believe her rhetoric against me is designed to drown out those who question her."

It becomes clear. The reason for our stop here was to find evidence of her misconduct. "Challenge her. The evidence will present itself."

He lunges to his feet and crosses the room in two powerful steps. He has never shown aggression toward me and my shock overrides my warrior's instinct. The second he's within arm's reach, he strikes me across the jaw with the back of his hand. It brings little physical pain, but the anger and humiliation are enough to make me stumble.

"Such sage advice from a brute." The words drip from his mouth. "Even with evidence, the backlash would have been powerful. But now, if I challenge her, she has more than enough ammunition to put our entire society back on the precipice." He moves to strike me again, but refrains. Instead he turns and slams his fist into the wall. It makes a dull thud and I watch his wrist collapse under the pressure. He will have a sprain tomorrow. "Pride, I can accept. Stupidity, I will not abide. You have served me well, but you will prove your true value in the coming months. Keep that in mind. To right your wrong will take great sacrifice. And I expect your immediate and unquestioning obedience when I call for it." He leaves before I can respond.

I sit down, my jaw tingling where Demetrius struck me, trying to understand what had just happened. Yes, I baited Castor into an outburst, and he took it farther than I expected. But, even after his speech, I fail to see the same ramifications as Demetrius. When we've disagreed in the past, he has been measured and fair. This outburst is a side I have never seen, yet he slipped into it so easily, I briefly wonder if it's as rare as I think.

"We leave at first light. Demetrius has just commanded it," Tori says. He crosses the room toward his quarters. As he passes, he hands me a cold pack. "We don't want it to look as if you and Castor got into a scuffle when the Aegeans see you tomorrow," he says.

I take the pack and stand, pressing it against my cheek. "You were listening?"

He pauses in his doorway. "We can discuss when we are home. I prefer the known dangers over the unknown."

Our quarters fall silent again. In my room, I shove my meager possessions into a satchel and lie down. Sleep doesn't come until hours later, after the sea winds have died down, along with the waves.

Chapter 13

It is good to be back in Celsus. We arrive to a crowd of our citizens gathered around the training facility. The second we step from my skimmer, Tori and I are surrounded by minidrones while we pick through our supplies. Demetrius approaches us for the first time since leaving Aegea with a warm smile and prolonged embrace. There is only pride and happiness in his eyes as he looks from me to the crowd of Celceans.

"To be home is to finally breathe again. Your newly liberated countrymen send their gratitude and delight to be grafted into the mighty nation of Celsus," he says.

The citizens cheer as loudly as I've heard outside of the Temple. We stand next to each other, the mightiest team in the world, while the drones drink in the image. He steps aside and pulls Tori into our huddle.

"These two," he pulls us as close to himself as he can, "are the perfect example of skill and discipline. Because of Tori's wise tutelage and Trajan's single-minded execution, countless citizens have been rescued from the tyranny of greedy leaders." Our crowd crescendos in wave after wave of adoration. Demetrius releases us and raises his hands. "But their task is not done. Even now, my ambassadors tell me of rampant abuse from Rulers who would otherwise appear charming and measured."

An image of the smiling Marcail, elegant hair and carefree robes, flashes in my mind. Then Mansa, strong headed and proud. I'm grateful for the battlefloor. Where the opponent is clear and the prize unmistakable.

"I'm sure you have heard the news," he continues, "of the challenge." His posture has changed, as has the tone of the crowd. Diverted from ecstasy to anxious uncertainty. "I cannot go against the will of the Twelve. So young, impetuous and aggressive Castor will face our Battle tested and immoveable Trajan in the Mid-Year."

There are gasps and moans from the audience. They are the brush and Demetrius the artist.

"Pray for them. And pray for Celsus. While our guards squabble in the bunkhouse, assassins creep toward our gate."

He says a few more things about the greatness of our nation and his burden to see the will of the Twelve carried out. The shame I feel for acting in a way that requires him to make this speech after having just brought a new nation under his rule turns my stomach. It is clear I have hurt him and I'm overwhelmed with thoughts of how to regain my status. Victory. That is how he came to love me and it will be how our relationship is renewed. Sudden, bloody, shocking and decisive victory. It is all I can do to remain by his side, the urge to enter the training facility and push myself harder than ever feels like a magnet pointed directly at me.

The axe blade reflects a burst of sunlight, leaving me briefly blinded. Tori stands behind me, his breathing a perfect rhythm. It is a cloudless day, but the heavy air hints at a coming storm. I lick my thumbnail and drag one side of the axe head across it, feeling the blade catch as it passes over. I flip the handle and repeat the process on the second blade. It does not catch as readily so I re-engage the file.

We are in the most desolate part of the Celcean wilderness and I must fell a tree in order to construct a shelter for us before nightfall. The humidity adds to the pressure. Tori's instructions were clear. A complete shelter from a standing tree, all done by hand before we're allowed to eat or rest.

We only stayed in Celsus for three days after returning from our trip before Tori announced we would spend the rest of our time before the Mid-Year isolated. We have trained this way before, but never for this long.

Once I'm satisfied with the sharpness of the blades, I repack the files and set my sights on a tree with a trunk just under two meters in diameter. The axe bites deeply on my first swing, causing me to step to my right to keep my balance.

"Know your foe. The deeper you penetrate the tree, the harder it will hold the blade," he says.

I wriggle the handle until the axe head comes free, then readjust my stance, placing my feet wider and shifting my weight to accommodate the slope of the ground. The next swing I angle upward. My aim is true, sending a chunk of moist wood flying and leaving a perfect wedge.

Tori moves close to the tree mid-swing, which causes me to adjust slightly, throwing off both my momentum and timing. The axe clunks against the pulpy wood and sends a shiver up the handle and into my arms.

He says nothing, but the lesson is clear. I failed on two fronts. I swung before considering what could interrupt my attack, and I allowed an unplanned action to disrupt the course to which I'd already committed. He remains uncomfortably close to where I've been chopping. Rather than change positions, I continue my swings so they miss him by centimeters before they dig into the dwindling trunk.

Time slips from my mind as we remain locked in this silent match. My shoulders and back begin to burn in a pleasing acknowledgement of my activity. It does not take me long to learn the weight and length of the axe. By the time I'm halfway through the tree, it feels as if the tool has become an extension of my arm. I switch sides, quickly biting through the bark, forming the hourglass needed to topple the giant.

Ten swings and I hear the fibers begin to stretch, then snap as the tree succumbs to the attack. Tori steps back in anticipation of the unpredictable kickback of the trunk. As it falls, it catches the branches of a nearby pine, causing it to jolt violently to the left. If Tori hadn't moved, he would have been crushed in an instant.

"Even a mortally wounded opponent can kill you," Tori says.

As the branches sway from the impact of the ground, I jump on top of it and begin severing the limbs which will prove to be part of our structure for the night. Two hours later, our shelter is completed, a fresh fire warming the small space as Tori prepares our meal.

"Why did you choose this tree?" Tori asks.

"It offered the most material for the shelter. And it proved the biggest challenge."

He does not respond which means he has found something in my thinking which requires his attention.

I wake to gusting winds and the sound of pelting rain. Tori is already awake, stoking the fire with the driest wood he can find. Even still, it puts out more black smoke than heat.

"The firewood was left outside," he says.

He needn't say anything more. I allowed my pride in preparing the shelter to overshadow the subtle hint of a storm. It is a stupid mistake. So stupid, in fact, I would chastise even a preteen for making it.

I immediately rise and lace my boots.

"We will wait for the storm to pass before training," he says.

"There are birch trees nearby. I'm sure their canopy shelters some burnable timber," I say. Before he can respond, I am out of the shelter. The rain is heavier than I thought, coming down in sideways sheets. I'm briefly impressed by how sound my shelter is, but the soaked pile of firewood near the entrance brings me back to reality. A half victory is a full failure.

The rain is thick enough to make me move slowly, sure to keep my bearings in relation to the shelter at all times. After searching for fifteen minutes, I finally stop under a heavily branched and gnarled tree. In spite of the storm, the ground remains dry here. I take a moment, allowing my eyes to adjust to the dim light, then begin to methodically search for dried twigs and branches.

My search yields a small pile of finger thick wood. It's not much, but it's better than what we have. I take off my shirt and wrap the twigs, first insulating it with leaves and needles to ensure the rain won't ruin these as well.

When I get back to the shelter, I am shivering and my fingertips have lost feeling. Tori says nothing as I kneel over and use the few coals to light the meager pile of dry wood. I allow myself a brief few seconds of warmth from the flames before I head back out into the storm.

This process repeats for the next two hours, the rain showing no signs of relenting. Every time I return, the fire has burnt out enough that my next pile of wood is barely enough to sustain it. At least, I think, I'm keeping Tori warm. The cold and exhaustion I feel is a fitting punishment for my sophomoric laziness.

I drop what must be my tenth pile of sticks and turn for the door when Tori says, "Sit."

I pause, then do as he says. Clearly irritated, he sighs, stands and wraps a wool blanket around me. "Even animals have enough sense to know when to allow a storm to run its course."

The storm rages through the day and well into the night. Rather than continue to forage for dry wood, I move a few small logs into the shelter. We wait in silence for them to dry. Late in the night, after I have given in to sleep, I feel the fire radiating against my back. When I wake the next morning, the shelter is warm, Tori has moved the rest of the wood inside and a cup of steaming tea sits on one of the warmed rocks lining the fire pit.

"The rain has eased enough for us to have a little fun," he says.

The training is intense. We move from one discipline to the next without rest. While I enjoy the strain, it is obvious that Tori is taking out his frustration on me. I say nothing, accepting my punishment in the hope that his anger will fade quickly, the same way I hope Demetrius will forgive me for my behavior in Aegea.

Just before lunch, Tori points to a dead, limbless tree which stands at least fifty meters tall and tells me to climb. The bark is slick from the rain and he offers me no gear to help with my ascent. As I begin to climb, I feel my forearms tighten under the strain of my weight. My fingers shake ever so slightly, warning the rest of my body of my calorie deficiency, but I ignore it, eager to give Tori a solid showing.

At twenty meters, my right foot slips from a tiny knot in the bark, but I'm able to catch myself before dropping more than two meters. The flesh on the inside of my left arm stings, then burns. A clear indication that I have gouged it on the rough bark of the tree. I take a couple of breaths and look down at Tori. He watches me intently, but offers no encouragement. Rather, he looks impatient. As if disappointed with my slow progress.

My legs have begun to shake as well, begging for more fuel to sustain the pace I've demanded of them today, but I press on. Faster than before the slip. First Demetrius, now Tori. Pleased when my performance reinforces the investment they have made in me. Angered and vengeful every time I fail to deliver even the slightest of rewards. Castor would crumble under this scrutiny in less than a week. I have been bred and groomed for this, and yet I still come up short. After years of dominance, both of them, it seems, feel no hesitation to throw me aside at the first mistake, no matter how small.

The surge of anger-borne adrenaline is a welcome gift and I pounce on the strength which follows. In less than a minute, I am five meters from the top. My mind is empty, save for the utter focus of hand and foot placement. So focused, in fact, that I fail to hear the snap of the old, dead wood. Weakened after so many years of exposure to the elements, my weight is simply too much for it to bear. The fall takes two, maybe three seconds before I impact the ground. Just before I hit, I realize Castor has won without having to lift a finger.

Pain rarely shocks me, having experienced enough of it to last three lifetimes. But the anguish shooting through my body is like nothing I have felt. I'm not sure how long I have been unconscious, but when I open my eyes, the tree from which I fell still looms over me. Tori is at my side, quiet and emotionless, with both syringe and bandage in hand.

"Be still," he says as he plunges the needle into my neck. Compared to the pain in the rest of my body, this tiny pinprick feels as if a fly landed on me. I immediately feel the tingling of the fluid in my veins.

"Have you called for medical transport?" I ask.

"No need."

The painkillers begin to work, making each of Tori's touches feel like a thump through a thick wall.

"Moto-San, I fell from fifty meters."

"Do you think so little of me? Why would I deny you the help you need? Your wounds do not require such drastic measures."

I lie quietly, too disoriented to argue. Tori is right, however, it is in his best interest to ensure I receive treatment commensurate with my wounds. Even though I may heal faster or more comfortably in a Celcean hospital, Demetrius would not be pleased to hear about Tori putting me in such a dangerous situation without precautions in place.

"Demetrius would declare Castor default winner if you showed up like this so close to the Mid-Year. If you want the chance to defend your place, we will remain here. Plus, the fall looked worse than it was. You have very little tissue damage. Just a broken collarbone and separated shoulder."

I take a deep breath and feel the broken ends of my collarbone grind against one another. "How is that possible?" I ask.

"Sleep. There is ample time to review."

It is raining again when I wake. Somehow, Tori managed to get me back to the shelter while I was knocked out by the serum. The fire warms us and the sound of the drops landing with chaotic uniformity makes me want to roll over and drift back to sleep. But I have no idea how long I have been out and I've never been one to allow myself extra indulgences.

I sit up slowly, testing first my shoulder, then my clavicle. Neither carries any pain from my movements, but I quickly notice a slight ridge where it healed. Another in a long line of scars which tell the violent story of a General.

"How do you feel?" Tori says. He drops a handful of leaves and berries into a kettle which is placed on a flat rock near the fire.

"There seems to be no lasting pain. I'm eager to test my strength and range of motion."

"In time."

He stirs the tea with a stick he has whittled into a makeshift spoon. The image makes me laugh. Here I sit, healed almost instantly from an impossible fall by using the most advanced technology on the planet, about to drink tea prepared with a tool as old as humanity itself. He looks up and sees me smiling. "I have grown unaccustomed to any expression other than frustration or determination from you. For a moment I thought someone else had come to the wilderness with me." He pours, then hands me a cup of tea.

Before taking a drink, I wrap my hands around the container in an effort to warm them. "There has been little reason to rejoice of late," I say.

"Much has been asked of you."

"A General sacrifices so others may be carefree."

"If a General forgets his humanity, can he effectively Battle to protect it for others?"

"You confuse me, Moto-San," I say. "I disappoint you when I'm human enough to fail, then you rebuke me when I deny myself for the sake of perfection." Between Tori and Demetrius, I have begun to doubt my ability to succeed at anything.

"I do not know what voices you have heard, but they have certainly not been mine." As always, his voice is controlled and he sits with utter calm.

"I am weary of games. You have calmly tolerated mistake after mistake ever since we came out here, but I cannot learn from your silence. At least Demetrius respects me enough to lose his temper when it's called for."

He has been idly stirring the fire, but he stops and places me under his scrutiny. The only movement of his body is the pulsating flex of his jaw muscles. "Very well," he finally says. "You have yet to face an opponent as powerful as you. Or fast. When you fight, you hold nothing back. Celceans love you, not just because you win, but how you win. You are decisive and unstoppable." He places another log on the fire and the flames instantly begin probing the bark for weakness.

"You make my job as Mentor simple. I ask and you give. I teach and you learn. Sometimes I wonder if you were genetically engineered to be a General."

I listen to him, embarrassed at the rare outpouring of encouragement. "I did not ask the question for the sake of my pride," I say.

"And you are stupid," he says.

It takes a second for this to sink in. When it does, I straighten my back. "Mentor?"

He shakes his head and adjusts his weight. "You have believed a lie. Your speed, your strength, your determination, these things are merely the top polish, easily scuffed and worn away. If you think they compile your core, you value yourself too little. And those who try to make you believe those falsehoods squander your loyalty."

He sits forward slightly, causing the flames to reflect a faint, flickering orange against his skin, "If you never stepped foot inside the Temple again, I would continue to serve you. If you are killed in your next Battle, I will die alongside you.

"I delight in you, Trajan. Not because of your talent. Or your genetics. Those you would have regardless of your position. It is your character which sets you apart." He pauses, as close to emotion as I have ever seen him. These words are foreign and unexpected. I look away, unsure of the proper response.

"Look at me," he says. I do, although it feels as if I willingly place my face in the path of a projectile. "If I did not highlight this flaw, I would be no better than one of your enemies. If you think I would punish you for not placing wood inside of a shelter, or for stumbling after swinging an axe, then you are too focused on your own perfection to know my character. If you were punished this week, it came at your own hands, not mine."

"Why the silence?" I ask.

"Would you have believed me if I told you differently?"

I don't say it, but I know he is right. No matter what he said, I would have heard displeasure. "So the tree was just an exercise?"

"No," he says with a humorless laugh, "that was a lesson."

This revelation angers me. "Reckless at best, wasn't it?"

"There are times when it is necessary to take a man's sight in order to help him see," he says.

"And if the fall had killed me? As it should have?"

He stands. "Come with me."

The rain has intensified again, but I don't notice the chill this time. We march through the mud and rocks until we reach the dead tree. He motions for me to stand next to the base and I comply.

"Jump," he says.

I do, unsure of his point until I land. Upon impact, the ground beneath me compresses as if made of foam.

"The harder you hit, the softer it becomes. Your life was never in danger. In fact, the only reason you suffered injury is because you landed on the part of the tree which broke. A painful but acceptable consequence if it helps you understand the lesson." He turns and begins hiking back to our shelter.

I remain in the rain, gently bouncing on the rubbery surface as he disappears behind the falling water.

Chapter 14

Mid-Year Battles are not held in the Temple. Since there is no danger of one nation conquering another, they don't need to be on neutral ground. Instead, they are held in the defending nation's capital. My Battle with Castor will be held just a few kilometers from where I sleep. It's an odd sensation, fighting at home.

The morning of the Battle, I sit in a lush dressing room. If the preparation rooms in the Temple are stones, this is a cloud. Tori hands me a glass of water then checks over my uniform, made of a synthetic, kevlar reinforced weave. Knowing Castor, there will be no trickery. His pride will insist on blunt hand to hand combat.

Ever since the forest, Tori has been more relaxed than I have ever seen. Today is no different. "Don't try to prove a point. A victory is a victory."

His lesson continues to stir inside of me, especially with the Battle looming. To separate myself from the role I play as the Celcean General feels as unnatural as a body without flesh.

"I have not anticipated a Battle more than today's," I say. "It will be liberating to remove this pebble from my shoe."

"Just don't lose your balance while fishing it out. He's been a more attentive student than you realize."

Our lights pulsate, signaling the imminent start of the contest.

He nods and leaves. I spend the remaining moments clearing my head of anything which may distract me from the task at hand. When the door to the battlefloor opens, the only things left in me are tactics and violence.

The Crowd is frenzied as I walk onto the battlefloor. For many of these people, this is the first and only time they will get to see their General in a live Battle. Only the most wealthy and influential are fortunate enough to journey to the Temple. The floor is covered in roses and trinkets, cast down by the audience to show honor and respect. A dozen attendees scurry around the fifty meter oval trying to clear it so the Battle can begin.

I feel good. Pure. Powerful. There is a spear stuck in the ground in front of me. Another in front of Castor. I heft it, feeling the perfect weight. Three meters long with a hand carved, jagged piece of onyx for the head. These are the ceremonial weapons of Celsus.

Castor looks like a man standing on burning coals. Jumping, pacing, running in place. He alternates between those movements and stabbing the hard-packed gravel with his spear. I'm still. Focusing on my breathing and heart rate. As I wait, I begin to take inventory of Castor's movements.

His strength is predominantly in his legs, which will make his spear thrusts incredibly powerful, but they will be slow and easy to predict. He favors his right side, but leads with his left. When he shadow boxes, he throws more elbows and knees than fists and kicks. He will try to draw me close if we lose our weapons. Just as Tori predicted, it's obvious he will be the aggressor, betting his youthful speed and strength will overwhelm me. I've never felt more confident.

As always, minidrones buzz around the battlefloor and over the Crowd. Their blood thirsty presence annoys me more than usual.

The lighting in the arena dims and the Crowd grows silent. I can feel the surging energy of these spectators as they await the commencement. Castor won't take his eyes off me. When our gazes lock, he begins jumping higher and faster.

The giant video screens come to life as the face of Demetrius appears. The audience remains silent. Anxious for him to set the rules and unleash us on each other. He smiles that gentle smile which has earned him the adoration of his nation.

"My glorious citizens," he says, his voice booming. "Today is a first for our humble nation. Two demi-gods stand before you, prepared to earn the honor of defending your children, your culture, your very way of life."

The Crowd roars and Demetrius happily pauses, pleased by the response.

"Yes, cheer. These titans deserve it. Without them, who knows what darkness would consume us." He stops speaking and adjusts his posture, immediately seeming less proud than he did just a moment ago.

"Cheer for them, but weep for us. Two Generals from the same nation fighting in the Mid-Year Battle, is a dubious first. There are nations watching right now who see a different Celsus than they used to. And what they see does not strike fear in their heart. It gives them the confidence to oppose us."

No one moves. Not the Crowd, not Castor. Even the video drones hover in frozen silence.

"I respect and submit my nation to the mandate of the Ruling Elders, but know that with each strike, with each parry and every drop of blood spilled today, Celsus will fracture a little more." He bows his head in solemn introspection.

"May the victor be valiant and tempered. May the victor be as much a healer as a warrior. May the victor be glorified."

He says a few more things to bring the energy of the Crowd back. By the time he's done, they are as happy and excited as they had been before the opening of his speech. I can't help but think those admonishing words were meant only for Castor and me. Or possibly just me. Either way, I can't dwell on it. My opponent knows me better than any opponent ever has. He's not only studied me, he's studied with me. I've been his instructor, baring my secrets and making him better for years. And now he stands opposed to me.

The rules are given quickly. No death. If a General is killed, the other will be executed immediately. The fight will last until one General is both unarmed and neutralized. That's it. Vague enough to allow brutal and irreversible injury, which I plan on exploiting.

There is a pause between the rules and then we're signaled to start. In this tiny eternity my mind fills with what I must do. I must crush him. I must remove any doubt that I've lost my edge. I cannot simply survive this fight. No, this victory must be decisive. It must be overwhelming.

Drums, deep and cruel mark the start of our Battle and neither of us hesitate. Tori told me to be aggressively defensive, but something in me bursts when I hear the drums.

Castor and I barrel toward each other, two battering rams unwilling and unable to yield. Everything becomes palpable. The air as I rush through it, the gravel shifting and settling under my every footfall, the grain of the spear's handle. It all feels more real than ever. And Castor. I see him more clearly than I should. It's as if I've been listening to the world through a pillow and it's suddenly been ripped away.

There are Battles that are nothing more than physics. Two giant bodies imposing their will on each other. The body which summons the most power wins. These Battles are fought in straight lines.

As Castor and I converge, it's obvious our Battle will be different. It will be a chess match. Calculated and measured. More about angles and ground gained. This was my plan, but I was not expecting it from Castor.

We're mirror images of each other, side-stepping and jabbing our spears. Both of our thrusts are easily parried and we immediately circle, looking for the smallest opening.

Castor fakes high with his spear, then drops, attempting a leg sweep. I easily counter with a knee that knocks him off balance, but not long enough for me to take advantage.

The drums stop abruptly and for the briefest of moments, it's just Castor and me, studying, searching for a subtle crack in the other to pry apart and exploit. If the Crowd is cheering, I have no knowledge of it. We may as well be in a desert, just two predators vying for supremacy.

I'm undeterred. The plan Tori and I established is sound and I know I can outlast Castor. There is a difference between changing one's character and adhering to a strategy. He's doing the latter, but the former will always win. Somewhere Tori is smiling. Regardless of the surprising strategy, we both know Castor is incapable of holding this line.

We continue to circle each other, finding our distance, testing our timing. It feels like a dance, these measured movements. We're so in sync, it seems as if I know what he's going to do before he does. Judging from the way he almost preempts my movements, I'm sure he's as in tune with me.

In a strange way, I enjoy the technical nature of this. It feels refined, almost mature, but I know we can't continue this way. The fact that I need to prove a point hasn't changed just because Castor has chosen to emulate me. I need to advance our violence, but I need to do it in a way which jolts him out of this faux discipline. Somewhere, just below the surface is the power-hungry and careless child I so easily chided into an outburst in Aegea.

Jab, shuffle, sidestep, jab, jab. He's been using this rhythm since our initial clash. But he's not fully committing to the cadence, which makes it clear he's just waiting for me to over commit.

The technique is borderline insulting. We do this to novice Hopefuls to prove a point about staying focused and not allowing your opponent to dictate the altercation. I can use this to my advantage. If he thinks I'm susceptible to such a pedestrian technique, it will make it that much easier for me to get him to overreact when he thinks I've taken the bait.

I start subtly. Moving in step with his shuffles, dropping an elbow or shoulder split seconds before I should. Minuscule markers only a warrior could read. We even start breathing in the same pattern. It seems so obvious, what I'm doing, but Castor clearly thinks he's won the upper hand. I even see a small smile creep across his mouth. If we were training, I'd halt the action and berate him for gullibility and arrogance. But I'm not his teacher anymore.

If I simply wait him out, I'll easily defeat him. But that won't be decisive enough. Demetrius doesn't care about a technically won Battle. He cares about the sensational ending and images that can be used over and over in order to remind lesser nations of our dominance.

Jab, shuffle, sidestep, jab, jab. There's a pause between each salvo and it's in this slight respite I decide to push the action. After the final jab in his series, instead of aligning myself to his shift, I plant my weight on my back foot and explode forward, cutting the gap between us in half. Castor is shocked and he clumsily tries to reorient his spear between us, even though we're too close to use the tip. I plant my spear to my right, making it a temporary fulcrum and swing both of my knees up. One of them crashes against his chin and the other snaps his spear in half.

He recovers quickly and parries with the blunt end of his spear. It grazes my ear and makes direct contact with my collarbone. The strike is more defensive than a counterstrike and it's effective to keep me from continuing forward. Too late, I realize I've just given him the close quarters advantage of two shorter weapons rather than one long one. We won't be mirroring each other anymore, which both pleases and frustrates me. In order to maximize the effectiveness of my weapon, I'll be forced to play defense.

Castor lunges forward, closing the ground between us quickly. In less than a second, he's close enough for me to smell his breath, landing blow after blow with the broken spear. The blows do nothing more than irritate me, but I'm mindful of the onyx tip that he continues to slash toward my neck. I drop my spear and use my forearms to parry the attack.

There's an intimacy in the feel of the wood as it strikes me. The years spent using my forearms as shields has taught me where they are strong enough not to break, and has succeeded in deadening the nerves that would traditionally cry out.

He's relying too much on his weapons, not realizing he's doing nothing more than increasing our heart rates. We could do this all day long and neither of us would gain an advantage. But it looks as if I'm backpedaling, which only serves to make me look weak in front of the Crowd and my Ruler.

I've succeeded in one thing, however. In his excitement, Castor has completely abandoned his measured approach. He's unleashed the animal I expected. There are no more angles in his approach.

My mind does strange things in moments like these. Rather than strategizing the best defense, I begin to notice inconsequential details. The stretch of the new flesh on my most recent scars, how the dust clouds produced by our clash look strikingly different. Mine, gentle bellows of white. His, jagged pillars of grey. The delicately chiseled artwork that runs along the second level of the stadium. I don't panic when I do this. In fact, when I begin fixating on these things, I know I'm about to do what is needed.

When I was younger, I would do it so much, it would infuriate Tori after a Battle as he tried to get me to articulate why I took the line I did, or why I chose to attack one joint over another. For a long time I was ashamed of it. The inability to think my way through a Battle, I thought, was a sign of my mindlessness. Proof I was made to do nothing more than play the part of a brute. But now I just let it happen, confident that whatever causes this phenomenon will result in my victory.

The blows continue, each more powerful and sloppy than the next, which tells me Castor is becoming frustrated. The Crowd has begun chanting my name, stressing the second syllable, TRA-JAN, in an effort to help me weather this storm. I could easily just jump out of range, but that would be a sign of me backing down.

Castor alternates his strikes from one hand to the other, which leaves little time to counterattack or regroup. It's obvious I won't be able to take advantage of a gap in the attack, so I meet force with force. Instead of blocking his next hit, I allow it through my defenses which frees me to connect with a perfectly placed shot to his face. I can only do this when he swings with what used to be the end of the spear. Because he's wildly chopping at me, his strike glances off my shoulder.

His nose immediately begins to bleed, but he's in such a rhythm he's left unfazed. We do this for a few rounds. I dodge the spear's tip, strike when he comes at me with the other hand. The sharp part of the spear is in his left hand, which means I'm blocking with my right and striking with my left. Not really a disadvantage for me, but I don't feel as accurate or powerful.

After my fourth blow, Castor's lip is cracked open, his nose is bleeding and his right eye has begun to swell shut. The shots I've taken from him have resulted in a blood blister on my shoulder, a few chipped teeth and a cut on my forehead that's beginning to drip into my vision. My strikes are faster than his, which means I'm getting more accurate and he's getting less focused. His fifth shot does nothing more than glance my shoulder, while I simultaneously burst the hematoma over his eye.

The Crowd erupts as it sees Castor's blood spatter across the right side of his face. He's blinded briefly, which interrupts the rhythmic chaos of his attack. I immediately move to my right with the intention of taking the spear tip from him, slicing the tendon which holds his calf to his leg, puncturing his lung with a quick thrust from behind him and blinding him with a couple of quick wrist flicks.

I can see all of this as clearly as the canyon left by a river cutting through limestone. Feel his flesh part as the spear enters his body and releases the air from his lungs, judge the gentle resistance of his eyes as the very tip of his own spear slices the membrane and renders his retina useless. If I go deep enough, I'll end him as a General. The physicians will be able to give his sight back, but even their knowledge goes only so far. He'll be able to see, but not clearly enough to be a General. He will live the rest of his life in a mist of dulled shapes and blended colors.

The sequence is clear and simple, but it all hinges on my ability to disarm him. It should be easy. There is a nerve cluster on the top of the forearm that, when struck correctly, causes the hand to weaken its grip. All I have to do is strike that cluster and the rest will happen on its own. As I move to my right, I grab the spear and raise my hand to strike Castor's forearm. But as I bring my fist down, my foot tangles in my discarded spear on the ground. I thought I had thrown it out of the way, but I was wrong, and because I've moved with such purpose, it throws me completely off balance.

I go from attempting to disarm Castor to desperately trying to keep my balance by holding on to the spear in his hand. My feet continue to shuffle, trying to catch me as I fall backward, but they only get more tangled in my spear. I hear the Crowd as everyone stands at the same time. My shifting weight sends us both to the ground. As we hit, I use his momentum to push him over me, rather than let him land on top and give him the advantage.

Castor must be as confused as me, because I don't feel him move once he's on the ground. Briefly, I wonder if I've knocked him unconscious, but the way his body hit, there was no danger of that, his back and shoulder taking most of the impact. I spin my body, looking for a temporary arm lock in order to give myself time to evaluate my next approach. Castor's arm offers no resistance as I pull it back. He doesn't try to fight my legs off when I plant them, one on his neck, the other on his chest, and arch my back. There's a gentle pop from his arm when I snap it, perfectly, at the joint.

Silence. Only my breathing and the breeze swirling through the stadium. I look across my body and see Castor's under mine. There is blood. Lots of blood. Too much to come from the few cuts on our faces. I release Castor's arm and sit up. As I do so, I see the tip of my spear, covered in red, jutting through the center of Castor's torso.

Blood continues to pool under us as I kneel over him. Visions of Seth come back to me as I check for a pulse. For the subtle rise and fall of his chest. Anything to tell me he isn't dead. Anything to tell me I haven't broken the rules of the Mid-Year and killed both of us.

The next moments are frantic. I find a faint pulse and can feel his breath, although it is sporadic. I'm not a physician, but I've seen them work often. In order to save both of our lives I begin to emulate them as closely as I can. First, I pull the spear from him body. It releases cleanly, without any noise, but blood immediately begins spilling out of the hole it leaves. I rip my shirt off and begin to shove it in the wound. Once it seems as if the top of his wound is as packed as it can be, I flip him over and do the same to the hole in his back with my pants. There is no modesty in me as I crouch naked, pressing the cotton pants into the wound in his back.

There are some screams from the Crowd, then the screen comes to life. Demetrius coldly declares me the winner as the lights dim. After what seems like longer than necessary, I'm surrounded by physicians. Most of them begin tending Castor while a couple of them cover me with a robe. They inject Castor with at least ten different medicines and wrap his body with linens infused with gels. It's amazing watching these people. They work more efficiently than I've ever seen the Generals. After he's been triaged and stabilized, they move him to a plank which immediately morphs and encapsulates him within seconds of being placed on it.

We all walk out of the stadium together. Castor's capsule hovering between four physicians, me ushered by two others. Once we leave the arena floor, I'm met by a team of security guards. They don't need to say anything. It's clear. I'm a prisoner until Castor either lives or dies.

Chapter 15

They take me to an empty, grey room. I will not leave here until Castor's fate has been determined. In less than a year, I have gone from celebrated General of Celsus, the Gem of the Earth, to a prisoner for the possible murder of a comrade. Failure. Utter failure from the moment I decided to show mercy to Seth.

My body aches as I begin to evaluate myself. I'm mostly covered with bruises and cuts and my cheek throbs deeply enough to make me think the bone underneath may be cracked. Blood begins to drip from my nose. As a prisoner, I'm not guaranteed medical treatment, but Demetrius will need to hedge his bets in case Castor lives. If he does, there will be no excuse for Demetrius to deny me the right to compete in the next Battle.

Tori is somewhere in the building, negotiating, no doubt. He won't be allowed to visit me, but he will try to find a way regardless. I wonder what will happen to him if Castor dies and I'm executed. Likely, Demetrius will end him as an example to other Mentors. This thought makes me even more desperate for Castor's survival. I'm willing to pay the consequences for my mistake, but to have a man like Tori held responsible for my indiscretions is almost too much to bear. I am who I am because of him. Every victory, every accomplishment, every well-spoken word has come from him. From his insight and tutelage.

The door of my room opens and Demetrius walks in. "I hope he dies," he says. "Your arrogance and stupidity weaken this nation as much as the worst enemy I've ever faced." His voice shakes, his face is contorted with such hatred that I prepare myself for another attack.

"Lord," I begin, but he stops me.

"No words, Trajan. I will do everything in my power to ensure he lives and that he's able to succeed you after the next Battle. But I have lost faith in your ability to champion this nation. So I hope, against myself, that he dies. I'm more willing to have our third represent us than I am to have you."

I want to tell him what happened. That I stumbled. That I would never willingly bring my protege so close to death. But I know this would infuriate him even more. And it would give him grounds to declare me incompetent. He can tolerate a defiant General, but he would never abide a clumsy one. Instead I wait. Something Tori has taught me. Allow the onslaught, capture every attack and catalogue it for analysis later, deny myself temporary and spontaneous reaction in order to gain an edge.

He stops speaking, most likely realizing his anger and how his control has slipped. We face each other in silence for what seems like hours. Neither of us willing to break eye contact. I can feel his consuming anger radiating from him.

Just like in Aegea, he raises his fist and I prepare to accept his strike. I wonder if these outbursts from him, after so many years of temperate and calm governance, are what other Rulers use to decry his ethics. His lack of control cannot have been limited to his interactions with me.

"I will accept any punishment you deem appropriate," I say as I angle my cheek to meet his fist.

His fist hovers over me, shaking with his rage, but it never drops. "No," he says, as he lowers it. "I want you to stew in your failure. A beating would make you feel forgiven. My mercy and forgiveness are not so easily attained. If Castor lives, you will learn what it means to earn my favor once again."

After he leaves, the light in the room blinks off, surrounding me in absolute darkness. My first thought is of Tori. For his sake, and the sake of my citizens, I will do what it takes to earn my Ruler's love back. I owe it to Tori. I owe it to Celsus. I owe it to myself. Demetrius will love me again.

Chapter 16

The only time I'm given light is when my meals come. An aluminum tray appears through a temporary seam in the wall. On it a cold, mostly broth, soup, water and a protein supplement. If not for the meals, one in the morning, one at night, I would have no conception of time. The lights come on for five minutes only.

Late on the fourth day, after my meal has been taken, there is a faint hum, then the far wall fades into an image of the Temple. My thoughts, wandering freely from childhood to long dormant images which lack context, have become so vibrant, I do not know how long it takes me to understand this image is not from my imagination.

The image pans around the Temple, then a narrator begins speaking.
Countless years of human suffering, eradicated by the vision of twelve extraordinary men. Each of these saviors suffered for their dedication to rescue us from our own brutality. But the Temple you see, where our noble Rulers settle issues of tyranny and liberation through the expertise of their Generals, was not always available. Indeed, the peace we take for granted as a matter of law, was not always so.

The video on my wall fades to grainy footage of stern-faced politicians standing behind ornate podiums, addressing giant Crowds of chanting people.

As has always been true, people rarely give up their madness, opting instead to cling to the very thing which draws them under.

I prop myself against the wall opposite the video, fascinated by the footage and happy to have something to distract me from my own, private, insanity. The video flicks to the battlefloor, where two men stand across from one another. They do not look like the Generals I have faced. These men have not trained to fight the way I have. They are men who have proven themselves in truewar, slaughtering hundreds for the sake of their cause.

The first Battle was a failure before either General threw their first strike.

The two Generals begin fighting. At first, they are tentative, but once the first drop of blood is spilled, they change into animals. There is no technique, only the base desire to mangle, humiliate and kill. It is settled when one of the Generals allows his back to be taken. He is quickly choked into unconsciousness, then his neck is snapped.

The win was vulgar. But it was a win. It seemed the will of the Twelve was fulfilled. But within seconds...

My room is filled with another voice. I quickly understand it to be the speech of the defeated nation's Ruler.

"If even one of the Twelve were still alive, he would agree with me. This Battle was instigated under false pretenses for the gain of a subversive and greedy Ruler. I do not acknowledge the victory of my adversary's General, other than to accuse him of outright murder. If any delegate from any nation approaches me to convince me otherwise, I will consider it an act of truewar and will defend my nation as such.

Another abrupt switch to a different but equally angry Ruler, decrying the actions of the previous. Then such terrible images fill the wall, I am forced to turn away. Squadron after squadron of soldiers march forward to meet their death. The weapons they use on each other deal death efficiently, without discretion. The sounds of truewar turn my stomach and I wretch the meager contents of my meal.

This continues, hour after hour, day after day. Every time my food arrives, a new story with the same narrative. Two Generals meet, fight a pointless Battle which leads to a horrific truewar. When I sleep, I'm awarded no reprieve. Rather, my dreams meld into the same horrific scenes, only when I sleep, I can't turn away.

The sheer volume of footage astounds me. Every citizen is taught that, when the Twelve finally established order, truewar ended. To see the will of the Twelve discounted so easily, even when Generals were willing to die for their nation, is like watching a tiger being gutted by a mouse.

I have lost track of the days in spite of the rhythm of the meals. All at once, however, it is over. My door opens and a guard steps a hesitant foot into the door. "Demetrius has called an audience," he says.

I open my mouth to speak, but I find my tongue is too dry and my throat too raw to form discernible words. On shaky legs, I stand and hobble behind the guard. The fact that he did not end my life when the door was opened tells me Castor is alive and I am still the General of Celsus.

Demetrius breaks into tears when he sees me. "Your appearance mirrors my emotion," he says as he approaches me with open arms. I do not return his embrace.

"I have been harsh," he says as he releases me. "It is true, but I do not apologize. Even though you are still General, and you have been disciplined, it does not change the precarious position in which we find ourselves because of your carelessness. I needed you to understand the stakes. Do you?"

Again, I attempt a response, but my mouth fails me. Instead, I nod.

"I'm not sure you do. Your eyes betray you. I see your anger toward me. That is fine. Your defiant spirit is one of your gifts. But know your place. Mine is to rule, which means I carry the burden of being second guessed and made into a villain. I must also understand the balance between empty rhetoric and credible threats." He returns to his desk where he sits heavily.

I finally find my voice. When my words come out, they are whispered through desiccated vocal cords. "My intent has never been to undermine you or weaken Celsus. Although, it seems a waste of breath to say so."

He sighs as he sweeps his hand over the desk, revealing a control panel. "Intent. Only those concerned with reputation use intent to justify themselves. Those who understand consequences apart from purpose seek to make the course right at all costs." After a few keystrokes, a holographic letter appears in front of me.

"I'll save you the effort of reading the entire message," he says. "In short, Marcail has sent this to every Ruler, save me. In it, she accuses me of being obsessed with world domination and you of being, at best an oblivious puppet. At worst a willing participant in my campaign." The image fades. "Do you recognize her wording? It is the same rhetoric of the early Rulers who allowed their Generals to fight, only to subvert the will of the Ancestors with truewar when things did not go their way. I do not care about your intent, General. I care that your stupidity has given her the means to question my integrity."

My defiance from a moment ago feels like the behavior of a spoiled child. "What are we to do?" I ask.

To think truewar is even being hinted by a Ruler fills me with a terror I have never known.

Demetrius stands and looks out his window. It is several seconds before he answers. "So many citizens think the peace which we enjoy was secured by the Twelve. History is often distilled to the easiest to understand concepts. The truth, however, is much more complicated." He turns to me, eyes sagging under his need for rest. "There are times I hate the Twelve."

The vulgarity of his words takes my breath away.

"You see?" he says, gesturing to my reaction, "the lore which has built up around them has made them into gods. But the reality is less flattering. Yes, they gave us an ideal. But they lacked the forethought to sustain it. Did they really think rule of entire nations would just be handed off because of an overhyped wrestling match?"

I am silent, unsure of his point or how to act in light of such shocking rhetoric.

"They put their mandate forth and, at the time, everyone feared them, so the mandate held. As soon as the last Ancestor died, so did the peace. That is the footage you saw in your cell. Rulers call it the second fall. If left unchecked, it would have landed our world back into chaos. That is when the majority of the Rulers convened and instituted the Justification Protocol." He does not pause to see if I react. "Before your predecessor, when Battles were rarer than today, the Justification Protocol was a standard practice. A delegate from the aggressing nation would be sent to the challenged nation to gather evidence of wrongdoing. That delegate would then return and present his findings to any Ruler who might question the validity of the original challenge. It was once an elegant solution to the lingering distrust and greed of early Rulers. It was certainly an improvement on the naive ideals which the Twelve left us with. I thought, however, we had evolved past it. But given Marcail's threats, it appears we must dust off the Protocol once again."

"Why is this the first I have heard of such things?" I ask. The realization that my role as General has not been the final say in disputes between Rulers makes me feel like a child who has been playing dress up.

"What would be the point? The citizens of this world do not care how it is held together. As long as they feel safe and happy." He waves a hand toward me as if dismissing a servant. "Regardless. Now that you know, you have a part to play."

"Of course," I say. "the Aegean General will not last a minute against me."

"You speak truly. But your role will not be so simple." His features soften. "I envy you. Your skill. The ease with which you execute your gift. You fight and win and, in so doing, you conquer the hearts of the citizens. No one questions you. In fact, the only misstep in Marcail's letter is her accusation of you. She has retreated from that line in subsequent communications. Which is why I want you to be my ambassador to Aegea.

You will find fault and you will report it. Then you will crush the Aegean General. And the world, which has tilted because of your mistake, will be made right because of your service."

"Sire. I will follow you to the end of this life and beyond, and I will serve you now. But is there no other way? A General is not trained for such things."

"A General is trained to defend his nation. Your nation is under siege. Will you not fight for her?"

"To my last breath. But trusting a warrior with the intricacies of politics is like storing dynamite in a candle shop. There must be someone more qualified who has the trust of the citizens?"

"Do you hate me so much that you would make me plead with you? Or worse, command you? This is how you can serve Celsus. Will you do it or not?" The room suddenly feels cold and sharp.

"Forgive me. You need do neither. I will serve. Of course. Thank you, Father, for trusting me with such a great responsibility." These words, which I have spoken so often to Demetrius over the years, feel brittle. I am not sure if it is because of the gravity of Marcail's threats which weighs us down, or because it feels like I'm speaking with a calculated politician rather than a loving father.

Either way, I hate Marcail. She has caused Demetrius to question me, and me to doubt my king. I will find fault. And after the world is convinced, I will wipe Aegea from this earth.

Chapter 17

"Did you know of the Justification Protocol?" I ask Tori. We leave for Aegea tomorrow. Today, while servants pack our meager belongings for the journey, he has mandated we train.

"Only in story. For the longest time, real Battle occurred once a decade at most. Before Demetrius attacked my nation, I had only fought in exhibitions."

The facility is silent. Tori has ensured we are not distracted by Hopefuls today. We begin as we do every session. Stretching. First legs, then the back, shoulders, arms, core and finally neck. As we hold each stretch and focus on the rhythm of our breathing, I can tell how my body has suffered from my time in the cell. I want to ask him what he went through while I was locked away, but I refrain. If I were to learn he suffered the same fate as me, it would be too much. It is already crushing to know I have opened the door for Marcail's obscene campaign.

"What was the reason Demetrius challenged your nation?" I ask. We have never spoken of such things, mainly because I have never asked. As the question leaves my lips, I feel embarrassed for never asking.

"Switch," he says. We move our legs in unison. My right leg tingles as the blood flows through the elongated tissue. "He claimed my Ruler was imprisoning and executing anyone who spoke against him."

We adjust, focusing on our hamstrings. "Was he?" I ask. To think Tori would have stood by while his Ruler acted in such a way is preposterous. Even more ludicrous to imagine Tori would have fought to sustain such actions.

"It does not matter now. If you read the histories, there is evidence of such things. But histories usually justify the intentions of those who emerged victorious. I loved my Ruler. I loved my nation. If such things were happening, I was not aware." He pauses as we roll onto our backs, allowing a moment of rest. "I can think of no man who would consider himself a villain. Most, if they are honest, believe themselves to be heroes."

I feel my vertebrae relaxing, then I hear them pop as I bring my body back into submission. The Battle will be here sooner than I would like and I have slipped too far. This will be the first time I will enter the Temple in less than peak shape. The path before me. The Battle, the visit to Aegea, the Justification. All of it feels like punching a ball of tar. "Is the truth that flexible?"

"Truth does not bend. Because of that, few are willing to consider it. Rather, we dress it up, put it in a shiny and shimmering wrapper and marvel at how difficult it is to describe. But it is there if we have the courage to dig deep enough. The difficulty lies in what we do with it once we find it."

We continue the same pattern we have followed since my childhood. It feels good to grasp onto something so familiar during a time of such confusion. As we draw the stretching to a close, I notice a fresh welt on the back of Tori's shoulder. "Moto-San," I say, "is that because of me?"

He pulls his sleeve back over the mark. "It is," he says. There is no emotion in his response.

"Forgive me. I do not know how things have turned so drastically."

He stops and instructs me to do the same. "There is pain which we cause. There is pain which we encounter because we do not control the world. And there is pain which is thrust on us. This," he points to his shoulder, "is not yours to own. Even if it were, you would need not ask my forgiveness.

129

Whatever difficulty I encounter on your behalf, I gladly accept."

The rest of the practice is quiet. After stretching, we spar. At first, our movements are slow and the strikes controlled. As we feel the blood begin to flow again, and our muscles remember what it is like to be tested, our attacks are faster and increasingly severe.

Usually, we train for a minimum of four hours. Today, however, he stops us after two.

"It will be a few days until we can sustain much more than this. Go rest. Tomorrow will be taxing in other ways."

He turns from me and lifts the bottom of his shirt to wipe the sweat away, the same way he has done thousands of times. This time, as the shirt rises, I see a patchwork of welts, gashes and scabs. None of which were there before I was locked in my cell. Demetrius punished my mind and punished Tori's body. I understand why he did what he did to me. I needed to understand the true stakes. But I cannot understand what he gained by such brutality against my Mentor.

I have been dreading my trip to Aegea. But seeing the toll this situation has taken on Tori, I am suddenly happy for the time away from Demetrius. The irony is not lost. I will be traveling to a nation to find evidence of tyranny while the proof of my Ruler's cruelty is in the same room with me.

Chapter 18

The landing pad looks deserted as we circle it. A perfectly white sanded beach frames the north shore of the island. The rest of the tiny fleck of land is overgrown. I'm surprised that a nation with such little land mass hasn't taken advantage of every piece of dry earth. If this were Celsus, the trees would have been cut and replaced with rows of farmland or identically designed housing units.

As the drone settles gently on the landing pad, a single dignitary emerges out of the forest and stands patiently, hands clasped in front of him. His eyes are locked on the leveled ground and his loose clothes whip around him, bullied by the powerful drone engines.

Tori stands at the door, a small bag of belongings in his hand. He turns to me as the seal breaks and gives me a quick flick of his head. I'm not sure if he's reassuring me or giving me a subtle warning. Either way, the door is lowered and all I see is a landscape untouched by man, tangled and confusing and untamed.

"Welcome, General."

My eyes are still adjusting to the lack of light when I hear a familiar voice. We're in a crudely dug series of tunnels, maybe five meters from the surface of the island. The entrance, just on the perimeter of the landing pad, looked at first to be a crack between two rocks. When approached from the correct angle, however, it opened into a one meter hole with a perfectly woven rope with which we used to lower ourselves. Once at the bottom, we followed the tunnel around two or three corners until we emerged into a larger room. It's hard to believe a jungle is directly above us. The smell of earth and organics is such a stark contrast to the industrialized surroundings of Celsus.

"Please excuse how rushed we are. Usually, we'd greet a representative from another nation with a feast and quarters in which to rest. Sadly, our time today is limited."

Tori, standing to my right responds, "No apologies necessary, Prince. We're honored by your presence, no matter how rushed. Our goal is to learn from you, not to be entertained. We will do everything in our power to ensure we're of no burden during our stay."

I feel him shift his weight and I assume he's bowing with his usual formality. William doesn't respond but my eyes have adjusted enough to see a slight smile on his face.

"Forgive me, William," I say, "if I had recognized you earlier, I would have surely greeted you more affectionately." This feels overly formal, but I imagine Tori saying something similar, and I figure emulating him is the better course to take.

"No apologies necessary. A storm is coming and I want to be sure we get you safely to your quarters before the sea gets too choppy. It will take some time for you to be able to navigate the waves when they decide to take over.

A pesky problem that comes with living at the mercy of such a powerful force of nature."

The room in which we're huddled, if it can be called a room, is like nothing I've seen. Five meters high, twenty meters square, a tunnel entrance at the center of all four walls. A faint blue glow emanates from the soil above.

"We genetically engineered those from plankton and roots. They're the perfect source of light in situations when you don't have access to fuel for generators, which we rarely do, so far from any power grid," William says. They're beautiful, and now that my eyes have adjusted to incorporate their light, I'm amazed that the glow they offer provides complete clarity without any glare.

He kneels down and begins sifting through three packs. From the size of them, they look to be about twenty-five kilograms a piece. "May I help you?" I ask.

"We're not so barbaric as to ask a guest to prepare for his own journey, but thank you. I'll be done shortly."

Tori and I amble around our man-made cave while William finishes his task. I feel like a child, overcome with curiosity in this strange environment. The soil walls are pleasantly spongy to the touch and the residue they leave on my hands is gritty without feeling grimy. Tori beckons me, and when I join him, he hands me a worm, ten centimeters long.

"Eat. It's pure protein."

I glance at William, who has stopped rustling in the packs and watches us with a small smile. I'm embarrassed by Tori's antiquated directive. "I'm sure our hosts would be appalled to see a delegate of Celsus sucking down such a grotesque thing," I say, forcing a lighthearted chuckle.

He laughs, "On the contrary, I was happily surprised to see your openness. The consensus in Aegea is that citizens of Celsus have forgotten mankind once subsisted without chemicals and altered foods."

Tori withdraws the worm from me and pops it in his mouth. "I think you'll find, young Prince, at least these citizens will fit here quite nicely." He picks another, longer worm out of the wall and hands it to me.

The worm itself has no flavor or much substance once it's in my mouth. I taste, more than anything, the specs of dirt that cling to its moist body. William stands and hands us each a pack.

"We'll travel through the tunnels for the sake of speed, which is indeed a shame. It's so rare for us to experience land and trees, but I fear we've tarried too long. Unfortunately, your welcome to Aegea will include whipping wind and angry waters."

Chapter 19

William moves surprisingly fast once he's shouldered the pack. I'm used to the weight, but I assumed it would be cumbersome for royalty. Imagining Demetrius running through tunnels with survival gear strapped to his back is enough to make me laugh as we bob and weave through the tunnels. As soon as the humor starts, it fades as I wonder what will become of Aegea after I defeat their General. The pressure of these last few months seems to have changed Demetrius so much.

We run for about five kilometers, through what I realize is an intricate system of tunnels that must run through the entire island. For a moment, I realize that if William wanted, he could disappear down through a series of fast turns into offshoot paths and strand us. In fact, I'm so disoriented, I begin to wonder if I'd have the ability to find my way to the surface. The other thing that stands out to me is how uniform these tunnels are. What I thought were roughly dug holes are actually very expertly engineered. I doubt if we've changed elevation since we started and the ceiling and walls have remained perfectly uniformed. This level of exactness would be difficult aboveground, much less executed in darkness and without a horizon to orient against. It seems I will learn more than Battle strategies and political posturing while I'm here.

We emerge onto a beach with glaring white sand. "I would offer you eyewear, but it wouldn't do you much good with what we're about to do," William says. He's squinting as intensely as Tori and I are, but it's obvious he's used to the drastic lighting changes. As my eyes adjust, I'm awestruck by the perfectly crashing waves. Everything about them, their shape, the sound they make as they fold over themselves, the way they rush up the sand, then gently retreat back into the ocean. I want to sit down, close my eyes and listen to that perfect rhythm.

"General, Elder, this way please." William shouts. He is about one hundred meters away and I can barely hear his voice above the wind and waves. Tori and I quickly catch up to him. "Again, please forgive the rush, but if you look to the south, you'll see we're being chased by a storm. We won't want to get caught in this one."

He's right. The sky to the south is almost black with fast moving clouds. I look around for a structure in which to weather this storm, or possibly a vessel that will outrun the wind, but I see neither.

"Are we taking to sea? Maybe the tunnels would offer some shelter during the worst of it?" I ask.

William smiles. "We certainly could do that, but our destination isn't on solid ground and if we wait out this storm, the currents will have carried our target so far away we would be searching for days. I'm sorry to say we don't have enough rations for that. There is a transport waiting for us a few kilometers off the coast, but we're merely hitching a ride and it can't wait too long."

He drops his pack and pulls out what looks like a second skin. Tori and I do the same. We have similar suits in Celsus, but they are pedestrian compared to this Aegean technology. In Celsus, they are synthetic fibers woven over composites of flexible resins. What I hold now feels organic. It's translucent and slightly moist.

"It only works if it's in direct contact with your skin," William says. He's already naked and has the suit halfway on his body. Tori follows William's example and is securing his suit to him arms.

136

Once I've stripped, I step into the suit, pulling it up my legs and wrapping it around my chest. The most striking aspect of this odd material is that it allows my skin to breathe perfectly. In fact, once it's on, I feel as if I'm still naked. The wind, the heat of the sun, even the floating granules of sand feel as intense as before I'd put the suit on. I look for the mechanism to attach the suit to itself but can find none. However, as I look at the seam of where it would join, I'm astounded to see the suit move on its own and form a perfect seal. My amazement washes away when I look at the churning ocean, already bending to the winds of the approaching storm.

"Come, I've stashed three canoes just off the coast," William says. We run a few hundred meters further and he pulls the canoes out of the tree line.

They appear to be trees which have been carved in an oblong shape in order to pass through the water with the least amount of resistance. The interior has been hollowed out, and there is a hole in the side of each. We're meant to climb in the hole so the majority of our body is inside the canoe. Only our head and the top third of our chest will protrude. William hands us each a rod with a paddle attached to both ends. "We've looked at every technology available, but we just haven't been able to improve on the design of our ancestors. I suggest you pull the headpiece of the suit over your face too." With that, he hefts his canoe and darts for the water. Tori is on his heels.

I'm surprised by how light the canoe is when I lift it. As soon as I set it in the water, I jump through the hole. The workmanship of the wood is astounding. It's as if they had my exact body specifications when carving it.

Just before the first wave hits, I remember to pull the headpiece over my face. Even still, I expect to feel the shocking chill of the water and the force of the wave pushing water up my nostrils. Neither happens. This suit seems to open me up to every element but water. Amazingly, even though it now covers my entire face, I can still breathe and my sight isn't impaired one bit.

Without thinking, I yell with delight and cut my paddle into the water just as the second wave crashes over me. I slice through the water and emerge on the other side of the wave. Tori and William are a few yards ahead of me, laughing as well.

We make it past the breaking waves relatively fast, but the storm has caught up with us. Now that I'm wet, the suit acts as an insulator against the wind as well. I can hear the water splashing and the wind whipping, but other than that, I'm as comfortable as sitting in a gently rocking boat.

William's lead has diminished and I can tell he's running out of strength in his shoulders. Tori has eased his pace as well. My shoulders are burning as intensely as I can remember, but I've learned long ago to push through the pain. As I draw next to William, I see him slump his shoulders and rest the paddle on his canoe.

"We made it through the worst of it. I'm impressed at how aggressively you conquered those waves," I yell.

"Thank you for the compliment," William says, "but we're not through the worst of it. This storm is matching perfectly with high tide, which means we're fighting a pretty strong current. I also fear I've asked too much of my strength, too early. I can't see myself paddling the remaining three kilometers successfully. Especially with how intense this storm is going to be." As soon as he says this, I hear the first splatters of rain falling on the ocean. If William wasn't so worried, I'd be in complete awe at these new phenomena.

I hear Tori behind me, panting. I know he's tired, but I also know he'll push himself past exhaustion and never say a word. Even though we've only paused for a moment, I can tell William is right. We're still so close to the island and the waves that I can feel us drifting toward it. Not slowly, either.

"Allow me to be your engine, then. Do you have any rope in your pack?" I ask. William nods, but it's obvious his shoulders are too spent to release his pack. "Moto-San, fish out the rope. Tie one end around yourself, then loop it over the prince. I'll take the other end."

Tori works quickly, securing the rope with the precision of a sailor. It never ceases to amaze me how deft he is at nearly every task. Once the knots are in place, I quickly loop the rope around my waist.

"If you can paddle," I say to Tori, "please do. We're almost in the surf again and I don't know if I can drag all of us out." The ocean has become increasingly choppy. Both because of the storm and the fact that we're mere meters from entering back into the breaking waves. I don't wait for his response to start paddling.

"Bear southeast," William breathes.

"I may as well be a blind man when it comes to directions on the ocean. Just tell me when to go left or right," I say. The burn returns to my shoulders immediately, but I don't think about it. It feels as if we're crawling through wet clay.

"Don't try to do too much, too fast," William says. "In weather like this, you must bend with the sea as much as fight against it."

I have no idea what he means so I just keep paddling. The pain in my shoulders spreads into my neck, then down my back. The lactic acid feels as if it's bubbling just beneath my skin, but I keep moving, focusing on form and efficiency of movement. I tense my stomach but concentrate on relaxing my legs in an effort to reroute that energy to my upper body. The muscle burn turns into sharp knots which feel as if they are pulling the fibers apart one by one. That, too, fades into a thick numbness. For a moment, I lose all feeling and have to look at my arms to ensure they're still pushing the paddle ends into the water.

Cadence becomes the center of my focus. The way my breathing corresponds to my movements. When to flex my core and when to relax certain muscle groups. It all becomes an intricate choreography and I find I must not only focus on the sequencing of my body. The way the ocean tilts affects my movement as well. I quickly learn that one movement when climbing a wave produces much different results when descending. I vary my rhythm and aggression as quickly as the wind and waves change. Everything else fades. I no longer feel the tug of the two canoes behind me, nor the torrents of rain around me. I hear my breath and I feel the ebb of the ocean. In fact, after what seems like hours, I find I've closed my eyes. Not because I'm tired, but because I can feel a better path without relying on my sight.

"You may stop, General. We're here," William says.

I find myself saddened a bit. The synchronicity of my task feels incomplete. In spite of my desire to continue, I stop paddling and open my eyes. The rain continues to rage around us. I turn as far as the canoe will allow, but I see nothing to distinguish our position. "How do you know?" I ask skeptically.

William laughs, "These waters are as distinct for me as a forest is to a squirrel. We're exactly three kilometers from our island, right at the edge of one of the most powerful slipstreams on earth. It won't be long. Just promise, no matter how startled you get, you won't fall out of your vessel. Your arms are too weak and your legs too knotted. You would sink like a stone."

Tori adjusts the rope around his waist. A subliminal gesture that tells me he's ready to drown alongside me, if that's what it comes to.

There is a subtle change in the water. I can't describe it, other than to say I feel a brief wave of nausea and the waves feel as if they begin to move side to side, rather than up and down. Even though the surface of the water looks as if it's boiling because of the rain, the ripple patterns seem unnatural. I look at William and find he is laughing.

"You two look as if I've brought you out here to kill you." As he says this, the sound of the rain changes pitch and the ocean loses whatever sense of consistency it had a second ago.

A huge wave forms underneath us and in an instant we're at least three meters above the rest of the ocean. The wave is about fifteen meters in diameter and completely smooth. It occurs to me that we're not on a wave at all, but at the top of an enormous bubble which is rising out of the sea. I feel a deep frequency in my chest which turns my stomach violently. The bile burns as it rises up my esophagus and I rip the translucent hood off my face just in time to wretch over the side of my canoe.

The upheaval leaves me completely depleted. I remain draped over the side of my tiny vessel. It is tipped precariously close to capsizing, but I can't muster the energy to right myself.

There is movement beneath us. At first, it looks as if we're drifting over an underwater landmass, but the longer I look at it, I realize we're not moving. Rather, whatever is beneath us is rocketing to the surface. The bubble we're on continues to grow, as does the shape rushing toward us.

"Prince," I yell, but my voice is drowned out by the sudden crashing of waves. Waves shouldn't be crashing three kilometers out to sea.

William glances at me and smiles, "Welcome to Aegea's most advanced transportation system." As he says this, I feel a grinding at the bottom of my canoe as we're all lifted above the water. I drop my paddle and grab the sides of my tiny vessel, which tips to the right. Moments ago I was floating in the middle of the sea, now I'm lying on my side as an enormous vessel comes up for air.

The first thing I notice is how smooth the material of the machine is. It's dark grey, seamless and without blemish. There are slight rises or dips at certain points, but they are tapered perfectly, as if they were formed by the ocean itself. The other, and equally fascinating, detail I notice is that the skin is springy.

A foot appears in front of me. "Allow me," William says, offering me his hand.My shoulders reluctantly engage as I push myself upright once again and accept his help to get me out of the canoe.

The vessel has stabilized into a sort of platform. "Clever," I say, "an instant island". William smiles, but doesn't say anything until I'm upright on wobbly legs. "I've never once in my life thought of it that way. More like an irritating interruption in the sea."

"Is that how you view continents too? We're not fish, after all," Tori says.

"Spoken truly, Elder. Come, let us get out of this storm. There is much to show you."

A sliver of the material rises from an opening in the machine. Three tan, wiry boys emerge and bow slightly as they pass us on their way to our canoes. By the time we get to the opening, the canoes are gone, as are the boys.

The material silently seals shut behind us and the same low, bluish light we experienced on the island fills the space. It's not cramped, but it's not spacious either. The surface inside is the same material as the outside. Smooth, springy and monotone.

"Come, the pilot will want to be underway soon. But there are procedures to follow," William says. He turns his back to us and leads us down the corridor.

Chapter 20

The craft doesn't rise and fall on the ocean. At least, I can't feel the effect of the waves as we make our way to the command room. There is no sound as we pass through the ship. Our steps, the power source of the vessel, even our breathing seem to be absorbed by the material which surrounds us. The deeper we go, the more people we encounter, all of whom politely nod to William but quickly continue with their job. For his part, William does his best to ensure we don't get in anyone's way.

After countless turns and dips, we round a corner and see the command room. I've sat in the pilot seats of Celsus landskimmers countless times. They are full of brightly lit monitors, holographic interfaces and wires. Lots of wires. This command room is nothing like those spaces. There is a window as wide and as tall as an entire wall of the vessel, five chairs, perfectly spaced in an arc in front of the window. An older man, clearly the captain, paces back and forth, his hands clasped behind him.

Before we enter, William stops us and turns. "We're not allowed in this room unless the captain invites us individually. Obviously, he's aware of who you are, but he may be hesitant to welcome you. If he chooses not to, please don't be offended. I've only been allowed in a handful of times. This ship is Aegea's pride."

The captain is a small, deeply tanned man with pure grey hair. He wears a perfectly manicured beard and, if I had to guess, carries no more than three percent body fat. As he paces, he pauses to whisper to each person seated in the five chairs. Even from here, I can tell he's an equal mix of gentleness and unwavering authority.

I look out the window, beyond the captain and the people in the chairs, and see we're moving at an incredible speed and yet there is no shaking, no climbing and descending waves, there isn't even vibration. Tori seems entranced by the sensation as well, but he's following William's instructions perfectly. The three of us stand there for a long time before the captain notices us.

He motions discreetly to William to enter, but it's clear the invitation does not extend to us. William steps forward and greets him with a bow. I'm amazed. William is the Prince of Aegea and he's the one bowing. This subtle humility feels absolutely right. It is also in direct contrast to most of what I have seen from Demetrius, especially in the last few months. To compare William's deference with the pride Demetrius showed toward Mansa is to compare a planet to a pebble.

Their conversation ends after a few moments and William beckons us both to join him. Although there is no physical difference between the command room and the hall where we stood, entering the captain's space feels as if we're entering a holy place. I instinctively lower my head and step lighter.

"Welcome, General," the captain says. He doesn't offer me a hand, nor do I extend mine. He turns to Tori, "Mentor, I've heard of you. In fact, I've seen you Battle. Long ago."

Tori nods a slight bow but says nothing. We stand in silence, waiting for a cue from William or a question from the captain. After a few moments, I grow uncomfortable with the stagnation.

"Forgive me if I'm out of turn, but this vessel is astounding. It's like nothing I've ever seen," I say.

"That is kind of you. In honesty, if I had my way, it would have remained that way."

I smile, happy, at least for the moment, to be outside of false ceremony. "I understand. I wouldn't want to show this to many people either. Your honesty makes me appreciate the honor even more."

It's the captain's turn to smile. He turns to William, "What would you ask of me?" With that question, William's demeanor changes. His formality is replaced with relaxation. Whatever happened in our brief conversation, apparently we've crossed some threshold.

"If it pleases you, I'd like for our guests to witness our pilots and navigators as they lead us home," William says.

"As you wish," the captain says. He walks over to the person sitting in the center chair and whispers something in his ear.

"He's speaking with the pilot right now. The two people to his right are the navigators. One for above the water, one for below. The two on his left are in charge of safety." William says to us. His voice is barely above a whisper. "We keep this room as quiet as possible because they have to be able to hear the captain's voice without distraction."

As the captain stands back up, our ship begins to rise above the water. I didn't think it was possible, but the ride gets even smoother. I realize the spongy material had been acting as a buffer for a very faint jostling, but as we rise, the jostling stops completely. We reach a height of about two meters and level out as our speed increases dramatically.

"Help me understand," I say to William. "This vessel submerges, floats and flies?" I say. This is the first question of many. The second, and equally important, is how the pilot made the ship respond to him. I witnessed no movement and I see no control panel in front of him.

William doesn't look away from the window, "We're not flying. More like suspended above the water. The vessel won't raise any higher, but this allows us to use the energy of the ocean while not fighting against it. It's released us, but we're still tied to it."

This sounds more like a riddle than an explanation, but I don't pursue it any further. For now, I'm captivated by the sensation of skimming over the ocean's surface. We're not terribly high, which means that, from time to time, the belly of this silent missile breaks the water's skin in a cloud of mist. Even when we do this, our speed doesn't waver. In fact, I'm only aware of it because the enormous window fogs over before the sprinkles streak toward the top of the vessel.

The captain walks lightly over to Tori and stands to his right. "General Motodada, it truly is an honor to have you as my guest."

These two men, standing side by side, look like statues paying homage to a time long forgotten. Before Demetrius, before even the Ruling Ancestors.

"I was a young man when I first saw you Battle. It was against the giant that championed Balkavia. No one gave you a chance. But your precision. Your brutality. And at the end, your mercy. It was breathtaking."

"Thank you, Captain," Tori says. His stance straightens even more and he continues to peer through the window–as if he's waiting for some leviathan to emerge from the ocean to devour us.

"I couldn't sleep for a week after your final Battle. Waiting to hear whether or not you'd live. You have no idea the relief I felt when your survival was announced. I only wish you had been victorious." His voice drops as he says this and his eyes drift toward me. I'm not surprised, nor am I upset by the statement. This is a gazelle standing next to a lion. But I notice Tori's discomfort in a way only a son could and I'm overcome by the desire to end the conversation.

"Your kindness is appreciated," Tori says. His eyes have glazed over, allowing him to see a different time. Perhaps an alternate ending where he was victorious and his family still lived and I was nothing more than the son of a politician. He blinks rapidly and takes a deep breath. "Yes, you are very kind, sir, but that time is so far away, I don't think either of us can remember it truthfully. I'm sure I was less swift, void of mercy and brimming with brutality. We tend to remember things how we want them to be, rather than how they were." He turns to William, "I pray you don't think me ungrateful for your hospitality, but I find myself spent. Is there somewhere I may lie down?"

146

William motions to a man standing silently in the doorway behind us. He is like the rest of people I've seen since boarding. Thin, tan, unassuming.

"Of course. We have quarters prepared for you," William says.

Tori bows to each of us and follows his guide down the hall. The captain watches them until they are out of sight, then turns back to the five people silently navigating us over this vast expanse of water.

William brushes my elbow. "Please do not take offense at his attitude. He spends too much time in isolation, pondering impossible eventualities. I fear he feels a false kinship to your Mentor."

"If there were an offense, it would not be yours to mend. I expect no one, other than politicians, to maintain the illusion that I'm anything other than a predator stalking his prey. If my presence upsets your captain, I'm happy to take my leave." Even as I say this, I hope he doesn't take me up on it. I'm wholly captivated by the control of this ship and anxious to understand something so foreign.

"Not at all. Stay as long as you desire."

Given the silence of the room, our captain has heard our entire conversation, yet makes no attempt to clarify or rectify. I prefer it that way.

"How is it that we're being controlled?" I ask to no one in particular. "Our direction, speed, height. All have changed since I entered the room, yet I've seen no controls manipulated."

"I'm afraid I can only give you a cursory idea, as my understanding is stilted at best." William pauses to look around the room. I can't tell if he's looking for the right explanation or the perfect lie. "When you live on the ocean, you must learn to tune your needs with others in order to prosper. There is no subduing the ocean the way one would tame the land. You learn it. Embrace it. Become one with it. You felt this, I think, when you were towing us. You would not have dreamt of telling the waves to stop. Rather, you learned when to bend to their power so you could exploit it when you were at the crest."

"He's not looking for a love note, Highness," the captain interrupts. "He's a soldier. You want to know how it works? We're efficient. We have to be, living here. We don't have time to realize that we need to go to port, then tell our hands to move a control, which then has to engage some gears, which finally begin to turn us to port. We simply think it and the ship does it. These pilots are somewhere between crew and vessel. Same with the ship. When they're engaged, the vessel is another member of the crew. It's not mystical. It's technology. And it's the most elegant thing I've ever seen." He says this without inflection, barely above a whisper.

I'm grateful for the straightforward response, but it serves to cause more questions than answers. "Thank you, but how is that possible?" I ask.

He turns to me. It's the first time he's looked me directly in the eyes. "And now I see how efficient you are."

William steps forward, ready to correct the captain. But I've never needed a champion and I'm not about to ask for one now. I say, "Your hospitality is much appreciated. As is your candor. I've walked into this situation seeking to understand. I believe I've demonstrated that so far. And until I demonstrate anything else, I suggest you refrain from accusing me of anything different." I've matched my inflection, tone and volume to his.

"This man is our guest, Captain, and you will treat him as such," William says. His voice matches neither the tone nor the volume of the room. It's so jarring, the vessel wavers slightly, causing we who are standing to check our balance through the quick shifting of our feet.

The pilot adjusts his position in his seat and the vessel smooths back out. It is the first time I have seen him move since entering the command room.

"Maybe this is a better conversation to have in a different venue," the captain says.

"As you wish. We will discuss, civilly, over dinner this evening," William says. He turns to me, "The trip has been long and I'm afraid I'm overly exhausted." He bows to both of us and heads for the door. "I'll arrange a proper feast for us." As he leaves, I bow, instinctually, in a way I've never bowed to my Ruler.

We're silent for a long time. The captain continues his vigilance over the pilot and his crew while the combination of the sea's rhythm and the low hum of our vessel lull me into a waking dream.

"Celcus used to be the least of all the nations, you know," his back is to me, posture stiff. "When I was a boy there was rarely a Battle. We looked forward to the exhibitions, but when it came time for official challenges, the nations, for the most part, remained at peace." He speaks as if telling a child of a time of dragons and magic and unrealistic human courage.

"Then Demetrius took power. The first few years were without incident, but he began focusing on your Mentor's nation. Making speeches about supposed atrocities by their Ruler. His ruthlessness and hunger for power."

He whispers something to the pilot and we gently glide in an eastward arc.

"Demetrius kept challenging Tori, year after year. All the while, his rhetoric against Tori's Ruler grew more and more accusatory. Other Rulers investigated the claims, but never found the horror of which Demetrius spoke. But he kept insisting disenfranchised informants were coming to him, begging him to end the oppression. So he kept throwing Generals at Tori. And Tori kept winning. He was amazing. The perfect balance of viciousness and honor. The world loved him. Regardless of the validity of Demetrius's speeches, the world adored Tori's precision, relentlessness and creativity. His brutality. You're so much like him."

The narrative of conquered nations is largely controlled by Demetrius.

What little I've been able to learn has been footage of exactly what the captain is referring to. Speeches, mostly by Demetrius, sometimes by other Celcean politicians, that decry corruption by opposing Rulers. All of them justifying our need to rescue a nation's citizens from depraved despots. Every child in Celsus is taught the same thing in school. The Ruling Ancestors set a perfect system to keep people from mass killing each other, but the system is tenuous because of the greed of other nations and Celsus has the moral responsibility to ensure we protect the ideals they set in place. It's why we identify Hopefuls so early in life. It's why we keep the Ceremonial Guard. So our nation will never lose. Because if we do, the peaceful way of our world may come crashing down. I've seen myself as not just the champion of Celsus, but of the world. Winning Battles and guaranteeing the continued vision of the Elders. My conversation with Demetrius surfaces from the back of my mind. The weakness of the original rules. The Justification.

"But there are checks put in place to mitigate such a thing. If what you're saying were true, Celsus would have been conquered by Tori's nation," I say.

"Yes, if they would have followed the letter of the law. But they didn't. They never took land from Celsus, even though they had every right. Demetrius made it clear he would go wage truewar if they tried. He said he wouldn't let Celsus fall in the hands of such a vicious Ruler. We were all so scared of the idea of truewar, we let ourselves become convinced. His persistence in Battle and his insistence Tori's Ruler was a monster began swaying world opinion. The only thing that never wavered was our love of Tori. We began dreading each Battle because we thought Tori was an honorable pawn of dishonorable Ruler."

It is as if the captain was listening to my audience with Demetrius and attributing Marcail's rhetoric to my Ruler.

"Then Tori lost to your predecessor. Almost died. I remember the tension across the world as we waited to hear if he survived. He did, and we all celebrated because we loved him. Then Demetrius had free reign to tour the nation and highlight, firsthand, the squalor. The overcrowded slums and political prisoners. He even found evidence of mass graves."

The captain stops talking. We both stand next to each other, watching the ocean pass beneath us. The scenes he describes flash through my head. I've seen all of it, of course. I took it all for truth. Examples of our responsibility to ensure justice reigned across the world. Evidence that, if I ever lost, I'd be letting people in similar circumstances remain in their version of hell.

"There is no way. It's impossible Tori would have fought so hard to defend a nation which treated its citizens that way. You know him. His honor. Could a man like your Mentor come out of a nation like that?" He stares at me. Tears pool at the bottom of his eyes, threatening to spill over and streak down his sun scorched skin.

"I like to think I fight with honor. Tori tells me I'm beloved. Maybe not as much as he was, but I hear the Crowd. They cheer for me the way I'm sure they cheered for Tori," I say. The ocean looks to have gotten more violent and our vessel, in spite of hovering above the waves, feels as if it's being jostled from side to side. I'm grateful for an empty stomach.

"Of course. You do your Mentor justice," he says.

"If that's true, then the thing you find so impossible of Tori, you willingly accept of me. And if you question me, then you assume it of Tori, as he's the one who has equipped my hands to kill, focused my will for victory." The words sound true, but they don't sound like they're coming from me. The voice that forms the sounds is too clear, too confident. Even as I say these things, my hands feel out of place. My skin seems awkward against my muscles and no matter how I adjust my weight, my clothing feels as if it reveals my every flaw.

Chapter 21

It's late. Dinner was like any other feast. Delicious food, polite conversation. Nothing of significance discussed. Both William and Tori showed up promptly and were pleased to see the captain and me without any lingering quarrel. Now, as the crew of the vessel sleeps, my cabin feels small. The monotony of the floors, walls and ceiling no longer interest me. The lack of stimulus sets my mind on a single course. In fact, I haven't stopped thinking about it since my discussion with the captain.

I knew Tori was a formidable opponent. People have even ventured to tell me he would have bested my predecessor ninety-nine out of one hundred times. Tori, they've said, simply had a bad day and my predecessor took advantage of it. Out of respect for Tori, I have mostly refrained from bringing it up, assuming the memory of loss too great of an embarrassment for a man with as much pride as my Mentor. But now it's all I can think of.

A simple voice command converts the wall opposite of me into a viewing screen. "Battle archive. Tori Motodad," I say. Seven tiles appear, arranged sequentially, by date. "Motodada versus Celsus." Three of the tiles disappear. Four Battles. When the captain mentioned multiple Battles, I thought there had been two at the most.

This means Tori defeated three Celcean champions. "Play from the beginning, I say."

The first image I see is a young Tori, naked except for a loincloth. He's small, even for a General of two decades ago. But what he lacks in bulk, he makes up for in tone. His skin clings to every twitching muscle on his torso. His opponent, my nation's champion, looks young. Inexperienced. Scared.

Since Celsus was the aggressor, Tori's nation has picked the Battle. No weapons, just simple hand to hand combat. To the death.

I'm not surprised by the rules. And the meaning isn't lost on me. Tori's Ruler, no doubt, sees the challenge as an offense and trusts Tori's superior skill. He, therefore, wants to make an example out of Demetrius and his General, hoping to quell any ongoing challenges by fast, severe and overwhelming dominance. I respect the choice, but, with the benefit of history, it's obvious the choice only served to stiffen the resolve of Demetrius. In fact, if what the captain said was true, this was likely used as evidence of the brutality of Tori's Ruler.

The camera switches to Tori's Ruler. This is the first time I've seen him and I'm stunned. It's clear I'm looking at Tori's father. Not only is the resemblance uncanny, but I see the subtle fear in his eyes. The same expression I see when Tori sends me into the Temple each year.

I then see Demetrius. Thinner, his thick hair perfectly arranged atop his head. After a few uncomfortable moments, he takes a breath and launches into what I've come to accept as a typical speech. I'm spellbound. Not because his words compel me. On the contrary, viewing his performance with the buffer of time, the speech is less compelling than what he's capable of now. But I watch this young Ruler and I see uncertainty. I see hunger. I see ambition and the focus to achieve a dream at all costs.

I skip the rest of the formalities and queue up the start of the Battle. The Crowd is silent, knowing they will see a man die. Something my Crowd craves. The yearly sacrifice to the Ruling Elders.

Tori moves toward his foe in a straight line. I see no fear or hesitation. There is only the singular focus he has made so instinctual in me. Win. No matter the cost. No matter the pain. Win. Win decisively.

The two Generals meet at the center of the battlefloor and one lone voice screams out. *Kill him!* It's as if that simple, guttural exclamation ignites a wick which detonates the collective Crowd. At once, the roar I'm so used to fills the Temple. It's so loud and so sudden, both Tori and his opponent flinch as if dodging an unseen opponent. They recover quickly and tear into each other. Neither trying to block the other's strikes.

Tori lands three cutting strikes across the face of his opponent, only to receive a vicious knee to the solar plexus, which doubles him over. The Celcean champion wastes no time in bringing his elbows down on the back of Tori's head, which forces him to his knees. The Crowd gets even louder, sensing a fast victory for Celsus. But Tori dodges an attempt at a stranglehold by rolling out of the way. It's one of the first moves he ever taught me. Feint weakness to entice an aggressive opponent to overcommit. As Tori rolls out of the way, he slashes a heel up, catching his opponent across the jaw as he rushes to lock his arms around Tori's neck. If the Crowd wasn't so loud, I'm sure I'd hear the snap of his jaw.

Tori is on his feet as his opponent stumbles. In an instant, his opponent is at Tori's feet. Dead. I have to replay the footage three times to understand how it happened. Even after reviewing, the best I can understand is that Tori snapped his neck with a series of perfect strikes, at least 4 in less than a second, to his spine. As fast as that, Tori defended his nation. I'm in awe. And I immediately feel slow and awkward. Seeing this Battle, I wonder how Tori has ever been able to trust my ability to emerge victorious from any contest.

He doesn't wait for victory to be declared. Instead, he walks across the battlefloor, eyes on the ground until he reaches a point directly in front of his father's seat. Without looking up, he bows deeply, then walks out of the Temple.

The screen goes blank for a moment, then the next tile appears. One year later, Tori against another Celcean General. This General I know. Tori spoke of him often. His name was Lemuel. Much bigger than his predecessor, still not as big as me.

I progress the footage past all of the formalities. The rules are the same. Hand to hand combat to the death. Tori is dressed in the same loincloth. Lemuel has body armor. Nothing in the rules prohibit how he's dressed. I can't help but wonder if this is a mistake on the part of Tori and his team, or if they had so much faith in Tori, they knew he'd win no matter what. Another statement about Tori's dominance.

I know about Lemuel because Tori would constantly refer to him as the General who should have beat him. I slow the footage as the Generals snap into action.

Tori rushes toward Lemuel much faster than the last Battle. However, Lemuel stays in one spot. The only movement he makes is to drop his left foot back so he's not facing Tori directly, and bends deeply at the knees. Tori closes the distance and, at the last second, instead of launching himself at Lemuel as I expect, he drops to the ground and, using the momentum of his advance, spins so his left leg sweeps the back of Lemuel's right leg. The strike is flawless and causes Lemuel to stumble, but not fall. Tori is up in an instant, having continued through his spin and he catches Lemuel with a crushing elbow to the throat.

A droplet of blood trickles from Lemuel's mouth and he drops to his knees, slumps and goes motionless. Tori, with two strikes, has killed him. I feel as if it was my windpipe which was crushed. Two strikes. This is the man Tori thought should have beaten him. He didn't even feel his power. As the screen goes blank, and the next tile pops up for review, I realize I've never really known my Mentor.

Battle three. Tori's last victory. The Celcean General is back to a loincloth. Tori looks relaxed, as if resigned to the task before him. Rather than starting the Battle, Tori's Father stands. The entire Temple falls silent.

He faces the camera. Rigid, hands behind his back, he looks exactly like

Tori when I've stumbled through a drill. He says, "These attacks against Niponuzi tire me. It's clear the Celcean leader has a personal vendetta and is perverting the Battle structure given to us by the Ruling Elders. My son, the mighty Tori Motodad," at the mention of Tori's name, the Crowd erupts. It seems like minutes until Tori's Father can speak again. "My son continues to fight valiantly, defending the honor of his nation and his father. Many have asked why I have not ended this. Taken my rightful prize and removed Demetrius from power. Many have called me a fool for expecting Demetrius to act with honor. That foolishness ends today." He looks to his right where a beautiful young woman sits next to him, cradling a newborn, cupping her hands over the child's ears to shield it from the noise. "My son has been granted the greatest gift one can receive in this life. And I will not allow this child, this royal heir, to grow up watching his father Battle year after year, simply because Demetrius wants to conquer my nation."

I pause the recording. Tori was married. Tori was a father. And at some point, he was separated from them. My stomach knots. This whole time, he's secreted their existence far away from me. This man. The person who has nurtured me, taught me, protected me. This man who I've learned from and sought refuge with, as a son would a father, once had a son of his own. The resentment he must feel for me makes me want to jump into the ocean and drift until my strength gives out. The hatred he must feel for me. In spite of my shock, I begin the recording again. Now, more than ever, I need to understand this man who has formed me.

"And it is in my power," Tori's father says, "to end this charade. Demetrius, I have been kind enough to leave your nation unconquered, even though your Generals have proven grossly incompetent. If you insist on pursuing this after today's Battle, I assure you, Celsus will suffer. You will not only cease to rule. You will cease to exist."

The Temple is silent. Direct address from one Ruler to another is unprecedented. As soon as Tori's father is done speaking, I know he has made an enormous mistake.

"Niponuzi's leader must be very proud to see his family grow. Indeed,

General Motodada is an opponent of the highest caliber. No doubt, he will be an unparalleled father as well," again, the adoration of the Crowd interrupts Demetrius.

"I mourn each of my valiant Generals that have lost their lives trying to free an impoverished and tortured nation. How a General as valiant and honorable as Tori Motodada continues to defend such a dictator is beyond me. And how the rest of the Rulers can stand by and allow me to shoulder the burden of freeing a noble citizenry such as Niponuzi breaks my heart. I truly wonder if I'm the only Ruler, as meager as my nation may be, who is dedicated to ensuring the Ruling Elders didn't labor in vain. Know this, King Motodada, I will continue to fight for your citizens to my last breath. Tori is not invincible. He has a weakness and I will find it. And when I do, the world will finally see you the way I see you. And you will reap the consequences of your brutality. I will continue to operate within the edicts passed down by our Elders to free the citizens of Niponuzi from a tyrant. I don't care how mighty or popular his General is. Eventually human decency will prevail."

He doesn't waver. He hardly blinks. The speech is perfectly delivered. In a few short sentences, Demetrius has turned this carnival atmosphere somber. This is the Demetrius I know.

Before the Battle begins, Tori looks up to his father's suite and places his hand over his heart. The gesture is returned by the young woman and a camera zooms in to capture a tear trickle down her perfectly angled cheek and land on the baby's swaddling blanket. It's the first time I've seen him take his focus off his opponent while on the battlefloor. This tenderness, and divided focus, is almost more than I can handle.

The Celcean General begins walking toward Tori, following the arc of the Temple wall. Tori stays in one place, waiting for the General's strategy to be revealed. This goes on for at least five minutes and it's obvious the Crowd grows restless, as do I. I progress until I see the two Generals converge. The Celcean General looks to be in perfect condition. He's not huge like some of the other Generals, but his toned physique rivals Tori's. They almost look like mirror images of each other.

When they finally clash, it looks more like a dance than a fight. This is a Battle of torque and balance. The strikes aren't meant to incapacitate, instead, they're meant to gain the slightest advantage through forcing the other to shift his weight just slightly. Each strike is met with a block, which was also a strike. A perpetuating cycle until one of them overcompensates in the slightest. Their precision is amazing. Tori has run similar drills with me before and I can't last nearly as long as these two have. Each minute that goes by, the intensity ratchets up. The need for continued perfection more evident with each move. The Crowd, it seems, has grown bored and I begin to hear jeers from people who crave a more vulgar form of violence. But this Battle is one for Generals. Even the rhythm of their breathing plays a part in gaining a strategic advantage.

After ten minutes of nonstop movement, I see it. The Celcean extends his fist three centimeters too far, which allows Tori to connect his block slightly above the General's elbow, which forces his torso to angle slightly farther from Tori, which allows Tori to shift his foot closer to the General's heel, which makes it impossible for the General to adjust his weight, which makes him have to arch his back on his return strike, which makes Tori's knee to the hip knock him completely off balance. And since they're so close, the General falls directly into Tori's clench, his arm wrapped around the General's neck in a vice. The Crowd gasps, shocked at the seemingly instantaneous turn of events.

I see him look up to his young wife and new child as the General tries in vain to wriggle out of the stranglehold. Tori nods, a tiny, almost imperceptible gesture, and his wife returns the nod. A hidden communication between husband and wife, something I'll likely never understand, which tells Tori all he needs to know. In an instant Tori twists at the waist, fast and powerful. The Crowd goes silent as the Celcean General slumps in Tori's arms. Dead.

The Crowd erupts, happy to have their fill of violence. They have no idea what they just witnessed. Likely the finest technical fight in history, settled in centimeters. And in the midst of it, a silent conversation between a man and his wife that decided the fate of another man. All these people know is that one man defeated another. The scandal of death trumping beauty and nuance.

It's almost morning and I have no idea what the day holds for me, but I must see Tori's defeat. In these few hours, my Mentor has grown from knowledgeable coach to demi-god. I must know how it all unraveled so quickly.

The next Battle queues and flashes on screen. I don't listen to the speech of either Ruler. The adrenaline coursing through my body makes my hands shake.

I slow the recording just before Tori's father reviews the rules. The camera focuses on the Niponuzi booth. Like the previous year, Tori's beautiful wife sits next to the king. But she is dressed in all black, save a string of pearls around her neck. The dress of a woman in mourning. And next to her, instead of their young son is a small chair, painted black with a tiny stuffed animal placed on the seat.

"This Battle will continue until one of the Generals is unable to continue. Either due to death or incapacitation. The one rule, if a General is already incapacitated, the other may not kill him. Doing so will result in immediate execution of the conquering General. This has been agreed upon by both Rulers," Tori's father says with a quivering voice. "Forgive me. But I'm moved to ask for a moment of silence for my grandson. Just last night, he succumbed to a week long illness. His fever simply grew too high. Please bow your heads."

The Crowd immediately drops into an eerie silence. Thousands of people, silent, unmoving, possibly not even breathing. It's likely the first they've heard the news and, like me, they are utterly shocked. How can Tori be expected to fight? The morning after losing his son. It's impossible, even for someone like Tori. The camera switches from face to face in the Crowd. Blank stares, covered mouths, bowed heads. Then it focuses on Demetrius, his head bowed, hands clasped reverently in front of him. For a split second I think I see the upturn of the corner of his mouth. After that, the camera finds Tori, tears streaming down his face, hand over his heart, identical to his gesture from a year before.

The Battle begins with a whisper. It's not followed by cheering. In fact, everyone remains silent. The only one to respond is Augustus. General of Celsus. My predecessor. The one destined to defeat Tori and set Celsus on a trajectory of dominance.

In spite of knowing the outcome, I watch, hoping it doesn't happen in this recording.

Excited to see Tori's preoccupation, Augustus advances on him quickly. I want to scream at the video, warn Tori that a substandard General is about to take advantage of him at his weakest. But I know it's futile. Of course Tori loses. I'm amazed he even made it to the Temple.

Within seconds, Augustus is on top of him, landing blow after blow. After the first, Tori snaps out of it and takes a defensive posture, his instinct finally kicking in. Augustus is sloppy. Every time he rears back to strike, I see countless ways Tori could exploit the onslaught, but Tori never does. He simply continues to retreat without form or strategy.

After what seems like an eternity of vulgar bullying by Augustus, he lands what I know to be the first in a series of Battle ending strikes. While Tori simply covers his head from the relentless fists and elbows, Augusts jumps and sends the side of his foot directly into the side of Tori's knee. Even though it's an unimpressive strike, one that Tori would have dismantled on any other day, it makes perfect contact. Every ligament in Tori's knee is instantaneously shredded.

On my command, the video goes dark. I can't stand to watch any more. He loses. To an inferior opponent. One Battle and Niponuzi is wiped off the map. One Battle which opened the door for Demetrius to rise to ultimate power. One Battle which led me to Tori, and my eventual rise as the greatest.

I drift into a violence filled sleep. The final dream I have, I stand in the Temple across from a young Tori. Demetrius smiles at us from above while the Crowd calls for my blood.

Chapter 22

I'm not prepared for what I see when we reach the surface of the vessel. Instead of a dock that leads to a land mass, we're moored to a man made, floating city. It takes me a few moments to understand what I'm looking at, but eventually it dawns on me that the city is made up of hundreds, maybe thousands, of individual modules which are linked together. Because of this, the city drifts fluidly on the water, forming hills and valleys as the waves pass beneath them. It also looks as if the modules can attach or detach from each other as they see fit, which creates impromptu canals for small vessels to pass through. Each module is roughly one hundred meters across and supports different structures. None of the structures, however, stand more than three stories tall. The architecture of this place has the soft curves of the ocean. It seems as if the pathways flow and the walls themselves flex. It's clear the water and wind provide the energy needed to power these structures. Everywhere I look I see turbines, kites and propellers turning the waves and wind into power.

As I step onto the city, I expect to feel the platform beneath me continuing to rise and fall, but the moment both my feet are on the city, it feels as firm as Celsus. The jolting sensation turns my stomach.

"Don't worry. The nausea is normal. Once you're deeper in the city, and can't see the ocean, your senses will stop fighting with each other," William says, as he walks unsteadily next to me. I turn to see Tori, stone-faced, measuring each step.

William is right. Once we're fifty meters in, I feel as if I'm in a remarkably beautiful city, firmly planted on a continent. Not only do the structures please my eyes, but each is adorned with subtle artwork. Mosaics, paintings, carvings, poetry. I'm surrounded by creativity.

"Who created all of this art?" I ask, trying to imagine the endless granite and marble monoliths of Celsus with anything other than straight lines and sharp angles.

"Aegea did. Our citizens. Each piece of art reflects a story about the forming of our nation. How we learned to embrace the water and bend to it. Captured here is our history. Told and retold through celebration." He says this as easily as one may give directions to a tourist.

I'm surprised we're not met with any sort of transportation, but, the farther we walk, I find myself grateful for the chance to stretch my legs. Above us, a flock of seagulls floats on the breeze.

"They never leave our floating city. My mother complains that we've made them lazy. Rather than hunting the fish beneath the surface, they lethargically float there, waiting for a child to drop some bread or a shopkeeper to discard some leftovers. Amazingly, no matter how we reconfigure our city, they seem to know where the main passages are. Our captains tell us they know when they're close because the clouds of birds flocking in the middle of the ocean," William says.

Tori glances up and smiles briefly. I can't tell if it's actually a smile, or if he's squinting against the sun. Either way, it's such a difference from the pain I saw in the footage last night, I wonder what's boiling under the surface of that calm exterior. I wonder, if every time he sees something beautiful, or hears something which causes genuine joy, if the image of his dying son flashes into his memory, turning it into regret, or anger, or hatred.

We enter a smallish structure with a flowing piece of purple fabric for a door. As my eyes adjust to the dimmed lighting, I see Queen Marcail round the corner, smiling and rushing to embrace William. If this is Marcail's royal chamber, it is appalling in its simplicity. The only extravagance I can see is a floor to ceiling mirror which is framed in a mosaic of seashells. I am suddenly reminded of my last conference with Demetrius. If he is right, this woman has brought our world closer to truewar than we have been in decades. Yet she acts as if she is simply the host of a quaint dinner party.

Tori watches the reunion of prince and queen without expression. I can't help but assume he's thinking the same thing. My conspiratorial musings fall completely apart when we are joined by Fiona. It seems our paths have been destined to intersect. First as my escort when battling Seth, then as our servant at the Aegean feast. Even from across the room, her green eyes glow against her tanned face. She doesn't look at me, rather, she rushes to William and they embrace. The smile on her face, framed between William's neck and shoulder, reflects pure joy. I look away, feeling the same childish awkwardness as when I began watching the footage of Tori's Battles last night.

Queen Marcail has turned her attention to me, smiling the same smile she had for William. Only a person with much to hide can greet her would-be conqueror with the same expression she showed to her son.

"Please believe me when I tell you what a pleasure it is to see you. I only wish it was under different circumstances." She reaches out and embraces me. I've experienced few embraces in my life. Rather, I'm much more used to the grappling clutch of an opponent than one expressing care.

I return the embrace with clumsy, stone hands. She's much smaller than me, but has put her arms around my shoulders, which makes me have to stoop and thread my arms under hers. As I pull away, my hand gets caught in her robe. We begin a strange, lumbering dance as I try to dislodge from her laughing arms. After a second that feels like years, Tori reaches over and helps free my hand from under the Queen's arm.

"Your graciousness is a gift, Highness. We are unused to any sort of affection other than the kind that leaves bruises and drips blood," Tori says. Bowing instead of returning her offered embrace.

She continues to laugh, "If that is considered graciousness, I would hate to see indifference." She turns back to me, "And thank you, that was one of the best dances I've had in years."

I smile and mimic Tori's bow, knowing better than to respond and make an even bigger fool of myself.

William and Fiona walk over to us. "I know you two have had run-ins before, but allow me to officially introduce you to Fiona, Princess of Aegea, my sister," William says.

Princess. Sister. The revelation makes me inexplicably happy, even though I should likely question why her royalty is only now being brought to light. She watched Tori and me as we prepared for Battle, heard our conversation. Witnessed our strategic reasoning. She even took the opportunity to try to distract me before I entered the battlefloor.

The Battle I'm about to fight with Aegea, apparently, has been brewing much longer than I thought. As we politely greet one another, a Battle surge of adrenaline flows through me. Only this Battle can't be won with fists or weapons. This Battle has been waging against me as I slept and ate and marveled at a foreign culture.

My thoughts are interrupted by Tori, "Such a pleasure to meet you, Highness. The architects of this lovely city must have used you as their muse, only now that I see you, I realize they failed miserably at capturing your essence." He says this as he gives his customary bow.

She curtsies and turns to me, extending her arms the same way her mother had. I step back with wooden legs and offer Tori's bow, "I think I've made enough of a fool of myself today."

Her smile fades slightly, but she stops and gives me an identical curtsy. "Such a shame. You're so elegant in the Temple, but when it comes to human interaction," Queen Marcail puts a hand on Fiona's arm.

"We often forget that our customs are much different than most other places. Come, let us begin our official audience." Her eyes widen in exaggerated excitement as she says the last two words.

William leads us into a second room. This one is slightly more formal, but it still seems like the dwelling of a commoner. Cushions for lounging have been arranged in a circle and Marcail gestures for us to pick any. Fiona grabs my arm and leads me to one which is between her and William. Tori takes one next to the queen. I sit, doubting more and more the wisdom of Demetrius sending me as his ambassador.

"Let's begin, shall we?" Marcail says. She looks between Tori and me, waiting for one of us to speak.

Tori defers to me with a nod. I almost begin laughing. General and Mentor, struck dumb and ineffectual with a few hugs and some laughter. The first rule Tori ever taught me echoes in the back of my mind.

When outmatched, accept it. Expose it and allow your opponent to believe they are on their way to an early victory. Then wait for them to act lazily.

I slowly look from the queen to William, then to Fiona. Catching their eyes just long enough to avert my gaze before they do. Finally, I rest my stare on the ground in the middle of the room. "I find myself at a loss. I was given no training in the world of politics. If we were standing on the battlefloor, I would know the next ten moves. But seated here, with the knowledge that you know much more about me and these official proceedings than I do of you, I can do nothing but defer."

"Well, this is refreshing," Queen Marcail says.

"Honesty. In a meeting of state," William says, smiling at his mother, "if I wasn't sitting here, I wouldn't believe it."

Marcail nods, "We do have a dire situation then. You see, as long as I've been queen, we've never been challenged. Not even for a Mid-Year exhibition. In such, young man, we were hoping to rely on your considerable experience."

Fiona sits up straight and pulls a strand of hair from her face as if it's the string of a bow, "It would be much more expedient if they would just tell us what justification they hope to find. Demetrius obviously has a narrative which he hopes to strengthen with their presence. Even if they find nothing, I'm sure some evidence will magically emerge against us."

"If you're not going to act with the dignity, self-control and respect that is required of your place," Marcail says to Fiona, "I'll have to ask you to leave." Her voice is soft, but there is no doubting her authority. "This is why we asked her to serve food during your last visit. Can you imagine Demetrius and her at the same table?"

Although it's obvious Fiona wants nothing to do with me, I feel bad for her. Every official interaction for her is layered with family nuance and political ceremony. It must have been the same for Tori, although I can't imagine him doing anything close to rebellious toward his father.

"In all honesty," I say, "I am uninterested in political posturing. Demetrius has sent me here and I am happy to obey. I only hope to learn enough about your culture so, when the time comes, our two nations can join without pain or resentment."

Fiona lets out a deep breath and William's face flushes red. The queen smiles, "Assuming we will be joining. You're talented, but don't be so hasty as to assume an outcome, regardless of how likely it is. I believe there are countless proverbs about such pride which predate even the Ruling Ancestors."

I look to Tori, but his head is bowed, either praying for this meeting to end, or too embarrassed to look up. I rarely feel vulnerable, but when I do, the only response I know is violence. I fight the surge building inside me by regulating my breaths into perfect rhythm. The tangled tassels on the fringe of my pillow give me a rare anxiety and I begin to straighten them as quickly as I can. As I align each tassel, I feel a small amount of control return.

"Of course, Your Majesty," is all I can muster.

We're silent for what feels like an hour. The queen sits patiently and William mirrors her. Fiona stands, clearly as uncomfortable as me, and leaves the room without saying anything. I'm about to follow her lead when she comes back, holding a tray of food. If Demetrius had a daughter, he would never let her serve anyone. The thought of royalty doing anything other than sitting, scheming and projecting power is so foreign to me that I stand and take the tray from her.

"Allow me. It's the least I can do," I say. She begins to protest, but sits instead.

The platter looks to be woven from dried seaweed, but feels incredibly sturdy. Piled on top is an assortment of food I have never seen before. Even though most of it looks as if it has not been cooked, the smell reminds me I skipped breakfast this morning. As I kneel to present the platter to the queen, my stomach lets out an audible groan.

She clearly hears but, in her elegance, says nothing, correctly assuming I'm at my limit for humiliation. The kindness is unexpected and, as almost everything today, completely alien. After I've made my way around the circle, I drop to my cushion, the tray still half full.

"Please, eat," Marcail says. I comply immediately.

"I must admit," says William, "when I woke this morning, I did not expect I was going to be served lunch by the General of Celsus. This has been an interesting day so far." His levity and candor break the tension immediately.

Fiona laughs in between bites, "Nor did I plan on the little dance we saw between mother and Trajan." Marcail shakes her head at her daughter, but the gesture is full of love and humor.

They go on like this for a few minutes. Each comment is a lighthearted joke at the expense of another, lacking any trace of malice. Tori and I remain silent. This interplay, loving and gentle and playful, is the strangest thing I've seen since setting foot on Aegea's island. They may as well be speaking a different language. I wouldn't be able to contribute no matter how hard I tried. It occurs to me that in all my years of studying gestures, movement and tone of voice, I was only studying the worst of human nature so that I might exploit it. When presented with kindness and humility, I can only stare in wonder.

I glance at Tori. He follows the banter with amusement. It makes me think of his wife and child. This could have been a regular occurrence if his son had lived and he had won his Battle with Augustus.

I try to think back to my family. What was it like, I wonder, to share a meal with my parents? No matter how hard I try, I have no memory of before my training. The barracks, the combat lessons, evaluating everything even as a child. If I passed my parents on the streets of Celsus, I'd never know it. I don't even know if I had a brother or a sister.

Fiona's voice stirs me from my reflection. "Mentor, my father used to speak of you as if of a legend." At the mention of Fiona's father, the queen's smile fades. I watch as she allows a brief daydream of her own. I can only imagine what she's remembering, but it causes her to sit a little straighter and her eyes to soften around the edges.

"That was a long time ago," Tori says.

"Even still, I'm happy to sit with you. It brings back fond memories of him. He would tell me stories about you and other Generals while brushing my hair when I was a child." Her face mirrors her mother's. I wonder if anyone will ever remember me with such fondness or intimacy.

"I would have enjoyed meeting your father, I think," says Tori. "I'm told he was a kind and fair leader. His loss was felt around the world."

"Thank you. But you did not come all this way to reminisce. We've wasted enough of your time," Marcail says, her eyes more focused. "We've discussed the best way for you to spend your visit. We'd be honored if you would accompany the prince and princess to our outer farming communities. You will get to see what Demetrius is calling the fringe of our society and we will get some much-needed help with the coming harvest. That is, as long as you don't mind a little manual labor. If you would prefer, however, I can have you sit with our small congress. I believe they will be debating a proposal to anchor our capital in the southern hemisphere this winter."

"We would be overjoyed to help with the harvest," I say, trying not to sound too anxious to leave these types of meetings behind me.

"Very well. You will depart the day after tomorrow. In the meantime, we have prepared one of our pods on the edge of the city for you. I trust you will find it relaxing before your trip. I'll do my best to keep our politicians at bay."

Chapter 23

My room only has a bed and three walls. Instead of a fourth wall, it opens directly to the ocean. Tori's room mirrors mine on the opposite side of the building. Between us is a common space, littered sparsely with cushions and a cooking area. Outside, near the edge of our pod is a work table, complete with carving tools and a block of walnut. The only other structure on our pod is a training ring surrounded by various combat simulators.

Tori sets about inspecting things. I watch him, imagining his son walking next to him, inquiring about the curve of a wall or what he advises about being so open to the elements if a storm comes.

"Please stop," I say.

He pauses, his arm buried to the elbow in his pack. "You saw the footage?" He doesn't look at me and his voice betrays no emotion.

"I did."

He sighs. "As soon as the captain started talking last night, I figured it would happen. This is probably one of the only nations which still has that record." He continues unpacking our bag. This simple act of unpacking for me, the way a father would do for a son, is too much.

"Please. Stop. Allow me."

"Why? Because you saw me lose a Battle? You've known that. I am the shamed General of a defeated nation. Did seeing my defeat disgust you that much?" He stands as he says this, turning directly toward me.

"No, Moto-San. We all lose. You taught me that. But your son. Your wife." I stop, not knowing what else to say. "What was his name?"

He turns back to our bag, "That does not need to be discussed. We can talk about any of my Battles. There is much to be learned. But you will learn nothing of how to be a General by talking about them."

The pain of their memories paints his face. But that is his pain. Made worse, no doubt, by having to teach and care for me all these years. He has been my father. I have not been his son. That much is painfully clear. I have been nothing but an assignment. A duty to perform as a consequence of his loss. And as such, he has fulfilled the exact mandate of his job. Today has been a painful example of this fact. I am a mighty General. But when asked to sit at a family table and navigate things like kindness and relationships, I bumble. I am more machine than human.

Tears come to my eyes for the first time that I can remember. I am not angry with him. He has survived the only way he could. I am angry at myself for believing the fairytale. Of course he would never be my father. Nor could I be his son. He is a slave and I am his lifelong assignment.

"You're right. It won't." My voice sounds small and distant. Tori must hear it too because he takes a step toward me but stops. Standing with my training bag behind him, framed by the gentle slopes of an Aegean structure, he looks as awkward as I've ever seen him. Before he can move toward me anymore, or say anything, I turn, "When you are finished unpacking, I would like to train."

In my quarters, I push these strange thoughts of doubt and anger and fear as far away as I can. I focus on what is normal to me. Emotions do not win Battles. It is the might in my body, and my ability to control what I feel, which makes me great. I relax my muscles as I stretch, allowing each fiber to release as much lactic acid as possible, priming the tissue to be tested and respond immediately. But my mind doesn't clear the way it's supposed to. Every measured breath brings a vision of Tori's dead son, or Fiona laughing lazily with William, or myself as a child rushing to Tori for comfort, hoping for a word of approval after a drill or waking him early on a day off from training. None of it is true.

Before I realize what I've done, I launch myself into the ocean. The water is cold. Refreshing. I allow myself to sink, focusing on the air in my lungs. The way the water fills my ears and distorts sound, the sting of the saltwater when I open my eyes.

Cream then blue then purple then black. The deeper I sink, the more the water absorbs the light. Above me, I see the underbelly of the Aegean capital. It too is smooth and contoured, as if shaped by the sea. When my lungs begin to burn and as the water grows colder, I finally kick my legs and push down. I reach the surface just before my instincts take over and I inhale a lung-full of water. Just a few more seconds and I wouldn't have surfaced.

The city has floated away from me. Something I didn't expect while I was under the surface. William would probably laugh, ask if I'd ever heard of currents. I begin swimming hard and in a few minutes, I can tell I'm making progress, but it won't be as easy as I thought. This feels good. Jumping into the ocean without considering the ramifications and having to fight to get back to safety. I'm reminded of my first few Battles. Before I was the Lion of Celsus and just an impossibly young General who got lucky against the General who dethroned Tori.

I pull myself back into my sleeping quarters, water pouring off me, the ocean breeze chilling my skin.

"Did you have fun?" Tori asks. He stands in the entrance, his hands behind his back. His usual pose when he doesn't approve of something I've done.

"I did."

"I would advise caution out here. There are currents which could separate you too far from this city." His tone, like always, is measured and respectful. A slave doing the job given him, nothing more.

"Don't worry, I won't do anything that would keep me from being the General Celsus needs. Please prepare the attackpad. I'd like to work on my hand speed. This Battle won't be won by strength." Tori bows slightly and leaves. I step away from the puddle of water on my floor and quickly change into my training gear.

The courtyard is perfectly set up when I arrive. It's as if we're back in Celsus, ready to run drills before the rest of the Hopefuls show up. For the first time in what seems like months, I think about Castor. The brutality of our Battle already a distant memory. He will have mostly recovered by now. Probably not fighting yet, but surely aerobic sparring, drilling the Hopefuls, teaching them to be like him. Brash and arrogant and overly aggressive.

At some point one of them will challenge me and I'll be past my prime and they will become the new General. It won't be Castor. He had his chance and, even though his body will recover, his mind won't. I've learned him. Mapped his strengths and exposed his weaknesses. He will fade into obscurity, relegated to the faceless group of people in history who almost won. But someone will. And if they don't kill me, I'll become a Mentor, or be put on display as a cautionary tale. And the next General will rise, then another after him, and yet another after that. Until this way of governing falls short and people find another way to exist.

"Are you ready?" Tori asks.

I take a deep breath, forcing those thoughts from my head. If I don't focus, my defeat will be sooner rather than later.

The attackpad is the perfect training apparatus. A composite cylinder, one meter in diameter and four meters tall connected to a platform. The platform has thousands of microscopic holes, each filled with a one millimeter long needle. Each needle contains a toxin that, once released into the bloodstream, causes excruciating pain. If the user doesn't strike the cylinder appropriately, the needles under the pad spring up, punishing him. Perfect and stunning feedback. It's simple and elegant. If you don't want pain, don't falter.

Tori sets the protocol so the cylinder lights up on random spots, at random intervals. My goal is simple. Strike the lit area before it dims and I avoid the needles.

"Set it for speed. The fastest possible," I say, as I remove my sandals and step onto the pad. My feet sink in at first, but it adjusts to my weight quickly, providing just enough traction.

"Let's work up to that. No need to make you suffer too soon."

"Do as I ask. I've eased into my recovery too much already. I have no interest in being pampered any more." I don't look at him as I say this and I immediately want to apologize to him for my disrespect, but I refrain. If he is only my trainer, then it is time I act accordingly.

Without expression, he sets the controls accordingly. A holographic number appears above the cylinder, starting a countdown. I relax my shoulders as the numbers get lower and lower. At five seconds, I shift my weight onto the balls of my feet and rock from left to right, ensuring my balance is even.

As soon as the number disappears, a small circle flashes at the bottom right of the cylinder. I barely make contact before it fades. I only have one second to identify the light and strike it. The attackpad will speed up as the training circuit progresses.

It's impossible to predict where or when a light will flash. At times, the light will flash on the opposite side of the cylinder, and at this speed, it's impossible to circumvent the whole distance in time, which means I'm guaranteed pain at some point. The first minute is a blur of lights and awkward strikes, but I manage to avoid any needles. I settle into a rhythm after a couple of minutes by allowing my instincts to take over rather than trying to think my way through the circuit.

Flash, strike, balance. Simple and effective. Times like these, when the tasks are clear, with no hidden agenda, are what I'm made for. I don't worry about saying something wrong, or being someone I'm not. It's just coordination and conditioning. I don't know how long I go, but even the few needle strikes don't disrupt my zone. This is what I needed.

"Your ability continues to amaze me," Tori says.

The words only register as sound, but I'm so focused on the drill, it takes at least ten seconds for me to realize Tori just gave me a compliment. When I do realize it, I'm so surprised, I completely miss a light directly in front of me. The sole of my foot immediately bubbles with pain. I try to re-focus, but another light flares out less than a second later and my other foot is hit with another injection of the toxin. A light, barely visible on the left side of the cylinder, flares and I whip my fist around, striking it just in time. I shift toward it, assuming the pattern is rotating around the attackpad.

"Thank you," is all I can muster. Two lights pop up simultaneously, one high and one low. I hit them both, but the movement throws me off balance and I miss the next three sets of lights. My feet are burning from the toxin building in my system, which means my ankles and calves will soon feel as if something is trying to tear its way out of my body.

"Three more minutes. You're at a ninety-three percent contact rate. Well done."

He's trying to apologize, but he's doing more harm than good. If I didn't have to focus so much on the sequence, I'd tell him so.

"Relax, fight through the pain. Refocus your body."

I strike a lit spot at waist level and my fist explodes in pain. The next spot lights up and I hit it with my right knee, which blossoms with searing pain as well. "Moto," I say, before three spots on the cylinder light up. Fist, elbow, heel. I hit them all, and each part of my body screams with toxin. It isn't punishing me for missing, I'm being injected even though I'm keeping up with the algorithm.

"Fight through it. Realize success can bring pain as well. Meet it head on. Your hit rate has fallen to ninety percent. One more minute."

At this point, my entire body, with the exception of my face, feels like it's about to burst. The pain changes every time I'm injected, as if the toxin finds new ways of damaging my tissue. The cylinder lights up in the same place three times in a row, bottom right, which means I strike it with the top of my right foot three straight times. On the third hit, the skin on my foot splits open. My polluted blood bubbles over, smearing the attackpad with the evidence of my torture.

"Fifteen seconds. Finish strong."

I miss the next light, and I feel both feet ignite. I'm being injected when I miss and when I make contact. The pain has saturated my body. Even my vision is affected by it. At this point, the cylinder lights up in so many different places at once, it's impossible to coordinate a sequence of hits to cover them all. Delirious from so much pain, I flail, trying to cover as much of the cylinder as possible. Every time I touch it, a new, more intense and terrible pain awaits.

After what feels like an hour, the cylinder collapses straight down and the injections stop. I collapse with it. The toxin has no long term effects, but I know the next thirty minutes will be excruciating. Celsus has used the attackpad for as long as I can remember, but I've never seen it be so devious. Either this is a new iteration of the tool, or Tori chose this moment to prove some kind of point.

"Your hit rate was ninety-three percent." He covers me with a damp sheet, bringing a slight relief. But the toxin continues to shred my veins, knot my nerves and pulverize my organs.

My head rolls to my side and I see a pair of small, delicately sandaled feet. I follow them up, past flowing material draped around a slender body until I see the dazzling green of Fiona's eyes. Tears stream down her face. I can't tell if she's looking at me with pity or disgust. My vision blurs as I slip into unconsciousness.

Chapter 24

I wake to the sound of water lapping at the side of our floating structure. Tori, or possibly Fiona, has hung a light canvas over the open wall, so my room is dark, but the breeze sneaks through the sides. It feels good as it swirls through the room. My limbs still burn from the lingering poison in my body. Voices filter through the wall. I can't understand what they're saying, but the sound of Fiona's voice alleviates some of my pain immediately. Even though I know I should stay in bed, I stand and take a step toward the door.

My movement turns my stomach and I barely make it to the edge of the pod before I'm sick. There's nothing in my stomach, so most of what splashes into the ocean is bile and saliva. I control the heaving noise as much as I can. The last thing I need is for a Ruler of the nation I'm about to Battle to see me so weak. After I'm finished, I search the room for a pitcher so I can clean myself. I find it, perfectly prepared with a soft cloth next to my bed. Fiona's work under Tori's purposeful direction. In spite of our earlier conversation, I allow myself to believe that, if I were nothing more than an assignment, surely he wouldn't have been so protective, so kind in my weakest moments.

Once I gather myself, I slowly walk into the common area. Tori sits across from Fiona. He looks calm, but I can tell he's not.

"How long have I been out?" I ask, unable to muster the formality of addressing royalty.

They both stand. Fiona is closest, so she reaches me first and leads me to one of the larger cushions. I don't resist, although I should.

"Tori has been trying to get me to leave, but I saw you pass out and I simply wouldn't go until I was sure you were ok," she says. Being this close reminds me of almost a year ago, when she escorted me to the Battle. Now, as then, I'm unable to fully appreciate her beauty or attention.

"I tried to explain to her that our physicians designed the serum to cause pain, but leave no lasting damage," Tori says. He waits at the cushion to help guide my weight down.

Every touch from either of them sends ripples of pain echoing through my frame. They think they're helping, so I bear it.

"I thought physicians are supposed to heal, not hurt," she says.

"There's a difference between hurting and harming," Tori says. "Would you rather the toxin be developed by someone with no knowledge of the human body?"

She sighs as she lets go of me. Even though her touch was painful, I miss the closeness immediately. "I'd rather the toxin not be developed at all."

"That is not the world in which we live. And as brutal as it seems to you, I credit the attackpad for teaching me how to maintain focus through pain, as well as the price of failure," I say.

"It looked like success came at quite a price today." She shimmies her shoulders a bit, realigning the straps which hold her gown in place.

She's right, of course. That was a new wrinkle I'll need to discuss with Tori, but I'll save that for a more appropriate moment. Right now, I notice the cut on my foot has reopened and left a stain on Fiona's dress.

"Apologies, Highness. It looks as if I've ruined your garment. Celsus will reimburse you, of course," I say, pointing to the red blotch my bleeding foot left on her hem.

She looks down and laughs. "Two things, General. First, please call me

Fiona. We'll be spending quite a lot of time together over the next couple of weeks and I can't bear the thought of you having to remember all of those royal terms. Second," she stoops down, rips the stained part of her gown off, along with plenty of extra fabric, "this, and any piece of clothing I wear, is nothing more than a covering. Worth far less than your suffering." She takes the torn cloth and begins to tie it around the wound on my foot.

"If it pleases you, Princess," Tori says, "we have some salve that will heal his wound overnight. I'll retrieve it before you've bandaged too much."

She stops wrapping my foot. "Excellent. It looks like your physicians actually do practice healing. But the same goes for you, Mentor. Please address me as Fiona."

"With pleasure," I say. "But please return the favor." I point to myself and Tori, "Trajan and Tori."

She laughs and, while that sound carries across the room, I feel no pain. I'm reminded, again, of the first time I met her in the preparation room before my Battle. Her eyes were the loveliest things in a cold, dark room. Now, her eyes are the loveliest things in a room designed to rival the ocean.

Tori returns and hands her the salve. We're quiet, again, as she gently applies the balm to the top of my foot, then tightly wraps it in the portion of her dress. The cut immediately stops throbbing.

"I'm sure you didn't come here to tend Trajan's wounds. How may we help you?" Tori asks.

"I'd completely forgotten. I was going to ask if you'd like to depart a day early? Leave in the morning?" She offers no explanation as to why and neither of us ask.

"I'll leave the decision to my General. He's taken in more toxin than I've ever seen. If he feels up to it, I see no issue. However, prudence would call for a day of rest."

If we stay another day, I'll likely just push myself in another exercise and I'll still be recovering on our journey. And the idea of seeing Fiona tomorrow, rather than waiting another day, is much more appealing.

"We'd be delighted to leave tomorrow."

She nods, clearly pleased. I see her mother in the measured elegance of her gesture. I let the two of them work out the details. Instead, I get up, slowly, and make my way to the courtyard. Our training equipment has been packed away. The only structure left is the work table.

I pick up the block of walnut, then one of the carving tools. The wood is a bit waxy and dense and the tools are all in pristine condition. Without thinking, I set the block down and press the blade of one of the carving knives into it. A perfect ribbon curls off the block and falls to the floor. The fragrance of fresh lumber drifts into my nose as I continue to slice sliver after sliver from the block.

"I'm glad you found that. It's one of Aegea's favorite activities. Although we mostly carve synthetic material. I've only carved true walnut once before," Fiona says.

I quickly put the tools down, embarrassed at how clumsy I must have appeared.

"Don't stop. In fact, be sure to pack them with you. In the meantime, I will take my leave. We will depart at dawn tomorrow. There really is nothing like the adventure of the open sea. Rest up, Trajan." She turns quickly and disappears behind a wall before I've found my tongue.

"Lovely. And kind. She reminds me of my mother," Tori says. He glances at the slivers of wood on the table and hands me a small chisel. "In my nation, artists spent a lifetime trying to form a perfect sphere from blocks just like that. They were the most focused people I've ever met." He turns and disappears behind the wall of our quarters.

Alone, holding the chisel and mallet, I realize the pain is still there, but bearable. As I secure the walnut into a small vice and place the chisel, the pain seems to fade completely. I swing the mallet and a chunk of wood falls away, then another. Place, strike, replace. I like the method. I like the solitude. Before I know it, the cube has become a cylinder and I start to see where the wood needs to be cleared away. I see the sphere in there, waiting to be revealed.

Chapter 25

The people of the farming colony don't stop their work when we arrive. There is no defiance in their behavior, rather, it is as if Fiona's presence is as common as the breeze. Such a contrast to the carnival atmosphere which surrounds a visit from Demetrius to the Celcean frontiers. A few people pause briefly to consider Tori and me, but they quickly resume their tasks.

The living structures line the outside of the pods, leaving the center flat with perfect rows of various forms of produce. It's an odd sensation, standing in the middle of the ocean, yet smelling fertilizer and soil. I am immediately struck by how manually all of this work is done. My second observation is how calm everyone seems. There's a space, off to one side where small children totter around, scooping dirt and bumping into each other, but other than that, everyone appears to be working.

"We weren't expecting you until tomorrow, Fiona." A tall, well-toned man says as he approaches. He removes dust covered gloves and drops them on the ground just before wrapping her in a tight embrace. Fiona grunts a little at the unexpected greeting and begins to laugh.

"My escorts were kind enough to agree to an early departure," she says while wriggling from his hold. "May I introduce you to Trajan, General of Celsus and his Mentor, Tori Motodada."

I extend my hand and give a formal bow in the way I've seen emissaries do hundreds of times.

The man's hand feels like stone when he grasps mine. I can't tell where bone stops and muscle starts, surely the byproduct of a lifetime tilling the ground and harvesting.

"You can call me Colin," he says. "We're glad to have you. There's some heavy equipment we've been wanting to install and having your strength will be just what we've been waiting for." He turns to Tori, "Welcome, Mentor."

Colin's eyes are bloodshot, likely from working in the sun and dirt for so long. He's as tall as I am, but much thinner. If I had to guess, I'd say he's my age, maybe a couple of years older. Other than the hard handshake, he shows no malice toward me. Like the captain of our vessel, he seems to hold Tori in high regard.

"You're in your usual quarters, princess. As for our guests, I've set them up next to you. In fact, can you show them? I'm teaching a class on preparing soil. If I'm gone too long, I'll spend the rest of the day trying to get their attention refocused." He doesn't wait for an answer. After a few paces he turns and yells, "Come find me once you're settled. I'll put you to work."

"I hope you're not offended by Colin's informality. He wasn't raised to entertain dignitaries. No one here was. Which is why I love visiting so much. If I could, I'd live here indefinitely." She gathers her garment bag and motions for us to follow. "We're over here, by the infirmary."

Tori and I are the first out of our quarters. We both stand silently, watching the activity of the colony. It is close to a perfect circle, about one thousand meters in diameter.

Four pods each at ninety degree angles appear to hold all of the farming equipment and grains. Even though everything appears to operate at peak efficiency, it is impossible for me to imagine how they are able to pull this off.

The water for these crops must come from filtering salt from the ocean, and the soil must have been transported by a vessel. Either that, or the entire platform can be navigated over long distances. I remember studying a map of Aegea before leaving and there being only one main land mass, other than a few small islands. They must mine that for their resources.

"Beautiful, isn't it?" Fiona's voice brings me out of my analysis.

Tori turns to her, "I was thinking the same thing. These people look like they're of one mind. They're as precise as an army."

"Funny. If you gave me all the paper and ink in the world and asked me to describe what I'm looking at, I don't think army or precision would appear once," she says.

Colin is surrounded by a group of teenagers. They watch his hands and listen to him without distraction. He speaks with authority and commands the soil like a master. I'm reminded of my first lessons as a young General in training. Augustus demanded unwavering respect. I once drifted off during one of his lectures, one moment I was standing with the others, thinking about something other than what Augustus was teaching, the next, I was on the ground with a broken jaw. Our physicians quickly healed the break and Tori chastised me for my fickleness. The next lesson, I watched as Augustus did the same to another boy. As I watch Colin, I can't imagine any of his students drifting, nor can I imagine him attacking them.

He sees us and nods slightly, but continues the lesson. I listen for a few minutes, but realize I won't likely be given the task of soil preparation. Fiona touches my arm and whispers that she is going to go help another group trim and tie some tomato plants and I should wait for Colin to finish. She doesn't mean for her touch, or the closeness of our faces while she whispers, to be intimate, but it is. I feel immediately alone when her hand slips off my arm and when I can't feel her breath on my ear. I watch the way she embraces each person without pomp or pageantry as she joins the other group. Every so often, she glances toward us, once giving me a subtle wave.

"Thanks for waiting," Colin says, waking me from my daydream.

I turn to see his students wandering off in random directions. He greets Tori first.

"That group is close to running their own crews and I want to be sure they're able to spot lazy prep work. We can't afford it. The slightest imbalance and we could lose an entire season." His eyes never leave Tori's as he speaks.

"Are you the only farming colony in Aegea?" I ask.

Colin pauses before answering. "No, we have many others. But they all must produce exactly the right amount. It's the same for our hunting colonies."

"I'm eager to help. From the looks of it, your colony takes their jobs seriously," I say. The easiest way to break down any walls that may be hiding information, it seems, is to match their work ethic. Something I will have no problem doing.

"This isn't just a job to us. Most were born in the colony and have known nothing else. It's our way of life and something we're proud of," Colin says, playing the unnecessary part of a sage cousin.

"And I'm anxious to learn your ways. Consider me your student. Or, more likely, your workhorse. I'm likely too slow to grasp the nuances of harvesting in such a foreign environment." If he hopes to goad me into an altercation, I've already won this Battle. Compared to Demetrius, Colin is a cub, hanging from its father's mane.

He leads us to the outskirts of the colony, across from our quarters. From here, Fiona is out of sight, which means I can concentrate on the task at hand.

We enter a fairly large structure, the inside of which is much more industrial than any I've seen in Aegea. Without the need for explanation, I can tell this is where the majority of the mechanics for the colony reside. It's nice to know that even in Aegea, there are places like this. No matter how something appears on the outside, there's always the dirty, clunky, grease covered places which keep it alive.

"Our water filtration system is due for a cleaning," Colin says. "We usually dock with the maintenance vessel, which has the equipment to make the process simple. But, since you're here, I thought it would be best to let it help other colonies, as long as you're up for a little heavy lifting." While his words are innocent enough, there is an underlying antagonism.

For the first time since we entered the structure, Tori speaks. "I'm sure my General is capable. However, it would be a tragedy for both of our nations if he is injured while helping. We'll need to evaluate both the part and the space before committing."

Colin nods, "Of course. I would never think of harming such a valued member of the Celcean government."

I smile at his sarcasm. Tori, also unfazed by his tone, nods to him and we are led through the engine room. We round a corner and we see the filtration system. Most of it just looks like tubes and hoses randomly connected, but I immediately see why they rely on specialized equipment. In the back corner, suspended above a two meter wide hole, is the main engine. The hole is placed so that it almost touches the edge of the wall, and the ceiling above it dips. I'll have to straddle the hole, and hold the motor while stooping. All the weight will be in my shoulders and lower back. To make matters worse, this room doesn't seem to be immune from the rise and fall of the ocean, which means I'll be constantly fighting for balance. Depending on how heavy the part is, if I fall, my arms will likely get caught, or severed, between it and the edge of the hole.

"How heavy is it?" I ask, nodding toward the impeller.

Colin hesitates before saying, "About one hundred fifty kilograms, give or take," he says.

Which means it's closer to two hundred kilos. I'm not worried about the weight, but the balance combined with the weight will stretch me.

"I assume you can close the opening?" I ask. Straddling the hole and stooping while holding something so heavy would be impossible for anyone.

"Certainly. We'd just build a platform to hold it, but the installation process requires the engine to be moved around periodically. Like I said, with the proper equipment, it's a simple job. If you'd like me to call the maintenance vessel, we can find a less taxing assignment for you."

"If this is the most danger I face while in Aegea, I fear I will be overly bored. When can we begin?" I say, without consulting Tori. It will feel good to test myself in a new way.

"The sooner the better." Colin flips a switch, and the hole is sealed by the same composite flooring as the rest of the room. Lights trigger as well, casting odd shadows around the various mechanisms. "You'll need to hold the engine in place while I remove the supports." He sifts through a wall-mounted toolkit.

"If your grip slips at all, you will be crushed," Tori says. His voice is low, not wanting to show Colin his disagreement with my decision.

"I don't deserve to be General if I am so easily undone by a piece of machinery."

He nods, realizing he's not going to sway me. "Then listen closely to Colin. Respond immediately to his instructions. I'll help you focus."

The motor is encased in a web of carbide rods which allow it to spin freely. A series of steel beams and cables hold the encasement in place. Each one has to be released sequentially in order to disperse the weight correctly. My role will be to lie underneath, support the increasing weight and adjust the placement in order to release it. Once it's free, we will clean it, then reattach it in reverse order.

"I'm not worried about the motor," Colin says, "I'm worried about the support apparatus. If any of these rods or beams are torqued out of place, the entire filter won't work properly."

"This seems unnecessarily complex," Tori says.

"Like I said, we can call the maintenance vessel. It is in the south, helping a hunting colony repair its navigation after weathering a hurricane." He says this with his back to us, still rummaging through the tools.

"Just tell me when you're ready. All I ask is that you work as quickly as you can. Isometric tension seems easy, but it will quickly sap my strength," I say.

"I have no interest in taking my time. If you falter, our entire system is ruined. You'll get a chance to rest for as long as you need while it's being cleaned."

We work in silence for the next ten minutes. Colin methodically lines up all of the tools he's going to need on the closest open surface he can find. I crawl under the filter and begin inspecting it from every angle. It's close enough to the floor that I won't be able to lock my arms, which will exponentially increase the difficulty.

Tori inspects the connections which hold the engine in place. He finally breaks the silence, "There are ten of them. Don't exert yourself unnecessarily. Wait until you see one of the supports start to shift before you increase your resistance. Your strength is unparalleled, Trajan, but don't rely on your body. This requires focus and mental discipline. Your body will give out. There's no doubt. But your mind can overcome it."

I position myself so my chest is directly under the motor. When I place my hands on it, my arms are still bent thirty-five degrees. Not ideal, but it could be worse. Colin loosens the first bolt and I feel the structure shift slightly, so

I add enough pressure with my left hand to stabilize. The second bolt shifts it forward, still on the left side. After the fifth bolt, my triceps burn. By the seventh, my shoulders are on fire and my arms have gone numb. Sweat beads on my forehead and my breathing increases. Tori was right, with weight this great, holding it this way, my strength drains faster than I could have anticipated. If I drop the motor now, the final three rods will torque beyond repair and this colony will slowly stop producing, which will put a strain on the rest of the farming colonies. The ripple effect of three bent rods will be felt across an entire nation.

Colin ducks under cables and beams as he tries to loosen the bolts on the other side of him. Every time one of the supports is loosened, he hands the hardware to Tori, who arranges them in the same pattern as when they're installed. The eighth and ninth come out quickly.

"Almost there," Colin says. He's out of breath as well, which makes me feel better somehow. I've rarely been part of a team like this. Most of my trials are solely dependent on my ability to execute well. This time, success depends on us working together. The forced camaraderie is foreign, but empowering too.

"You can drop it," he says.

I lower the motor as gently as my arms will allow. It hits the floor with a sickening thud. I'm panting and my arms feel like ribbons flapping in the breeze.

"The easy part is done. What comes next will make that feel like throwing pillows around." It's meant as a joke, but no laughter follows.

Tori silently evaluates my ability to continue. I can tell he's doubtful, but he won't show any disagreement in front of Colin. "Is there no way to provide Trajan some help for the installation?"

Colin looks at me, splayed on the ground. The question bites at my pride, but I am too exhausted to save face.

"We have passed the point of no return. If we can't get the motor back on after the cleaning, it will be as if the entire unit fell in the ocean. Our crops would be severely damaged," Colin says.

With my eyes closed, I say, "Stop fretting, Moto-San. I will meet this challenge the same way I have met every other." I open my eyes and look directly at Colin, "Your system will be running perfectly before dinner."

While Colin's team cleans the system, Colin and Tori quietly discuss the best way to reattach the engine. I doze in and out of sleep, letting the jostling of the ocean perform an impromptu massage.

It takes them a little more than an hour to finish their task. As they pack their instruments, I hear Fiona's voice.

"Have we tired you out so quickly?" She stands over me with her hands on her hips and a crooked smile.

Colin turns and makes his way to us while I stand. I push myself up, testing the strength in my arms.

She glances at Colin and the smile fades. "I remember our conversation about cleaning the filter a little differently than you."

Colin looks at his feet and folds his arms, the playfulness of their initial encounter erased. "This far from the capital we use every resource available. That includes honored guests." He looks at me when he says the last part.

She cocks her head but refrains from the obvious rebuke of Colin's disrespect. I'm shocked by her restraint. I have never known royalty to allow blatant opposition such as this, especially in front of an outsider.

I twist my hands, flexing my wrists and testing the amount of blood still concentrated in my forearms. They are fatigued, but not overly. "Far be it from me to interfere in an official conversation, but I am happy to help. Colin offered to send for the maintenance vessel," I say.

"Of course he did. I'm sure it was immediately after appealing to your pride as well," she says. The edge in her voice remains, but her expression has softened.

"My pride is not so all encompassing as to force me into stupidity," I say, half joking.

"That remains to be seen. My issue, however," she says, "is with the opportunity for pride, not the pride itself."

Colin shifts his weight and says, "Of course, Highness, we will call for maintenance immediately."

At this, Fiona lets out a long breath. "I am not so petulant as to delay the crops in order to prove a point. If a vessel is needed, then summon it. But if Trajan can match the task, then let's get on with it."

Everyone looks to me, waiting for my response. For the second time since we arrived in this strange country, I am at a loss for how to respond. If the will of Demetrius had been challenged the way Colin challenged Fiona, there would be no deferral. There would be punishment. Until this moment, I would have never questioned the severity under which Demetrius has exercised his authority. To think of authority being handled gently and with temperance is intriguing, but it also feels incomplete. "I have never made it a habit of backing away from a challenge, however, it is not my nation which would suffer from a mistake," I say.

"And it is not my nature to shirk decisions, however," she says, looking from Colin to me, "we find ourselves staring at an incomplete statue. And the two bumbling artists stand before me. I can't feel the remaining strength in your arms, General. Either you can or you can't. Just tell us."

Patient one moment, insulting the next. I prefer the consistent and unrelenting control of Demetrius. "We are wasting time," I say, turning my back to the group and positioning myself for the installation.

As I lie down, Tori and Colin return to their preparations. Fiona watches me, clearly irritated.

"It was never my intention to undermine you," I say.

Her features relax slightly, "Nor was it my intention to offend you. We are in your debt."

I smile, "You may want to reign in your gratitude until the job is done properly."

It's her turn to smile, "If it's not, we may have to feed you to the sharks."

When they are confident they are ready Tori and Colin return.

"Last chance," Colin says, his earlier antagonism gone.

"Let's get this over with," I say.

Just getting the motor situated on my chest so I can press it into place nearly exhausts me.

"It's now or never," I say as I lift it upward.

Colin stands with the first bolt assembly ready. I notice his sweat drenched shirt and realize my failure will be even worse for him with Fiona watching. Even though I just met him, and most of his interaction has bordered on hostile, I know the feeling of losing favor in a leader's eyes and I will do everything I can to help him avoid failure.

"There," he says.

I stall the press and commit myself to the burn that begins immediately. Colin works as quickly as he can, but I can see his hands shaking. He must be perfect or I will falter.

"Calm, Colin." I say. Even though I want to say more, I can't.

He finishes with the first and steps around me to the second as Tori hands him another set of bolts. Any slip now and the entire afternoon will be for not.

"Tilt up with your right and ease it toward your head," Tori says. "Ten degrees more."

I obey, more from instinct than anything else. My hands grow slick with sweat, which makes me squeeze the motor even tighter. I'm using precious energy needed for my arms, but it's too difficult to isolate the individual muscles.

"There."

Fiona's voice grabs my attention, "The first time I set foot on true land, I saw an ant skittering across the dirt. I had no idea what it was, but I couldn't take my eyes from it."

The second bolt is in place. "Down with your left, five centimeters, rotate it toward your hip simultaneously."

I move too quickly and feel the strain on the two rods. There is no damage, but I see Tori and Colin exchange glances. "Easy General," Colin says.

"For some reason, I dropped a rock on it," Fiona says. "It must have been three times bigger than that little thing. I thought I'd killed it. But a moment or two, the rock began to move, and the ant emerged."

With every secured bolt, the engine should get lighter, but it doesn't feel that way, and the way the supports are arranged, it appears it will remain insecure until the last rod is attached.

"I was so amazed, I continued to drop things on it. Leaves, clods of dirt, sand, jewelry. Anything I could find. And every time, it would falter, but it would overcome. Throw the weight off and keep going. I never thought I'd see anything like it again."

The eighth and ninth bolts are secured. My arms are completely numb, which means I can't feel the shift of the engine. I simply push with everything I have left. Eyes closed, my heart feels as if it's fighting my lungs for space in my chest. The body fails. It always does. So does the mind. But the will draws from something else entirely. It short circuits the brain's impulse to quit, it infuses strength directly into the fibers of failing muscles. If the motor drops, it's because my will is too weak, and I won't allow that to happen.

"Done."

I don't register the word at first, but Tori places his hand on my leg and I realize it's over. My arms drop, one of them hits my face, unable to control the trajectory.

Someone begins to laugh. The type of expression which comes from surviving a brutal fall.

I try to speak but I can only gasp for air. My head starts swimming as I drop it to the side and open my eyes. I see Fiona's feet. The same angle as after my session on the attackpad and realize, if I pass out, it will be the second time in as many days she has seen me at my end. Slowly, the spinning stops and my breathing slows.

"Two hundred kilos. Suspended for ten minutes. I hoped it would work, but I wasn't sure it would," Colin says.

"That makes two of us," I say.

Chapter 26

After dinner, which consisted of the freshest seafood I have ever tasted, the entire colony gathers on an impromptu cove that's created by detaching three smaller pods and swinging them away from the rest of the floating island. The result is an instant beach. They even slope the platform so it provides a gentle ramp into the depths of the ocean. The children immediately begin splashing and diving into the water.

"Aren't you worried we'll drift away from them?" I ask Fiona. We're sitting with Colin, Tori, and three older, silent Aegeans.

She laughs, "Those children are as close to fish as possible. If anything, we should be worried about sharks. These pods attract packs, no matter how hard we try to dissuade them."

I think back to when I dove out of my room at the capital. The idea that I could have been devoured by a shark never crossed my mind and now I wonder how close I was to that reality.

"And yet you allow them to splash around like that?" I ask.

"What you don't see is the underwater barrier we engaged when we swung the pods out. No shark could get within one hundred meters of them."

"An elegant solution," Tori says.

"When you live in an environment such as this, one where mankind is the outsider, you quickly learn the value of protection without upsetting the natural order of things," one of the older Aegeans says.

"It's certainly different than Celsus. I think every square meter of our nation has been brought into submission," I say, speaking more freely than I expected.

"If you paused to point out the differences between Celsus and Aegea, I don't think you'd have time to do much else," Colin says. His antagonism from earlier is gone. This statement is merely an observation of culture.

Fiona stands, the breeze catches her robes and hair simultaneously. Her silhouette against the field of stars looks like the statues of old. "I'd like to walk. Trajan, would you be my escort? Unless, of course, you'd like to take a swim." More and more of the adults have joined the children. It appears as if everyone will end up swimming before the night is out.

I stand, more clumsily than I'd like. "A walk sounds nice. If I tried to swim, I'd sink like a stone. My arms aren't quite recovered from today's fun."

We walk in silence for a few minutes, the sounds of the party fading behind us as we follow a path through row after row of crops.

"Aegeans don't usually make a fuss over individual efforts," she says, "but that party back there is because of what you did today." Her voice is barely audible over the breeze.

"We just cleaned a filter," I say.

"Certainly. But you did it sooner than we expected, and with impressive strength. Also, we've had to change the way we operate as of late. We've never faced Battle before, and we fear being even more isolated if you prevail. Certain leaders are taking extreme measures to save our natural resources."

Her demeanor is the exact opposite of her words. If I were deaf, I'd think we were two infatuated teenagers, convinced nothing else mattered but finding a reason to brush shoulders or innocently entwine our hands together. If I were blind, we could easily be sitting around a negotiating table, jostling for political victory through rhetoric.

"Why would Demetrius liberate you, only to cause you suffering?" I say.

"What suffering have you seen? Either it's non-existent, or I'm covering it up. If I'm covering it up, what sort of monster would I be?" she asks.

"And if it's non-existent, what sort of monster would I be? Maybe not a monster. Maybe the blunt object swung by the monster. Either way, neither of us seems willing to explore the worst of what may be true about ourselves."

"And equally willing to explore the worst of the other."

We're quiet over the next several meters. For a split second, I allow myself to imagine what things may be like once I win and we share the same banner. Maybe just the two of us sharing a life free of politics.

"Just promise me one thing," she says. "Then we can walk and talk as if we're just two people, strolling through a field like our ancestors did before the chaos and rules and segregation. Promise that, as you learn about us, you'll give equal consideration to our position as you do to your Ruler's."

I almost ask her if she'd do the same for me. Ask her to consider the agenda of an opposing king over her mother's. But I don't. It would only serve to feed an already exhausting conversation. "You have my word," I say.

They shut off almost every light on the island at night. At first, I thought this would leave us in utter darkness, but the stars are vibrant, and the walls of the structures glow in response. When I say so, Fiona tells me they coat the walls with a material which is designed to pick up the slightest light source and magnify it. No energy required. Another technology engineered by studying ocean life. The outcome is a gentle, bluish glow radiating around us. Barely casting a shadow, but providing enough light that even our expressions are easy to see.

"What was your childhood like?" she asks, apparently as anxious as I am to turn the subject from matters of state.

"I don't think of my life in terms of childhood or adulthood. There was preparation, then there was General. Nothing before, nothing in between."

Fiona looks at me as if she's triaging a wounded animal. "And your parents?"

"Tori. I don't remember anyone before him. Logically I know they must exist. In fact, they're likely still alive. They probably watch my Battles with an odd sense of pride. But I was chosen at such a young age, they left no impression on me."

"You speak so factually. Doesn't it bother you?"

"You assume I see myself the same way you see me. But I don't. I don't consider a different destiny any more than a tree would yearn for a different patch of land for its roots. I was planted where I was. These roots aren't going to become legs. It would be the same as you wanting to place Aegea in a desert," I say.

We've made it farther into the crops, which means there is less light from the structures, but my eyes adjust easily. The smell of soil and leaves and water combine so powerfully it's as if I can catch it in the air, form it into a shape and present it as a gift to Fiona.

"But we have legs. Not roots, Trajan. To be human is to dream of something else. We'd never have come out of the Great Chaos if we just accepted our position."

No matter how hard we try, we can't seem to forget we're in the center of two nations about to go to war. "True," I say, "but if all we did was try to change, we'd never stay the course long enough to accomplish anything."

There is a faint humming from behind us. The island rumbles just enough to shake the leaves of the plants. An earthquake in the ocean.

"They're closing the bay for the night. We should get back to the path. We don't want to get caught in the field when they turn the generator on." She leads me quickly through one of the rows of what looks to be small corn stalks.

"What happens when they turn on the generator?" I ask.

"I'll show you. It's pretty amazing, actually. But dangerous. I guess that's how most amazing things are."

We get back to the exterior path a few seconds before the rumbling stops.

"Now watch," she says.

At first, it looks as if a fog has formed in the middle of the island and is spreading through the crops. My knowledge of atmosphere tells me this can't be true, but I have no other way of categorizing the phenomenon. After about a minute, the fog has spread to cover all of the crops, but stops once it reaches the perimeter. I reach my hand into it and wave it back and forth. Not fog. Mist. They're watering the crops with some sort of controlled mist.

"Since the plants are so weak from not getting water, we're letting the mist soak in. It's the best way to nurture them back without shocking them. Too much water, too fast, would be just as bad as continuing to starve them," Fiona says. She too reaches out her hand and traces a curving arc through the cloud.

"While the technology is impressive, I don't see the danger. Unless the Aegean Princess is afraid of getting wet," I joke.

She smirks. "It's not nice to mock royalty. Just wait. Try to keep from attacking what you see next."

After a few minutes, the mist disappears. There's another hum and, within an instant, each plant begins to glow. The change is so dramatic, I step back, unsure of what's happening. Fiona's admonishment to not attack seems less like a joke now.

"What happened?" I ask.

She picks up a clod of dirt, about the size of my fist and throws it as hard as she can at the nearest stalk. I expect to see the fragile plant shudder and fall over, possibly even break. But it doesn't. Instead, the clod of dirt disperses as if it hit a wall.

"Go ahead, you try," she says, handing me another clump. This one is even larger.

Curious, I take it from her and, after hesitating for a moment, throw it as hard as my tired arm will allow. The same thing happens to my clod of dirt as hers.

I reach out to the plant closest to me and give it a gentle shove. Instead of the plant giving, I'm knocked off balance slightly. I realign my balance and push harder this time. The plant remains unmoved as I increase the pressure on it. After I've maxed my strength, I stop, slightly out of breath.

"It's easiest to compare it to a force-field. The plants are safe inside. We're pumping just enough oxygen through the soil so they won't suffocate overnight. But we've covered them in a layer of perfect, pure energy. Nothing can get through until we switch it off. It's used to protect the plants from the salt in the air, or from a rogue wave in the middle of the night."

I feel like a child, witnessing what must be magic with my limited mind. "How?" I ask.

"You'd have to ask our engineers. Something to do with light waves, and an enormous power source. Other than that, I have no clue. I just like throwing things at them," she smiles. "Come. I'm tired. Walk me to my room."

Reluctantly, I walk with her, staring at the glowing plants. Every so often, I throw something at them, just to be sure each is as sturdy as the next. Every time, the rock or clod ricochets harmlessly away.

Chapter 27

The night with Fiona is so fresh in my mind that I can still feel the brush of her robe carried by the wind and the melody in her voice. I part the curtain which hangs over the open wall and watch the changing oceanscape as it catches the water differently with every rise and swell. Even though my body begs for rest, I know sleep is far away. Rather than fight my mind, I pull a seat closer to the opening and remove the walnut block from my bag. Other than the tools for carving and a few changes of clothes, it is the only item I've chosen to bring. Up until now, I've carved with the grain of the wood. But it's clear that if I'm going to form a sphere, I need to begin challenging across the grain. I rotate it over and over again, looking for the easiest entry point but none are apparent. For a moment, I contemplate choosing another shape, one that would let me continue to glide with the grain, but it's as if the sphere I saw inside this block beckons me. I put knife to block, pausing briefly, realizing I have neither vice nor protective glove. One slip and the flesh on my hand will fall open, revealing muscle, tendon and bone. In spite of the danger, I begin carving.

The first few slices come off in awkward chunks. But after a few minutes, I fall into a rhythm. Instead of forcing the knife through the wood, I begin to hold the knife steady and push the block into it. This keeps the knife from choosing its own destructive path. My forearms burn. Asking so much of them earlier brings them to the end of their capacity faster than ever. Regardless, I continue. Now that I've found a process, I want to see it through. At first my mind drifts between Tori's Battles, Fiona's gentle opposition, and the accusations against Demetrius. But as the block falls away and a lumpy, splintery ball takes shape in my hand, everything fades. I may as well be in the Temple. Nothing exists in this moment except me and the task before me.

"They know you better than I. All these years and I never contemplated carving as a means to peace." Tori stands just inside my quarters, his hands behind his back in his usual perfect posture.

"Moto-San, I thought I was the only person still awake. Is it time to train?" I say. Since arriving in Aegea, we've done little else than train and plan. We seem more and more like partners than friends.

"There's something elemental about the smell of freshly cut wood. Your quarters seep it."

"I can stop, if it bothers you," I say.

"No complaint. In fact, it brings back a flood of pleasant memories."

My hands cease the dance of walnut and blade. "You needn't do that. Your memories are yours. You've made me great. I'm owed nothing."

"Do you remember our first meeting?"

My past lacks a narrative thread. At best, when I look back, I see disjointed images, as if from video highlights. The only things I remember with clarity are my Battles. If I needed to, I could choreograph each one to perfection.

"I've seen would-be Generals meet their Mentors. Children entering a contract with a person focused on giving them fame and glory. I imagine it was like that."

"It was. Except I had just recovered from losing a Battle and my country and every member of my family. I had gone from prince and son and husband and father to slave. Overnight. Forced to fight mere hours after holding the lifeless body of my only son. And then defeat. And then you.

And I hated everything about you."

My stomach immediately feels as if I've been poisoned. But if I'd been poisoned, I'd know what to do. What's actually happening, what I'm hearing, has no easy fix.

"I'm tired. As are you, I'm sure. Some other time." I idly begin scraping small amounts of wood from the block. It suddenly feels vulgar in my hands. Every uneven peak or valley magnified.

"You were huge," he says, as if I hadn't spoken. "They didn't tell me how old you were, nor did I ask. Unused to Celcean customs, I assumed you were at least eight. Maybe even ten. Not just big. You were well spoken and coordinated. There was no reason to think otherwise. So that's how I treated you. That's what I expected from you. If I'd known you were half that age," he's moved across the room and stands with his toes hanging over the edge.

"I was harsh. Even for a ten year old, the things I demanded of you would have been nearly impossible. And yet, you responded. Powerfully. But there were signs. While your body was practically a teenager's, your mind and your emotions were still a child's. I was so full of wrath, I didn't see it. Every time I looked at you, I was reminded of my son. Dead."

I try to match my sparse memories with what he's saying. I never once thought of him as cold or harsh. He was easily disappointed. But that was because of my shortcomings. Because he knew what I was capable of and demanded I deliver without fail. If he had been easier on me, who knows if I would have reached my potential. "This needs not be spoken, Moto. We're here now. And we need to focus on what's at hand." I feel guilty for my earlier outburst. If I had kept myself in check, he would not feel the need to open such deep wounds.

"Quiet. When you asked, I realized this conversation was long overdue. Then the attackpad. You could have just stepped off. But that option never entered your head. It should have. That it didn't is my fault." He takes the knife from me and absently twirls it between his fingers. It's as natural there as it is in my hands. "After six months I chose a trainee much bigger than you. He must have been fifteen or sixteen. I had you spar him. Full contact.

It was a Mid-Year exhibition and Demetrius was there. A few Mentors tried to talk me out of it, citing the age difference. I was still so destroyed, I had no idea there was a decade between you and your opponent. You were scared. Even began to cry before the Battle. It's the only time I've ever struck you."

These things he's saying, it's as if he's speaking of a different person. When I try to conjure my own version of this, I'm met with nothing but blurred snippets of indistinguishable gibberish from my mind.

"You started timidly. The other trainee bloodied your nose quickly, then he cut you just below your collarbone. You retreated and looked to me. I shook my head and turned my back to you."

This image is cemented in my mind. I can feel the torn skin and dripping blood on my chest. I can hear the other trainees yelling, laughing. My first experience of the energy of a Crowd. Tori continues to describe the contest, but I don't hear him. My Battle memory takes over. The boy was stronger and faster. Definitely better with weapons. I was so scared, I even contemplated running away. But then I saw Tori. Saw how I was letting him down. I knew he would never match me against someone I couldn't defeat. The boy, cocky, came at me again. A teenager staring down an oversized toddler and I saw his flaw. When I saw it, I was excited. I knew I would live up to Tori's expectations. So I struck. In his overconfidence, he rushed me without protecting his left rib cage. I rolled my shoulder back to dodge the trajectory of his knife, which gave the upward thrust of my knife even more power. It was the first time one of my blades actually pierced human flesh. I was surprised by how easily the skin parted for my blade. Then there was blood. Pouring down my hand. The strike was perfect because I knew Tori wanted it perfect. Up and into his lung, which collapsed immediately.

I didn't stop there. He was so much stronger and driven by the desire to impress Demetrius, I knew a collapsed lung wouldn't stop him. Without interrupting my momentum, I rolled under him, redirecting his weight into a body slam with my knife still in his chest. Then I was on top of him. Slashing. Stabbing. Here, my memory blurs again. All I see is blood. All I hear is silence. The stunned Crowd of trainees shocked by the turn of events. Then Tori pulling me off. I don't remember seeing that trainee after our Battle.

"It was an impressive victory. But it's not what stands out for me," Tori's voice picks up where my memory stops. "We put you in a room while the Mentors met. You were so brutal, they were worried the other trainees would lose their nerve, having seen a real Battle so intimately. Demetrius came in and embraced me. It was the first interaction we'd had since..." his voice trails off for a moment. "That put an end to the debate. The other Mentors realized you had just jumped to the front of the list. Which meant their livelihoods were in danger.

"They dispersed, offering their tokens of congratulations. When I went to get you from the holding room, I paused outside. Watching you from the window. You were covered in dried blood, sitting on the floor with your legs crossed. One hand, forming imaginary people with your pointer and middle fingers. You walked them up and down your legs, making them speak in a made up, high-pitched, language. You were sucking the thumb of your other hand. That image will never leave my mind. For the first time, I saw you for your true age. A baby in a man's body. That I turned into a killer."

The sky is lighter. Fewer and fewer stars are evident. This is Tori's confession. I wonder how I'm supposed to react. How he expects me to respond. With indignation, or shame. I wonder if it's wrong that I feel pride. At the age of five, I defeated a well-trained, sixteen-year-old Hopeful.

"I was given a son in my previous life and I couldn't protect him from death. Then I was given you. And I was too hate filled to realize you were my second chance. And I failed you. I tore your childhood from you. Made you do things most men wouldn't be able to. And I've been watching you on this trip, Trajan," something about how gently he says my name makes me more uncomfortable than everything else I've heard. "I made you a General and neglected the man you could have been. Forgive me." He doesn't wait for a response. His speech was never about my response. He leaves as quietly as he entered.

The horizon blurs from dark blue to orange, then yellow, back to blue. My eyes burn. Maybe from the story, or the salt in the air, or how long I've been awake. As a new day drops into place over the Aegean waters, I hope something drops into place for me too. This trip. Fiona. Aegea. Tori. And everything before it. Castor. Seth. Demetrius. There is no solid ground I can find where things feel right. And I need it. Weeks away from my Battle, I'm a log, drifting down a river, into the ocean and deeper to sea.

Chapter 28

We arrive back to Aegea's capital a few days later. In the short time I spent with Colin on the farming community, I grew to appreciate the life they live. It was uncomplicated. Wake, receive an assignment, work hard all day, relax with friends and sleep. No schemes. No conspiracies. It reminded me of being a Hopeful, focusing only on preparation and execution. Visiting Colin showed me how far removed I've become from that way of life.

Our vessel arrived in the middle of the night, so Tori and I were ushered quickly into our original quarters and left to fend for ourselves. Neither of us had any trouble finding sleep again.

After a breakfast of fruit and thinly sliced tuna, we begin training. The facility is small compared to the Celcean equipment I'm used to. Like everything else in Aegea, the room is lit by natural light and is open to the elements on one side. None of the equipment is automated and there are no cameras ready to playback a drill in order to reveal the slightest miscalculation.

Tori and I begin slowly. Stretching, breathing, stretching some more. After his visit to my room, we have been at a strange ease with one another. He's more relaxed than I've ever seen. Our conversation strays from Battles and training more often, drifting into philosophy and thoughts of a life after the violence that comes from being a General.

We begin a circuit of controlled grappling. Neither of us trying to gain an edge. Rather, focusing on technique and balance. The drill is as much mental as it is physical. I'm heavier and stronger, but Tori's technique is better, which puts us at a stalemate. Every few minutes, Tori reminds me that if he were in his prime he would easily incapacitate me.

"I don't think I've ever walked into a room and seen them doing anything other than fighting." I immediately recognize the voice as William's.

We break our entanglement and stand. The intensity of the exercise has left us both covered in sweat.

William is not alone. There are two men standing on either side of him. I immediately identify the person to his right as the Aegean General. He's a head taller than William, which makes him shorter than me by at least eight centimeters. I also outweigh him by twenty kilos.

He's between thirty and thirty-five years old. His weight is unevenly distributed, holding about forty percent of his weight on his left leg. Either he's nervous, or he's protecting an injury. It doesn't matter which. Without knowing, he's already shown me an explicit weakness.

"It is a pleasure to see you again," Tori says. He walks forward and gives a slight bow before offering his hand in greeting. William accepts his hand, then pulls him into an embrace.

"We'll get you Celceans to lighten up if it kills us," he says.

I register this interaction as background noise. Even though I want to let my guard down, I can't help but continue the evaluation of my opponent. For his part, the General holds my eye contact briefly, then turns his attention to William and Tori. When he does, he shifts his weight fully to his right leg while simultaneously bending his left. He does this twice. The injury is to his knee. The constant flexing is his subconscious way of testing the pain.

Tori taught me long ago that Battles are only finished in the Temple. They are planned and executed long before. I feel bad for this General. He has no idea he's in the thick of Battle right now.

"Allow me to introduce Liam, Aegea's General." All eyes turn to me as he's announced. My expression doesn't change. I remain so motionless, even my breath ceases while he turns his attention back to me. I offer as little information about myself as possible.

Tori, as is our custom in these situations, breaks the silence by offering the traditional Battle salutation. "We salute your valor, General. May our blood be the only shed between our nations."

Liam smiles, "I'm probably supposed to return some scripted response to that. My inexperience in these meetings leaves me ignorant. Instead, I'll say this. Mentor, it is an honor. Truly." He turns to me, "General, I've never seen a more vicious fighter. I'm both excited and terrified to test myself against you."

His honesty, like every interaction in Aegea, puts me off guard. "And I'm anxious to learn the truth about you in the Temple. I've never faced an opponent of whom I know so little," I say. I step toward him and offer my hand, as is customary for two Generals. He takes it without pride. Most of these embraces turn into a stalemate with neither General willing to let go first. But his grasp his firm and brief.

Liam addresses Tori, "As far as bloodshed, without giving too much away, there will be little. My strength isn't with a sword. Dedication and reflex are my virtues. Since Trajan's dedication is unquestioned, and reflex can't be taught in so short a time, I'm comfortable sharing. There is no sense in you or Trajan wasting strength or risking injury while training unnecessarily."

We should assume he is lying, but our experience with Aegea tells us he's not. These people approach life from such a different angle than we've ever experienced. And if he's not lying, then he's confident he possesses a superior skill than me. I've only fought one Battle which wasn't a physical confrontation. Instead, we played a game of strategy. The Crowd was just as enraptured as we moved pieces against each other on a small board placed in the middle of the Temple. I won decisively.

William laughs, which brings me back to the present. "I believe you broke him, Liam. Trajan rarely lets down his mask, but you dropped it within the first five minutes. This Battle will be epic."

I take a deep breath, contemplating the proper response. He's right. Liam, while I judged him for his lack of gamesmanship, was attacking a front I had left unguarded. The Lion of Celsus, fighting a shark in the depths of the ocean.

"Come, let us play a game. I will tell my grandchildren of this, one day," Liam says. He leads us to the center of the room.

Tori brushes my shoulder as we walk, which is his way of sitting me down in the midst of turmoil and giving me a lecture. When I meet his eyes, it's clear he's telling me to focus on Liam. Learn his habits. Let him reveal his strength and study where it comes from.

Liam sits, cross legged, and motions for us to join him. I sit across from him, Tori to my left and William on my right. After we're settled, Liam drops a small silver cube in the middle of our circle. "Simple. Choose your opponent. The first one to grab the cube wins. If you lose, fifty pushups."

A simple child's game to test and refine one's reflexes. It was one of my favorite ways to pass the time between sparring sessions with other Hopefuls.

William looks at me and says, "Would you do me the honor?" He smiles, then draws a finger across his throat. We may as well be twelve, our parents lounging in the background. At least, that's how I imagine a normal childhood.

"With pleasure," I say. "On your signal."

Before the last word is out of my mouth, he yells, "Go!" and swipes at the cube. Instinct takes over. I treat his attempt on the cube as a strike. An instant later, I've knocked William's hand out of the way and I sit with cube in hand. My mind catches up, remembering the motion rather than willing it.

William laughs, "Leave it to Trajan to turn this game into a contact sport." He rubs the spot on his wrist where I struck him.

"It's difficult to rewire decades of training," I say.

"No apologies," Liam says. "Your aggression is your signature. William, as a future Ruler, you should accept the lesson he just gave you. When the rules are ambiguous, tighten any loopholes you can. In order to preserve our forearms, however, let's outlaw the striking of your opponent."

It's Liam's turn to be overly confident. Even though he addresses William, it's obvious he's using this contest to craft our official Battle.

I place the cube back in the middle. "Mentor," I say. We sit silently, motionless and without expression for what must be thirty seconds. Both waiting for a shallow breath, a twitch in the corner of the eye or the pre-emptive flex of a forearm. While exhaling, I strike. My hand darts straight out, following the straightest path I can cut. Tori moves immediately after. His shoulders must have been more relaxed than mine, which allows his arm to move faster than mine, but the lag was too great. In an instant, I sit with the cube in the palm of my hand.

"Well done, General," Liam says. "If I may?"

I put the cube back and relax. Studying Liam.

He shifts his weight, scratches the palms of his hands, coughs, then, before I can respond, he's holding the cube. His approach was sloppy. After scratching one of his knees, he swept his hand in a wide arc to grab the silver trinket.

For the second time today, I've allowed myself to believe the lie that he is a bumbling old man. He may as well have pointed behind me, a stunned, plastic, look on his face, and warned me of a fictitious attacker.

Even though losing at anything makes me want to snap the first thing I can grab, I'm pleased. He's revealed a trend. He's calculated and, once he finds a weakness, he will exploit it without drawing attention to what he's doing. He likes to play the oaf. An assassin who kills with an embrace. But he's proven too proficient. Too greedy. If he had changed his approach after the first misdirection, I likely wouldn't have connected the dots. But he went back to the well too quickly. The next time he drinks from that water, he'll find it laced with poison.

"One more time?" he asks.

"Yes," I say.

Liam places the cube back and begins a similar routine, this time by cracking the knuckles on one of his hands. Before the last joint has popped, I've snatched the block from the floor.

I don't say anything, nor do I reveal any expression. My move may have been too premature, but I want to put him on the defensive. I want to see how he responds after losing.

He laughs, "Amazing. Prince, did you see that? Aggression. I barely had enough time to take a breath and the next thing you know, he's holding the trophy."

"If we know anything about Trajan, he plays any game on his own terms," William says.

They may as well be commentators at a sporting event. I've dialed into the technique, though. Even this banter is meant to hide their strategy in the shadow of exuberance and naïveté.

"One more time? I cannot abide leaving things at a tie," I say.

"Of course. I wouldn't have it any other way," Liam says.

The cube drops on the floor with the thud of metal on wood. For Liam, this is the most telling match. He's betting that my obsessive need to win will highlight my base strategy. If he can learn that, he can structure a Battle and its rules so I'm guaranteed to lose.

I'm left with a conundrum, however. If I'm too obvious, he'll extrapolate what I'm covering up. He'll also realize I've figured him out, which will cause him to act out of character when we meet in the Temple. I have to give him something to match his preconceptions of me. This is my gamble. I have to be a flower releasing poison laden pollen.

Aggression. That's his assumption. It's correct. I am always the aggressor. But aggression can wear many masks. Most interpret it as impatience. If that were true, I'd be no better than Castor. My aggression is different. I'm willing to wait until I've revealed a weakness. Then I exploit it without mercy. A piece of steel, coiled and under pressure. Stored energy waiting for release.

In this case, I need to act like Castor, not Trajan. I forget about the cube and go for Liam. At least, I make it look as if I'm going after him. Rather than strike out with my hand, I plant my fists on the ground and swing my legs toward Liam's face while screaming the most guttural noise I can muster. Liam instinctively reacts by rolling to one side and bringing his hands up to protect his face. Millimeters before my feet strike him, I pivot and plant myself in between him and the cube, careful not to touch him. I calmly reach behind myself and pluck the cube off the floor. Liam, still leaning away from the fake strike looks around, trying to process what just happened. There is the briefest smile on his face before his regains his composure. I've given him what he expected. In his mind, he's bested me. Learned my flaw and can now devise a Battle which will put me on tilt.

"There again, Prince. He's tightened another loophole. Turned a game of reflexes into attack and parry. Used intimidation to strike me without ever making contact. Masterful, General." The pleasure with which he speaks is genuine. He's smelled the flower and is enjoying the scent, filling his head with a sweet smelling toxin.

"You speak as if you're the Prince's Mentor," Tori says to Liam.

Liam and William are silent for a moment, each waiting for the other to respond. "In a way, I guess you're correct," William says. "When Demetrius offered his challenge, we found ourselves with an inexperienced General and without a succession plan. It was Liam who asked my mother if I would shadow him."

"I pray he won't have to take my burden, but the lessons I'm teaching will equip him to rule one day," Liam says.

They treat me as a trusted confidant rather than as the General seeking to conquer their nation.

"And you, General? Have you found the justification Demetrius is looking for?" Liam asks. It's the closest to outright antagonistic he's been.

"With respect, Celsus doesn't challenge, then find reason. The reason has always been vetted well in advance. I've seen little of Aegea." It is as if someone else's words are coming out of my mouth. I remind myself of

Marcail's threats of truewar, but even that feels like trying to remember a distant dream. "But I'm not here as a spy. Rather, an emissary, hopefully building a bridge that will allow our nations to join in mutual benefit."

"I'm not a politician, and I haven't been groomed in the ways of state as you have," Liam says, "but if it were that simple, I don't think a Battle would be necessary." He looks at William, likely measuring whether he's gone too far. The prince looks at the floor with his hands behind his back. "Do us a favor. If you find any violation, then by all means follow through with the Battle. If you don't, exercise your right and refuse to attack."

His breath is short, face flushed. Clearly this was not rehearsed, nor sanctioned. This is Liam, acting on his own, hoping the repercussions don't outweigh the risk.

"If only it was that easy," I say.

Chapter 29

"I would call that meeting a draw," Tori says.

It's mid-afternoon and it appears we have been left alone for the rest of the day. I find myself thinking about what Fiona is doing and whether I will get to see her today. "He played the part of the clueless idiot well," I say.

"He was a snake with the markings of a branch, waiting for you to step over him."

"But he was too obvious. He won't surprise me again."

Tori turns and considers the ocean. "They're attempting a coup. They know Demetrius won't relent and they know you can't be defeated. But they hope you can be changed. All of this is meant to give you doubt. To test your loyalty." These words are spoken as if giving directions to a lost traveler.

"Am I so easily manipulated that a few moments of kindness would usurp my loyalty to Celsus?" I ask.

"Is that the question we need to ask?"

"Stop being so formal," I say.

"You can't fault yourself for their tactics. Nor can you fault them for trying something new against you. But your response is another matter. We've identified their tactic. Our parry is what's important. Remove your pride. Remove your expectations. Remove what you think of them. Do that and you've made this new battlefield yours. Don't, and you may as well let Castor take over."

"You speak as if I have a choice," I say. "If I were to relent, Demetrius would be undermined in front of the entire world."

"We always have choices. And it's not the outcome we should pursue, rather, the reason."

"You would have Demetrius undercut and Celsus disrespected?"

"I'm not advising a course. Just know I will follow your leadership, no matter what you choose," he still doesn't face me. I wonder what future he sees, floating above the waters.

"Is it so hard to believe William and Fiona could simply be sheltered children? Unaware of the suffering throughout their nation? Why must we consider them so manipulatively calculated?" With this, I do sit. It's easier to talk about the motives of others than be forced to consider my choices. Things were simpler when Demetrius kept me at bay until I was to be unleashed. If he were here, I'd ask him why he sent me. Why he would expose me to such doubt and distraction.

"Their actions may not be manipulation. They may merely be presenting an option which hasn't been available before. An option exposed by a lack of foresight by Demetrius. He sent you here to intimidate, assuming your desire to earn his love back would overshadow anything else." He moves away from the ocean and sits across from me. "Regardless, they have struck. And struck well. You must decide your next move."

The sun dangles above the horizon. Dinner will be soon. Another opportunity for them to demonstrate the difference between Aegea and Celsus. To poke holes in my opinion of Demetrius. "You're right, Moto-San. Of course you are."

Demetrius couldn't have foreseen this. Yes, his tactics are strong. Unwavering. But he provides for his nation. And he provides for the nations as I bring them to him. This last year has tested us. Tested his trust in me as his General, and my trust in him as my Ruler. But he found me. Made me the Lion of Celsus. Gave me the best Mentor and nurtured the truest part of me. Allowed me to grow into who I've become. These Aegeans, no matter if they're manipulating me, or if they truly are this way, have offered me nothing other than happy ideals and fascinating examples of adaptability. But it's all been by their scripting.

There is movement at the door. "I would be honored if you two would escort me to dinner this evening," Fiona says. In spite of myself, I stand immediately but I keep myself from inviting her in.

"Of course," I say. "Please wait for us in the courtyard. We are finishing with some matters of Celcean importance."

My stomach turns as I watch the corners of her eyes drop into a formal, cold posture. "Certainly, General," she says, emphasizing General more than necessary.

After escorting us to dinner, Fiona excuses herself, claiming the need to help with preparations. Marcail begins to question her, but after a silent exchange, restrains herself. I don't see Fiona for the rest of the night. Rather, Tori and I sit among the politicians of Aegea. For the first time since arriving, it feels as if I'm back in Celsus. My mind wanders as different men and women politely insult each other over differences in ideology. For their part, Marcail and William remain mostly silent.

As dessert is served the queen positions herself next to me. "I'm told your assistance on our farming colony saved the day. We are in your debt." Her voice is low, insinuating this is not a conversation she desires the others to join.

"It was the first time I've challenged myself since the Mid-Year Battle. I've missed the exhilaration."

"The Mid-Year. Yes. I must admit, that was more violence than I could handle watching. My advisors were sure you'd killed Castor. I cannot say we mourned the possibility."

"How long have you ruled Aegea?" I ask. If this is somehow a manipulative maneuver, I don't want to walk down her path too easily.

She pauses so long before answering, I almost turn my attention back to the jockeying of the politicians. Finally she says, "A little more than five years. My husband's death was a shock to all Aegeans. They needed leadership. They," she motions to the group of advisors, "offered to take over until my mourning was over. But the people needed me. Not because of my leadership, but because I was at least a shadow of the king. And even a shadow of him was better than a group of people who would blot out his memory."

"It sounds like they should be kept at bay, rather than given a place at your table," I am shocked by the freedom with which these words come out. I would never think of saying such things to Demetrius, yet with Marcail, a person who has willingly brought truewar back as an option, I lack even precursory tact.

She laughs, "That's what Fiona says. But these people care about Aegea as much as I do, and when they're focused, working together, they're mighty. We all have weaknesses. Their's just happens to be greed. Take the option of more power out of the conversation and they're able to concentrate on the interests of the nation."

It's my turn to laugh. "Sounds like a dangerous game. People will invent ways to gain more power if they crave it enough."

"But if I eliminated them, who would keep me in check? I'm not immune to it either."

She grabs another cushion and hugs it against her ribs, allowing her to lie on her side, propped on her elbow.

"Too much acceptance, however, leads to acquiescence," I say. "There are times when the unpopular decision is the right decision."

"Too true. You would make a great Ruler, you know. You see the grey. You're humble enough to listen, but confident enough to stay the course. No matter how difficult. I see much of my late husband in you." For the first time in our conversation, she looks at me directly. There are tears, puddling in the corners or her eyes. She lets out a stifled laugh as one breaks free and traces down her cheek. "Enough of this," she says with a wave of her hand, "if you're willing, tomorrow William and Fiona leave to inspect some of our outlying colonies. The trip will take a couple of weeks. They would love you to join."

"I would enjoy that. Many more of these dinners," I nod toward the politicians, still debating, "and I believe I may throw myself into the ocean."

The queen sighs and sits up, "Yes, they do tend to melt one's mind. I will ensure you have an uplink at all times. Demetrius sent word today that he would like to be able to connect with you before your return."

We sit next to each other for another hour, listening to the politicians argue over increasing the yearly allotment of grains throughout the colonies.

When the queen finally rises to leave, she squeezes my shoulder as she stands. I feel as awkward as when we entangled in our embrace on the first day of my visit. She bids an elegant farewell to the group, then stoops down and puts her mouth close to my ear, "Thank you for the conversation. I rarely get to tune this group out. I'm grateful to you for that."

Chapter 30

The second Tori enters my quarters, my eyes open. It's still dark out, which confuses me. We aren't supposed to leave until mid-morning.

"Demetrius is waiting," Tori says.

I'm out of bed and into the common room within seconds. A shining Demetrius greets me. It's not him, rather a conglomeration of intersecting light beams that project his image. He can't see me yet. I need to stand in a specific spot so my image can be scanned and reproduced back in Celsus. When I step into the circle of light, my image materializes in front of him. He opens his arms, as if to hug my apparition.

"My child! These old eyes of mine have ached to behold you."

I bow, immediately more at ease. "And mine you, Highness."

"I trust you're well? You left us so quickly, before full recovery." He drops his hands and clasps them behind his back, a father asking after the health of his son.

"Tori has taken care of me as always. I'm grateful you provided me such a caring and competent Mentor, my lord." When he dotes on me like this, I feel how a gem must feel in the hand of a jeweler, but the rarity of it makes me uncomfortable.

"And the Aegeans? It appears you've become quite comfortable there.

Still sleeping at this hour."

I'm about to remind him of the time difference, but I do not want to make him feel foolish. "Their style is much different than ours. Staying up much later, which leads to late mornings. Trust, however, my readiness has not suffered."

"I'm told you visited one of their colonies. What news?"

I straighten my shoulders. Even though his tone is light, I feel the urgency in his question. I am not on vacation and this report carries more weight than is comfortable. "They are hard workers, and they have to be. Resources are scarce in Aegea. But they're resilient. And inventive. Their technology is strange, but impressively effective."

"Yes, it will be a burden, taking them under my wing. I'm already planning the logistics of how to provide better for them. I pray they will have to work less, yet be better nourished once they are freed. But I'm interested in this technology. I've heard little of that. All reports tell me they are significantly behind the rest of the world." His image wavers as he shifts his weight. It's odd, seeing Celcean hardware in the gentle confines of Aegean decor.

"Their technology appears backwards on the surface, but some of it is quite impressive. The methodology is opposite than ours, but no less effective."

He raises his eyebrows and cocks his chin back, instructing me to continue.

"It's like comparing a bird with a drone. The bird uses the currents of the wind to fly, while a drone forces the air to lift it. Their technology adapts to their environment. Ours, it seems, bends the environment to our needs."

"You speak of it lovingly. I can't recall any poems written about drones." The hint of offense in his voice confuses me.

"Not at all. While impressive, it is limiting," I say. Outside, the sky blurs as the sun begins its ascent. So similar to a couple of nights ago, as I listened to Tori's confession. It's amazing how the sky can be so similar, but the conversation so different.

"Describe the impressiveness to me. What has grasped your imagination so powerfully?"

I pause, considering all that I have seen. It really doesn't matter what I find the most intriguing, Demetrius needs to know the implications of what I have seen. I'm about to describe the stabilization of their artificial islands. Instead, I blurt, "They have an energy field which can be contoured to any shape. It helps protect the plants from the salt in the sea air." Inventiveness and adaptability.

He asks me to tell him more, so I describe the way Fiona ensured we were out of the way before the field was engaged, and how, no matter how hard I tried, I was unable to move the corn.

Demetrius drops his head and begins pacing. The sensor follows him and the lasers on my side fire manically in order to accurately represent his movement to me. The effect is mesmerizing, as his image begins pacing through our quarters. A thoughtful and concerned ghost. "Such strong shields seem like a lot of trouble to go through when a tarp would suffice, don't you think, child?"

"In honesty, I didn't question it. They are at extreme odds with their environment. Such measures seem to be necessary."

"I sent you because you see things for what they are, and what they could be. It is troubling to hear you so easily write this off. I need you to think critically. To see through the veil of deception that has kept this nation off the world's radar for so long."

"Forgive me, Lord. My intent was not to justify. You're right, of course." How we've gone from doting to disappointed so quickly makes my head spin. But I understand his perspective. He has not seen Marcail navigate her politicians, nor Fiona's humble leadership.

"My son. I know I've asked much of you. But I want to see a life for you after you've handed the mantle of General to Castor. Please don't make me reconsider that. I'm recalling you in two weeks. Your instincts are good. There's a reason you mentioned this energy field. Dig deeper. Report back to me. What they're calling a protection for plants sounds like prototyping for a dominant armor. I can't afford for you to let your guard down. Think of the people living in poverty. Forced into near slavery so an upstart nation can develop the means for truewar. Stay vigilant. I will hail you again soon." His image fades away as the uplink is severed.

Tori and I are silent until I've disconnected the uplink's power source.

"Are the justifications for Battle so subtle?" When he sent me, I envisioned finding half-starved children and political prisoners. But if I'm to find a shield disguised as farming equipment, it seems anything would suffice for my Battle.

"Likely. But no matter what technology you chose to highlight, the outcome would have been the same."

We're both still. Both of us remembering the conversation in order to understand the new expectations put on us.

"Come, we must get ready. The prince and princess will be expecting us soon."

"How I long for the days when I was told to fight and I fought. Nothing more. Just you preparing me. And me executing."

"Yes, but there comes a time when the risk of falling is less daunting than the reality of crawling through life."

"It's so nice to leave. I just wish the queen would come more often," Fiona says. She, William, Tori and I stand on the surface of one of their high speed vessels. We drift from the Aegean capital as our crew makes the final preparations for our trip.

"I'm sure she does too," I say, remembering our conversation from last night. The sea air is perfectly humid as always, brushing the sun's heat from our skin. It's easy to understand why Aegeans are so tan. In fact, I realize my skin has grown a few shades darker since I've been here, which pleases me.

We're silent for the few remaining minutes we have before we're beckoned below deck so the vessel can whisk us away. Each of us, undoubtedly, consumed with very different thoughts. For my part, the conversation with Demetrius keeps me from savoring this moment as deeply as I would. Fiona and William act as if we are leaving for a whimsical vacation and Tori remains respectfully curious. If I am to give Demetrius what he needs, I will need to see through the adventure in order to understand the underbelly of these people. As hard as I try, however, Fiona's joy, William's honesty and Marcail's respect make me wonder if the belly isn't equally as clean as the surface.

"Where to, Trajan?" Fiona asks. She doesn't look at me. Her eyes are closed, her head tilted toward the sun, and her whole body seems to be smiling.

"I thought there would be an itinerary," I say. I mean to express surprise, but even to myself, I sound accusatory.

"There's always an itinerary. Which makes deviating from it even more exhilarating." She and William laugh to each other, likely remembering a scene from their childhood.

"Any true islands we can visit? Other than the one where we landed?" I ask.

"There's a fishing colony which patrols the waters near our biggest island. We will visit them first."

"You just want to show off your spearing skills," Fiona says.

"Spearing sounds fun to me," I say.

Fiona shakes her head, "Of course it does. Too bad I'll put you both to shame."

Tori lets out a deep breath. He's been standing with his usual perfect posture while the three of us pretend to be nothing more than children. "I've heard of your fishing communities and have always wanted to see them in action. Now, quiet down and let me enjoy this breeze just a while longer."

We oblige for the next ten minutes. When one of the crew members beckons us below, none of us move until he threatens to submerge the vessel with us still on deck.

The trip is six hours through a storm. I know this because, every so often, we venture to the control room so we can see outside. The storm is so intense, it's hard to distinguish the clouds from the surface of the ocean. It just seems as if we're hovering in the middle of grey matter. Even our speed is impossible to detect. However, our stabilizers perform so well, it feels as if we are immobile on dry land.

"Come, let's make the time pass," says Fiona.

We find a quiet room with two chairs molded to the floor on opposite sides of a small table. When we sit, Fiona waves her hand over the table and three small lights appear on her side. "I know Tori has taught you strategy well, but I'd still enjoy playing you." She presses the middle light and the table's surface looks as if it begins to boil. In seconds, a chess set grows from the churning surface. It reminds me of the obstacle course in my training facility in Celsus.

"It's been quite some time since I last played. Most Generals focus on strength of body over strength of mind these days," I say. Chess has always been my favorite strategy game. It makes me think of a time before the chaos and the Ruling Ancestors.

"Which is likely why you continue to win," she smiles.

She starts in a traditional defense posture, staggering her pawns in a zig-zag pattern and moving her bishops behind them. If I want to break through her line, it will mean sacrificing one of my more valuable pieces. It is a sound, but easily defeated, strategy.

We chat idly while we move. Neither of us want to admit how much

226

we're focused on ending the stalemate. The way she's set up her board, it's obvious she over-values her knights.

"Tell me of your childhood. Celsus has no princes or princesses. What's it like growing up constantly required to represent an ideal?" I move my bishop into an enticing position for one of her pawns, testing her resolve to stay on defense.

"Much like yours, I would imagine," she says. "You attained General so quickly, I bet your responsibilities outweighed mine. Father was determined William and I should have as normal a childhood as possible." She brings her knight into position to take my bishop.

"Then what is a normal childhood like in Aegea? Celcean children are identified early in life to fulfill particular jobs, based on aptitude." I move my bishop to a space which would let her pursue with her knight, leaving her slightly more vulnerable.

"Lots of play. Learning to swim and read the ocean. We're made to learn navigation and crop rearing, which takes up most of our time. Survival is more of a focus for us than most. But there's an emphasis on education. We study the philosophers of old." She pauses before her next move, struggling to stay passive. After a long bout of contemplation, she takes my bait, jumping her knight past her line of defense.

The moment she lands her knight, I take it with my queen. She flushes with anger. After a moment's pause, she does the obvious thing and takes my queen with her pawn in an attempt to even the score.

She looks at me triumphantly, "You just can't help your aggressive nature, can you?"

The next series of moves between us are fast and bloody. By the end, there's a gaping hole in the middle of the board and she's missing the two pieces she values the most. While I, on the other hand, still have my most powerful pieces primed to invade.

It takes her a second to realize what just happened. "That was probably the most violent series of moves I've ever played," she says, "it's amazing how an ancient board game can get my adrenaline flowing."

I smile, moving one of my rooks to put her king in check.

Most people would realize their tactical disadvantage and surrender. Not Fiona. She makes me play to the last piece. By the end, she's lost every piece but her king and has whittled me down to my king, a rook and a bishop. It takes me a painstakingly long time, but I finally trap her king to put her in checkmate.

"We're never playing again," she says.

"I should apologize. It's impossible for me to approach games like this without compete intensity. I don't know what a casual game of chess is," I say.

"Why would you apologize for your nature? I don't know you well, but that fire is one of my favorite things about you. I just wish it was loyal to someone other than Demetrius."

It doesn't appear as if she meant this as anything other than a passing remark. I don't sense any overt manipulation. Regardless, what was once a fun moment between a beautiful woman and me is shattered.

"I should rest before we get to the colony," I say, standing to leave. In the doorway, I stop. "Hopefully, one day you won't see him as such a monster. Even more, I pray you won't always see me as his unwitting tool." I hear her inhale as if to respond, but nothing comes.

Chapter 31

"The sharks, I'm told, are much more aggressive than they used to be. Before the chaos," William says. We're standing on the deck of the hunting community, watching as the crew finalizes the rigging which will suspend us over the ocean, above a thrashing school of the biggest sharks I've ever seen.

We woke at dawn, much to Fiona's protest, to prepare for the truehunt.

"It's simple, really," William said as we ate a light breakfast of salt cured fish and candied nuts. "We draw the sharks in with chum, wait until they're spun into a frenzy, then we go after them with nothing more than a one meter long spear. Because of how short the spear is, we have to be suspended as close to the water as possible to have any chance of actually hitting one. One stab isn't enough to kill a shark, but it is enough to anger it. And these sharks don't run once they're injured. They seek revenge."

The rain has stopped, but the wind and high waves continue to jostle us. Tori and I have the most difficulty staying upright, but after a few embarrassing tumbles, we manage to adjust.

"I'll go first to give you an idea of the process," William says. He's virtually jumping up and down with excitement.

Fiona, standing to my left, says, "Relax, brother. The sharks aren't going anywhere."

"Why are they so agitated?" Tori asks. "Do you put something in the chum to trigger them?"

He's right. Even though there's blood in the water, these creatures appear to be unnaturally upset.

"Do you remember the energy field we put over the plants at the farming colony?" Fiona asks. "Once we attract the sharks, we surround them with the same field. Right now, they're in a sort of bowl, twenty meters in diameter and fifteen meters deep. If there's one thing these beasts don't like, it's confinement."

I'm surprised to hear such excitement in her voice. For some reason, I would have imagined her disapproving of this type of tradition.

"It seems as if you can do pretty much anything you want with that energy field," Tori says. The prince and princess are too focused on the hunt to pick up on the nuances of Tori's comment. Demetrius would be very interested to learn of this ability to manipulate the unique technology.

"We're ready!" Jacob, the colony's captain, calls from the control panel of one of the hydraulic arms. He is the most severe looking Aegean I have seen yet, covered in brightly colored tattoos, most of which look to be ancient symbols. The tattoos even carry to his face, but they do not take away from rusty eyes which seem to weigh and measure my character every time he locks gazes with me. "My crew grows bored of your hesitancy. Who is first?" he bellows, his voice puts even the wind at bay.

William turns and slaps me on the shoulder, "If this is what you feel before a Battle, you must want to fight every week. The adrenaline. It's like I can see a whole new spectrum of color." He doesn't wait for a response before he straps himself into the harness. To Jacob, he yells, "Take note, captain, I'm about to give you a free lesson in hunting."

Jacob's laugh carries across the colony as he lifts the machine's arm, which swings William horizontally. I can tell I'll have difficulty keeping myself in a good striking position. As he's swung over the sharks, William flips himself upside down and wraps one of his legs around the cable which holds him.

"Show off," Fiona says, smiling and shaking her arms as if she's trying to flick mud from her hands. "He gets one shot. If he misses, he's brought back and has to wait until we've all gone. The person with the fewest strikes to register a kill is victorious."

"What prize accompanies the victory?" I ask.

"Pride. Surely you, of all people, understand that."

"Seems our nations aren't so different, after all," I say.

William is directly over the corralled sharks, about four meters above the water. "Lower," he yells. Jacob drops him a meter, then pauses. "Lower," William yells again.

He's barely two meters above the water, which means every couple of seconds, a wave washes over him. I glance at Jacob. His eyes are fixed on William and his hands clutch the levers that could yank the prince from the water in less than a second.

"I can't wait until you're out here, Trajan," William shouts, "I bet you've never faced an opponent as fierce as these monsters." At the same time he says monsters, he thrusts his titanium spear into the water.

There is a brief pause, then a curse as the spear returns without blood on it.

Jacob immediately pulls the prince back to the safety of the deck.

"They're so fast," William says once he's back on deck. "You really can't understand how agile they are until you're out there."

"Thank you for the lesson, Highness. We are better hunters for experiencing that brilliant demonstration," Jacob says through gritted teeth. It is a loving joke run through a harsh filter. William shakes his head and nods a conciliatory acknowledgement toward the captain. "Next!" Jacob yells.

In spite of Fiona's displays of excitement, she doesn't volunteer. If I wait too long, Tori will step forward. I won't allow my Mentor to precede me in this. I step toward the swaying harness and give Jacob a wave. It's amazing how quickly I've adjusted to the rocking of the vessel. Less than a day ago, I could barely stay upright. Now, the jostling is a mere distraction.

"I've got my money on a first strike for you, General. The spear has always been one of your truest weapons," Jacob says.

I nod while I attach myself to the system of spring loaded carabiners and loops that are integrated into our sea-suit.

"If the spear doesn't make contact with anything in the first three meters of water, it will automatically return. Keep your arm extended. The spear is attracted back by a sensor in the arm of the suit. If your arm is behind you, the spear could impale you," Fiona yells. She may be trying to scare me, but I won't test the advice.

Without any warning, Jacob lifts me from the deck. My adrenaline flows so mightily through my body, I barely register his maniacal laugh. I begin to spin, so I stretch my legs out, and use my core to extend my upper body, which slows me. Tori and I lock eyes in the same way we lock eyes just before entering the Temple. That single look holds reminders, encouragement, and warnings, but the end result is calm and focus.

Rather than dangle upside down like William, I plant my foot on one of the carabiner's joints and push myself into a standing position. This gives me a much better vantage and it's a more natural striking position. Within seconds, I'm centered above the melee of sharks. William was right. Their movement seems unnatural and they change direction faster than I thought possible in water. Even when they look to be coasting, they move faster than any human can swim.

At first, I focus on one place in the water, trying to find a spot where the sharks tend to conglomerate, but their collective movements are too complex for me to quickly decipher. Instead, I pick out one of the beasts. It's of average size, but there is a jagged chunk missing from its dorsal fin. By focusing on the abnormality, I'm able to track it. After two laps through the swarm I see its pattern.

It stays close to the surface when on the right of the group. After five meters, it turns left and dives low, presumably following the arc of the energy field all the way back to the surface, thereby avoiding the majority of churn. Once back at the surface, it glides around the side of the field closest to the fishing pod until it returns to the right side.

I decide to strike just before it dives, waiting four revolutions, to ensure I've mastered the timing.

This will be a good kill. The spear feels true in my hand, the weight distributed evenly, it's an extension of me. William is right. The clarity of any sort of Battle is a cleansing thing, offering a focus beyond any drug or emotion. The shark begins its journey toward the center of the group.

I time its progress. Everything slows as it gets closer. When he's two meters from diving back down, I release my grip on the cable, sending myself into a free-fall, building the momentum necessary for my spear to strike with as much devastating force as possible.

Just before I expect my harness to catch the rigging, I release the spear. It slides from my hand cleanly. Even before it's fully out of my grasp, I know this is a lethal strike. Tori will surely scold me for so easily mastering a sacred right of passage, but this moment is too perfect for restraint.

The tip of the spear slides into the water without making a ripple and I watch as, in the very next moment, it parts the flesh of the shark directly in the center of the head. The blood comes out in clouds as the spear continues through, severing muscle, piercing brain tissue, carving its path through the shark's skull. This will be the last I see of the kill, I think.

My harness will stop my fall in less than a second, so I brace myself for the inevitable snap when the cable abruptly halts my descent. But the snap doesn't happen. Instead, I feel a gentle tug where I know the loops to be, and I'm spun ninety degrees. But the tension releases as fast as it started and the next sensation I experience is the sound of my body falling into the center of the frenzy.

The sharks are as surprised as I am, but they recover much faster. I begin flailing in an attempt to gain my bearings, which only entices the monsters more. One of the biggest of them banks left, then right, spinning himself completely around in less than a second, and charges me. Razor sharp teeth fill my vision. I put my left hand out to push the beast away, realizing too late that the diameter of his jaw will easily envelop my entire upper body.

Just as the jaws begin to descend around me, I feel a sharp pain in my right forearm and I'm jerked straight down. I watch as the enormous shark passes over me, then I look down to realize I was saved from sudden death by another shark, clamping around my arm and pulling me away from competition. I feel the pressure of the water around me and for the first time I realize my lungs are burning.

If given the choice of my death, I would have opted for the single bite of the leviathan, rather than being forced to drown by this smaller predator.

Every General ponders his own death. In all my life, this scenario never occurred as my end. No gasping Crowd. No cameras. No hero's burial. Rather, a broken suit and a hungry predator. In the midst of all of our technology, all of the perfectly researched supplements and training regiments, my death is no different than the death millions of sea creatures have suffered every day for millennia.

I look to the surface, where the majority of the sharks continue to teem when the water begins to hum around me. We must be approaching the bottom of the energy field. Suddenly, my suit flashes red hot. In an instant, it has gone rigid. I try to kick my legs, move my free arm, turn my head. All are impossible. Even where the shark bit me has been suspended. It still radiates pain, but the intensity of the attack has eased.

There's another rumble in the water, followed by what look like transparent tentacles, almost like watching a current run through still water, jutting toward every shark above me. One second they're thrashing above me, the next, there's an explosion of red. Mists of blood burst from each of the sharks and they're immediately motionless.

It's all so surreal, I assume I'm hallucinating. Likely the effect of an oxygen deprived brain. As if to reinforce the apparitions, my vision blurs, then darkness begins creeping in from the sides. I always thought drowning would be a panicked struggle until you're forced to draw a final gasp of water into your lungs. But this is peaceful. My last thought, before I lose consciousness, is wondering which young Hopeful Tori will begin Mentoring once he returns to Celsus.

Chapter 32

My hearing returns before my vision. Disembodied voices drift around me. I'm not coherent enough to understand what they're saying, but I can tell they're discussing me. It's Tori's tone which snaps me back completely.

I don't know how they got me out of the water, but I find myself back on the jostling deck, surrounded by Tori, Jacob, William and Fiona. Without thinking, I reach for Fiona's face, but I'm unable. It's as if my skin has hardened into a rigid shell. I can move my eyes from side to side and I can breathe, but other than that, I'm completely incapacitated.

William stands and shouts over his shoulder, "Shut his field down!"

An instant later, I'm able to move. My initial desire to caress Fiona's face has been tamed, but the need to move, to take command of my surroundings, is overwhelming. I jump to my feet, pushing Jacob back with such force, he's barely able to keep himself from falling overboard.

"Peace, Trajan," Tori says.

I realize I'm acting irrationally, but I'm unable to control myself. Panic. I never feel panic. But I continue to back away from the people who clearly pulled me from the water and revived me, gasping for breath.

Fiona begins to move toward me but Tori stops her, realizing I'm just as likely to strike as embrace her.

"Give him space. He'll come around," Tori says.

Just then, my legs give out from a wave and I black out again.

I wake this time in a grey room. No one hovers over me, discussing my condition. My breathing is normal and I'm able to move without restriction. There's a light blanket over me, slightly fluttering from the sea breeze. For a moment, I wonder if I'm back at the Aegean capital, waking from a nightmare. A fly lands on my nose and I move my right arm to swat it away. Pain. Pure, white and aggressive, it starts at my elbow and shoots straight to my fingertips. Clearly the sharks weren't a dream. I sit up as fast as my spinning head will allow and bring my arm into view.

Mangled. My entire forearm is covered in stitches, desperately trying to pull together the zigzags of jagged gashes. The pain is deep, but I quickly overcome it. What frightens me more is how damaged it is. This type of wound seems permanent. Maybe not if I was in Celsus, but on the outskirts of a primitive nation like Aegea, this will end me. Castor will step in. Demetrius will claim Aegea purposely tried to kill me. No more cheering Crowds. Trajan, the once mighty warrior, will be no more than a cautionary tale Generals and Mentors tell their pupils about the need to always be on guard.

"It's not as bad as it looks."

I jump and spin, the movement tugs on the feeble stitches, shooting a renewed surge of pain through my arm. Fiona sits in the corner nearest the opening to the ocean, watching me. The concern in her expression is embarrassing.

"Where is Tori?" I ask, sounding harsher and more panicked than I'd like.

"With Jacob. We're navigating to our main medical facility. Tori is making sure we're going as fast as we can." She looks at my arm and clenches her jaw. "You've torn some stitches."

I look down to see blood dripping from my arm, forming tiny pools in the sheets. "No loss, I guess."

"Just like that? Giving up? Don't put yourself out to pasture too quickly," she smiles.

I flex my hand, introducing more pain. I want to know how deep the wounds go. From what I can tell, there's significant tendon and ligament damage. And the muscles along my forearm are shredded. I'll be lucky to regain twenty percent of the strength I once had.

"Here," she hands me a sling, "put this on. I don't want you passing out from loss of blood."

I clumsily begin to wrap it around my shoulder with my left arm, trying to keep my right as still as possible. After a couple of minutes of struggle, I say, "Would you mind helping?" The question causes as much pain as the pulling stitches in my arm.

She offers a smile and gently takes the sling. The tenderness of her movements communicates that she is protecting both my arm and my pride. This is the lowest point I can remember and I am grateful to share it with her. ,

"Come, let's go see Tori," she says.

We exit my quarters to a sunny day with a slight breeze. The ocean is as calm as I've seen since visiting Aegea.

"How long was I unconscious?" It's jarring to see such a drastic difference in weather.

"Just a day. The sea changes as quickly as the loyalties of a politician," Fiona says. She walks slightly in front of me, but keeps her pace slow, accounting for my tentative steps.

We make our way across the deck, weaving our way through blurry lumps of grey. My eyes struggle to adjust to the brightness of the day, but once they do, I realize we're walking around dozens of shark carcasses. "Fiona," I say, "Are these," I pause, unable to articulate the question.

"They are," she says, as if speaking at a funeral.

"How?" I ask.

"One issue at a time. Let's speak with Jacob and Tori about our progress first."

We make our way past shark after shark, each one with a perfectly round puncture straight through the body, gill to gill. The last body we pass before entering the control room is the shark with the chunk missing from the dorsal fin. My prey before the tables were turned. There's no puncture through the gills, just the hole left by my spear. I stop, replaying the entire scene in my head. "Did I?"

"Yes. One shot. You really are terrifyingly proficient at death," she says. Without waiting for me, she enters the control room.

Tori meets me at the door, his face strained. Before he says anything, he inspects my arm. "Some torn stitches. There is severe damage. Not the worst I've seen for you, but you're usually sedated while you heal," he pauses, then leans nearer to me, "your attitude is as important as the physician's ability to heal you." He pulls back and locks eyes with me, testing my mental state. Looking for fear or determination or anger. He nods. No matter what he sees, he now knows the score, and how to guide me.

"We're less than a day from the island," Jacob says. "We've been pushing for shore since we retrieved you from the water. Tori is quite the task master. No wonder you're as dominant as you are." Of all the things I have seen since waking, Jacob's determined focus on getting me to the Aegean doctors underscores the gravity of my wounds the most.

Tori turns his focus back to the ocean. "We've maxed our speed, and have been fortunate for the change in weather. Jacob is a fine captain. You should go back to your quarters. We have no sedative, but you should try to rest. Your arm needs all the help it can get."

"With respect, I don't think I can rest until I know what happened."

"Unfortunately we don't have video for your review. From what we can tell, your fasteners gave way. Ripped clean off your suit due to your weight," Tori speaks as if reciting a history lesson.

"We don't have very many people as large as you. And we certainly don't have anyone who would pull the maneuver you did. The suit never stood a chance," Fiona says.

"That much I pieced together," I say. "But what of my inability to move. And the sudden execution of the sharks? And why was there no water in my lungs?"

Fiona places her hand on my shoulder and runs it down my back. "In short, the energy field. All suits are programmed to engage if their wearer goes deeper than five meters. And there's a fail-safe which redirects the energy of the containment bowl around the sharks into a type of energy spear. It kills anything that's not human if triggered. Jacob launched it as soon as we didn't see you emerge."

There are implications here. Everyone in the control room knows it. Aegea has an energy field that doesn't just protect plants and herd sea creatures. They have something easily weaponized to target with perfect precision and can serve as body armor.

Her statement hangs in the air, this has obviously been discussed while I was unconscious. "We use the technology to survive and protect. Nothing more."

"Another discussion for another time. Although, I am flattered you think I am so obsessively loyal to Demetrius," I say.

Tori turns from the controls, "Every second you are awake syphons needed energy from your arm." To Fiona he says, "You can offer your defense once Trajan is further down his path toward recovery."

He leads me out of the control room, around the carcasses and back to my quarters. The bloodied sheets have been changed and fresh bandages have been prepared.

I sit and slip the sling off my arm. While Tori sorts through the bandages, I inspect the gashes further. Even through the stitches, bone is visible in places. I'm fortunate no major arteries were severed, but that is where my luck ends. Muscle, tendons and ligaments are all shredded.

"How long until the Battle?" I ask.

"A little under a month," Tori says.

Even if I do recover fully, there's no chance of it happening that quickly. How odd it will be, I think, to see Castor fight for Celsus. I've known nothing other than the Battle for so long. Will Demetrius allow me to watch from his chamber, I wonder.

Tori beckons my arm, which I tenderly offer. His methodical tending of my wounds is both familiar and much needed. My mind stops spinning. We will figure this out. I'll be General again. Celsus will absorb Aegea and Marcail will become an advisor to Demetrius. All of this political posturing and manipulation will cease while I set my focus on recovery.

"I don't know what help they can offer at their hospital. Whatever it is, it will look different than what you're used to. Keep an open mind. Remember, your mind will be just as powerful as any healing compound they offer."

"Can we keep this from Demetrius?" I ask.

He stops his work to look at me. "His only focus is winning. He'll have you inspected from head to toe before you even travel to the Temple. With Castor pacing in the wings, he would never risk sending you in at less than one hundred percent."

Chapter 33

The island is barely one kilometer in diameter. Structures cover the majority of the land, but there are pockets of trees and crop boxes scattered about. This is, by far, the most industrialized segment of Aegea I've seen. The buildings lack the wispy, curved architecture of their capital. In fact, this scene much closer resembles Celsus. I take all of this in as I'm led down a rubbery path toward the high-walled central structure.

"What's the hour count since we pulled him from the water?" Fiona asks over her shoulder.

Jacob answers from behind us, "Just over thirty-six." Rather than dropping us off and returning to the sea, he has chosen to remain.

No one reacts, which makes me think this is not very good news.

I think back to the Battles in which I've suffered the most damage. In those cases, I've been barely conscious at best when being taken to the hospital and therefore unaware of the urgency of the physicians. That ignorance would be a welcome reprieve right now.

We're met by a tall woman in her mid fifties with her greying brown hair pulled back. There are no introductions or formalities. She immediately begins asking curt questions and giving detailed instructions to the people surrounding me.

Eventually, she turns to Fiona, quickly grabs her hand and says, "Good to see you, my dear. I hear you've already started treatment?"

Fiona nods and quickly looks at me out of the corner of her eyes, "Yes. We didn't have much on hand, but when he was initially passed out I applied some salve. I don't think much took, though. He was bleeding pretty heavily. I purposely left the stitches loose."

"Excellent," she says, "sounds like you've given us a strong start." She turns to me, "Welcome to our community. I had hoped to show you our healing capabilities a little differently, but this way will surely be much more meaningful. My name is Lilith. I'm in charge."

She puts her hand on my shoulder as she speaks. Her purposeful way of initiating contact, but being mindful of my wounds, reminds me of Fiona. The majority of Lilith's face is unremarkable, save her teeth, which are the brightest white I've ever seen on a person.

"We haven't much time," Fiona says. "We're past thirty hours."

Lilith gently guides my arm into the sunlight and pulls back one of the bandages. "More bone here than muscle." She looks at Tori, then me, "You're lucky to have an arm at all."

"We moved as quickly as possible," William says.

Lilith chuckles, "I'm sure you did. And the General owes you his life." Still holding my arm, she turns and leads me into the building.

The interior of the hospital is sterile and efficient. Unlike Celsus, there are very few machines or monitors. Instead of rooms separated by walls, simple curtains separate the patients from each other. Physicians and assistants mill about with hushed tones, occasionally breaking the silence with laughter. Lilith leads us halfway down the hall and reveals a small bed with two chairs.

"Part of recovery here is the patient's encouragement," she says. "Which two people would you like to sit with you?"

Without hesitation, I point to Tori and Fiona. She nods and smiles.

"Everyone else, out. We've prepared quarters for you deeper into the island."

The next hour is filled with physicians shuffling in and out of my space. Each one asks slightly different questions. Both Tori and I grow more impatient with each visit.

After the final physician leaves, Fiona grabs my good hand and says, "What comes next will seem strange. Possibly barbaric. But I ask you to trust us. We're not skilled in healing wounds from man against man violence, but we've become quite adept at recovering from the wounds caused by our environment. You will see. Lilith's skill borders on that of a magician."

"Our young princess is too kind. I prefer not to get the hope of my patients too high," Lilith says. She's accompanied by three assistants. They don't look at me, instead, they begin pulling what looks to be restraints from under the bed.

"We're fortunate, in a way, that Aegea is in such a harsh environment. It's forced us to turn to the creatures who have survived in these conditions for eons in order to carve out a way of survival. Some of these creatures are quite remarkable." She pulls out a Sea Star as the assistants check and test the straps. "For instance, not too long ago this gorgeous little thing was a single, mangled arm. But look at it now. Five perfect arms, a digestive system. There aren't even scars which designate where the new cells cling to the old."

They begin to strap down my legs, starting at my ankles, then my knees.

"There will be pain, then?" I say, nodding to the restraints.

"Yes. Quite a lot of it. I've seen you Battle, so I have an idea of your pain tolerance. Even still, I'm confident what you're about to experience will be orders of magnitude worse than anything you've felt."

I'm only able to move my arms, shoulders and head. Lilith turns to a small table against the wall and opens a sealed container. A pungent, fishy odor fills the space immediately.

"When our bodies experience any sort of trauma, they immediately go into lockdown. Blood starts clotting, and healthy tissue begins to reserve the blood and oxygen for itself. Our friend the sea star does the exact opposite. As soon as it's damaged, it begins pushing nutrients and energy toward the wounded area, turning it into a fresh construction site. Unfortunately, it's been so long since your attack, your body has effectively shut off the wounds. We need to re-open them. Then we can begin teaching your muscles how to rebuild themselves."

The final strap is cinched across my forehead. For the second time is as many days I've been completely immobilized. Even though I'm not about to drown nor surrounded by sharks, I'm closer to panic than I was the first time. I'm about to ask them to sedate me when Fiona leans over, smiling.

"You probably thought your time in Aegea would be full of boring dinners and pre-arranged demonstrations of our peaceful nature."

I manage a small smile, "Makes me wonder what you would have done to Demetrius if he were here."

"You should feel fortunate. We don't usually give our best tech to outsiders. This is just another day for most Aegeans."

I'm reminded of the first time I met Fiona. Not even a year ago as she walked with me before the Battle. Her beauty was so captivating, it annoyed me. Now, as Lilith stretches my arm and begins snipping Fiona's feeble stitches, causing my arm to light on fire with pain, it's as if her beauty has matured. I've seen her demonstrate her impetuous youth and I've seen her act beyond her years by leading her subjects. All of these experiences serve to make her eyes more vibrant, her skin more flawless and her hair cascade all the more elegantly.

"Your stitching was perfect, Fi. Just tight enough to avoid too much blood loss, but not enough to start the scarring process."

Fiona doesn't respond. Rather, she puts her hands on each side of my face. "Take deep breaths. The worst is about to begin." Tears glisten across her eyes.

My arm immediately feels as if the remaining flesh is being torn, fiber by fiber, from the bone. My nerves simultaneously catch fire and explode in rivulets of lightning strike torture. I tense my entire body and open my mouth but the pain is so intense, even my lungs seize. Somewhere in the distance I hear a protest from someone that sounds like Tori. Pain this intense can't last too long, I tell myself, so I force myself to calm. But the pain intensifies as it moves from the top layers of my skin into the deeper muscles and tendons. The shark bite which caused the wound seems like a mosquito bite in comparison.

Fiona's grip on my face grows tighter and tighter as she watches my reaction to whatever Lilith is doing to me. The tears flow freely from her, landing on my forehead and cheeks. One lands on my lips and for a moment the pain is gone, replaced by the salty sensation. But it returns with renewed aggression. This time, it's as if millions of ants have begun a parade up my arm, destroying every cell along the way. My vision begins to blur as blackness creeps in from the edges. Just before I pass out, Fiona leans down and softly kisses me.

Chapter 34

I wake to silence and darkness, still strapped to my bed. The entire right side of my body is numb and I'm shivering.

"Tori," I whisper. There is no response.

"Fiona," I try.

"Here." Her voice is heavy with exhaustion.

I wonder how long I've been out. The intensity of the procedure on my arm, combined with my blood loss and overall exhaustion makes me think it's been a few days. I'm surprised Tori isn't here, but I don't begrudge it. Even he deserves rest. In fact, I'm embarrassed by Fiona's presence.

It's so quiet, I'm hesitant to speak for fear of waking the others around me.

"How do you feel?" she whispers.

It's too dark to see her, but I try anyway. Her voice comes from my right.

"I don't know. Whatever they gave me to dull the pain is working. I can't feel anything on my right." I say.

She lets out a long breath. "I'm glad you're not in pain. But we didn't give you anything. You've likely shut off input from that side due to the intensity of the pain. Feeling will return. Probably just a few hours from now. Enjoy the reprieve while you can."

"What did they do to me?" I've been patched up by physicians all of my life. Recovered from being within seconds of death, and I can't conceive of any healing procedure that would cause that amount of agony.

"If we had gotten here earlier, it wouldn't have been so bad. But your body is incredibly proficient at healing. In this case, that's a bad thing. We had to open the wounds back up to allow the mixture to work. Basically, they took what was left of your skin and muscle and shredded it into strips, one centimeter thick. Then they packed in the mixture. A composite of the gene which allows the sea star to regrow its body and various cells and proteins. It has to interact with fresh wounds. Any clotting or decomposition will stall the process." She moves to my left and grabs my shackled hand. "That meant scraping out the early scar tissue, clots and dying flesh before initiating the fresh cuts."

Her words are clinical and factual, but her touch is gentle and loving. "Why not just knock me out or dull the pain?" I ask. "No matter how behind Celcean technology you are, Aegea must have painkillers."

"We're not barbarians. And we're not behind." She lets go of my hand. Her voice becomes cold and distant. "The pain is essential. It causes your body to release vital elements of the healing process. Adrenaline, oxygen, extra blood and a thousand other things all rush directly to the wound with a heightened urgency. All because of the pain. If you were blissfully unaware, the reaction would be much less productive."

"Of course," I say. There's so much more. I want to apologize to her. I want to berate her for being so easily offended by my questions. I want to ask her to hold my hand again because it's the one thing which brings me calm. But I know it will all come out wrong. Instead, I say, "Demetrius will use this."

"Only if he finds out," she says. The gentleness has returned to her voice.

We remain in silence for the rest of the night. I listen to her breath slowing to a perfect rhythm as sleep claims her. More than anything else, I want to reach out and find her hand. Instead, as I hear her relax, I feel the numbness give way in my arm. It starts as an ache. As if I'm a teenager, lying awake as my joints groan under the pressure of a rapidly expanding skeleton. The ache gives way to red-hot currents of pain. Instantaneous and random flashes across my arm. As I watch my room turn from black to deep grey, the arm feels as if my bone is a heating rod, causing the remaining flesh and blood to boil. When Lilith peeks her head through the curtain a few minutes later, I'm soaked in sweat.

It's been three days since entering the hospital. The torment has been so intense, I'm barely able to remember a life in which I wasn't bound to a bed while doctors mutilated my arm. The only other constants have been Fiona and Tori. I haven't been alone once.

"Today's the day, General," Lilith says. "How do you feel?"

The second they release the strap from my head, I look at my arm. It's covered in blood soaked bandages.

The pain is a part of me now. A dull ache highlighted by random flares of searing acid-fire. Tori stands just out of reach, watching as Lilith begins to snip away tiny strips of spongy gauze.

"The first time we tested this procedure, we had to keep stepping outside to vomit. It seemed so counterintuitive to inflict more damage in the hope of achieving a better recovery. If I hadn't run the tests myself, I would have called it off a dozen times," Lilith says. She whispers the words as if reciting an ancient and holy mantra. "Our first true test was a child who had wandered out too far from the beach and got caught under wave after pounding wave. Each one crushed her against the jagged reef. When they pulled her out of the water, I could barely tell they were carrying a human body." Her fingers are nimble, careful not to apply too much pressure, but lacking any tentative movement. "Imagine the pain you felt amplified over every centimeter of your body. We shredded and scraped for twenty-three straight hours. The girl's parents had to be taken off the island because her screams could be heard from shore to shore. But after it was all over, as we lifted the bandages from her, we knew the suffering had been worth it. Staring back at us was a gorgeous little girl, pink-skinned and scar-free." She's reached the final layer of bandages. The smell of sweat and sea and blood are almost more than I can handle. "I think of her every time I peel these strips from a patient. I think about how we live, so focused on keeping pain and suffering at bay and how, sometimes, it's the things we would run from if given the slightest opportunity which offer the greatest benefit. If we only had the courage to face the suffering."

My arm screams as she pulls off the final layer. For a moment, I fear she's gone too deep and has begun to tear the remaining skin from my mutilated arm.

"Calm, Trajan. We're almost there," Fiona says.

Seconds later, the pain eases. Everyone in the room stares at me. At my arm. Each with the same shocked look. I find Tori, who has moved to the side in order to inspect the result. He is paler than I've ever seen. I tell myself to look, but I'm seized with fear. All that pain. My years of single minded focus on my duties as a General. All of it comes to this. Lying on a glorified cot on a remote island with a room full of strangers staring at me. I'm the General of Celsus. I've always been the General of Celsus. But if I look down to see a mangled stump where my mighty arm should be, my very existence will change.

The room is silent. No breathing. No beeping monitors. We don't even hear the commotion from the rest of the hospital. I don't know how long we stay suspended between the present and the future, but with each passing second, the stakes seem to become more dire.

I hear a sob. It's the first noise since Lilith ripped the final bandage from my arm. Then another sob. Without looking, I know it's Fiona. And I know she's mourning the failed procedure. Tori steps around Lilith, his face still unreadable, then turns to embrace her. More sobs fill the room as Fiona's emotion jumps from one person to the next. Then a new sound. Laughter. Then sighs. I watch as physicians hug and shake hands.

Tori releases Lilith and turns to me. "This is a gift I did not think possible."

I finally look down, wondering if everyone has lost their mind, to see an arm. Pink skin. Healthy veins. Defined muscles. My arm. Perfect, scar free and healthy. Tenderly, I bend it, lifting my new hand to my face, half expecting it to remain limp and immobile. But it responds perfectly. As if the last few days have been nothing more than a drug-induced nightmare.

"How," I say, looking to Lilith.

"Honestly, I don't know. We've never attempted to heal something so badly damaged so quickly. And we've set a new record given how long it took us to initiate the procedure. If Fiona hadn't prepped your arm so perfectly, this would not have been possible." The tears in her eyes match mine.

"You're not out of the woods yet," Fiona says. "Everything below your elbow is brand new. It possesses the same amount of strength, but it will not be used to the strain. You'll find yourself tiring faster and the pain will be significant."

"There will be time for that later, princess. Let our patient enjoy this moment," Lilith says. She turns to her team and begins to usher them from the room.

Suddenly, it's just Tori, Fiona and me. Just as it's been. We're quiet as we examine my new appendage. Every few seconds, one of us shakes our head, or laughs. Too overcome to articulate anything other than awe.

Chapter 35

"You never received the spoils of your victory," William says as he enters my quarters.

We're back in the Aegean capital, only two days since my miraculous healing. I glance up from the wooden block to see him carrying a tray of thinly cut meat. It's got a pinkish hue, but the cut is so fine, it's almost transparent.

"Is that," I begin, but pause. Images of the truehunt flash through my mind. The perfect throw, the cloud of blood, the bite, the energy field, my arm, the pain, the healing. They churn into a whirlpool which turns my stomach.

"It is. You're a legend. One shot kill. Then the plunge. Then the recovery. Folks are starting to wonder if there's some sort of protection spell you cast over yourself every day. Whatever it is, this is delicious and well deserved." He picks up a slice of the raw meat and pops it into his mouth. It's all I can do not to vomit.

"If it won't offend you too much, I must respectfully decline," I say.

The block in my right hand grows heavy. Fiona was right. This new flesh tires quickly, which has Tori concerned for our return to Celsus. He's convinced Demetrius will notice the difference and demand an account. I'm determined not to let that happen. I've spent every possible moment focused on rebuilding the stamina I once possessed.

"I understand. If you don't mind, I'll continue to indulge. And, in case you change your mind, I'll be sure to leave a sizable cut for you on ice." He motions toward the block, "May I?"

I hand him the block, the muscles in my forearm burning from the strain.

"Very nice. You'll need a vice soon. As you cut more angles off, the need for complete immobility is paramount. The cross grain cuts look good, but your chisel is skipping a little too much. You'll need to sharpen it." He rotates the geometrical block as he speaks, holding it close to his eyes, then caressing it. "The feel of it is more important than the look. It looks pretty symmetrical, but I can feel a few plateaus that are lower than the rest. Doesn't seem like much now, but it'll wreak havoc if you don't fix it now."

"I'm less interested in perfection than the reciprocal benefits. Holding it with my new arm seems to be the best way to regain my strength," I say, motioning for it back. There has been an unease between us since the accident, as if we've both committed a crime and we're unsure the other knows.

"Trajan uninterested in perfection? Not likely."

"Sometimes pride must relent to necessity. Even a king will beg if hungry enough." Tori's words coming from my mouth.

"So you're hungry to remain General."

"If you were in danger of losing your position as Ruler, would you not fight for it?" I say. He's right, the block is lopsided.

"An impossible question to answer. A man can't presume to know what he may do in extraordinary situations until the situation is upon him. We're arrogant enough to think our best intentions would supersede our instincts." He grabs one of the larger chisels and begins to file the bevel. His movements are slow and articulate.

"Spoken truthfully. The insinuation, however, is that my animal instincts have taken over. That, if I were to rise above my circumstances, I would concede my position."

"Ours is an odd friendship. Wouldn't you agree? You laugh with us. Care for us. Are healed by us. Yet you prepare to usurp us. Have you witnessed any barbarism that necessitates removing my mother from the helm of this nation?" He continues to sharpen the chisel. I place the block on the workbench and rest my hand next to one of the smaller chisels.

"It is. I imagine it's my fault. Ambassadors don't usually immerse themselves as much as I have," I say. "I'm much more skilled at executing a strategy than justifying it."

"In previous years, you may have been able to hide behind the limited amount of information you were given. Played the loyal statesman. But with knowledge comes accountability. If you haven't seen reason for an attack on our nation, yet decide to follow through with the Battle, how are you any better than a power-hungry warlord?"

"There are only two people who have spoken to me this way. One is my king, the other my Mentor," I say. In spite of the awkwardness I felt earlier, I lock eyes with William and hold his gaze in the same way I measure an opponent before a fight.

"I mean no disrespect, but I'm at a loss. You've inspected my nation and found no wrong. You've helped people and seen our goodness. Do we really pose a risk to this world? To our citizens?"

There are many things I could say. I know I've only been shown the side of Aegea they want me to see. In reality, I've only known these people for a few weeks. Anyone could present a perfect front for that long. Every nation we've ever challenged has claimed the same, only to have the truth revealed once their Rulers were removed from power. But I know that would lead to an even more tense situation.

"You make the mistake of believing I am the only one with an agenda. What of Marcail's campaign against Demetrius. Or threats of truewar? And you've tested me," I say. "You know my weaknesses and strengths. I believe in the Battle. Our Ruling Ancestors set up a perfect system. We could debate for the rest of our lives. But the Battle is pure. It removes all of the politics and posturing and leaves two wills. When one faces death, or the potential of allowing a dictatorship to rule, it doesn't matter which General possesses the larger body or faster reflexes. The will overcomes everything else. When everything is stripped away, a man will give his last breath for something truly pure, but a man with the slightest doubt will hesitate."

William puts the chisel down, his head bowed so I can't see his expression. "That's a beautiful sentiment. I now see why you've won so decisively and consistently. People focus on the enormity of your body. The power of your strikes. But few realize it's the size of your faith which carries you. I can only pray your faith is placed in the correct entity."

We allow the silence to settle over us. It's my turn to inspect the block, feeling the unevenness of it. Disturbed by how different it feels from how it looks. "Can it be reversed? Seems like it would be easier to start over, rather than try to restore balance. I fear I'd just cut too deeply, or spend the rest of my time adjusting to its imperfections."

William takes the block from me again. "It'll always be imperfect. If you started over, you'd just make another, different mistake. Stay the course. It'll get messy. It'll even feel like you're doing more harm than good, but eventually, all the jagged edges will get knocked off and you'll finally be able to shape its core. You're still just clearing away the distractions." He hands it back to me smiles. "That was a lot more intense than I expected. I was just planning on eating some shark with you."

Chapter 36

I plug the last cable into the projector and wait for the uplink. Demetrius requested my audience just after William left, and this time I'm prepared early. I stand directly in front of the sensor, head bowed, hands behind my back.

Light flickers throughout the room as the projector casts a perfect version of my Ruler. It's as if he's made the long journey to see me in person.

"Celsus is not whole without her lion prowling her borders, General," Demetrius says. There is no pageantry in his tone. Nor is there warmth. "We approach the end of your tour. And with it, we prepare to welcome a new flock of Celceans. Do you know what I hate about tyrannical Rulers?" He pauses, waiting for my response.

"One would imagine, Highness, the hatred could not be summed up in one thought," I say.

"Wisely spoken, my son," he says. "And yet, there is one thing. One terrible by-product of prolonged cruelty which is so sinister, it causes the weak to fight for the very cruelty which presses its heel against their neck." The projector is so clear, I can no longer see the subtle curves of the Aegean room in which I stand. Even the sea air seems to desiccate. "When a person is abused for long enough, their brains rewire and they begin to crave the very thing they hate. We see this with children who are abused by their parents. When they have children, they find themselves hurting their offspring in the same fashion as when they were young. Only now, when they finally have the power to break the cycle, they look at their behavior and call it love.

"And, as this happens, generation after broken generation, each progeny will swear all the more vehemently to their happiness and safety. I fear Aegea is a nation of beaten and deceived children."

He pauses, allowing his words to settle, waiting for me to affirm his assertion. I make quick fists with my right hand, feeling the new muscle flex beneath the new flesh. This feels like the opposite side of the conversation I just had with William. Two leaders vying for the agreement of one man. Generals shouldn't be put in this position. It's too easy to confuse and distract with words and half-truths.

The behavior makes sense coming from William. Try to win the Battle before it's even started by inflicting a wound by way of doubt. But Demetrius is my Ruler. There is no reason for him to convince me. The people he has set free, through me, live without fear of oppression or cruelty for the first time in decades.

"I am grateful to have a Ruler who sees the shadows within the shadows. I fear my eyes have no such filter."

"If only every citizen held your faith. You trust the system of governance the Ruling Elders gave. There is no variation. But Marcail's rhetoric continues to eat away at our foundations. Her cancerous words have even taken root within our very borders." His shoulders are slumped and his head lowered, revealing a small circle of thinning hair. I turn away from the projection, feeling, for the first time, as if Demetrius is nothing more than an aging man, coming to terms with his own limitations.

"This Battle, if left alone, has the potential of unraveling the tenuous peace our Ruling Ancestors brought us, my son. And I fear there is no good way through it."

My chest begins to burn with tension. This whole conversation feels wrong. As if I'm in the body of one of his advisors, rather than his General. The silence grows awkward as he waits for a response I do not have. My words come out slowly, as if twisting and rolling my tongue for the first time. "I have always trusted you, Father. Even the recent times when I appeared in opposition to you were nothing more than benign rebellions from an immature child. Please understand my heart has never wavered from your wise leadership. When I say my next sentence, I pray do not lose sight of that." I pause, imagining our world devolving back into darkness and brutality. "If what you say is true, might it be prudent to back away from our challenge to Aegea? Even if Marcail holds her citizens under a knife, isn't it better to have one nation of oppressed people than a world once again in chaos?"

He shifts his weight a few times and takes a deep breath. "Would that I could see the world through your eyes. It's the warrior in you. No middle ground. Life or death. But the arena of public opinion is not so simple."

I'm thrown briefly off balance as the ground beneath me lurches and I'm forced to stumble a few steps. I'm about to ask Demetrius if he's alright before I realize I'm still in Aegea and he's in Celsus. What I thought was an earthquake was just a larger than normal wave. I'm likely the only person on this man-made island to even notice.

"But let's consider your counsel, for a moment. If I were to relent, there are three possible outcomes. The first would tell other oppressive Rulers that all they need to do in order to keep harming their citizenry without fear of retribution is to mount a publicity campaign as soon as they are challenged in Battle. Marcail has done this beautifully. A second outcome would be to make me, and Celsus, appear to lack the courage to follow through in spite of opposition. Which would make us appear weak willed and vulnerable to an attack outside of the rules which govern our world. Or, thirdly, it would insinuate that my original challenge was done out of impure motives and I relented only because I was found out by more discerning leaders." He sighs and shakes his head. "No, to turn around now would mean the end for our noble nation."

He's right, of course. I've seen the evidence of a jealous world even on this short trip, and my guides were likely hand-picked to be on their best behavior.

"Even still, if we stay the course, we will be accused of tyranny. And I'm not being overly conspiratorial. Just this morning I received communications from no fewer than five Rulers who have vowed to break the rules if we insist on conquering Aegea. They are preparing makeshift militaries to physically oppose us at Aegea's border." The specter of Demetrius looks directly at me. Either the projector is catching a particle of dust in the air, or there is a tear streaking down his cheek, "For the first time in generations, we are on the brink of war."

The fear I feel is deeper than anything I've ever experienced. Compared to this, pre-Battle prep is nothing more than stretching before a long run. An urge to distance myself completely from anything associated with this begins to creep up. I'm prey, backed into a corner, willing to do anything to get away. Like a coward, I'm about to tell him about my slowly healing arm. Hang the mantle of the Peace-Shattering General on Castor. He's stupid and arrogant enough to accept it in spite of the consequences. I hold the soft flesh up and inhale, ready to absolve myself completely, when Demetrius speaks again.

"But the Crowd, Dear Trajan, is a fickle thing. Yes, they hate me. They see me as a scheming, power hungry tyrant. But you. You have won them over with your valor in the Temple. You have won while sitting at death's door and you have won by showing mercy when none was warranted. They look at you and see what they wish to be. They hear your words as if they are thoughts in their own minds." He wipes a tear from his face. "Which is why we must stay the course. And you must lead the way. It is time for you to be more than a General in the Temple. You must be a General and the Crowd must be your army."

I know I should be connecting the dots between his words and his meaning, but I'm not. All I know is, if I can somehow have a hand in stopping our world from degrading into murder and citizen against citizen violence, I will do it.

"Convey your appreciation to Marcail and your hosts. Begin your preparations. I will send for you in two days. My eyes ache to see you in the flesh, my son." His image fades to black with his last words and I stand in the darkness, feeling the ground beneath me rise and fall in an uneven and unpredictable rhythm. As hard as I try, I can't predict the next wave.

Chapter 37

The queen seems to have aged since I last saw her. And yet, she remains as beautiful and elegant as ever. Tori and I are seated with her and two of her counselors while young servants shuttle food and drink in front of us. The plates are ornately arranged, but I may as well be eating wood. All I can think about is my audience with Demetrius.

"Fiona and William apologize for not attending. Please don't hold it against them. I asked them to tend another matter of state this evening," Marcail says while handing me a platter of steamed rice, seasoned with ground cumin. "When I was alerted of your coming departure, I realized I couldn't keep you from our delegates anymore." There is a playful glint in her eye, as if I'm supposed to be sharing an inside joke, but it's all I can do to nod my thanks for the dish.

"We are honored your counselors are able to dine with us," Tori says, "from what we've seen of Aegea, it appears you choose your inner circle well, my queen."

The two politicians at the table couldn't be more different. To my right sits Francis, the elder statesman of Aegea. His hair is grey and closely shaved, making it appear as if he's dusted his head with metallic shavings. Across from me is Laurel, a young woman with sharp features and hair pulled into a tight bun. Francis smiles and comments on every dish as it passes him by, as if this is his first formal meal. Laurel is stoic, smiling only with her mouth and refuses to eat anything other than boiled seaweed.

"Our queen makes our job unbearably easy. What I wouldn't give for something interesting to happen. Instead, our citizens run around helping each other and refusing payment. It's like living with a bunch of priests," says Francis.

"You may get your wish, sooner than you know," says Laurel. She looks at me with the cold eyes of a statue as she speaks.

"You should try visiting one of your hunting colonies in a storm, father," I say. "We certainly had an interesting time."

Marcail scoops a delicate portion of fried squid onto her plate, "Yes. If I had you here longer, I'd like to find out just how interesting. William and Fiona refuse to tell me anything about it."

I finally find my tongue, feeling it warm as I sip on my second glass of wine, "Far be it for me to interfere in the affairs of a royal family."

"And yet, you're perfectly willing to interfere in the affairs of an entire nation," says Laurel.

Marcail pauses her fork halfway to her mouth before over-gently setting it down, "These are my guests, Counselor. As are you. Please don't make me rethink my invitation."

"General, I am an old man and I fear my days are numbered," Francis says. "Aegea has been my home my entire life. In as much, I have never set foot beyond our borders. Would you allow me to see with new eyes by describing my nation?"

Francis seems more like a retired businessman than a counselor to a queen. "If only they had sent a more eloquent person. My simple observations and limited vocabulary may indeed leave you wanting, Elder," I say. Countless experiences and scenes run through my mind. "And yet, I've experienced so much in my short trip, if I took all bridles off my tongue, I fear I could usurp the rest of the evening."

All but Laurel laugh. "You flatter us," Marcail says. A quiet settles on the table as we slowly eat. What I wouldn't give to have Fiona and William here, breaking the tension with their banter.

After a few seconds, I say, "Your will. If I had to focus on one thing about Aegea, it would be the will of the people. You have figured out how to live in an environment that is not only barren, but hostile to humankind. And instead of bending the environment to suit your needs, you have chosen instead to partner with it. Find a way to benefit from the most inhospitable aspects of it. Remarkable."

Francis puts his utensils down and chews slowly on the last bit of food in his mouth. "I've never thought of it that way. What do you mean by, bending the environment to our will?"

I pause, looking to Tori for any sign that I'm wandering into a trap. But either he sees none, or his mind is elsewhere, so I press on – confident in my observations and comforted by the kindness of Francis. "There is a small city in Celsus. It is one of our main sources of certain minerals and metals that help sustain our industry. It's located far from our capital, on the southern coast. What's unique about this place is that it's right on the water's edge, yet below the sea level. In fact, the land on which the city sits used to be on the seafloor. When we discovered how rich the deposits were, we immediately set out to push the ocean itself back. And we did. We grew our land mass by forcing the waves into submission. But it comes at a price. The people who live there are in a constant war with nature. The sea, it seems, wants to reclaim what belongs to it. Every storm brings leaks in our levies, and the deeper we dig, the more the waters look to burrow under our walls." I pause to take another sip of wine and I notice that the entire table, even Laurel, is captivated. "Try as I might, I can't see Aegea making the same decision as Celsus. You would likely still find a way to the deposits, but I'm willing to bet it wouldn't be by opposing the sea itself."

"You give yourself too little credit, General," Marcail says. "You have summed our two nations perfectly."

Laurel clears her throat and looks at Marcail, "Forgive me, Highness, but I did not come here to indulge the very person who will, in just a few days' time, put his life on the line in order to take away everything we have worked so hard to accomplish." She turns to me, "If you truly are so in awe of us, then how can you justify going through with the Battle? Is Demetrius so terrible that even the mighty Trajan is too frightened to oppose him? Tell me, in the weeks you have spent with us, have you seen one starving person? One injustice? One questionable act of government?" Her voice fades toward the end of each sentence–if I were in the Temple with her, this would tell me she's suffering from an instantaneous dose of adrenaline and her lungs are struggling to keep up with the demand to oxygenate her faster flowing blood. "Or are you so complacent in your duties that Battle is a foregone conclusion? Was this entire visit simply Celsus going through the motions to fulfill the Ancestors' Law? Invasion, regardless if caused by an army or by the dominance of one man, is still invasion."

I have stopped eating and the slight wine induced blurriness of my vision is completely gone. Laurel and I have not broken eye contact since she started speaking, neither of us willing to feign weakness. This must be the same rhetoric Demetrius was referring to earlier. There is truth to her words. Any such narrative has truth. But there was an equal amount of truth to what Demetrius said. What must be inspected is the lens through which the information flows. The decision I must make, sooner rather than later, is which lens reflects the correct angle of truth. I finally break eye contact with Laurel, ready with my rebuttal when Marcail speaks.

"You have spoken your peace. In direct opposition to my wishes and directives. Now you are excused, Laurel. Both from my table and from my counsel." Her tone is flat and her stare is that of a person on the edge of violence.

Laurel takes a breath to speak again.

"If you value your comfort, Lady, you will restrain yourself and do as I say," Marcail says.

Francis places his hands on the table, "I think I will take my leave as well. Come, Laurel," he offers his hand to the now pale woman beside him, "allow me to escort you home."

We are silent while Francis and Laurel collect themselves to leave. There is no formality to their leaving. We remain seated and they scurry away without parting comment or acknowledgement.

As soon as they are out of the room, Marcail says, "I knew that was likely to happen, but I hoped better."

"We appreciate your desire to protect us from your politicians, Queen," Tori says, "but I pray the difficulty of our presence does not undo any trust you have for your advisors."

"There are times when ideals must be set aside for the sake of relationship. If my advisors can't control themselves enough to understand that simple truth, then I must find their counsel in all other areas flawed."

"Tell me, Highness," I say, "do you agree with Laurel?" I feel my heart rate increase slightly as I ask the question. This is likely my last conference with the queen and it seems as if so much is still unsaid.

"No leader, regardless of political structure, wants their ability questioned. However, I find myself in the odd predicament of having your Ruler doing just that. Which has caused me to indulge in quite a bit of reflection. If I were to find no fault in my governance, I would need to remove myself based on hubris alone. And if I were to find too much flaw, it would reveal a lack of confidence not suited to rule. The same goes for someone asked to audit my nation from the outside. Which is what you have been asked to do. You have seen but a fraction of my kingdom, and still you're asked to go back to your leader and give him justification for a course that cannot be altered. It seems, given the situation, you and I have both been placed on a train and are being asked to stop it by placing a twig in its path."

In consecutive conversations, two Rulers have confessed their utter helplessness. If our Ruling Ancestors really did set up such a perfect system, I fail to understand how this could be true.

"Is that it, then?" I ask. "We find ourselves in an impossible and unfixable situation?"

"It depends. There are myriad fixes and outcomes. But I don't see a fix, nor an outcome, that gives all parties the resolution they want. Such is the way of life, sadly." She reaches across the table and places her hand over mine. The palm of her hand sizzles, while her fingertips are ice. "What is worse is that Demetrius and I are reliant on you. You have the public. Because we are Rulers, and are naturally at odds with our subjects, we will never be as loved as you. Which is why he sent you. Your words and your actions will decide all of this. I'm sorry, child, but that is the ugly truth set forth by our Ancestors. Ultimately, we Rulers are at the mercy of our Generals."

I look to Tori, who was both a General and a Ruler, for his reaction. "My father was not unaware of this when he made me his General."

These words are so different than what Demetrius said, but I now realize the meaning is the same. This whole trip has been one giant campaign to win me over. The tactics have been polar opposites, but the strategy has been identical.

Chapter 38

We arrive back in Celsus without fanfare. It's the middle of the night when our drone lands. There are no bags to unpack, nor souvenirs to show off. Just Tori and me, bleary eyed and cold. A lone sentry greets us with a salute, then hands a note to Tori before returning to his post.

"It's less than a month to the Battle, so Demetrius has placed us in adjacent quarters," he says, then folds the paper in half. His voice echoes off the flat cement surfaces around us. I stand still for a moment, looking at the cloud covered sky above me, waiting for the gentle rocking I've become so accustomed to. The stillness of the air and the ground beneath me is jarring.

Our quarters are less than a kilometer from the landing strip. We cross the distance quickly and silently. My mind is still in Aegea, upset to have missed saying goodbye to the princess. Even more concerned about the task before me.

My room is like every room I've ever had in Celsus. A cot and desk are the only furniture. The only break in the cement walls is the door. A low ceiling adds to the stark message. I'm meant to sleep here. The rest of my time is dedicated to training and education.

"We were in Aegea for less than a month, yet it feels as if this is the foreign land," Tori says from the doorway. In the darkness, he looks older than I've ever seen him. This trip has taken its toll on us both. Being moved into adjacent quarters highlights the fact that Demetrius expects us to already be Battle ready. Single minded and well-tuned. Most of my life, I have been able to read Tori's thoughts without hesitation. But looking at him now, I realize we have barely spoken or trained since my injury.

"Moto-san," I say, "are we ready?"

His shoulders sag and he leans on the frame of the door. "If you have to ask, then I suspect you have your answer." He straightens and steps into my room. "Our task this time is different. And I find myself unable to equip you for what Demetrius expects for two reasons. I've never trained a politician. And I lack motivation to see you be successful."

It's as if he has stabbed me in the chest. I step back from him, trying to see him better through the darkness.

"Don't mistake me. If asked, I would cut out my heart and place it in your chest."

"How can you say you desire my failure in one breath, then tell me you'd die for me? I've already heard doublespeak from two Rulers, I don't need it from my Mentor as well."

Our voices are mere hisses, slithering through the inky blackness.

"But your success or failure is not in the power of your body this time. It's in the strength of your words. The queen was right. Your words and yours alone hold the outcome. The Battle is a formality with you. You're unbeatable. Which means Demetrius is unbeatable once the Battle begins. His only vulnerability is outside of the Temple. But if he convinces you to wage war on the opinion of the masses with your rhetoric, then you're not fighting one single opponent. It's the same as if you led an army of men against the world."

"And what would you have me do? Deny the man who has built the greatest nation this world has known? Commit treason because we were wooed by a charming woman? Throw a lifetime away because of one month's delight?"

I'm angry and scared and confused. This feels like more than a mere argument. This feels like the tearing of flesh from bone. Tori has been my father. Demetrius my lord. Until this moment, following one meant following the other.

"When he asks you for evidence of Marcail's tyranny, what will you give him? When he stands in the Temple and levels his final accusation against Aegea, will you be able to, with a truly clear conscious, agree? What country did you see while I was sleeping?"

"Why do this now, Father? We are not men who manipulate nations as if they're pieces on a game board. We have trusted our leader without question. Battle after bloody Battle. Why stop now? Do we stop believing in gravity when a magician takes the stage and makes a man float?"

We're silent. Standing in darkness. My mind races with too many thoughts. Too many opinions and manipulations.

"I will question Demetrius. Aegea was peaceful. They healed the very man that seeks to conquer them. But they're also a cornered animal. In the last month, I have experienced more politics and lies than in all of my years combined. But know this, Moto-san. I can't lose you. I can't fight, I can't walk, I can't breathe, if you're not by my side. You are my foundation. Without you, my decision does not matter." Tears stream down my face and my voice quivers in ways I didn't know possible.

He places his hand on my shoulder and allows me my weakness. There are no other words between us tonight. We both know we've said more than we should have. After a minute, when he feels my sobs ease, he removes his hand and leaves.

Chapter 39

At some point in the night, Tori left my incomplete block of wood in my doorway. When the lights of my room flickered on, in sequence with dawn, I grabbed the block and the knife next to it, and began carving. What was once a cube is now a nubby, lopsided sphere. If Fiona were here, she would likely laugh in a way that would both humiliate and energize me. The only course I can see is to continue chipping away in the hopes of slowly correcting the miscalculation.

The young muscles of my arm feel good. They still tire faster than I'm used to, but the discrepancy is much smaller than even a few days ago. In spite of all the advanced therapy techniques, I honestly think tinkering with this block has been the most effective.

"I had forgotten just how imposing a figure you are, General." Demetrius stands in my door, arms spread and smiling. He is wearing a golden robe with black trim. When he looks past me, to my wood chip covered desk, he begins laughing. "I see you have picked up some primitive pass times while away."

I stand, then kneel and take the hand he offers me. "Thank you for greeting me this morning, Highness."

"Stand my son and allow me to look upon you," he says as he removes his hand from mine. "At least their meager diet has not caused you to wither away. Tori has served you well. Remind me to commend him. Come, let us dine. My chefs have prepared the perfect welcome breakfast for my Lion."

The sun is still low in the sky, but the intensity of it causes me to pause as we step outside. There is no breeze and the air is crisp, not yet warm enough to cut through the frost which blankets the ground.

"This is a fortunate day. You have brought the first frost of the year. I trust the omen is a good one," Demetrius says.

We pass three different groups of young Hopefuls, running in tight cadence.

"We must have been gone longer than I thought," I say, "I scarcely recognize these trainees."

"Much has changed since you were away. The rhetoric of the nations who oppose me has forced me to recruit more. It saddens my heart, but the threats are so dire that we have begun training our Hopefuls not only to fight in the Temple, but as a unit to protect our citizens."

I stop walking. "Sire, you're training an army?" These are words I never dreamt I would say.

"Would you have us remain asleep while a tiger roams our borders? Our world is on the brink. And while I have no intention of leading it over the edge, I will do everything in my power to pull it back on solid footing. Even if that means shedding more than your blood."

"I had no idea. Forgive me, but I thought these threats were likely just rumblings from jealous leaders." We begin walking as yet another group of Hopefuls run by. I think of Castor and the role he may be playing in the training of these men.

"We can pray I'm overreacting. If I am, then we can send these lads back to their families. And I hope you will have a hand in that happy ending. But the day is too young to dwell on rumors of war." We arrive at his dining hall and as the doors are opened for us, I see a table full of fruits, nuts, meats, breads, sweet wines and pastries. "I will allow you this one indulgence, but then it's back to sculpting your body for Battle."

Demetrius eats with a voracity I had forgotten. For my part, I choose some freshly cut tomatoes, a slice of walnut bread, six hard boiled eggs and water with lime slices. The bread is my indulgence.

"How you remain so large is a mystery to me," Demetrius says in between mouthfuls.

"If you wouldn't mind, Highness, I haven't heard anything about Castor in quite some time." The question has been nagging me since Tori and I boarded the drone. I'm not scared of him, but I want as much knowledge about him as possible before we're in the same room.

"Yes. An ugly business that was. The Battle was exciting, but I wonder if it wasn't the weakness our opponents needed to start these threats. As for Castor, it appears it took his near death to humble him. He has embraced his new position as Corps General with a dedication and seriousness I wasn't aware he possessed."

"Corps General?" I ask, even though I know the answer. I've studied all of the great militaries and their leaders for years.

"These new recruits aren't training themselves. Castor has graciously altered his path as your successor in order to select recruits and govern their transition from citizen to Guardian. I must say, he has surpassed my greatest expectations. He is planning a demonstration for you later in the day. I'm eager to see your reaction."

I'm stunned beyond response. It's one thing to have a standing army. It's another, much more dangerous, thing to have that army built by one as power hungry as Castor.

"Enough of these questions. You were sent as my delegate. Time for your report. What have you learned as the Aegeans?"

I swallow the last bite of food from my plate. "First, Lord, please allow me to express my gratitude for you choosing me as your emissary to Aegea. In my travels, I have collected the finest examples of the people and their culture that you will be welcoming into your kingdom," I say, channeling the pageantry of the previous delegates I have heard. I'm about to continue with my rehearsed monologue when he interrupts.

"I sent a General. Not a sniveling aristocrat. Stop pretending to be one and tell me what you saw. The world waits our final verdict, child."

"Very well. There are three things I have learned of the Aegeans," I begin. While I was carving this morning, I decided to describe my experience to Demetrius with as much accuracy as I can muster. Then wait to see his reaction. Marcail's words continue to ring in my ears. If Demetrius is the Ruler I think he is, my report will force him to take more time to decide on the right course. Possibly reexamine the sources that accused Aegea of such horrible actions. "First, they are much more advanced than I was aware. Second, they work in harmony with their surroundings in a way I have never witnessed before. And third, Marcail is both a gracious and fierce Ruler."

Demetrius takes a long drink from his gold rimmed cup, then pushes his plate away. "You have my attention."

"Their existence relies on very understated, yet powerful, technology. Most of it seems to be a combination of organics and mechanics, using the ocean and its inhabitants as inspiration. They use this methodology for lighting, healing, protection of both themselves and their crops, and various other necessities. I have not only witnessed these technologies, I have experienced them firsthand." I speak as if reading from a prompt, trying not to give additional weight to any one thing.

"Tell me of this protection. There are murmurs from those who have fled Aegea, but nothing specific," he says. In his hand is a small recording device. My every word and movement are being captured so he can review and present it whenever he sees fit.

I pause, feeling as if I'm somehow betraying Marcail and Fiona. The hesitation angers me. I was shown nothing in confidence, but because of the way they treated me, I was made to feel like an insider, and Demetrius was painted as a tyrant.

He sits forward in his chair. "Son, I know you were given a nearly impossible task. I know how persuasive Marcail and her court can be." He disengages the recording device and stands. "Come, let me introduce you to someone."

We leave the dining hall and cross through his personal gardens. They are vibrant with perfectly trimmed hedges, flowers, herbs and trees. Our pathway follows a winding creek, just shallow enough to bubble over silk smooth rocks. We're both silent as we cross through. There was a time when this was one of the most serene places I could imagine. Now, with the Battle and truewar looming, all I can see is how artificial and perfectly controlled it all looks.

He leads me to a small door, stashed behind a side garden, full of purple and yellow carnations.

"Before we enter, all I ask is that you listen with an open heart, question with prudence and allow your intuition to respond." He slides a key in the lock and turns it until he hears a gentle click.

The entryway is bright. While it appeared there were no windows, I now see that the entire wall on the garden side is a one way mirror. We climb a small flight of stairs and emerge into a small room, overlooking the entire garden. The view is immediately calming.

There's a rustling behind one of the white walls, then a man appears. At first, he appears to be bending over, as if to pick something up, but when he sees us, he doesn't stand. I quickly realize that he's horribly deformed. From the looks of it, one of his legs is much shorter than the other, and his left arm looks to be fused with his ribcage. The left side of his face has been badly burned at some point and his eye socket is vacant.

"Your Highness," he says through slurred lips while he attempts a bow.

Demetrius hurries over to him, "I've told you, there is no need to bow, my friend. It is I who should be bowing to you." Demetrius takes the deformed hand of the man and leads him to one of the cushions in the middle of the room.

"It is my pleasure to present to you my General, The Lion of Celsus and Liberator of the Oppressed, Trajan." He turns to me, "General, I am humbled to present to you Caleb, Aegean scientist, exiled and left for dead for crossing Marcail." He turns to Caleb and smiles, "But don't take my word for it. I'll allow Caleb to tell his own story."

I've never seen Demetrius act with such gentleness or deference toward someone, which causes me to channel Tori and address him with the highest formality. I drop to one knee and bow my head, "My lord, I am your servant."

"Nonsense," he says. "I'm no man of court, I'm a man of science." His speech is difficult to understand and every time he pronounces an S a small amount of saliva leaks from the side of his mouth. "Demetrius tells me you have just returned from Aegea."

I nod and take a seat across from Caleb once Demetrius has settled in.

"In spite of myself, I still miss the ocean. Once it's in your blood, the draw is overwhelming."

"I can understand. I was there but a short time and I'm continually reminded of the beauty."

He nods and wipes his sleeve across his chin. "It must be fitting. Only a place with so much beauty could hide such horror." Through the slurs, I can hear the anger.

"Our guest has just returned, and I'm afraid he's still a bit enamored with the pageant which Marcail arranged for him," Demetrius says. "I'm not accusing you, General. Before I met this brave man, I held Marcail and Aegea in the highest regard. I can only assume the spell she cast over you while you were there."

Caleb shakes his head. "In nature, the most dangerous animals are the ones who draw their prey to them with their beauty. Marcail is proof that we are no better."

"Teacher," I say, "I'm afraid you have met me at a time when my mind is more muddled than ever. If you can help clear my vision, I ask you to delay no longer."

Caleb does his best impression of a smile, but his deformity makes it looks as if he's snarling at me. "In due time, General. But first, is your king aware of the injury you sustained?"

It feels as if my lungs have collapsed. Since arriving, I'd determined to tell Demetrius what happened, but it was going to be at a time of my choosing. Now it appears I have been keeping something from him. "He does not," I say.

Demetrius looks saddened. "May you live five lifetimes and never feel the betrayal of a child," he says to me. "No matter. We are here to speak as men should. Truthfully, logically and unblinkingly. Let's not weaken our resolve with emotions."

To Caleb, I say, "Impressive trick. I assume you're proving a point?"

"I spent the majority of my adult life perfecting the salve which repaired your tissues. One of the ingredients, a composite of octopus blood and a rare seaweed, gives off a subtle yet unmistakable odor. Apparently your wound is fresh enough for it to seep from your pores."

To Demetrius, I say, "Father, you would have learned of this from my mouth, I assure you."

He waves his hand across his face and nods toward Caleb.

"Give me your hand, child. I want to see the healing progress."

I reach across the room, pulling back the sleeve of my shirt. The skin of my forearm looks suddenly pink and childish. Caleb takes my hand and pulls me close. While he inspects my new flesh, I'm overwhelmed by how mangled this man is. This close, I can see that his hair is falling out, and the scalp beneath the thinning hair is cracked and flaking. His breathing is labored and his hands shake as they twist and bend my arm.

After what feels like hours, he releases me and settles back in his seat. "They're getting better. From what I can tell, you almost lost the arm. But it looks as if they've strengthened the salve. Tell me, how did they prep your arm before applying the bandages?" he says through quickened breath.

I quickly tell them of my time on the island hospital. How they reopened the wounds and deepened the lacerations, then applied the salve, then repeated it over and over, all without any pain blocker.

"They finally read my notes, apparently," Caleb says. "Although, I would

275

have given you something for the pain. Sounds like Lilith oversaw your treatment. She never takes the edge off. Sadist," he spits.

His knowledge of the inner workings of Aegea is impressive, which makes his appearance and his presence here even more confusing. "With respect, Teacher," I say, "you have proven your knowledge of Aegea. The mystery I can't solve is how we come to have you as our guest."

Both Demetrius and Caleb laugh. "He makes it sound like I'm on a happy vacation, doesn't he?" Caleb says.

Demetrius regains his composure, "Forgive us, my son. Caleb was Aegea's chief scientist until two years ago. Marcail's husband had passed away a few years prior and Marcail was struggling to maintain control over the politicians and influential citizens who sought to create an opportunity out of her husband's death." He pauses and looks to Caleb, "Forgive me. Would you like to tell this to Trajan?"

Caleb shakes his head, "I lived it. That was enough for me."

"Very well," he turns to me. "I've lived through so many details of Caleb's life, at times it feels as if I'm telling my story when remembering his." He looks down for a few beats, then continues, "losing a Ruler can throw a nation into chaos. Especially if the next in line is perceived as weak. And Marcail was seen to be exceedingly vulnerable. Her whole life she had been the elegant hostess of a gracious king. If she was to maintain control, she would need to eradicate that reputation.

"She began by removing the most vocal counselors from her circle. Then she focused on finishing the work her husband had started by making trade alliances with their neighbors. But the final treaty was skewed in favor of the other nation and the public outcry was louder than ever. She was on the brink of a coup."

Caleb stands and begins pacing slowly around the room. "She needed a distraction. An enemy her nation could rally against. Someone she could defeat easily and in so doing, win trust back from the public. She may be an incompetent Ruler, but she's a masterful politician." He begins coughing, which doubles him over even more.

Chapter 40

Demetrius stands. "We've stayed too long. And our conversation has caused Caleb too much pain."

Caleb tries to say something, but his breath is too weak and the hacking is too powerful. A group of four physicians come running up the stairs and begin tending to him without even acknowledging Demetrius.

He leads me back through the garden, across the courtyard which leads to the Celcean Parliament and Hall of Justice. My mind is racing. Concerned for Caleb's health. Anxious to hear how Marcail's rise to power impacted one of Aegea's scientists. How, I wonder, will all of these puzzle pieces finally fit into place?

We end our silence as we sit at the top of our Royal Amphitheatre. Usually the venue for political debate or royal speeches, I'm stunned to see an army below me, running through drills, marching in formation and sparring.

"My anxiety got the better of me," Demetrius says. "I forget that Caleb's mind is much stronger than his body. I'm glad you met him and I'm glad you were convinced of his authority. I just hope, in convincing you, he wasn't taxed beyond recovery."

"Has he always been so deformed?" I ask, trying to focus on Caleb, rather than the army in front of me.

"Caleb possesses the greatest mind Aegea has even known. Maybe in the world. But his body was always weak." Demetrius says. He looks down at the parading troops, casually inspecting their uniformity, "He will tell you it was his propensity toward sickness which propelled him to focus his intellect on medicine. He made breakthrough after breakthrough. First medically, then it grew into much of the technology you witnessed. But he was also prideful. He would push the boundaries too far. Performing experiments which pushed the ethical boundaries. And Marcail's husband sheltered him from scrutiny because of the benefit.

"He had been working on an integration point for the energy field you saw. A human integration point. Using the body's energy to power the field into a flexible, impenetrable suit of armor. They claimed it was to keep people safe when working in the water and using dangerous and heavy harvest machinery on unstable floating platforms. I have my doubts. When Marcail was about to be overthrown, she called an audience with Caleb and told him to speed his research. No matter the cost.

"He had worked through the math behind the latest iteration, but he warned her that he would need to test the theory on live subjects. This is where his pride got the better of him and Marcail was able to draw him into her web. She told him to proceed. And promised her support and protection." Demetrius turns back to me and I see tears in his eyes.

"He picked a small farming colony to test. The implants were placed on everyone. Adults, children, women and men. He had one placed on himself in a show of confidence. Catastrophe. When the implants were activated, the energy fields flared to life. But they were unstable. Melted flesh, severed appendages. Every nightmarish scene you can imagine sprang forth on that small colony. Caleb was the only survivor, but at the cost of the deformation you see today.

"Marcail captured the entire experiment on video and immediately broadcasted it to her nation. She had found her enemy to defeat. And she played the role perfectly. Caleb was put on trial and portrayed as a megalomaniac, obsessed with his own intellect. She tearfully renounced him and, in so doing, won the favor of her people."

As hard as I try, no words come. The thought of Marcail composing the slaughter of her own people, just to distract the rest of the population from her shortcomings, seems impossible. If she was capable of that, and simultaneously capable of the elegant and honorable attitude she showed me, she was more dangerous than I ever considered.

"The trial was fast. Presided over by Marcail herself. He was found guilty of subversion and purposeful manipulation resulting in the death of men, women and children. Because she had video of the massacre, Caleb was denied the ability to defend himself."

Demetrius raises his recording device and presses a series of buttons, turning it into a projector. In front of us, an Aegean courtroom appears. Caleb sits, covered in bandages except for his charred face, giving him an even more devilish look. The prosecutor stands, "The evidence is in front of you, my lady. I pray thee, what verdict do you return?"

The camera slowly pans across the room, full of delegates and politicians until it finally rests on Marcail. Draped in a flowing black gown and sheer veil. Even from behind the fabric, I can see tears flowing down her cheeks.

"Sir Caleb. You have served my late husband and this nation dutifully for decades. Many of the luxuries we enjoy today are the fruit of your unparalleled mind. The king loved and nurtured you. Perhaps too much. We now see the evidence that your hubris is even more unrestrained than your intellect. For you to willingly and secretly coax an innocent group of farmers to comply with your ill-fated tests is inexcusable. The evidence of your desire to hide your actions is clear from the marginalized colony you chose, and the fact that you brought no scientific or political oversight. These actions, along with the undeniable proof that your actions, and yours alone, led to the death of an entire colony in the most inhumane and tortuous scenario possible, leave me no choice but to find you guilty of premeditated and brutal murder."

While her tears continue to flow, her voice is strong and unwavering.

"In light of this verdict, Highness, what is the sentence imparted on the convicted?" asks the prosecutor.

"Because you showed no mercy or regard toward the lives of the perished innocents, I will neither grant you quarter. You are to be immediately set adrift in a raft, void of navigation technology or steering ability. Let the ocean inflict upon you even a fraction of the suffering which you inflicted upon your victims before She claims you."

There are shouts of agreement along with gasps at the severity of the punishment. Not just death. But torture, then death. In just a few sentences, Marcail was able to go from an overly soft imposter to a harsh and dangerous Ruler. She wasn't only sentencing Caleb, she was giving her opponents a preview of their fate if they continued to cross her.

Demetrius switches off the projector. "There is footage of him being taken away, but I have grown too fond of Caleb to watch his humiliation.

"He drifted for three weeks. I'll never know how he stayed alive. Dealing with his injuries while still figuring out how to distill water and catch fish. When we finally found him, he was delirious and at death's door. Our physicians spent months trying to coax him back." He's looking at the army beneath us, speaking as if telling a fairy tale. "That was three years ago. Since then, I have been inserting informants into Aegea. Their reports became more and more concerning. Marcail, it seems, continued Caleb's work on the energy field, as well as some other troubling experiments. And then, one year ago, the reports stopped coming. Marcail found our agents and had them killed."

"It's as if you're speaking about a completely separate person. She showed patience and understanding and harmony with her nation. If only you would have sent someone more used to the treachery of politics," I say. As I hear these things, I think of Fiona and William. Their lighthearted banter and kindness. No matter how hard I try, I only see the honor in William. The kindness and leadership in Fiona. I wonder if Marcail is manipulating them as well. Or if they have inherited their mother's duplicity.

280

"You are the only person I could send. And it was as if I had sent my own flesh into a den of vipers. Do you see, my son? Her power comes from her ability to appear overly honorable, maybe even a little weak. She wants people to see her virtue and be so enamored by it, they would be willing to move the heavens themselves to protect her. I knew it would be your biggest test yet. But I also trusted in your ability to weigh everything, no matter how painful."

Below, a figure breaks away from the rest of the trainees and begins moving toward us. I immediately recognize him. Castor. He walks with the same confidence, but there's a slight hitch in the way he swings his arms. No doubt due to scar tissue from the wound I dealt. I want to ask Demetrius if we can leave. Talk about Marcail in private. But I also don't want to appear weak. No doubt, Castor has seen me watching him.

"She is beloved," Demetrius says. "How could she not be? So I had to pit her against someone even more loved. And there is only one other person in this world who personifies honor, purity and dedication stronger than her. The masses have watched him year after year as he has put his life on the line to liberate the oppressed and oppose those who would seek to throw us back into chaos. It's you, Dear Trajan. It has always been you."

"But I witnessed no tyranny," I say.

"Didn't you?"

Castor is halfway up the stairs. He stops and turns back to the army of Guardians. Watching them with the same focus as I would watch while training him. I long for that. To focus on one thing. To be a General is to be of a single mind. Strength. Of mind and body and will. But always strength. And yet, I sit next to my Ruler, being asked to report on something I didn't see. I've never felt more weak or unprepared for a task.

"Maybe? Forgive my ignorance. I want nothing more than to honor you with this task the way I have honored you as General. But there was no training for this. My opponent embraced me. Healed me. Laughed with me and taught me. And yet I sit here being told the embrace was a strike, the healing was poison and the teaching was false."

281

He reaches over and rests his hand on my shoulder. "Such is the devastation wrought by deception. Tell me of your injury." His tone is gentle, the way one would coo a child to sleep after a nightmare.

I tell him of our turbulent landing on the hunting colony and sleepless night. As I describe the truehunt to him, Castor turns toward us once again and begins climbing. Just as I'm about to tell Demetrius of my perfectly placed spear, Castor reaches us.

"My king," he says as he bows. "Seeing you watch your army is like watching the sun crest the horizon in the morning." He turns to me, "General. Welcome back. Although, the Celsus to which you return is much changed. Our Father has been greatly tested while you were away."

I stand to greet him and realize that the last time we were this close, I had just pierced his chest with a spear. "It warms my heart to see you back to health, Castor."

His expression doesn't change. "Better than that, actually. While you were dining with our enemies, I have found the truer form of myself. Those men down there. You have not known courage until you look in the eyes of a young man and hear him pledge to give his life for you."

Same Castor, different words. He still desires to stand over me, more beloved and powerful than his predecessor. Nothing more than a child trying to outgrow his father. "I pray I never know that courage. The day I do is the day we have failed to carry out the peaceful dream of the Ruling Ancestors," I say. I see such anger flash behind his eyes that I almost step back and prepare for his attack.

Instead, he looks past me, "Father, our progress is quick. Not more than a week and I will have promoted my lieutenants."

Demetrius keeps his eyes on the troops below. "Tell me, Commander," he says to Castor, "how comes the armory?"

Castor smiles and attempts to push me aside with the back of his hand. I hold firm, making him wedge his body around me in order to stand before Demetrius. "I have the metalsmiths working in three shifts. Our power sources for the larger guns are delayed, so I have them focusing on the more primitive weapons. Rest assured, whether it's with the latest technology, or with swords and spears, your army will stand ready to defend Celsus."

"Sit, Commander. The General was just telling me of Aegean technology."

With all my heart, I do not want to tell Castor of the things I experienced. But he's here and Demetrius has included him. To do anything other than obey would bring irritation from Demetrius and ridicule from Castor.

"Rather than bore Your Majesty by recounting for Castor what you have already heard, I will continue on. Trusting, of course, in Castor's ability to come up to speed quickly." It's a childish statement, but I can't help myself. If Tori were here, I would certainly pay for my indiscretion through added drills. Castor rolls his eyes, and Demetrius simply waits.

I quickly describe the watersuit's traits, then describe the way I was strapped to the harness. In a moment of indulgence, I take the time to describe how I tracked the shark's pattern and timing, then I describe the thrust, the perfect strike of the spear and the failure of the suit. The ensuing attack is quickly summarized, as is the sudden change of the energy field from holding tank into protection for me and death for the sharks.

Demetrius sits up quickly and stares at me. "The energy field adapted that quickly? It changed shape, broke apart to surround you and acted as precision harpoons against twenty moving targets?"

I nod, feeling like I have somehow remembered the situation wrong. For me, the most impressive part of the story is yet to come. The way they treated my wound and caused new flesh to grow so quickly.

He turns to Castor. "This is distressing. If they mobilize against us with that kind of weapon, it wouldn't matter how we outfitted The Guardians. A weapon with that much power and adaptability would wipe us from any battlefield." To me, he says, "Were you able to determine the size of the power source?"

"No. I was on the colony but a short amount of time after, most of it unconscious. But when I helped repair the generator on the farming colony which used the energy field to cover the crops, the generator was no bigger than what we would use to power a small drone."

He sits back and looks to the sky, "If they can create such large energy fields, and manipulate them with such a small generator, they are certainly able to make them portable enough to carry with an army. Imagine an army of one thousand, with armor of impenetrable energy. We will be mere ants under their heel."

Castor stands quickly, "Your Guardians will be ready, Lord. Technology cannot replace will. Those men down there would die only to be resurrected and die again for you."

Demetrius laughs, "You should have been a storyteller, Commander. I'm more pragmatic than that. No, if it comes to truewar, we are outmatched the same way a forest lays down for one lumberman with a sharp saw." He turns to me, "Marcail knows it as well. But you are a greater weapon for the type of Battle we can win. If she knows she has opinion on her side, she will rise up and swallow this world. But if her true self is exposed by one more beloved, we may still be able to hold the dream of the Ruling Ancestors intact."

He's right. My Battle won't be in the Temple this time. The Ruling Ancestors foresaw this eventuality, which is why a justification for Battle must be given and agreed upon publicly. What I thought was always a formality I now see as the brilliance of the men who stitched this world back together. And Marcail knew this too, which is why she embraced me and gave me a family with which to bond. A mother and a brother I never knew. The hope of love once my servitude to a tyrant finally came to an end. I feel foolish for being so easily tempted. My fists are clenched so tightly, the skin over my knuckles begins to ooze tiny drops of blood through the stretched pores. She was a peddler of sweets and I was a child, taken in by the bright colors and promise of sugar dipped delight.

Quietly, with my head bowed, I say, "My king. I will Battle for you. I will plead your case and win. Both with my words when I justify your challenge, and with my might when I match their General in the Temple." Then, to

Castor, "I will prove my love for our Father by keeping the will of the Ruling Ancestors alive and making your command over an antiquated and grotesque army obsolete."

Demetrius stands and beckons both of us to do the same. "My sons. These last few months have broken my heart. My intentions have been attacked. My Generals have quarreled, almost to death. My first son has questioned his allegiance to me and I have asked my second son to go against the very principles which have pulled our world from the darkness. But, with a new, more sinister, darkness pressing against our borders, I stand with you both. And I feel your love. Love for your nation and for me. I am humbled and, for the first time in memory, I am hopeful. I can see the light of your love piercing the blackness seeking to consume us."

Chapter 41

Tori is already in the training facility when I arrive. We haven't spoken since last night and I find it difficult to look him in the eyes. I've never shown such weakness.

"What has happened is in the past. When an opponent strikes you, it lasts but a moment. Such is the case with many things. I have heard about the army as well as Caleb. The decision is made and there will be no more discussion from me. Our Battle looms. And I fear our politicking has delayed your preparation." He motions for me to join him as we begin stretching. The same routine he has led me through for years. It takes less than a minute for our breathing to synchronize and our movements to mirror each other.

After stretching, he examines my arm and tests its strength through a series of kinetic movements–each one adding more strain than the previous.

"Good," he says.

We move to cardio, then technique. I lose myself in the rhythm of the training. The familiarity and simplicity of it calms my mind and, for the first time in what seems like months, I'm able to enter into that zone where there is only the task and the execution. Utter focus on the movement of my body. That place where mind and body are welded so seamlessly that I can't tell which is in control. Hour after hour slips by. There is only Tori's voice and my response. When I complete a task perfectly, Tori's response is, "again." There are no encouraging words. Singular perfection is not the goal. Rather, repeated and uninterrupted perfection is the only acceptable outcome.

"Such a waste," shatters our cadence. Castor stands in the entry, arms folded. "All this attention on one man while my army, the true might of Celsus, toils outside with untested instructors." He makes his way toward us. "An old man, clinging to the old ways that have made him so popular."

"What is your business, Student?" Tori says. "Until Demetrius says otherwise, you are addressing the sole defender of Celsus. Your presence here can be considered an act of treasonous disruption."

"Calm yourself, slave. I'm here to pay my official respects to Our Lion, returned from grazing."

He is within striking distance and I consider ending him. There would be repercussions, yes, but Demetrius has made it abundantly clear how much he needs me right now. At most, I would be chided and denied the few comforts I'm granted.

"Say another disrespectful word to my Mentor and it will be your last. There are no cameras, nor are there rules in here," I say.

Castor stops. "General," he says, "it seems your time away has sharpened some of your edges. Threats of murder? Our Father would be disappointed."

"What is your business?" I ask.

"Father has asked you to address my Corps of Guardians."

"I will address the Hopeful Generals of Celsus, absolutely. But I will not acknowledge the abomination which you call an army. To do so would be to question the intentions and efficacy of the Ancestors."

"There it is again. You would do well to realize our perfectly scripted world of peace is melting away. There is too much hatred and jealousy in the heart of man to sustain such ideals. I will not sit idly by and watch as we are swallowed by those who callously disregard the system which binds them. Pacts and treaties will not keep a pack of wolves at bay. But rip the throat out of the lead wolf and the others will flee."

"Evil to combat evil is as logical as adding water to the ocean in hopes of drying it up," I say.

"Are you done, Castor?" Tori says. "You can save this debate for another time. You've made your request. Unless you plan on staying so The General can practice some simple sparring techniques, I'll ask you to leave."

"I am anxious to hear how you speak when the tide changes and you've been returned to your true position. A fallen General of a conquered nation."

Without thinking, I lunge, grab the back of Castor's head with my left hand, and pull his face into my swinging right elbow. There is a dull smack as his nose meets the sharp bone and I feel his legs give out beneath him. He staggers back, trying to find a fighting stance.

"I warned you, child. Consider that a gentle reminder. I will send word when I'm willing to inspect the Potentials. Have them ready."

He finally regains his balance and I ready myself for his retaliation. But it doesn't come. He wipes the blood streaming from his nose and smiles. "As you wish, General."

After Castor is gone, Tori says, "While I appreciate your protection, that was unwise. You just showed him a weakness. He won't forget, nor will he hesitate to exploit it when the time is right."

The rest of our session is lackluster. Tori is gruff and I'm unable to regain complete focus. Try as I might, I can't get Castor's smile out of my head.

Chapter 42

The army is assembled in groups of one hundred soldiers. Each one marched in, perfectly in unison, and wearing identical uniforms. They even seem to be grouped by height. It's like seeing the drawings of the old world come to life. I'm sick to my stomach.

Demetrius is on my right and Castor is to my left. Tori remained in our quarters.

"I have never seen a group of more dedicated individuals. Unwavering focus and obedience. And our physicians have outdone themselves. To see these men go from tiny and soft citizens to hardened soldiers in such a short amount of time is astounding," Castor says. "I'd like to see Aegea threaten truewar after seeing these demi-gods."

"Your pride makes you foolish, Commander," I say, almost choking on the word commander. "The very insinuation of this army would unite the entire world against us."

"And let them try to do something about it. The nations would fall faster than if you fought a Battle a week."

"And the devastation greater than our world could sustain," Demetrius says. He looks sad and old as he walks next to me. I consider offering him my arm to help steady him, but I don't want to offend. "Understand me,

Son," He says to Castor, "I am exceedingly impressed. But I do not delight in your work. It is the product of the jealousy and deception of our enemies."

"We will look back on this time, grateful for the prudence of preparation, saddened by implications, but delighted in seeing it not utilized," I say.

Demetrius rests his hand on my arm and Castor stifles a laugh.

Next, we pass by the weapons stockpile. Station after station of killing utensils. Guns, spears, swords, cannons, bombs for our drones.

"We continue to work night and day to get our armory prepared. I only fear it will not be ready in time," Castor says.

Demetrius is silent, as am I.

After looking at a newly designed weapon, designed to tunnel its way under a specific location, then detonate, causing the earth to swallow whatever may be above, I say, "I'm ready to address these people."

I make my way to the podium with shaking hands. They don't shake from fear of giving the speech, rather, from the implied desolation I have just inspected. It's one thing to embrace the violence of Battle when there are only two lives at risk. But to see the preparation and willingness to enter into truewar is almost too much to comprehend.

The army before me is silent and unmoving. Their eyes are locked on me as one.

"Citizens of Celsus," I say. "I am impressed. Your commander is to be commended. He has trained and built you into a group of men, ready to defend our home from the rumors of peace-shattering terror which swirl around us like a whirlpool, threatening to pull us under the waves until our sustaining breath is forced from our lungs. I have no doubt that if the sirens sound, you will answer the call of valor, sacrifice, bravery and pride." The crowd shouts their affirmation as one, guttural yell.

"I am also terrified. Not since the days of chaos and darkness have nations built armies with the potential of killing en masse. Our Ruling Ancestors saw a better way of living. One that assured peace for all, based on the sacrifice of a handful. When I was chosen as your General, I vowed to uphold the ideals and laws which the Ruling Ancestors sacrificed so much to enact." I look toward Castor. His face is contorted in rage, but he knows there is nothing he can do to stop me. "It is a vow which I consider more sacred than life itself. One that I will honor until the air is long gone from my lungs.

"There are some who say this army before me is the new way of the world. But I stand here and see the sins of our past resurrected. By no fault of your own, nor the fault of our Father. This is a dark hour for our world. But I declare to you, there is one who goes before you with strength of mind, body and soul who realizes that, even though you are mighty, you still need protection.

"My hope. My mandate. My promise to you is that you will look back on this day, decades from now as you sit comfortably with your family, and gratefully remember the time when you answered the call of valor, only to find silence on the other end."

There is another cheer, this one is more like the Crowd I'm used to-individual voices celebrating in their own way. It washes over me and I am filled with hope. I'm also overcome by the magnitude of the next few weeks and the role I will play in keeping these men and their families alive.

Chapter 43

"Our world awaits you, my son. Breathless and hopeful." Demetrius says.

We are in his royal transport, flying low across The Last Forest – the vast woodlands which sit on the eastern border of Celsus. Our destination is the Temple where the Rulers of each nation will meet tomorrow for The Final Accusation. The terminal event in the Battle process. Tomorrow Demetrius and I will stand before the world leaders, Marcail included, and level our evidence in order to justify the challenge. I always saw this meeting as superfluous. Just another chance for politicians to make themselves known to the masses. But, now that I'm involved, I realize how important it really is. If we don't succeed in convincing the other leaders of the reasons behind our intentions, the world as I know it could crumble.

"I will not let you down," I say through thick saliva.

"You could never let me down. Celsus is prepared for any eventuality, thanks to Castor. But this is not about me. It's about the millions of innocent lives around our planet. You're not my General anymore. You must be the world's General. I just pray we succeed so we can write your deeds in the history books."

The forest drops away and we skim over an increasingly barren landscape. The last bit of frozen land before we cross the Arctic Ocean. At this speed, we should be at the Temple in five hours.

I wish Tori were here. This is the first trip I've made to the Temple without him and it feels as if I've left home without any clothes. Demetrius made it clear, however, that Tori was unwelcome. As was Castor. Just Demetrius and me. No fanfare. No political advisors or servants.

"These meetings are difficult. Politicians twist and distort everything. I will not throw you to the wolves, however. When we convene, I will bear the burden of articulating the atrocities of Marcail. All we need is for you to agree without hesitation. There is a possibility one of Aegea's supporting nations will ask you to testify, but that would be overly bold, even for this situation. It would also mean I haven't done the necessary job during the initial Accusation. Marcail will also present her case, but she will not be allowed to question you. Nor will I be able to rebut her."

Below us, a herd of caribou appear on the horizon, grazing on the frozen grass. Before they can react, we overtake them. I wonder how the rest of the leaders travel to the Temple. Specifically, I wonder about Marcail, at this very moment. No doubt speeding along the ocean surface in one of her perfectly designed vessels. More than anything else, I fear seeing her in person. And I wonder if her children will accompany her. The thought of resting my final agreement with Demetrius while Fiona looks on is enough to make my stomach turn.

"You will have my complete alignment, Father," I say.

"Splendid. Tomorrow, this world will sleep comfortably, knowing they have a General watching over them who is strong enough to win, brave enough to stand against evil, and smart enough to see the schemes of a snake for what they are."

The ocean comes into view and the drone gains altitude. "Leave me, Son. I must prepare myself. Like you, this will be my greatest challenge. I can't afford to miss anything." He closes his eyes and leans his chair back.

I make my way to my quarters and sift through my bag until I find the walnut block. I begin pressing the Aegean blade into the grain with just enough pressure for it to catch the tiny nubs that litter the surface of the lopsided sphere. I'm making progress. It won't be perfect by any means, but it has become my creation. There are mistakes which I can't cover, but I can also see where I was able to sufficiently correct a misguided stroke of the blade. It's childish, I know, but I desperately want to show Fiona my progress. To hear her laugh as she chides my pedestrian technique, followed by her genuine praise for the progress I've made. If only it were that simple.

The drone begins to shake and I feel us climb higher to avoid the turbulence. In just a few hours I will enter a Battle like none I have ever faced. Undertrained, ill-equipped and without my greatest ally. The opponent will be someone I have laughed with. The outcome of this contest more dire than I could have considered months ago. We continue to shake, no matter how high we climb, so I put the knife down and lie on the cot. It senses my weight and dims the lights of my quarters.

Usually, the night before a Battle, I sit quietly, reviewing my training. Visualizing my opponent and testing the techniques I'm most likely to use. As I drift to sleep tonight, Fiona's lovely eyes continue to float through my mind. At first, they look to be laughing, but then I see tears in the corners, pooling across the bottom. As the salty liquid spills out, I watch the whites of her eyes fade to pink, then an irritated red. There is no laughter here. These are bitter tears. Caused by some terrible tragedy. The whole time, the eyes never look away. They stare, unblinking and unceasingly at me.

Chapter 44

The room is smaller than I thought it would be. There is a podium at the front with ornate tables rippling out in the fashion of an amphitheater. We sit at the front, across from the Aegean delegation, made up of Marcail, Francis and two other politicians I vaguely recognize from my trip. When I realized neither Fiona nor William were present, it felt as if I'd dropped a fifty kilo pack from my shoulders.

Behind us, delegates from all of the other nations arrange themselves in what looks to be their pre-session alliances. There are only five delegates behind us. The rest crowd into the rows behind Marcail. Since she entered, she has floated through the aisles, smiling, greeting, solemnly discussing the events of the day. Demetrius has greeted his supporters as well, but their interaction is much more understated. I can't help but marvel at these two warriors, already embroiled in their Battle.

The moment I have been dreading finally happens as Marcail makes her way to our table. I stand, as does Demetrius.

"Gentlemen. I wish we were greeting each other under different circumstances. In spite of the situation, however, my heart soars at seeing you, General. You are the only topic of conversation from the prince and princess." She holds my hand in her's as she speaks. Then to Demetrius,

"My lord. I trust your journey was uneventful? Afterall, you've made so many of them in recent years."

"No matter how familiar the path to the volcano's mouth becomes, it still burns the feet, my lady," he says.

I couldn't have aimed a weapon with any more skill than these two aim their words.

She smiles the same smile I've seen her give since she entered the room, "I pray your tortured journeys are coming to an end. For the sake of your tired feet, of course."

An old man, dressed in a black silk robe, wearing a sash with the words of our Ruling Ancestors stenciled on it, enters from a small door on the left side of the room. The Rulers immediately quiet down and begin taking their seats.

Lukas. Former Ruler of one of the Mountain Nations. He was so beloved as a Ruler that the delegates of the nations convinced him to become Global Arbitrator. He will preside over The Final Accusation and ensure the rules of our Ancestors are followed.

He reaches the podium and, with a booming voice says, "Lords and Ladies, Kings and Queens, Presidents, Chancellors, Emperors and Prime Ministers. No matter what your people call you, we are all one under this roof. We come together today because Celsus has challenged Aegea based on accusations of mistreatment, abuse of power and conspiracy against other nations." He pauses as he shifts his notes. "But before we begin the proceedings, I must address the rumors I have been hearing. Rumors which, if true, shake the very foundation upon which we have lived our lives and governed our people. I hesitate to even say the word, but it's already in your minds and on your lips, so I will. War. True, bloody, devastating and soul-sucking war. A word I prayed I would never hear spoken as a possibility in my lifetime nor the lifetime of my grandchildren's grandchildren. It is my hope that we are able to trust in the process of our Ancestors today and avoid the terrible thing so many of you seem so intent on bringing to life."

He points at me. "You only need to look upon this man, whom you have all watched fight for his nation and the lives of the oppressed around the world to see the effects of combat. He bears the scars of violence and hatred, both on his body and in his mind every day. He has been trained to bear these burdens since he was a boy and I am willing to wager he still suffers under the enormity of them. Just imagine what would happen to your farmers, cooks, artists, writers and teachers if the horrors of truewar were thrust upon them.

"He sits here willing to continue to bear that burden. I humbly beg each one of you to allow him his work, if Celsus so chooses to proceed with the initial challenge against Aegea. Let us not be the generation of Rulers who watches as we crumble back into the hell from which our Ancestors pulled us."

Demetrius stands and begins clapping his agreement, as do the Rulers seated behind us. After a couple seconds of delay, the rest of the room stands in ovation as well. However, that brief pause from Aegea's side of the room is enough to show me how close we are to the very hell Lukas describes.

The applause finally subsides and Lukas says, "Now, let us begin the Final Accusation." He turns to Demetrius. "Majesty, after hearing your delegate's report, do you still find Aegean citizens in need of liberation?"

Demetrius, still standing, bows deeply and with a barely audible voice, says, "Most honored Arbitrator, may I approach? My stance, I believe, is much more complex than a simple yes or no."

The room is silent and still while we await a response from Lukas. Finally, he says, "I yield to Demetrius, Ruler of Celsus."

The two leaders pass each other with a nod as Demetrius steps behind the beautifully carved podium. Tradition holds that this podium is a relic from the time before the Great Darkness. One side is charred with chunks of wood missing. The other side has fared better, showing the faded seal of a long forgotten nation.

Demetrius shuffles his feet, while he looks across the crowd. After a minute of anticipation filled silence, he begins. "We know one another. As

Rulers, we share the same burdens. We took the same solemn vow to uphold a new way of governing in the hope of avoiding the horrors of our predecessors. And yet, here we are. War looming over us.

"Some call me a dictator. Obsessed with world domination. Others call me misguided and prideful. And yet almost every one of you have sent delegates to my nation to find evidence of wrongdoing. Each time, your delegates return with stories of healthy citizens, hardworking politicians and a thriving economy." He pauses as if considering what to say next, even though I know every word and action has been rehearsed to perfection.

"I am known for my long winded speeches. But today I find myself disenchanted. Why not just walk away? Whither under the threat of truewar and let the Aegean people fend for themselves in whatever circumstance Queen Marcail has decided to levy on them? Yes, these are the temptations I find myself wrestling with. If Marcail, after all, is such a terrible leader, why would she have the support of so many other Rulers here today? It would be easy to fall in line with the prevailing mindset, wouldn't it? So many smart and caring people could not collectively be wrong, could they?

"Here is what is true of me and my nation. I encourage aggression in my people. You need only to look at my General to agree. Celsus boasts the strongest economy of any nation. We have the highest population. Ours is the best quality of life because of our focus on technological advances and the belief that one life is not as important as one nation. When I, with quivering hands, became the Celcean Ruler, we were landlocked, starving, poor and selfish. And yet, I still looked beyond our borders to help another, equally struggling nation gain freedom from their inhumane Ruler. When I did so, the very people in this room lauded me and helped Celsus with resources to minister to the destitute.

"In the early days, the world looked at us and said we were blessed because we did what was right. Even when the risk to our way of life outweighed any gain we may have reaped from our willingness to confront evil. But as our prosperity has grown, other nations have stopped reveling in our success. Sadly, the revelry has turned into something much uglier."

There are murmurs of disapproval from the Aegean side of the room and, for an instant, I fear the eloquence of Demetrius has left him. If he continues down this path, there won't be a Battle for me to fight. It will have been replaced by truewar by the end of the session.

"Peace, Rulers. I mean no offense," he says. "Before I present my evidence behind the painful decision to stay the course into Battle with Aegea, I want to ask one simple question. Why? Why would Celsus risk so much by challenging Aegea? Our General, while great, is coming off a devastating injury in the Mid-Year Battle. Aegea would benefit much more than Celsus, should they win the Battle. And I run the risk of being even more ostracized than I already am.

"My answer is simple. It is the answer I gave all those years ago when Lukas himself, still the Ruler of his own nation, asked why I would risk the well-being of my nation by going to Battle against the most ruthless Ruler and General combination of the time. Compassion. It's an easy word to forget as a Ruler. So many of our decisions must be ruled more by logic than compassion or we would be overcome with guilt. But when I look at an entire group of people being made to suffer because of the decisions of one person, I know nothing else. I am not just a Ruler of Celsus. And you are not just Rulers of your nations. We, collectively, have been given the responsibility to oversee the well-being of every human in this world. That was the heart behind the system which our Ruling Ancestors gave us. It was not so we could build strong borders. It was so our borders could blur through the understanding that we cannot survive unless we are united to a common cause. The cause of compassion and the willingness to practice it regardless of how it may affect us.

"So I stand in front of you. Stripped bare, knowing the hatred some of you feel toward me. Asking you to put your preconceptions aside. Begging you to be the Rulers our Ancestors hoped for. Guileless, lacking jealousy, discerning, brave and compassionate."

I look around the room and am amazed to see how enraptured each leader is. In just a few sentences, Demetrius has them in the palm of his hand. He begins his accusation toward Marcail. Showing Caleb's recorded version of the tragedy on the farming colony. Then he shows the footage of the tragedy itself. Then Caleb's trial, stopping to give context of how Marcail shaped events to win the respect of her nation. Then he shows Caleb's punishment. The brutality of his treatment. Finally, he shows footage of Caleb's rescue. His sun scorched, withered body being dragged from a leaking raft.

While the footage of Caleb's ordeal plays, I notice movement near Marcail. The very thing I dreaded has come true. Fiona quietly takes a seat next to her mother. We don't make eye contact, but I can see the tears in her eyes as she wraps her arm around Marcail. Most of the leaders near them have stopped watching the footage and are now gazing on this scene of mother and daughter weeping together. The obvious tactic makes me sick to my stomach. The fact that Fiona agreed to such blatant manipulation is the most upsetting part.

"Yes," Demetrius says, drawing attention back to himself, "I wept too when I saw this. Which is why I sent some of my most loyal citizens into Aegea to better understand what was happening." He flicks his wrist and the holographic footage begins showing a series of images of young men and women. "Fearing Marcail's reaction, I made a mistake that I now deeply regret. I sent these men and women into Aegea covertly. At the time I was worried Marcail would attempt to cover up what was happening if she knew she was being watched. It was a terrible mistake because it gave Marcail yet another opportunity to practice her brutality."

The images fade and Demetrius begins to describe how Marcail found out about them and began a vicious manhunt, finding each one and mercilessly killing them one by one. "They did not die without valor," Demetrius says with wavering speech. "The reports they sent before their death detailed a citizenry terrified into obedience. Savage punishment meant to discourage any disagreement. Arbitrary and changing rules, all in service to ensure Marcail's reign continued without question. A leader obsessively focused on building technology, disguised as tools for survival when in reality they are designed for war."

There are more accusations. Things he has not shared with me. Terrible stories of how entire colonies in Aegea are conscripted into servitude and torture, all so Aegea and Marcail can grow stronger. As Demetrius speaks, I watch as Ruler after Ruler gets up and takes a seat on the Celcean side of the room. Not everyone is won over, but by the time he is done, the room is almost perfectly divided.

After almost exactly an hour, Demetrius stops speaking. Clearly exhausted. He turns to me, "And finally, I look to my sole advocate. A man so dedicated to the truth of our Ruling Ancestors, he has lived a life of exile and dedication to their rules. His honor and valor are unquestioned. You have all seen him Battle. Seen his mercy. Heard his humility. Experienced his purity. It is my greatest honor in life to know he stands next to me in times of turmoil like this.

"I asked him to serve as my official delegate after I challenged Aegea in Battle. When he returned, his stories were of a beautiful and prospering Aegea. But he also told of a nation too perfectly represented. Colonies posing as hunting and farming communities, only to be exposed as possessing military weaponry. Finally he told me of an elegant Ruler, but a Ruler so controlling as to keep her counselors from him and to banish her advisors for speaking out of turn. I would ask him to recount everything for you, but there is no point in reiterating the things I have already shown. I will simply ask him," he stares at me with an intensity I have rarely seen, "to be as dedicated to honesty now as he has been his entire life. Trajan, do you doubt my decision to ask you to Battle one more time in the hopes of rescuing the people of Aegea from their Ruler?"

All eyes are on me as I stand. I feel as if I'm lifting the entire Temple as I do. I turn, looking first at the people behind me, then across the Rulers behind Marcail. My last few months swirl around me. My time with Fiona as I healed. Sparring with William. Arguing with Tori. Dancing with Marcail. All of it led me to this very second, with the Rulers of the world looking to me as the final voice. Demetrius and Marcail. Two leaders as different as mountains and the sea. Both of them brutal. Both of them wise. Marcail showed me kindness. Demetrius built me into General through unrelenting demands. But in his willingness to show me his dark side, he also showed me his honesty. Marcail, on the other hand, showed me only her gentleness. I can see now that she was a viper, posing as a branch, waiting for me to walk underneath so she could strike when I was weakest. My eyes finally meet hers and, with a Battle-like clarity, I say, "I have no doubt, my king. I agree with your accusations and I willingly enter into Battle in the hopes of liberating the Aegean people from Marcail."

The room erupts around me. Rulers from both sides begin yelling either their agreement or disgust. Fiona and I lock eyes and I see not just anger. I see such hatred, it makes feels as if I've been stabbed.

Lukas takes the podium and calls for order. It takes a while, but the room finally quiets. "These accusations are indeed troubling. Let us remember our roles. Let us honor the process of governance which has guided us peacefully for decades. Demetrius has had his say." He turns to Marcail, "Queen Marcail, we will hear your rebuttal."

She approaches the podium, backed by the applause of the Rulers who have remained on her side. Like Demetrius, she takes a few moments to collect herself. Her tears are gone, but the evidence remains through swollen and bloodshot eyes. The rebuttal is traditionally used as a final plea against Battle to the accusing nation's Ruler. It is clear neither Demetrius nor I will be dissuaded. Today, however, her speech holds a heavier weight. Depending on what she says, the rest of the Rulers will make a final decision for either truewar or trust in our Ancestors. We are a world balanced on a wire. One gentle puff of Marcail's breath could send us tumbling into an abyss.

"Distinguished Rulers. I stand before you with a broken, yet full, heart. Seeing the footage presented by Demetrius rips open tender scars. Caleb served my husband and my nation honorably until the very end. I am grateful to Demetrius for nursing him back to health. Regardless of his actions, I hope he has learned from his hubris and is able to put the past behind him.

"There are many things I could say, but Demetrius has set his course. As has Trajan. If there is one thing I learned about Trajan while he was my guest, is that once he has committed to something, he does not quit. I admire that. To the rest of the Rulers here today who remain dedicated to my innocence, you have my eternal gratitude. However, I fear some of you may have allowed your emotions to run unchecked. No matter how deeply you support me, or despise Demetrius, threats of truewar are simply unacceptable. I beg you, if you love me, if you support my innocence, if you believe in the Rules of our Ancestors, put these threats aside and allow the Battle to take place.

"When Trajan was with me, he told me of his unwavering faith in the system given to us by the Ruling Ancestors. So deep is his faith that he believes winning is less about the prowess of the General and more about the purity of the nation. Today, with the horrendous accusations of Demetrius squarely imposed on me, I choose to place my faith similarly. I will not argue my innocence. My innocence will be decided when Trajan faces Liam." She fixes her eyes on me, "Aegea accepts your challenge." To Demetrius she says, "Whether under the Celcean or Aegean banner, I look forward to our two nations uniting."

She leaves the podium and takes her seat amidst a stunned silence. Even the controlled exterior of Demetrius reveals his shock. We have been saved from truewar. Not by the power of Celcean accusations. Not by winning Rulers over through my loyalty. We have been saved by the very person Demetrius thought was pushing us toward chaos.

Lukas asks if there are any Rulers who wish to offer opposition or support for the Battle, but after Marcail's speech, all remain silent. "Very well," he says. "In two weeks' time, Celsus and Aegea will pit their mightiest Generals against each other in order to settle the dispute of their Rulers. Whichever General prevails will present his Ruler with authority over the fallen nation. May you both Battle with might, glory and honor. And may the pain of the few prevent the pain of the many."

I navigate the rest of the day in a fog. There are meetings and receptions. Mostly with other large nations where Demetrius negotiates trade deals and advocates for certain leeway. From time to time, a Ruler or a delegate will wish me luck, or ask if I would be willing to take one of their young Generals under my wing. But for the most part, I remain in the background, which allows me to play Marcail's speech on a steady loop in my head. I want to ask Demetrius about his reaction. Just days ago, Demetrius pleaded with me to stand beside him because of Marcail's secret campaign to go against the Ruling Elders and start truewar. If she really were as brutal as Demetrius claimed, and had the military technology to force nation against nation in bloody Battle, then why didn't she? Either Demetrius was wrong, or Marcail sees other options which remain outside of my grasp.

After the final dinner of the evening, I separate myself from the politicians and wind my way through the cold tunnels of the Temple. The smooth, colorless cement calms me. Reminds me of my true place in this world. Each tunnel is perfectly straight, leading inevitably to the battlefloor.

I step into the giant space, void of any Battle configuration. The stands rise into blackness all around me. This is the first time I have been here and not heard the roar of the Crowd. In spite of the subdued atmosphere, adrenaline pumps powerfully through my veins. I am a predator, standing at the site of his first kill. The nature of this place and who I am are inseparable.

Each of my previous Battles seem to meld into one victorious and blood-filled memory. Tori's preparation, Braddock's voice, the Crowd's adoration, precision strikes and pain filled retaliations. All of these moments have led me here. Will draw me here two weeks from now.

I close my eyes and remember Tori's guidance. Just breathe. Control what I can control and the rest will fall into place. So I inhale and exhale and inhale and exhale.

"I thought I would find you here."

I instantly recognize Fiona's voice in the darkness. Looking around, I see no one and briefly wonder if I imagined it.

"Up here. In the stands."

The perfect acoustics of the room carry her voice to me with immaculate clarity.

"It's amazing how comfortable you look down there. Standing where so much blood has been spilled." Her voice grows louder and I hear the wisp of her clothes as she makes her way toward me.

"Fiona," is all I can manage. This reunion has haunted me since leaving Aegea. I've tried to figure out the perfect words to say to try to make her understand my decision, but now that she's here, nothing seems adequate.

"Trajan," she says as she steps into the fading light of the front row.

We stand still, looking at each other, then around the Temple, then at our feet. All of our titles and accomplishments set aside. No government or Battles to distract us. Just two people trying to find something to say.

"My mother wants you to know she's not angry with you. This political avalanche was already too powerful for any of us to stop it."

"The queen is more kind than I could hope for," I say. Equal parts grateful and disappointed for the distraction.

"The queen is. I, however, am not," she says.

"I understand. My hope is that once this is over and we're all citizens of the same nation, you and I may be able to see each other without the fog of Battle. Maybe then I can meet the real Fiona and you can see the true Trajan."

"Your hopes carry a lot of assumptions. The least of which is that you will emerge victorious."

"Do you wish my death?"

"I wish for you to lose in Battle. And after hearing you blindly stand beside Demetrius as he lied about my mother, I am ambivalent toward whether that loss comes with life or death."

I understand her anger. And her honesty, while hostile, is a refreshing change from the conversations I've been suffering through. "I would wager you are in the majority." I kneel and brush my hand over the chalky dirt. "My death will come soon enough."

"Stop being so controlled. I didn't come to talk with a wall."

"I think you possess enough emotion for the both of us right now."

We're quiet, both realizing this is not the conversation we wanted to have.

"My sphere is almost complete," I say, hoping to talk about anything other than the collision course of our two nations.

She lets out a short laugh, "Based on the last time I saw it, are you sure you can actually call it a sphere?"

It's my turn to laugh. "You certainly offer a lot of criticism, and yet, I've never seen you put knife to block."

"One doesn't have to be an artist to appreciate art."

"Those who can't, teach."

"Let's ask Tori how he feels about that."

It's amazing how quickly she can make me forget all of the stress which plagues me every other second of my day. Even when she's insulting me, it feels like swimming in a cool lake. "I've missed you, Fiona."

"I've missed you too, Trajan."

Chapter 45

The Crowd is loud today. My Battle will be the highlight of the three which have been scheduled. Tori and I have been in my preparation room for the previous two. The first sounded as if it was over almost immediately. Judging from the Crowd, the second was a much closer and violent match. It spun them into a frenzy. Even though there is almost an hour until I'm scheduled to take the battlefloor, I can hear them chanting my name.

"He will try to use your confidence against you. Remember the game we played when we were in Aegea," Tori says.

I'm silent, focusing on his direction and the scenarios we have rehearsed.

"They may think Liam has a mental advantage over you. Rather than hand to hand combat, they may choose a puzzle, or strategy game."

It would be unlikely. Strategy games, while technically allowable, are not used anymore. The Crowd hates them so much, there was almost a riot the last time it was utilized in Battle. "Do you think they will have Fiona escort me again?" In spite of my attempts to push her from my mind, I have not been able to stop thinking about her since I saw her at the Final Accusation.

"It would be poor form for the princess of the challenged nation to escort her would-be conqueror. But given your obvious infatuation with her, she may. Let us not forget how manipulative Marcail has proven herself to be."

This is the closest he will come to rebuking me so close to a Battle, but his point is sound. I take a deep breath and, upon exhaling, force every image of Fiona from my memory. It's time for me to put everything other than victory aside.

My armor is delivered. From the looks of it, I will need to use my speed. I'm given light leggings and a sleeveless tunic.

We are silent as I dress, both of us listening to the Crowd. They have gotten so loud, I can feel the reverberation of their screams in the concrete.

"I miss that," Tori says. "The adoration. The strength which comes from so many people willing you to win. When their energy is focused on you, there is no better drug." His eyes are closed and his face is tilted to the ceiling, as if he's soaking as much of that energy as he can.

I think back to my first Battle. The Crowd was ambivalent toward me, the upstart General who dethroned Augustus. But about halfway through, after taking a spear to the side and not missing a beat, they began to cheer for me. It was what gave me the strength to overtake my much older and more skilled opponent.

"Do you think this will be my last?" I ask.

"I thought last year was your last. But Demetrius realized how beloved you actually are. You will be done when you decide, Son. No one else has the power to remove you without an all-out revolt." He holds his hands toward the Crowd above us, "Listen to them. They would follow you to the end of the earth."

"Which means they would follow Demetrius as well."

He finally turns to me, "As long as you follow him, yes."

A messenger pokes his head through the door, telling us we are fifteen minutes from my audience with Demetrius.

"I know you despise him, Moto-San, but I know nothing else. He has been no more dishonest nor harsh than anyone else, save you."

"What have we come to, when our most honorable Ruler is the least deceitful, rather than the most trustworthy? You deserve a better lord."

"Would that have been Marcail?" I ask. The Crowd continues to chant, reminding me of my need to focus on the Battle, just moments away.

"We will only make you weaker for your task if we continue down this path. We are here. And our steps are outlined in the dust in front of us. Win. Then, maybe we can sit back and pretend to be philosophers."

It is clear from the explosion of applause that the video feed has switched to our prep room. Tori and I immediately settle into our final routine. He runs me through a few agility tests, then stretches. The Crowd roars with each movement, as if I'm fighting some invisible opponent. He has me stand at attention. I think back to only one year ago. The moments before facing Seth. We had been focused solely on the task of winning at all costs. Winning in order to liberate an abused and withering people. Now, the ritual which gave me such clarity and focus feels as if it's a relic of a forgotten time.

Tori circles me as he's circled me so many times. I know the words before he says them. They have been the words to signify the importance of my task. The justification for why people like me exist. "One man, a nation on his shoulders," I don't hear Tori speak this. Nor do I hear the Crowd. I hear them as if remembering a story from childhood. "Another man, everything to lose. To the victor be the glory. To the victor, immortality."

The Crowd rumbles louder than ever. All of the rumors and threats of truewar bubbling over into an orgy of blood-filled anticipation, gratitude, nostalgia and vicarious excitement.

I see Tori's mouth move to finish his incantation, but the noise of the Crowd drowns him out completely. *To the victor, Trajan. You are the victor.*

The door swings open and my guide steps in with a timid bow. She is very short with sharp features. Her hair is cut at odd angles and she wears an outfit to match mine. Celcean. Demetrius has sent me one of the daughters of the Celcean elite to accompany me to his quarters.

I turn to Tori and, breaking from our practiced routine, embrace him. The Crowd above goes quiet for a split second before igniting into an even louder frenzy. Somewhere Braddock is recording this, zooming in, preparing to use it in his broadcast.

The walk to Demetrius is silent and I am subdued while listening to him. My mind is squarely on the Battle now. Tori is right. All that matters now, regardless of which Ruler is more right or wrong, is victory. I am on the world's stage. My part has been cast and rehearsed. The only thing left is to deliver the lines without deviating.

My audience with Demetrius ends with our usual embrace, then I'm back in the prep room. My last moment of peace before the Battle.

Tori is waiting for me, as always. He looks me over a final time. "You are ready, General." Then he drops his head. "My son was so young when I lost him. I never got to know his character. I never knew if he had a sense of humor, or a strong work ethic. When I remember my love for him, it is a simple, untested love. Stemming simply from him being my child. And it pales in comparison to my love for you. You are the greatest man I have ever known. Your only weakness is in your desire for perfection. You will fail in this life, Trajan. But your failures do not define you. You will be defined and remembered by your courage and your faithfulness." His eyes are full of tears. "When I look at my life, the thing I am most proud of, is you." He turns and leaves.

As I watch him go, the alarm sounds, signifying the start of the Battle.

Chapter 46

The north wall of my preparation chamber lifts, revealing the battlefloor. I step into the spotlights which will follow me relentlessly until I'm either victorious or defeated. The Crowd has become nothing more than background buzz for me. My mind is focused on one thing. Liam's defeat. My breath is steady, as is my heart. The clarity of Battle cuts through the haze of the last year. I finally feel at home.

A camera drone slowly spins around me at waist level. The giant screen above me shows the shot which makes me look larger than life. I slowly walk to my traditional mark where I will await Liam, then the terms of the Battle.

Braddock's floating platform lands a few meters in front of me and he steps onto the battlefloor, soaking up the Crowd's adoration. Bowing and waving, as he makes his way to me.

"Trajan, Lion of Celsus. Conqueror of Nations and Judge of the Unrighteous." He pauses to let the renewed cheering subside. "Your might looms over me, more formidable than the tallest mountain."

I nod, refusing to make eye contact nor break my concentration. I'm surprised Demetrius has allowed him to interview me so close to the Battle.

"I will not delay you too long, General. But I fear your adoring fans would revolt if they didn't get a chance to hear from you. After such a trying year: the Mid-Year, your injuries in Aegea, even the injuries you sustained in last year's Battle. Are you at all worried about your ability to face Aegea's General?" The Crowd is silent with anticipation.

The camera drone is now at eye level with me, surely zooming in to capture my slightest reaction. Now I understand why Demetrius allowed this. He needs one final justification from his General, standing on the battlefloor, for why Aegea must be conquered and why truewar is unacceptable.

"Our Ancestors gave us this system because of the horrors they saw during the Dark Years. When I committed to serve Demetrius, I also agreed to serve every citizen of this world. I trust my Ruler. And I trust our Ancestors. If that means fighting a monster until every last drop of blood spills from my flesh, I do it happily. I do it so no innocent citizen will experience the hell of truewar."

Braddock smiles, pleased with the soundbite, even more pleased by the reaction of the Crowd.

"Spoken like a true leader, General. Now, watch with me as the Aegean delegation enters."

The Temple screen switches to an ornate door, many levels above us. It opens and Marcail is the first to pass through. The Crowd is a mixture of applause and jeers. Behind her are a few of her advisors. Then Fiona, looking lovely, even though she is more pale than I have ever seen. The next person to walk through is Liam. Braddock gasps along with everyone else in the Temple, myself included.

He is dressed in the flowing attire of Aegea, which means I will not be facing him. However, more shocking is his right arm. It stops abruptly at the elbow with a thick bandage. Something has happened to sever his arm. Sometime between our last meeting and now, his life as a General was ended by a brutal injury.

Braddock is on his platform and piloting his way to the Aegeans before I can react. The cameras remain focused on Liam as he takes a seat and gingerly adjusts the sling holding the remnant of his arm.

"My queen," Braddock says after entering her quarters, "please keep us waiting no longer. What has become of your General?" The Crowd sits silently, awaiting Marcail's explanation.

"Liam has suffered a terrible injury while training to face Trajan here today." She reaches out and puts her hand gently on Liam's shoulder, "He has served Aegea honorably for many years and is devastated that he will not be able to represent us in our darkest hour."

There is scattered applause, which I join, honoring the General's dedication. While I pay tribute, my right hand, still tender after my injury, begins to throb. If they were able to save my arm in spite of the devastating injury I suffered, Liam's wound must have been catastrophic. I wonder what type of training could inflict such trauma.

"Even more heart wrenching, especially to me, is who we must send to Battle in his stead," Marcail says.

At her words, the door across from me opens. The Aegean General emerges. Small, young, squinting through the brightness of the lights. It takes me a moment, but when I recognize him, it's as if gravity has ceased to exist. William. Marcail's own son and a man I consider a friend takes the battlefloor.

The Crowd recognizes him a few seconds after me and ignites. This twist is almost too much for them to handle. A Battle has not seen a Royal General since Tori. To send someone so untested against a General like me is the same as surrender. It's worse. If Marcail would just surrender, William's life would be spared.

I scan the Crowd, looking for any sign of Tori. Now, more than ever, I need him. Marcail's manipulation is astounding. She is willing to sacrifice her son, all in the hopes of exploiting my friendship with him and baiting me into easing my aggression. My entire time in Aegea, she was building toward this. Putting the two of us in situations where we could grow closer together. Encouraging, for the first time in my life, a friendship. And now she's asking me to destroy her son. My friend. And she's betting I will falter. I'm drawn back to the present, only to realize I'm close to hyperventilating.

She has planned this Battle perfectly. Her first strike caught me unaware and wounded me in a way I have never experienced in the Temple.

Braddock lands in front of William and begins interviewing him. I miss his question, but William's words are unmistakable. "Before he left Aegea, Trajan told me something that has prepared me for this day better than any other training I have received. He told me that he trusted in our Ruling Ancestors so much that he believes the outcome of Battle is governed more by the will of the General than his might. At the time, I thought he was a little crazy. But as I stand here, on the battlefloor, ready to spill my blood for the sake of my nation, I understand what he meant. My heart is full, as is my faith. And I have never felt mightier or assured of victory."

The Crowd erupts. It seems they have found a new darling. With all of my might, I push my respect and care for William aside. Next, I fight the pain I feel when I think of Fiona's pain once William falls dead at me feet. I focus on how much I want Marcail to suffer by watching her son succumb to my might. I will end this fast and remove any doubt of Marcail's evil.

Soaking up the drama of the situation, Braddock jets back to me. "General, tell us what you are feeling," he says.

I look at him in a way that makes him take a step back. "I am done with this melodrama. We came here to fight, not perform an opera. Do your job and describe the terms of engagement." If the Crowd reacts to this, I don't notice. Everything has been removed. I want Marcail to feel more pain than she ever realized existed, and William will be my lever.

"Very well," he says as he boards his platform. He raises ten meters and navigates to the center of the Temple. "People of Earth!" His voice booms over the acoustic system, "You are about to witness perhaps the most important Battle in our history. Celsus has accused Aegea of atrocities beyond imagination. Trajan, the most dominant General to ever Battle in the name of justice stands ready to hold Queen Marcail accountable for her crimes. In his way is Prince William of Aegea. Trajan's friend and Marcail's own son."

The Temple shakes with the Crowd's excitement. I still can't find Tori, even though I see the Celcean quarters. Demetrius lounges in his traditional style. Behind him, Castor paces, clearly as spun up as the Crowd.

"This day, the true nature of what it means to be a General will be tested before you. No gimmicks. No weapons. We will not test the physical might of these two Generals. We will test the very nature of their wills."

No weapons. So it will be a race, or a puzzle. Marcail, it seems, is not so evil as to risk her son's life. A hole opens in the center of the battlefloor and a cylinder, maybe four meters tall, emerges.

"Generals, please step forward."

We do as he says. As I get closer, I see one single, chest high hole in the monolith. The cylinder is just tall enough that I can't see William on the other side. I was hoping to see his eyes in order to give me an idea of his level of anxiety.

"The task before you is simple. It is a test of sacrificial speed. There is an opening on each side of the cylinder leading to one single button. All you must do to win this Battle is push the button before your opponent. Simple, yes? There is, however, one contingency." Every person in the Temple is breathless with anticipation. Sacrificial speed. I have figured out the contingency before Braddock describes it. I should have known after seeing Liam enter with Marcail. "When the button is pushed, it will immediately release a blade which will sever the winner's arm. Here is your sacrifice. If you win, your nation will prosper, but you will cease to be a whole man. Your dedication to the truest intent of our Ruling Ancestor will be put to the test this day."

Win, and Celsus wins. Win and I lose. No longer General. Clearly not suited to be a politician. Too maimed to be a Mentor. Lose and Celsus ceases to be. The Crowd understands as well. They scream, not the usual yells of excitement for bloody Battle. Their screams are in protest of the impossible scenario Marcail has designed. This is not a Battle to please the onlookers. This is a Battle designed to turn our world upside down.

"We salute you, Generals," Braddock says, beginning the salutation which will initiate the Battle. There is a hint of sadness in his voice I have never heard before. "Your sacrifice will save millions."

Rather than begin their usual cheering, the Crowd falls silent. I take a deep breath, coming to terms with the start of the new life which will begin in mere moments. Teeth clenched, I raise my hand, ready to offer my sacrifice when I hear a deep tone reverberate through the Temple. At the same time, the hole on my side of the cylinder closes.

Then, Braddock's voice, "Aegea wins!"

Aegea wins. It takes longer than it should before I understand. While I hesitated, considering what would become of me, William didn't. I look toward the Celcean quarters, to find Demetrius standing, fists clenched, and Castor next to him yelling in his ear. I lost. My nation is no more because of me. When I was asked to give of myself completely, I couldn't answer the call. I cared more about my well-being than I did for my nation.

William rounds the cylinder. Pale and sweating. I look down, expecting to see a bloody stump, but both arms remain perfectly intact.

"How?" I ask. But there is no answer. Behind me, ten of the Celcean Guard, Demetrius's personal detail. rush toward me.

The Crowd begins shouting, as unsure as me about what just happened. As the guards surround and force me from the battlefloor, I hear William as he addresses Braddock.

"They told me Liam lost his arm testing this machine. I expected to lose my arm today."

The door to the Temple closes as Castor enters from the hall. His face is red with rage. "Hold him," he whispers.

They crowd in, then seize me. I'm numb, still coming to terms with what has happened. In all my life, I never considered the realistic possibility of my defeat. Even in my weakest moments the only defeat I contemplated was being killed. In those scenarios, the fallout of my failure was far from me. I never thought I would still be alive, facing my subordinates or my dethroned Ruler.

"You need not restrain me. I will accept any punishment Demetrius deems worthy," I say.

Castor vacillates between righteous outrage for the loss of Celsus and giddiness over my loss. "Don't be so sure. Father has kept his hand from you for far too long. It is time you learned of his true wrath."

Far away, I hear Braddock's voice, proclaiming William's final victory and, with it, the fall of Celsus. "Spare your anger until Marcail has spoken. She is our new Ruler." I say. Even as I speak, it is as if I'm describing the landscape of an alien world.

"Clinging already to your new Ruler?" he pushes his way through the Guard so we are face to face. "If you think Demetrius will simply hand over his empire, you are delusional." Before I can answer, he strikes me, clean across the jaw. Then again. And again. After the fifth blow, I feel myself losing consciousness. The last thing I see are Castors bared teeth, then his bloodied fist.

Chapter 47

One moment, blackness. The next, I'm ripped from my stupor by ice water. I gasp through cracked lips, covered in dried blood. My head aches and I'm barely able to open my eyes, but my ears work perfectly.

"One more time. I want to be sure he is completely aware," Demetrius says.

I'm immediately doused with another bucketful of water. "Enough," I say, weakly. "I am awake and ready for my punishment, Father."

"Don't be so sure," Castor says. He stoops down, inspecting the damage he inflicted. "If only I had a camera. I would capture every burst blood vessel and crack in your skull. You have finally been revealed for the traitorous weakling you truly are."

In spite of my wounds, I lunge for him, only to be stopped by the chains which are wrapped around both arms and my torso. "We're no longer bound by the rules of our Ancestors. Release me and you will understand the restraint with which I have been blessing you."

"Enough," Demetrius says. "It seems we have come to an end, Trajan." He has the calm of someone who has nothing left to fear. "I built Celsus into the mightiest nation through your strength. And through your cowardice, it all crumbled."

I don't recognize our surroundings. We're somewhere in the Temple, but it must be on the very edge, closest to the frozen winds and glaciers. "Father," I mutter, unsure of what to say next.

"Silence. I am not your father. I am no one's father anymore." He crouches down, "Marcail, in her magnanimity, has allowed me a few hours to put some final things in order. You should feel honored to know I'm focusing the majority of my time on you."

There is nothing I can say which will justify my failure, so I wait.

"After all was accounted for, your dedication was never to me. It was to your own glory. Marcail in her devious manipulation rooted your weakness out perfectly. She saw your flaw and exploited it beautifully. I, on the other hand, thought you truly loved Celsus. I thought you truly loved me. Shame on me." He pulls my head up and slaps my cheek. "But I don't only blame you. In fact, I think you were led astray."

Tori is dragged into the room. He's been beaten so mercilessly, he can't stand on his own. Judging from the odd angles of his legs, both are broken.

"Demetrius. Hold me accountable for my actions. Tori has served you without blemish," I say. My vision blurs from tears as I strain as hard as I can against the chains.

"It is as I have feared. You seek to protect him with more passion than you sought to defend Celsus," Demetrius says. He stands and walks over to Tori. "There has been a wolf in my own backyard, all these years." He beckons to Castor, who hands him a blade. "It is time to give the wolf what he deserves."

Demetrius grabs Tori's hair and drags the blade across his throat. Tori makes no sound, nor does he look away from me as blood pours from his neck.

There are no words for the pain I feel. Every strike, cut, stab and attack, combined and multiplied would not come close to what I feel. My scream fades to silence as air empties from my lungs. Tori's body crumbles to the floor and Demetrius uses his foot to push him away. To my left, Castor is laughing.

"As for you," Demetrius says, "death would be unjust. I want anguish to be your teacher."

I'm pulled to my feet by the members of the Ceremonial Guard.

"Since you prize your body over your nation, you must learn what it is to live in poverty." He raises the knife to my face, dragging it down my forehead, across my eye and down my cheek. "When I was a boy, my father caught me stealing from him. It was a simple gold bracelet. He owned dozens. But it was the principle which angered him. So he turned me over to one of his slaves. For the next month, I was the servant of my father's slave. I hated my father for it. But I look back now and I realize why he did it. He took what I valued the most and made me live without it. From that point on, it was no longer my master. Yes, I still desired it. But I was able to look back and know I would survive without it."

He rests the knife blade on the flesh of my right arm, just above my biceps. "Since you chose your body over me, I demand a just payment." His eyes widen as he applies pressure. At first, the pain is dull, but as the blade begins to sever muscle, then tendon, then bite into bone, it becomes electric. He slowly circles the blade around my arm, cleanly severing every piece of flesh from my shoulder. By the time the blade has made it back to where he started, I'd numbed to the feeling. Demetrius steps back, "Castor, end this General's reign and take your place as my new right hand."

Castor lunges for my blood soaked arm. In one, fast and violent strike, he raises my arm while bringing his elbow down on the exact spot where Demetrius separated my flesh. My bone gives way with a sickening crack. I begin to black out. As my vision fades, I see Castor walking around the room, holding my severed arm above his head. A madman's trophy. Pain gives way to a panic I have never known. The last thing I hear before I pass out is Demetrius order Castor back to Celsus.

"Go," he says, "mobilize your army."

Chapter 48

"I still don't understand why we saved him." I vaguely register these sounds as words. My bed feels as if it's floating and the sea breeze is cool on my skin. Somewhere in the distance, I can hear the call of a pack of gulls. Judging from the light, it is mid-morning. I have overslept. Tori will be waiting for me, impatient to get my training started for the day. In the back of my mind, I find myself secretly hoping to see Fiona today.

There is a dull anxiety creeping up, likely the remnants of a dream, slowly fading. Bits and pieces of it remain. The Temple, William, an attack by Castor, despair. I shake my head and open my eyes. Oddly, I am not in my Aegean quarters. This room is larger, brighter and I detect the faint smell of disinfectant. I try to remember the events of last night, but I cannot pinpoint what occurred.

The anxiety grows. Guilt for having overslept after a night of too much revelry.

"He's stirring," I hear to my left.

I look over and see two Aegean physicians. Curious, I push my elbows under me and am met with immediate and searing pain in my right arm. I look down to see the cause and my stomach immediately turns. Gone. Only a blood soaked bandage capped over what should be my arm. All at once, the events of the Battle and my punishment flood back. I wretch uncontrollably, faster than the physicians can reach me.

"We should have kept him sedated longer." One says to the other.

The scent of bile blots out the sea air. "How?" I ask.

They don't respond to me. Rather, they begin cleaning my sheets, rolling me from side to side as they swab me down, change the linens and redress me.

My shaking only intensifies as the memory of the Temple continues to solidify. My failure. Tori's execution. Marcail's manipulation. Demetrius's rage. Castor's delight.

"How did I get here?" I ask, after they have finished.

"Marcail knew Demetrius would deal horribly with you. Her spies weren't able to stop him, but after he dumped you for dead outside of the Temple, they were able to recover you in time. Barely." The tallest of the two says, while pointing to my left hand.

I look down to see my fingers, the skin black, swollen, blistered and peeling from the severe frostbite. As if seeing is feeling, they immediately begin to burn from the inside.

"We're not sure yet, but you'll likely lose the tips, at least," says the other.

"You need to rest," the tall one says, looking harshly at his partner. "Her Majesty will be here in a day or two. Until then, you need to stay still. There is too much trauma even for one as strong as you." He puts on a thin glove before scooping up a glob of translucent gel. Before I can protest more, he smooths the gel over my forehead. Within seconds, my vision blurs and I pass out.

I don't know how long I sleep, but I dream one continuous scene. I float in a dark pool, barely able to keep my head above water. My arms and legs burn, at the end of their strength. In a panic, I begin calling out for help. After a few feeble yells, a glaring yellow light shines through the darkness, highlighting Tori's lifeless body, suspended above me with blood pouring from his neck. As it tumbles down, it gains volume and turns into a waterfall of ice cold blood. It fills the pool higher and higher as my waning strength drags me lower and lower.

"Has there been any change?"

I recognize William's voice, but the drugs which knocked me out are still in my system. No matter how hard I try, I can't open my eyes more than a slit. Instinct takes over and I attempt to push myself up, only to be met by the same sickening pain from what is left of my arm.

"Take it easy, Trajan." Fiona. I'm overjoyed. Just to see her face, I force my eyes open wider.

"Princess," I slur.

There are tears in her eyes as she smiles at me. Such pity in her gaze, when it used to hold respect for me. "Easy. You can't afford any more trauma."

"So I've been told," I say, relaxing back into my bed. "Marcail should have left me to die. When the rest of the world hears about my rescue, there will be rumors of conspiracies and of my treachery. It will open her to more challenges." I hear Fiona sigh and sense William stand.

"You can tell her yourself. She will be here presently," William says. There is an edge to his voice which I would confront, if I were stronger. It was her manipulation which led me here and I don't take lightly to his offense.

"No need. She may have saved my life, but it is a life I do not wish. I choose the blackness of death over a life of reliance. Tell her I decline her audience."

"Your anger is understandable. But remember, Demetrius maimed you, not Marcail," William says.

"It's easy to pontificate after winning a Battle in which you knew the outcome, General," I spit. "Yours is a hollow victory."

"I didn't come here to argue. The Battle was fairly matched. I hope you come to see that in time. I wish you a fast recovery." He turns and leaves the room.

Fiona remains by my side, silent and patient. Exactly as she was during my earlier recovery from the shark bite. Only then, Tori was here too. Just the thought of him brings uncontrollable tears. He died because of me. Beaten, broken and executed, all because I didn't have the courage to do what needed to be done. He trusted me. I wonder, as the knife was raised to his throat, if he regretted what he told me before sending me into Battle against William. Tori is dead because of my cowardice and here I sit, broken beyond repair. Living the reality that, if I had chosen it, would have kept him alive.

I feel Fiona's hand on my shoulder and realize I have been sobbing. She says nothing and I'm unable to stop the regret and shame washing over me. "Just let me die."

In response, she leans down and wraps her arm around my neck, careful not to get too close to my wounds. We stay that way for what seems like hours. Her embrace, while loving and warm, does nothing to ease my pain. This despair is visceral. The inky blackness of standing in the heart of a cave. Somewhere inside me, the hopelessness takes shape and begins to soak into everything. Turning my blood into sludge, bone into stone. Devouring my flesh. Soon, I won't exist anymore. This shame will have possessed me. Made me its vessel. A tribute to my selfish pride and greed.

"It's not so bad. you can relearn to do almost anything one handed," Fiona finally says. Her words, meant to comfort, only serve to make me feel more isolated. "I would gladly give my other arm and both my legs if Tori were still standing here," I say.

She pulls away briefly, her eyes spilling tears as well. It looks as if she's about to say something. Instead, she just nods and wraps me in another embrace.

Chapter 49

Marcail does not come to visit me until two nights later. When she enters my room, it looks as if she has aged decades. This is not how a victorious Ruler should look.

"General," she says.

There is no emotion left in me to greet her with the anger she deserves. It has all been spent in mourning. I offer only a feeble nod.

"I'm told your body is recovering as well as can be expected. Naturally, I asked Lilith if she could perform her earlier magic on you. Sadly, your wounds were so severe, we must let them run their course." There is no compassion in her words. Nor is there delight.

I search for something to say, only to realize I am unequal to the task. This would be the time when Tori would step in to offer the perfect response. As it has for the last few days, just the thought of my Mentor brings on a new round of tears. I try to will them away, but it seems my will has long since given up the Battle for supremacy over my emotions.

"I can only imagine the enormity of the loss you must feel," she says. "You must think me a monster by now."

I swallow the next round of tears and finally say, "Would I be wrong?"

"Yes. And no."

"But mostly no."

"I don't pretend to be without blemish, Trajan. Sending William into Battle was the most difficult thing I've ever done."

I let out a bitter laugh. "Why? You knew he would not die. And he knew he would not suffer. Your victory was nothing more than a cheap magic trick."

She straightens. "You can question me all you want, child. But do not question William's courage. He had no more knowledge of the Battle than you. If we were to win, it had to be for the right reasons. I challenged you both equally. Rather than a challenge of physical strength, which we both know you would have won, I tested your will against my son's. And you, General, were bested fairly and soundly."

I hate her with every part of myself. "Is this why you saved me? To stand over me as my conqueror? I will give you no such satisfaction."

"Time, I pray, will show your error. Until then, I thought you should know," she swipes her hand and the wall in front of me comes to life with images of Celsus. In the images, Castor's army has surrounded the capital, cutting off all roads in or out. "Your valiant Ruler. The one who has respected the system given to us by the Elders, has refused to acknowledge Aegea's victory. He has stated that if we try to take control, he will launch an assault of truewar. And here you thought I was the one thirsting for blood." She stands to leave. "At some point in our lives, we all must step back and consider whether or not the truths under which we were weaned are worthy to carry us into maturity."

"We are a world undone," Fiona says.

My loss was less than a week ago and truewar is upon us. When Marcail's delegation approached the Cecean capital, Castor's army unleashed on them. The carnage was broadcast around the world in a matter of seconds. Of course, Rulers were outraged. In spite of a litany of accusations leveled against Aegea, most Rulers maintained there was no call for the bloodshed.

Marcail called upon her contemporaries to unite against Demetrius and his secret army, but the show of force had been enough. While he was being publicly chastised, no leader was willing to go against him. The fact remained, while the rest of the world slept, Demetrius had been preparing. After the slaughter of the Aegeans on the capital's border, Demetrius continued his show of force. He highlighted his stockpiles of weapons, showed how his drones had been retrofitted for combat and, in what was a shock even to me, showed the countless bases strategically placed in remote Celcean locations, each housing hundreds of ready and willing soldiers. In perhaps his most outlandish claim, he told the world he was only interested in what he considered his right. The complete and utter surrender of Aegea. He promised to return peace if only Aegea recognized him as their Ruler.

Marcail refused, of course. Since then, Rulers have called upon Aegean citizens to stage a coup. Claiming her vendetta against Demetrius was about to throw the entire world back into chaos.

Two days ago Demetrius grew impatient and mobilized two thousand Peacekeepers, led by Castor against one of Aegea's hunting colonies. It was a bloodbath. Immediately after the skirmish, Demetrius released a statement.

"Marcail's pride has caused the death of fifty of her loyal citizens. I weep for their senseless deaths, but I must carry the burden of pursuing balance across the globe, even if it means cutting down Aegea in the most brutal way possible.

"Before I sent my Peacekeepers, I contacted her. Giving her one last chance to admit her deception and forfeit what is rightly mine. Sadly, but not surprisingly, she was defiant. Even provocative. It seemed as if she was eager for the death of her own citizens.

"What I have feared for so long is clearly true to me now. The hubris and greed of this woman pushes her to see the people of Aegea as nothing but cows, meant to serve her every whim.

"Some have asked me why I would resort to the old ways. Aren't I equally to blame for my aggression? It is true. My troops have struck a blow against innocent Aegeans. But make no mistake. Mine was not the first salvo in this war. Marcail set this in motion when she corrupted and turned Trajan against me through her lies and hedonism.

"No, this war was started long ago. And if I must be the one to win, no matter the cost, I will bear that terrible burden and let history judge my actions."

Since giving his speech, the entirety of his army has been moving steadily toward Aegea.

"No matter how hard mother tries, no one will stand with her." Fiona sits at the foot of my bed. Her surgical clothes covered in the blood of the fallen Aegeans. She doesn't cry, having been emptied of tears long ago.

"They are all too terrified. If he wins this war against Marcail, nothing will keep him from turning his might against her allies," I say. In spite of all my logic telling me differently, I feel responsible. If I had won, Tori would be alive. The innocents on the hunting colony would be alive, and Aegea would be peacefully integrating into the Celcean Empire. "They are a herd of water buffalo, trying to appease the prowling lion."

"Do you realize you are likely the one person who has kept this from happening for all of these years?"

I'm unsure of her meaning.

She sees my confusion and says, "It's clear now. Demetrius has been on a rampage with you as General. He was happy to wage his war while still complying with the Ancestors as long as he possessed the most dominant warrior. It is not a coincidence that after suffering his only loss, he reveals a highly trained army. Your might has kept him at bay for years."

The way she describes his intentions eases my guilt at first. But after considering for a moment, I'm sickened. "If that's true, it means I am one of the most brutal conquerors in history. Even worse, it makes me the blind, yet useful tool of a madman. Rather than having the blood of one nation on my hands, I have the blood of dozens."

"Oh Trajan," she says, leaning forward, "that is not what I meant."

"I know. but it doesn't make it any less true." We are quiet for a few moments before I say, "Regardless, we no longer have the luxury of dwelling on what-ifs or lamenting our past choices. For right or wrong, Demetrius has locked a course. The way Aegea responds will likely determine the fate of this world for generations to come."

Chapter 50

"I thought there was nothing you could do for me," I say. We are still in my hospital room, but I am now surrounded by Marcail and the majority of her political advisors.

"In a way, that's true. You will never get your arm back as it once was," Marcail says. Her voice is low, but full of confidence. She is playing the part of self-assured queen. "But we could give you something that, in time, may become as useful, if not more, than mere flesh and bone."

"Such promises come at a high price. What would you ask of me? Further dishonor and disdain? A public oath of allegiance? Would you have me transfer my service from one deceitful Ruler to another?"

I can immediately tell which of the advisors in the room are loyal to her based on their reaction to this. One of them begins to say something, then thinks better of it. Clearly, they are under strict orders to keep quiet.

"If you are still wrestling with which Ruler walks the straighter road, then you are not as intelligent as I hoped."

She's right, of course. This realization has come after long, sleepless hours while staring at my severed arm. At first, I equated my punishment from Demetrius in parallel to what Marcail did to Caleb. But a General's loss in a Battle is not the same as a single man's hubris which caused the death of hundreds of innocents. That was the easy part to reconcile. After watching my Mentor murdered, having my limb amputated, being left for dead and now being accused of collusion with Marcail, it was easy for me to see Demetrius as a power crazed lunatic. The harder truth to accept is that Demetrius, in all likelihood, has been this way long before I became his General. Even thinking back to his multiple challenges of Tori's father, I can now see the obsession. And yet I couldn't see it before it was too late. I have been a simple minded fool, easily manipulated by Demetrius and instrumental in his patient campaign toward world dominance.

"It is not that, Highness," I say. "I see Demetrius for who he is. What gives me pause is that I am still unclear as to who you are. I have toppled nations because of my mindless obedience. What kind of man would I be if I simply fell into step with another such Ruler?"

The room is silent as these politicians await the fury of their queen. Rather than unleash on me, she gently sits on my bed.

"You have been betrayed by your Ruler. And you feel betrayed by me. So I understand why you would be so harsh. I wonder, though. If you had been an observer. A General simply watching a Mid-Year Exhibition, would you still see my terms of engagement as so devious? Are you not taught to observe your opponent and exploit his weakness? Is it really so wrong of me to have exploited so obvious of a weakness? A shortcoming, by the way, developed and nurtured within you by Demetrius himself?"

The truth in her words are too much for me to handle. If she had grabbed my other arm and lopped it off, I would be in less pain. For as long as I can remember, my worth has been defined by my physical ability. If not for my ability to impose my will upon others, I would not have lasted. And as I became more dominant, more and more people were assigned to ensure my perfect health.

"Trajan, for better or worse, you remain in the center of this crisis. You know the mind of Demetrius better than anyone. You have been the physical manifestation of his will for years. And the General who controls his army learned his tactics from you.

"I am not asking you to align yourself with me. I am asking you to oppose the obvious tyranny of Demetrius. And I am offering you a resource that just may give you the success for which our entire world prays."

She stands and says to her advisors, "Come. We have tired him too much already." As they shuffle out of my room, she gently grabs my hand and says, "I will return tomorrow in hopes of an answer. Demetrius is on the move and we cannot afford a long decision process." She pauses, and looks as if she's about to leave, then thinks better of it. "Most people in this world live easy lives. They rise in the morning and work a simple job. If they're lucky, they find love, and they drift into restful sleep each night, secure in the knowledge that tomorrow will offer them the same challenges as they have faced time and time again. But there are a select few who have been called upon to live a life which lacks comfort or regularity. They rise in the morning and fight the monsters which have been stalking them all night. Every day brings pain and confusion and solitude. The path they walk leads them through thorns, across violent oceans and past the dens of predators. Rather than sleep, they lay prostrate, begging for the strength to rise and face an even crueler reality than the day before. I don't envy the path which has been set before you, Trajan. But I beg you to rise one last time. There is a wolf approaching our gate. And he won't politely knock before ripping it from his hinges. Be our General and do what only the Ruling Ancestors before you have been able to do. Pull us from the darkness before it closes completely around us."

"You will be under anesthesia for about five hours, if the surgery goes well," Fiona says.

I have decided to help Marcail, rather than lay idly by while Demetrius and Castor break every truth I have ever known about war.

"And recovery?" I ask.

She puts down one of the many medical instruments which are scattered around the operating room. "That's the question, isn't it? This is new ground. It's never worked on a human before. Caleb's island massacre was the closest we've come to success."

The plan is to implant a chip at the base of my skull which will tap into the signals that travel up and down my spine, allowing me to manipulate a small energy field around my body. It won't give me my arm back, but, in theory, I will be able to project the field into an extension of my arm, briefly making it a weapon, similar to a white-hot sword.

"Seems like a lot of risk. You don't need an arm to command an army," William says.

I take a deep breath. "How did we come to this? Just a few months ago, truewar was the furthest thing from our minds. Now Celsus is on the move and I've agreed to do the very thing I've sworn never to do. Ask innocent citizens to take up arms and put their lives on the line."

"When you fight a man who honors no rules, sometimes you must suspend your honor as well," William says.

"With respect, Prince. But you know nothing of what you speak. If we become animals in order to protect our humanity, we risk our humanity never returning. This is a truth our Ancestors knew well. And it's why they appointed Generals. We few had to learn how to turn the monster on and off. Make no mistake. If we win this war, the men and women who joined in the bloodshed may not return."

"And if we don't meet their force with our own, we will not even have the chance of recovering from the horrors of war," he says.

"You are right. But it is not a reality I take lightly. Nor is there a reality in which I will lead an army as a broken man. I know what it means to spill blood and take lives. If I go into war unable to protect myself, I will fall almost immediately. And without me as the tip of the spear, your citizen soldiers will wilt. That is why this procedure is worth the risk."

"Enough. Both of you," Fiona says. "We need to focus on preparation and recovery.

"As far as we can tell, Caleb's experiment failed because the farmers couldn't control their panic response. If you watch the video, the implant was successfully placed in all of them, and they regained consciousness without issue. It wasn't until they started trying to control the field that things went wrong. Our best guess is that they experienced some sort of sensation when the field started moving which caused them to experience fear. That panic caused an overload on the implant which caused the field to intensify and turn against the subject. We're hoping you will be able to control your emotions better."

There is nothing left for any of us to say. We await the surgeons in silence, each of us lost in our own thoughts. I'm overcome by the absurdity of the situation. We speak as if my mere presence will mold a group of farmers, artists and hunters into Battle-hardened warriors in a matter of days. We will have only makeshift weapons to match against Castor's stockpile of precision killing machines. And we sit here, waiting to place an untested and unsuccessful technology into my body, putting our faith in theories and guesses–hoping I won't burn to death just a few hours from now.

Chapter 51

"It's time to wake up, General," I hear. For a moment, I forget what is happening, but the confusion passes quickly. I open my eyes, but stay as still as I can. The room is full of physicians and politicians.

"If I start burning up, we may want fewer people in here," I say. It's my attempt at humor, but judging from the reactions, it falls short.

"He's right," Marcail says, "all non-essentials out."

I close my eyes, forcing myself to remain calm while I search my senses for anything that feels askew. Nothing. Other than a dull numbness in the back of my neck, I feel normal.

"Alright, everyone is out."

Once again, I open my eyes. Just Marcail, a physician I don't recognize and Fiona. "Princess, I'm glad to see you, but please leave. If I were to harm you, even slightly, it would be the end of me."

She smiles and says, "Then don't do anything to harm me."

I focus on my breathing, letting the oxygen fill my lungs, then permeate my blood. "All good so far. Any suggestions on how to test it out?"

"From what we can tell, you should be able to move freely without engaging the implant. It seems to engage when you focus directly on the tech and try to manipulate it," the physician says.

"What is your name?" I ask.

"Daniel."

"Ok, Daniel, I'm going to sit up, then stand. Slowly. If something looks off, I want you to grab the princess and queen and get them out as quickly as possible. Understand?"

He nods, then wipes a bead of sweat from his forehead.

I slowly sit up, sure to focus only on the movement itself. Nothing wrong yet. Next, I stand, stretching myself to full height.

"Congratulations, so far you have lived the longest of anyone with the implant," Fiona says. Her voice has a slow, almost trance-like cadence.

"Let's get this over with," I say. I plant my feet shoulder width apart and settle my weight so I'm perfectly balanced. Next, I focus on the implant, imagining myself flipping a switch which funnels my energy into the device. "I feel some heat at the back of my neck," I say. It's not painful, but it's startling. Tori's training comes immediately to mind. All the hours spent forcing myself to control my emotions in the face of extreme fear and danger. I embrace it, name it for what it is, then detach from it.

"Has it intensified?" Daniel asks, his voice quivering.

I don't respond. Now that I have engaged the implant, I don't want to lose the connection. First, I try activating the energy field in the same way I would command one of my limbs to move. Nothing. The heat continues to pulsate at the back of my neck. "Sword," I say. Nothing. It's not tied to my voice.

This goes on for what feels like hours. I try every way I can think to make the device respond to me, but nothing is successful. Through it all, I remain in complete control of my emotions.

Finally, I turn to Daniel, Fiona and Marcail and say, "I'm out of ideas. Are you sure it is connected properly?"

Daniel nods, "We followed Caleb's notes exactly."

Fiona steps toward me. "I think, maybe, you are too controlled. Have you let in any emotion at all?"

I shake my head.

"Here," she says while lifting a fresh block of walnut toward me. "I brought this, sure you would master the implant and hopeful you would be able to begin a new sphere."

I reach out to take it with my left hand, but she pulls the block back.

"No. Use the energy field."

I clench my jaw and try again, imagining the field as an arm, reaching out. Nothing. "This is pointless. I've tried this already," I say.

"What would Tori say right now? Try? The Lion of Celsus doesn't try. The Lion of Celsus does what he wants. Do it."

The mention of Tori sparks something. A small, but powerful ember of emotion, which I quickly suppress. "Fiona, stop."

"Stop? So you give up? We've wasted all this time on you. You're not the General we need. Have you lost your will? Take the block, General."

Another spark. Larger, harder to suppress. The heat in my neck spreads to my shoulders, hotter than before. It fades back as I wrangle the rising anger.

"You're playing with danger, Princess."

"I don't think I am. I don't think you're dangerous anymore. I think you're too broken to be dangerous. They're coming, Trajan. The men who murdered your Mentor. Who murdered innocent Aegeans. That blood and death is because of you. You couldn't protect them and, unless you wake up, you can't protect us either."

Sudden and immediate pain. As if molten iron has been poured over me. My heart rate spikes and I go rigid. My knees buckle, but I don't fall. The energy field surrounds me, burning my flesh and sucking the air from my lungs.

Everything fades from my vision. There is only the pain and the fear. The experiment has failed and I'm about to be another casualty of Caleb's. They were right, emotion activates it, but that's where it stops. There is no controlling it.

Far away, I hear something. As if floating through mud, Fiona's voice filters through.

"Now control it. Own the pain. Fight through it. Think of what Tori taught you. He prepared you for this. Focus. Embrace it and make it yours."

The pain intensifies, as if the field hears her too and is fighting to take over. I think back to my Battles. All the deadly wounds I survived. I have lived through worse. The emotion is too powerful to suppress, but I begin to fight it the same way I would another General. I calm my fear, but allow the anger to stay. The pain fades from my focus and I imagine the field sliding across my body. Up my legs, over my torso, down my head. I can breathe again as I force myself to imagine a new arm growing from the tender stump that Demetrius created.

All of the pain has transferred to the tip of my arm, but I can feel the field taking shape. Forming into what was once muscle and elbow and bone and fingers. I'm drained, but I force myself to stay conscious as I command my new limb to slowly reach up and gently snatch the block from Fiona's hand.

At once, the anger is gone, as is the field. The block falls to the floor and I crumble with it, gasping for breath.

Fiona kneels beside me and rests my head on her lap. "You did it, Trajan."

Chapter 52

William is anxious to get me in front of the Aegean Militia. Celsus continues to press forward. Some of their scouting parties have come across more Aegea hunting groups. Each skirmish has been a slaughter. The one advantage Aegea has is the ocean, which allows them to continuously move their capital and all of their outlying colonies. Celsus has very few sea vessels, but they have deployed countless drones to identify and track Aegean colonies. Even still, finding the Aegean colonies is tedious. I'm convinced the brutality of the recent skirmishes are the result of Castor's overwhelming frustration.

I have had the implant for three days now. Thanks to the healing salve, the wound around it is completely healed. But my mastery of the field is pedestrian at best. I've figured out how to engage it, and I've reconciled myself to the fact that when the field is live, it burns whatever part of my body it touches. The more I concentrate the field into one spot, the more intense the burn. My biggest issues are my ability to move the field quickly from one shape or position into another, and my ability to form it into a usable shape. Currently, the best I can muster is a sort of rectangle which sprouts from my stump and ends in a ball, about a half a meter away. At this point, I would be more effective in the war without the field.

It's night. All of my physicians have long since gone to bed. Fiona left about an hour ago. William has asked me to meet with his appointed lieutenants tomorrow morning, but I don't feel ready. They need a leader who will inspire them. Convince them they could actually emerge from this victorious. At this point, I'm not that leader.

The block of wood Fiona gave me after my surgery remains on the footstool of my bed. I pick it up and focus on the implant, activating the field. The back of my neck heats up and I close my eyes, anticipating the rush of searing heat about to cover my body.

The key, I have discovered, is to allow myself to experience enough emotion to ignite the field, but not allow the emotion to take over. When the field is active, I must exist in an uncomfortable equilibrium between emotional chaos and control. So far, anger and sadness have been the most effective emotions to manifest. They have also been the most difficult to control.

I picture my final moments in the Temple. Castor strutting around the blood soaked room with my lifeless arm over his head. The field flashes to life, covering me in white-hot, pure energy. I hold the image in my mind, but I force the anger into determination. I know I've struck the right balance when I feel the energy begin to ripple over me.

The next step is the most difficult. I visualize the energy as a river, flowing over my body and pooling at the tip of my severed arm. The pain is intense, but I'm easily able to minimize it. It's obvious to me why Caleb's experiment with the citizens was such a failure. If not for my training, my lifetime of managing the pain which comes from being a General, I would be overwhelmed. In a matter of seconds, the field has contracted into a ball at the base of my right arm. If only I could grab the field and stretch it into the shape I want. But it is as solid as lead. Now that I have moved it to where I want it, I imagine it stretching, as if it is molten glass and I'm an artisan, forming a slender vase. The field boils at the tip of my arm. It's invisible, but I can feel it elongating. Earlier today, I was able to stretch it to almost a meter, but it took close to an hour and completely drained my energy. If I'm to be effective in battle, I must figure out how to manipulate the field as if it has always been a part of me. Faster and in more specific shapes.

I move my arm, and with it, the field, and tap the frame of my bed. It's reached one meter, which makes me smile. Rather than taking an hour, I was able to condense the process to ten minutes. Next, I imagine the energy contracting and molding into a scoop at the end. This is the most frustrating part. All of the physicians tell me I should be able to form the field into any shape I want. Even make it fluid. But it's just conjecture and theory at this point. Even though I can't see the field, I can sense when its shape and density change. The physicians spent hours grilling me about this, but I was unable to explain it in a way which satisfied them.

My goal tonight is to form a scoop which will let me pick up the block of wood at the end of my bed. I try to imagine the shape, then project that image down my arm. There is a jolt in the field and I sense a change, but as soon as it happens, my focus wanes and I feel the energy begin to contract. I'm sweating and I can feel myself weakening. With one final burst, I imagine my entire arm bending into the gentle slope of the head of a shovel. The field begins vibrating and I can sense it morphing. When it feels complete, I reach down and slide my false appendage under the block of wood. In wonder, I see the block move back, just slightly before I see it tilt as I slide the spade-head under it. I lift and watch as the block appears to hover in midair. I'm panting as if I've sprinted ten kilometers.

Gently, I imagine the tip of the field folding inward and over the block. My mind sends the same impulses as it would if I were plucking an apple off a tree. I feel the energy rolling up and contracting over the block when there's a loud pop. In an instant, the wood shatters. I'm so shocked that I lose all concentration and the field immediately contracts. Exhausted, I sever the connection to the implant and the wood shards scatter on the ground.

As I lower myself to my bed I begin to laugh. Yes, I clumsily crushed the thing I was trying to hold. But, for the first time, I saw the amazing potential of this alien technology. I will learn it, and once I've mastered it, I will be unstoppable.

"Welcome, General," Marcail says. "You look to have recovered remarkably well."

It's been a week since the implant was installed and my progress has been steady, but not fast enough. I've been hearing updates from various sources and it appears as if Celsus is becoming increasingly aggressive and ferocious with each passing day.

"Thank you, Highness. Your physicians, as always, have given me superior care."

"They would have my daughter to answer to if not."

I smile and dip my head. Embarrassed by my childish reaction to her mention of Fiona.

"I wish we were meeting under different circumstances, but Demetrius and his butcher grow more relentless with each day. They have even convinced another of the Sea Nations to supply them with vessels. It is only a matter of days until we have all been found."

She is right. We must do something other than run. At first, defense seemed the best answer. The sea is vast and the Aegeans are unparalleled in their ability to navigate and survive in such desolate waters. Soon after the first skirmishes, they decided to break all of the pods into their smallest possible sections and set off in as many different directions as possible. In an instant, Aegea had dissolved into a thousand tiny bubbles on the ocean's surface. But the plan has revealed glaring deficiencies.

Castor has proven to be an excellent hunter. His fleet of drones has methodically scoured for the pods and, once they spot one, it takes less than a day for a squadron of soldiers to show up and wreak havoc. The second deficiency is the inability of such small pods to defend themselves. They have no strength in numbers and very few of the pods have anyone with a military mind to help prepare them for battle, or guide them once the Celceans arrive. It's also become apparent that Castor has inside help. His understanding of ocean currents and the hidden waystations of the Aegean Nation has made him incredibly efficient in finding and dispatching the pods.

"When I first started fighting, Tori taught me to begin the confrontation by using an inferior strategy. For instance, he would have me fight with my weaker hand for the first few minutes. Just long enough so my opponent could formulate an attack pattern based on what he had seen. As soon as he had committed, Tori would have me adjust my style to vastly different and more superior tactics. Of course, this only works on overly aggressive and untested opponents. But, given what we have seen of Castor's style, I think it may be beneficial for us." Just mentioning Tori brings tears to my eyes. No matter how hard I try, I have not been able to block out the pain of losing him. I long for his wisdom, guidance and calm. Without him, I feel as if I'm no better than one of these tiny pods floating in the ocean, waiting for a predator to swallow me whole.

"An interesting tactic. But haven't we already put our best defense into play?" Marcail asks.

"Indeed, you have, my queen. This, however, is the beauty of Tori's deception. While you have sustained casualties, you have accomplished something much more important. You have manipulated Castor into a very specific style of engagement." Here I stand, advising a foreign Ruler on how to defeat Celsus in a truewar. How did this world get turned upside down so quickly? One loss. My loss, and the delicate equilibrium of our Ancestors was destroyed.

Marcail nods, encouraging me to continue.

"He has been forced to splinter his army in order to find and dispatch so many separate pods. In essence, he is fighting a war on hundreds of fronts. His communication and adaptability on the ocean are nothing compared to yours. Even though your citizens are untested and untrained, if you were to pull them together and commit to a full assault on Castor's command center, he would be overwhelmed by the sheer numbers. It may not end the war, but it would severely weaken his ability to command such a dispersed group of soldiers. And, once you have taken out the main command unit, you could turn your might on his isolated, smaller cells."

"Won't the command center be the most heavily protected?"

"Likely. But it's still weakened due to how many units he has dispersed trying to root you out. There will be heavy loss of troops, but they will sustain the brunt of it." I pause, amazed at how easily I have slipped into speaking about concepts of truewar. Dismissing the loss of troops and units, rather than wrestling with the death of countless men and women. "Forgive me, Highness. I realize my proposal comes at the price of the lives of Aegean citizens."

She is silent for a moment, with her head bowed. "The apology is not yours to make. You did not start this war, nor did you help secretly plan for it. Your counsel is sound. As is your humanity. I ask only one thing of you." She stands, puts her hands on my shoulders and looks straight up at me, "You continue to speak of Aegea as a nation foreign to you. For better or worse, we are now yours, and you are now ours. The sooner you reconcile that fact, the sooner you will be able to lead us into this hell with a clear heart."

Chapter 53

The Aegean Army is comprised mostly of their hunters. They are strong, agile, aggressive, disciplined and incredibly arrogant. William and I walk among them as they train, watching them laugh and goad each other.

"I think we will fare much better than expected," William says.

After my audience with Marcail, the fleet responded quickly. In a matter of hours, almost thirty pods had rejoined us. Now, more than a day into our journey toward the heart of Castor's Army, we are two hundred pods strong.

"How many have volunteered?" I ask.

"There are over one thousand willing to stand against Celsus," he says, proudly.

"How many of those are your hunters?"

"Close to three hundred."

This is the first time I have seen what the Aegeans have to offer, and the first time the Militia has seen me. As we pass by each group, they stop and openly stare at me.

"There are more women than I expected," I say.

"Aegeans do not assign roles based on gender. If a person can handle the task, they are given the responsibility. I think Castor will find our women more formidable than most."

I stop and turn to William. "Your confidence in your citizens is encouraging. It would, however, be prudent to limit your predictions. Yes, your hunters are fierce, but throwing a harpoon into a defenseless sea creature is not the same as facing a well-trained and disciplined soldier with superior weaponry. We want them confident, but we want them fearful as well. If we face Castor without the energy which comes from desperation, we will not last an hour on the battlefield."

I can tell he wants to argue, but he stops himself. We begin pacing again when one of the soldiers approaches us.

"Excuse me, my prince," he says. His skin is dark brown and his long hair has been bleached blond from the sun.

"Good to see you again, Donovan," William says with a smile. "May I present Trajan, Aegea's Commanding General."

Donovan smiles and offers his hand toward me. I look at his hand, then lock gazes with him.

"Are you part of the Militia?" I ask.

He drops his hand to his side, "Yes, sir. There is no Aegean more accurate with a spear than I."

"In that case, even if I still had a hand, I would not offer it in greeting. This is not a party and I am not your friend. I am your General," I say, loudly. Other young and tanned Aegeans have taken notice and they begin to crowd around us.

"I meant no disrespect," Donovan says before I cut him off.

"I do not care what you meant. I do not care if you're happy or sad or tired. I care about your ability to face an opponent with courage, honor and determination. More than that, I care about your immediate and uncompromising obedience to my every order."

William leans close, "This isn't Celsus, Trajan."

I step back and raise my voice, "Your prince, apparently, wants me to be a little nicer." Then to Donovan, "Young man, did I hurt your feelings?"

Donovan has stepped back a few paces and doesn't respond. We're surrounded now. Close to one hundred young and eager Aegeans overcome by curiosity.

"I'll tell you what, Donovan, I'll let you have your satisfaction. You say you're the best spearman here? Prove it."

I pick up a discarded spear and hand it to him. "If you can draw my blood, I will apologize."

Donovan hesitates, then glances at William, as if asking for permission.

"Don't you dare look at your prince. Marcail has given me full command over her Militia. Either take the spear or get off this pod."

William seethes, but keeps his tongue as Donovan accepts the razor sharp weapon from me. The crowd around us is silent, but I can feel their apprehension. In all likelihood, the majority of them would enjoy seeing me impaled.

"If you're as good as you claim, you should have no problem dispatching a one armed fallen General," I say.

I'm patient as Donovan begins to test the weight of the spear. After a few seconds, a few of the onlookers start yelling encouragement.

"Either strike or I will," I say. "Do you think Castor's army will wait for you to consider your options?" I'm yelling now. This lesson needs to be learned by everyone, not just Donovan.

He finally springs. The thrust is powerful, but slow. I easily twist my shoulder out of the way while simultaneously grabbing the shaft, which throws Donovan to the ground. The crowd goes silent as I stand over him with the tip of the spear hovering one millimeter from his throat. "If you're one of the best, we should surrender now."

I move the spear away and gesture for him to rise. "What did you do wrong?" I ask.

He stands, hands shaking. His elbow is bloody from where he landed. "I telegraphed the strike."

"What else?"

"I was too tense, which made the thrust slow."

"What else?"

"I didn't exploit your weakness."

I hand him the spear and say, "Again. Cleaner this time."

He doesn't hesitate. The second his hands grasp the spear, he pivots, swinging the butt of the weapon toward my head. I duck and it arcs harmlessly overhead. He continues his spin and brings the tip toward my chest in a downward strike. All of his power is behind the movement, which makes it easy for me to anticipate. I lunge toward him and bury my shoulder in his chest, sending him sprawling across the ground."

"Pathetic," I bellow. "I'm not even a whole man and you can't draw a single drop of my blood. The men you will face have trained since childhood to beat me. Their General took my arm. And you assemble here, arrogant and self-assured, expecting to win?"

Donovan is still on the ground. As I approach him, he swings the spear at my ankles, hoping to catch me off guard. I casually raise my leg and stomp, splintering the shaft.

"Get up," I say.

He scurries to his feet, short of breath, eyes wide with panic.

"I'm clearly too much for you, even in my weakened state," I say. "William, bind my left hand behind my back."

William slowly approaches. I can see the anger is still there, which irritates me. If he doesn't know what I'm trying to accomplish, he has no business around this Militia.

As he ties my hand, he leans close, "You've made your point. If you push much harder, you will break their spirit."

"If you think you can do a better job, be my guest. If not, shut your mouth. We have days to prepare for a job which takes years to perfect," I say, loud enough for others to hear.

He puts his full weight into cinching the last knot, letting his anger get the better of him.

I face Donovan. "Chose three more people to help you."

Without hesitation, two men and one woman step forward. Their appearance is almost identical to his. Lean and tanned with wispy hair. They could be his siblings.

"Begin," I say.

They look at each other before moving, which gives me the opening I was expecting. I twirl around, dropping into a crouch and sweeping my right leg out, which catches the tallest of them just behind the knees. His legs fly out from underneath him and he lands hard on his back. There is a dull thud as the back of his head strikes the ground. His arms fall limply away from him.

I'm back on my feet before the rest of them know what happened. An instant later, I'm in the air, connecting my heel across the cheekbone of the other man with a spinning kick. It connects with a crack as he's sent to the ground, unconscious before he lands.

What started as a lesson in decisiveness has turned into a beating. I should feel bad, but I'm infuriated. These novices expect to face Castor's Army and win. These children who likely cheered when the call for willing soldiers went out. They need to know what I learned decades ago. In a Battle, to win means the warrior must forfeit his morality. The victor is not the more honorable of the two. The victor is the one who is willing to cross an uncrossable line. And, once that line is crossed, there is no coming back. They must know and be reconciled to this truth before they're confronted with it in the face of a true enemy.

Donovan and the woman split so one is in front, one is behind. The crowd is cheering for them, loudly now. I feint an attack forward, but drop to my knee just as the severed tip of Donovan's spear passes over my head. Apparently the woman warrior is comfortable with a blade. She made a mistake by watching the trajectory, which I exploit by rolling back and springing up directly in front of her. She freezes as I loom over her and I bring my forehead down across the bridge of her nose. An explosion of blood bursts from her face as she falls back.

I spin to face Donovan one final time. The violence of my strike on the woman has silenced the crowd. "Do something," I yell at him. "Your friends have fallen. Your weapon is gone. Will you simply wilt before me? And you," I turn to the crowd, my voice reverberating now. "You stand idly by as your compatriots fall by my hand. Rather than join the fight, you play the spectator, as if we're back in the Temple." I strain against the rope which William tied around my arm. One by one, I feel the fibers giving. In a final show of strength, I rip my arm free. "You are not soldiers. You are not mighty. Celsus is on the move and you think your numbers will overwhelm them. They are faster. They are stronger. They are better trained and have superior weapons. Unless you learn to be more decisive, more vicious and work as a team this war is already over." I turn to Donovan who still hasn't moved. "You are not welcome in this Militia. You are weak and you lack the will to win. If I see you in these ranks again, I will kill you myself."

I walk away as the crowd parts. Most of them look down and scurry out of my way. Others glare hatred at me before ceding ground. Let them fear and hate me. It will bind them together. I will be their adversary before they meet the true enemy. I only hope I can focus their fear and hatred of me into desperate camaraderie.

Chapter 54

As soon as William and I are alone he strikes me across the face.

"How dare you." The words come out as a growl.

I know I upset him, but this reaction surprises me. Unlike the sparring session with Donovan, this feels more real, which ignites the familiar sensation of adrenaline through my body. More importantly, I feel the pulsating heat of the implant in the back of my neck.

"We are not Celceans and you are not looking for your replacement. You forget your place."

"Be calm, William. There is a reason Marcail has asked me to lead her Militia. Perhaps this is a better conversation for you to have with your mother."

He strikes me again. "You are not addressing some underling. I am the Prince of this nation and you will respect me as such."

He reaches back to strike me again when his hand stops in mid-air.

"Respect is earned, not demanded, Child Prince. This tantrum will end poorly if you don't regulate yourself."

"Trajan," he says. His tone has changed, but his face remains contorted.

"Silence. When this is over, you can rule as you wish. It is my job to ensure you have a nation left to rule. There is skill in your Militia, but they lack perspective. They must learn to stay focused and determined when their countrymen are dying less than an arm's length away. They must remain resolute when they take their first life. It is not a thing which can be taught through gentleness or philosophy."

"Trajan," he says, louder this time, with a hint of pain.

"I must harden them. Forge strength of mind and will by breaking them down and building them up again. Some, like Donovan, will be sacrificed in order to make the others ready. It is not a job I take lightly, but I will not be undermined, nor will I be stopped."

"Trajan!" His face has transformed from rage to panic, yet his hand remains cocked, ready to strike. "Please, release me."

"I'm not restraining you," I say, confused.

"You are. You're burning and crushing my wrist."

At once, the dull pulsing in my neck intensifies and I realize I have engaged the energy field. More importantly, it is not just engaged, but without thinking I have wrapped it around William's wrist. I can see the flesh just under his fist growing more and more red. I immediately focus on the implant and disengage it.

"William," I say. "I was not doing that intentionally."

"I know," he says. "Looks like you have made the breakthrough you've been waiting for." He's cradling his arm, glaring up at me. Then, softer, "And I understand what you're doing. I hate it, but I understand. These people are the bravest I've ever met, and to see you abuse them feels as if I'm being abused."

"Which is why it is I who must play this role," I say. "Please trust me, my sole focus is to see Castor's Army decimated. But it will mean changing your volunteers. They may not understand it now, but they have offered themselves, not just to fight, but to be molded into something more brutal than they could ever imagine. If we had months, I would ease them into this. But we don't. We may fail, but if we do, it won't be because our Militia hasn't been prepared for the horrors they are about to face."

I'm surrounded by five militiamen. They are armed with various weapons and stand ready to use them on me. We're covered in sweat and each of us are bleeding from several wounds.

"One more time," I say.

They immediately attack. I feel the instantaneous surge of adrenaline. The implant surges. My mind clears and I allow the decades of training to take over. Rather than responding with my mind, I allow my instincts to govern. My entire body begins a type of violent dance, only this time, the energy field joins. One by one, my attackers begin to fall. Not dead, but incapacitated with extreme efficiency. I sense a blade arcing its way toward my throat and before I can think about it, the field condenses into a shield, causing the blade to skid harmlessly away. An instant later, the energy has formed into a type of whip, wrapping itself around the legs of one of the attackers, three meters away, and pulling him to the ground.

As quickly as the match began, it is over. I look around, triaging the five warriors sprawled around me, then I disengage the implant.

"That's enough for today," I say.

As they leave the room, limping and rubbing their various wounds, I drop to a knee. This new ability is overwhelming. It is faster and more powerful than I ever imagined. My mistake had been trying to control it as if it were an appendage. Instead, the field seems to tap into something deeper. The subconscious impulses which keep my heart beating, or an animal instinct to protect myself at all costs. The less I think about controlling it and the more I give it an agency to act unfettered, the faster and more accurate it becomes.

All this time I saw it as a weapon which I was trying to yield. I now see I was wrong. The energy field isn't the weapon. I am. And the field makes me sharper, faster, stronger and more deadly than ever.

Tomorrow, everything will change. More accurately, tomorrow, we will revert to the very chaos and brutality from which we have been rescued. I stand in the Aegean command center, surrounded by overzealous and excited Militia Leaders who, just weeks ago, were carefree citizens of a peaceful world.

"Our intelligence tells us the Celceans have spotted us and are preparing a defense for a full frontal assault," William says. There is a three dimensional display of the Western Aegean coast where Castor's Army sits. "From the reports coming in, the bulk of the Celcean Army is still at sea, likely two days out. Trajan's plan has worked. We will outnumber them."

I look around the room and see smiles when I should see a healthy amount of fear. "Don't proclaim victory yet. While they are outmanned, they are over trained and well-armed," I say. "Also, we'll be making landfall, which means they have the tactical advantage. I'd like to try to bait him into a sea battle, but he won't fall for it. Even though he's a brute, he's intelligent. Our element of surprise ended a week ago."

"All of which are realities we have considered," William says.

"True, my prince, but we must realize the glaring reality. We must be perfect if we are to win. The Militia has answered the challenge I presented. No more can be asked of them, given our restrictions. With time, these men and women would be the envy of any nation. But death finds those with unmet potential much faster than it finds those who have prepared methodically."

Fin, the youngest of my captains, says, "We will not make the mistake of arrogance, General. You have prepared us to understand the truth of our situation. Desperation and fear will propel us, they will not freeze us."

He is a younger and much smaller version of myself. Tori would have been able to mold this man into a true leader. I have only given him sticks and asked him to build a monument to withstand the ages. "Well spoken,

Captain," I say.

We return our attention back to tomorrow's battlefield.

"At daybreak," William says, "three quarters of our pods will break from the main section. Half will go north, half will go south. Each of your navigators have been given the proper coordinates. Our hope is to make ourselves smaller targets and to simultaneously spread the Celceans even thinner than they already are. Our command pod will slow, just out of range of their biggest guns and wait for our landing teams to engage. Once Castor is fully committed to the north and south, we will press forward."

The room is silent as they run through the plan in their minds. It is risky, but it is the best we have. "Once you split off, Castor will likely launch as many drones as he can. They will be faster than your pods, but their firepower is relatively weak and inaccurate. Unless they strike a direct hit, they won't sink you. Also, they are not maneuverable at top speed. If they're low enough, you may be able to lock on and bring them down with your harpoons. He will throw as much at you as he can while you're still in the water, so don't take direct routes to your coordinates."

We go on like this for another hour. I cover everything I can remember about Celcean war technology. There are very few questions. When I'm done, there are no more smiles. Each leader is quiet and contemplative with the horrible task at hand.

"If I could," I say, "I would clone myself and die one thousand deaths in your place. Not because I question your ability, but because I desperately wish to keep you from this terrible reality." I look slowly around the room, holding the gaze of each soldier for as long as I can. "We are seven hours from day breaking on an ancient hell, newly awakened. Brief your teams quickly. Then, go. Laugh with your children. Make love. Pray. Do what you must in order to focus your mind, body and soul on the task at hand. Tomorrow, you will stare death in the face. Tomorrow, you will be baptized into a new and loathsome order. But you will not be alone. Look around," I pause, "we walk this blood soaked path together. A family forged with the heat of desperation and pressure of hope. If I had the entirety of history from which to choose my companions, I would pick each and every one of you without hesitation."

The only sound we make as we leave the room is the shuffling of feet and gasping of breath. I stand at the door and salute those who salute me, shake hands with those who offer their hands and clutch those who offer an embrace.

Once outside, I see Fiona waiting for me. She greets me with a sad smile and eyes red from tears. "Demetrius took a poet and made him a warrior. If he were alive, Tori would walk with a father's pride. Those men and women are better humans because of you."

"And we're asking them to enter into the most dehumanizing engagement imaginable," I say.

She reaches up and places a cold hand on my face. Her touch, as always, is gentle, but there is a tremor in it. "How about you? How will you spend your time before the war?"

I take her hand in mine and say, "I would like to walk with you. To hear through your ears. See through your eyes. I would like for you to rescue me from this life, if even for a few hours."

We begin to walk toward the perimeter of our floating city, hand in hand, pretending we are adolescents, fearful only of awkwardness and unrealized dreams.

"General, all captains are prepped and in place."

I nod at the young warrior. His chest is puffed a little larger than it should, betraying the fear which hovers beneath the surface. I should know his name, but the time for pleasantries has long since passed. In mere minutes, countless men and women with names I was too busy to learn will launch themselves toward Castor's Army. Ironically, I likely know more names of the opposing forces than I do in the troops I command. "No movement until I say. If we split too early, it will give Castor time to adjust."

He offers an awkward and rushed salute, then scurries away.

The royal family stands next to me in full armor. No matter how much I protest, Marcail, Fiona and William are unwavering in their insistence to be part of the landing party.

"Allow me one final try," I say, "this skirmish will not end the war. Your nation will need a leader in the weeks following today. Prudence advises you all to stay in the command center in order to lead your nation."

Marcail smiles and says, "Noted, General. But ours is a deep tradition. If we cannot stand beside our charges, we are not fit to lead." There is a finality in her statement which closes any further argument.

"Very well. My queen, you and William will go north. Fiona and I will go south. If fortune is on our side, we will meet in the middle. Look for me. I will be the one lofting Castor's head, the same way he held my arm."

"May your revenge be sweet and liberating," William says.

The queen and prince depart, leaving Fiona and me with the last peaceful moment before this war rips our world in half.

"Stay close to me. If we win, but I lose you, there will be nothing left for me in this life," I say.

"I am but one of a thousand soldiers, General. Do not burden me with the threat of distraction. If I fall, Aegea still needs a defender strong enough to stop Demetrius."

Silence hangs heavy over us as we consider our next few hours.

"Promise me this, Princess," I say at last. "Either live or die today. Do not allow yourself to be captured. Castor will look to make a gory and degrading example of any Aegean Royalty he detains."

We feel ourselves begin to slow. "Three more kilometers and we will be within range of their guns," says the Chief Navigator.

"Give us five minutes to get to our pods. When you hear my attack orders, I want this city at a full stop," I say.

Fiona and I march from the command room and I drain myself of emotion. No more philosophy. No more strategizing. Our course is set. There is nothing left to do but fight. I'm reminded of the moments I would spend with Tori in the Temple, just before entering Battle. How I long to hear his voice, repeating the tiny truths which governed me, or to lock eyes with his purposeful gaze.

Today, there will be no Crowd, happily cheering for their favorite warrior. No Braddock to brief us. There will only be terror and death. I silently pray that my army will be more vicious than Castor's.

"Men and women of Aegea," I say into the Comm Link, "let us end this swiftly and in a way which leaves no appetite for future engagement. Trust your training. Trust the people next to you. Most importantly, trust yourselves." The sea is as calm as I have ever seen it, which will make our path to the shore fast and easy. "Remember, the battle will begin the moment we are in range of their weapons. While we're in the water, we have the advantage. Use it. Once on land, stop for nothing. There are no moral victories on that beach. Fight with desperation and unrelenting assurance. You will get no quarter from your adversary."

I look to the pod on my right. Fiona stands at the front, ready to throttle her vessel as soon as she hears my order.

"Your children and grandchildren will look back on this as the moment in which you either assured their safety, or consigned them as slaves. Their fate will be written by the power in your strikes and the valor of your will. Make them proud."

The sky is a faded and lazy blue. For the briefest of moments, everything stops and I feel as if I could crumble both armies into a tiny ball and throw them into the rising sun. But the moment passes as we hit a lone wave, rumbling to shore, as if carving a path forward.

"On my mark," I pause, considering the digital battlefield on the display in front of me. Everything is in place. Castor has staked his ground and I have formed my plan. All that is left is to turn our forces loose. "Now," I say.

The Aegean strike force breaks as if some unseen missile has detonated in the center of their city. We couldn't be more precisely coordinated if we had trained for years. Less than a minute later, the sea erupts as Castor begins his counterattack.

Chapter 55

Our pods are fast, but Castor's drones are faster. About five minutes after splitting, the first wave of them buzz above us. The first pass is just for calibration, but on the second, they strafe us with bullets. Our navigators prove skillful in executing my orders to avoid a direct route to the shore, however. As the drones circle for a third pass, our captains report no significant damage and zero casualties.

"They will run out of bullets quickly. Be prepared for their short range missiles," I advise.

As if Castor is listening, the drones launch their payloads with more accuracy than the bullets. We're halfway to the beach and we've sustained our first casualties. Five pods from the north team and seven from the south have been obliterated.

"They've got at least three more attack runs left, let's make them pay. They're low enough for our harpoons," I say.

The next few minutes are tense as we engage the drones with our outdated weaponry. When we hit the surf, it looks as if we've come out on top. At last count, we've lost twenty pods, but they have lost thirty drones.

Our navigators expertly ride the waves to the shore and, within seconds, we're off the pods, forming lose attack lines.

I can hear the team leaders as they work to get their troops in the proper formation. Castor's Army hasn't reached us yet and I want to take advantage by claiming as much ground as possible before they arrive. The same is true of the north. I can hear William's voice, urging his troops forward.

In the distance, I see the Celcean Army advancing. Slowly, but with precision, they churn toward us. A patient and devastating swarm of locusts, leaving destruction in their wake.

As we draw closer, I say, "Prepare yourselves. They'll seek to thin us out with explosives. We'll be in range any second." On cue, we see the smoke trails of their first salvo. "Now," I yell. Once again, we splinter apart just before the beach explodes harmlessly with sand and water.

Castor, in his arrogance, assumed we would remain in formation and aimed everything for the middle of our ranks. Before the last grain of sand has settled back to the ground we are upon them. It's clear we have caught them off guard.

The first wave of our soldiers tears through the Celcean Guard. I expect to hear shouts, attack bellows and screams as deadly blows land. But the soldiers are silent as they engage. I hear only the sound of weapon on weapon and the occasional grunt as someone is struck.

I am the tip of the spear, cutting a deadly path through Castor's troops, both with the energy field and whatever weapon appears in my other hand. The adrenaline of true combat has made the field even deadlier. It's as if it has a mind of its own, striking killing blows to opponents I can't even see. Within less than five minutes, we have eliminated the Celceans and stand, short of breath, with a clear view of Castor's command center.

From what I hear, the north has fared equally well. Slowly, the army realizes their triumph. There are a few shocked exclamations, then some laughter. I watch as my soldiers begin embracing and yelling with victory.

This all seems wrong. Castor would never extend himself this far, and he certainly would not surround himself with such untested warriors. I look at the Celcean dead and I feel my stomach tighten. These are not members of the Celcean Guard. They look like teenage peasants dressed in clunky and ineffective armor.

I am a fool. Even in truewar, Demetrius continues to play games. He baited us into what we thought was a battle with his Guard, when in reality, he goaded us into slaughtering what he will claim are innocent bystanders. There is a low rumbling in the distance.

"Back in formation," I yell. Then, into my Comm Link, "William, we've been tricked. These aren't Celcean Guard. He's drawn us in so we would let our guard down. Prepare yourself."

I'm cut off by the thundering of gigantic war machines as they come bursting from the tree line. Seconds later, a squadron of drones swoop overhead, dropping explosives which rip us apart. What was celebration just seconds earlier has become cries of agony.

I hear William shouting for his troops to regroup, but the transmission is garbled by the endless eruptions and screams.

The war machines are upon us in all their gruesome glory. Not only do they pound us with bullets and explosives, they shred wounded Aegeans under their massive tires. In less than a minute, my landing party has been cut in half.

"Fall back!" I command. Those who aren't either dismembered or already running away turn and run for the landing pods as fast as they can. I stand firm, however, trying to provide as much cover for my army as I can.

With all of my will, I focus the field at the lead war machine. My head begins to spin as a bolt of searing, pure energy slices the giant mechanism in half. I turn to the next and do the same. Then again. But no matter how hard I try, every time I incapacitate one, it seems to be replaced by two more.

"Trajan!" I hear behind me. I turn to see Fiona. "The north is gone and our capital was just hit. Their guns are stronger than we thought. We have to get out of here. If we lose you too, all is forfeit."

Just then, the ground under her feet bursts, sending her flying. Without turning, I focus my energy on the machine behind me and I hear it explode. I'm at her side moments after her limp body has landed.

She still has a pulse, but it is weak. It takes all of my will to keep from turning and unleashing my fury on Castor's Army behind me. But Fiona needs help. We have lost. Our army shredded in a matter of humiliating seconds. If there's anything left of Aegea, it will be at sea.

I lift her body, supporting her with my human arm and the field as I board the last pod left on the beach. The navigator lay dead at my feet. Clumsily, and under an endless barrage of explosions, I manage to get us in the water. Once we're past the breakers, the hurricane of war dies down.

The occasional drone passes over us, happy to track our movements, rather than annihilate us. As we drift further and further from shore, even the drones stop. It's only midday and the Aegean Army has been destroyed. Whatever is left of us is scattered across an endless ocean.

Fiona stirs, but remains unconscious. The left side of her beautiful face is charred, the fingers on her right hand are gone and both of her legs appear to be badly broken. In spite of myself, I break down, weeping. She trusted me. They all trusted me to know my enemy and lead them to victory. Instead, I led them into a slaughter. If I had been a spy, sent to Aegea to bring them down from the inside, I couldn't have inflicted more damage than I did today.

Demetrius has won. If he wants, he can declare victory and let the Aegean remnants wither and die on the waves. But if I know him, he won't settle until every last one of us are hunted down and destroyed.

Chapter 56

Our pod ran out of fuel after a few kilometers and we have been drifting ever since. Somewhere on this ocean, countless other pods are likely doing the same. We never prepared for this contingency. In our mind, there was only pure victory or utter defeat. This is worse. We are no more effectual than seafoam, floating listlessly across the water.

Fiona remains unconscious. She stirs occasionally, groaning with pain. Before nightfall, I found a small medical bag and was able to wrap the worst of her wounds, but my ministrations are rudimentary at best. If I don't find a way out of this, infection and gangrene will begin to take over in the next couple of days. By then, we will be on the verge of death by dehydration as well.

I imagine Demetrius and Castor, lounging on the beach of their victory. Laughing, fulfilling every post-battle desire. The humiliation of the scene, and of my loss, overwhelms me. Not only did I bring this war to our world, I was not able to stop it. I have been out matched in every way. The once mighty Trajan is nothing more than a punch line. The fool who dared oppose the will of Demetrius. Mine will be a story mothers tell their children to teach them the danger of stupidity and pride. For the first time since his death, I am happy Tori is not here. I could not abide his disappointment.

I've been so lost in my lamentations, I haven't noticed the low, growing hum until it sounds as if it's on top of us. The night sky lacks any stars or moon so I can only imagine what horror is about to overtake us. Likely, a Celcean sea vessel, finally come to destroy us. I am past the point of exhaustion. So much so, that I have not been able to engage the implant since nightfall. I stand on wobbly legs, awaiting the final, freeing blow which will take my life. My only hope is that Fiona dies in the night so they can't cause her even more suffering.

A blinding spotlight fills my vision and I stumble back, trying to see through the white light. There are voices on the other side, but I can't make out what they're saying. I hear a splash, followed by a second, higher pitched hum of a smaller boat. For a moment, I wonder if Castor himself is coming to end me.

Our pod is bumped and I see the silhouette of a man, much smaller than Castor, board. Seething anger boils over. This is how little they think of me. Sending an untested and underdeveloped subordinate to dispatch of me. Whatever exhaustion I felt earlier is replaced with indignant rage. Before he can say anything, I lunge, driving my shoulder into his chest. The force of my blow against his slight frame sends us toppling over the side of the pod into the inky water. We struggle against each other briefly, before the instinct to save ourselves takes over. Our heads break the surface at the same time, both of us gasping for a calming breath.

"General," he yells. "I'm not your enemy. We've come to rescue you."

The words don't register as I kick back toward to pod. I want to gain the upper hand by getting out of the water before him.

Another, more familiar voice rings out. "Take the light out of his eyes." At once the blinding light flashes away, providing me the ability to see my opponents.

Standing above me on an Aegean transport vessel is William. His left arm is bandaged and there is a nasty cut across his face, but he's smiling down at me. The prince lives and we have been found. More than anything,

I'm overcome by the realization that Fiona will survive.

"It was as if we weren't even there," William says. "I never dreamed they would be so powerful, or so ferocious."

We are sitting in the small common area of the vessel. Fiona is resting quietly, being attended by a young physician. In all, there are twenty Aegeans aboard.

"I was a fool. Castor and Demetrius baited me and I jumped with both feet. Please forgive me," I say.

"You didn't make the decision alone. We knew the risks going in," he says.

I know he's simply trying to make me feel better, but I don't push the issue. "How many of these vessels are still out there?" I ask.

"This is the only one. It left the capital mere seconds before it was destroyed. I was one of the first people they found and we've been scouring the ocean for survivors ever since."

"We are fortunate. As we find more survivors, we will be able to regroup and think of a new plan," I say.

William dips his head and clasps his hands. "There will be no more of that, Trajan. At midday tomorrow, I will fly the banner of surrender and give myself to Demetrius. I still have the rest of the Aegean citizenry to consider." He looks at me with tears in his eyes. "I could have never imagined how terrible truewar really is. If I can avoid that fate for the rest of us, I will accept whatever awaits me."

"If you were going to surrender so easily, why did we bother with an attack?" I spit. "Do you really think Demetrius will show mercy to the citizens of the nation which openly defied him? At best he will castrate the men and turn the women into concubines."

"We are survivors, Trajan. Yes, we will endure some torment, but at least we will still be alive. And as long as we're alive, there is hope that we can rise up. Maybe generations from now. But there will still be hope."

I slump into my chair. "These are conversations which should not exist. I am exhausted, as I am sure you are. Rather than decide the fate of a nation after such a terrible day, let us sleep. Tomorrow will bring new hope. I pray we will find the queen in the same way we have been found."

William holds back a sob. "We will not. She died on the beach. Crushed under one of those monstrous machines as she tended the wounds of one of her soldiers."

The quiet hum of the vessel is the only sound as we sit together, silently trying to grasp this new and terrible reality.

"You're right. We can talk about this tomorrow," he pauses, "in all my life, I never dreamt of inheriting the crown of Aegea under such circumstances. You think you have failed? I am the king of a decimated nation. Preparing to bow in weakness to my conqueror. Rather than lasting glorious decades, my reign will likely last a few violent and impotent days."

I wake after just three hours of nightmare-riddled sleep. The second my eyes open, I know there is no use fighting my wakefulness. I dress slowly, stretching strained muscles and trying to avoid pulling the material of my clothes across the myriad cuts and scrapes.

The command room is quiet, manned by only one pilot. He looks up when he hears me enter. "There's a faint signal a few kilometers out. It's caught in a pretty strong current, but we should catch it in a couple of hours."

"Are we worried about Celcean drones finding us?" I ask.

"Other than rescuing someone, we remain submerged. I'm not about to give our position away to that butcher." He turns back to his console. "There is some food in the dining area, if you're hungry."

I am hungry, but I can't fathom eating. The combination of stress and the memory of the beach slaughter is enough to seal my mouth for good. Without thinking, I end up outside Fiona's room. I know I should let her sleep, but just being near her calms me.

She hasn't moved since I left her. There are fresh bandages on her face and hands. Her legs have been straightened and each are neatly wrapped in a cast. In spite of the wounds, she looks peaceful.

"You did well with your field dressings."

I turn to see the young physician entering the room.

"I'm Katrina," she says.

"Will she live?"

"Yes. She will bear scars on her face and will likely walk with a limp." She skirts around my awkward mass and checks the bandage around Fiona's hand. "If we had some salve, I might have been able to bring her thumb and forefinger back. But alas," her sentence fades, preferring the implication rather than having to speak the words.

I shake my head, tired of hearing reports of death and destruction. "There is too much truth in such devastation."

Katrina sits down and looks directly at me for the first time. "What will we do?"

The whites of her eyes are stained red and there is sand caked along her jawline. "Were you on the beach?"

She nods. "The prince drug me onto his pod after the queen was killed."

"I'm sorry. My plan was clearly flawed."

"No person on this planet could have planned for the brutality we faced, General."

I rest my hand on Fiona's shoulder. "The defeated blame surprise while the victors boast in preparation."

"What's the answer, then?" Katrina stands and begins to unwrap the bandage around Fiona's face.

Choking back vomit when I see her charred and melted flesh, I say, "There was a time when I was young. I had just been injured in a sparring session against an older trainee. He was faster than me and dictated the pace of the fight from the beginning. Rather than force him into my way of fighting, I tried to beat him at his style. After the match, my Mentor unleashed on me. Not for getting injured, but for being prideful enough to believe I could win without dictating the engagement myself."

"Most of this will heal. But she is in for a long and painful recovery and there will be scarring."

I shake my head. "If not for me, she would never have had to experience such pain."

"It seems to me that there were no terms we could have dictated which would have given us the advantage."

"The enemy always has a blind spot, you just need to find it," I say.

"What's Castor's?" she asks. Her hands are fast, but they tremble every time she stops moving them.

"I thought it was arrogance. But today he fought with patience and foreknowledge," I say, clearing a wisp of Fiona's golden hair from her sleeping face. "Maybe William is right. Maybe we should surrender."

Katrina stops working on Fiona and, with a quivering voice, says, "Do you think all of those men and women died on that beach today, just so you and the prince could wallow in self pity? Do you think the queen met her end so we could cower to the likes of Castor? Do you think Fiona will wake and be awash in gratitude when she finds herself the property of Demetrius?"

I feel like a child under her glare.

"What did your Mentor tell you all those years ago? After you lost that match?"

It's as if the spirit of Tori has inhabited the body of this small, fierce woman. "He told me to regain ground at all costs. Even if that means doing something outlandish."

"Then do something outlandish. Strip everything away, and this is still simply a Battle between you and Castor. Your weapons just happen to be flesh and bone. But it's still you against him. Stop acting like it's more complicated. Do what you were built to do. Win." She finishes redressing Fiona's bandage and walks quietly to the door. "Until a few weeks ago, you were the most feared man in this world. Not your Ruler. Certainly not Castor. You. And it wasn't because of your strength. When Castor took your arm, he didn't take your essence. Stop acting like he did."

Chapter 57

William stands in the command room. From the looks of him, he's slept even less than me.

"Have you been to see Fiona?" I ask.

"After you and I spoke last night. Thank you for saving her."

He watches the monitor. There is a faint strobe which looks to be about three hundred meters from us.

"Is that one of our pods?" I ask.

"Likely," he says.

The pilot switches to a view of the surface. At first, the image is blurry, but after a moment, the picture focuses. The pod is smoldering and looks to be ripped in half.

"Circle," William says.

Without responding, the pilot engages the vessel and we swing around the left side of the pod.

"We started finding more and more damaged pods last night," William says, eyes still on the monitor.

As we come around, I say, "Looks like the drones are expanding their search."

"It's worse than that," William says.

We finally make it to where the pod has been ripped open and, among the smoke, we see the mutilated bodies of three Aegeans. Two of them have been decapitated and their heads have been impaled on makeshift stakes. The third is hanging from a piece of exposed scaffolding.

William slams his fist against the wall. "How are they finding them faster than us?"

"Tracking down and engaging a retreating enemy is one thing. This is genocide soaked in bloodlust," I say. "How many of these have you found?"

"This is the ninth. Each one more gruesome than the last."

We circle one more time, looking for any survivors who may have escaped the brutality. "This is a tomb, my prince," I say.

He drops his head, trying to hide the tears.

I place my hand on his back, offering a pale form of condolence. "Do you still want to surrender?"

He straightens. "What other choice do we have?"

"Demetrius has turned this into a personal vendetta. At their worst, the wars which predated the Collapse rarely devolved into this level of savagery. He seeks to punish, not win. What do you think he will do if we present ourselves as willing victims?"

"How do you propose to fight a war without troops?" He yells.

"I will be your army."

He doesn't respond, waiting for me to continue.

"Castor's Army has been built to win through sheer force. It isn't designed to fight one on one. We were beaten because my expertise is in engaging with a single opponent. Let's redefine this war. We fought on his terms yesterday. Allow me to engage him my way.

"Even the mightiest lion can be made lame by the tiniest of thorns in his paw. I will be that thorn." I point to the smoldering pod, "Let that be an image of Castor's pride, rather than the symbol of Aegea's death."

Chapter 58

"You can communicate with us through the Comm Link," William says. We are three hours from the dawn of the third day after our failure against Castor's Army. "If we see or hear anything, I will be sure to tell you. Please do the same."

"This isn't a reconnaissance mission," I say. "I'll start on the beach, making my way to the hub. If Castor is there, I will end him. If not, I'll be able to find out where the army has gone."

"To what end? You can't kill them all," William says.

"I don't plan on killing them all. Castor will die. As will Demetrius, if I'm fortunate. Right now, the army has not seen adversity. They are untested, which means they are fragile. If they question the ability of Castor to protect them, they will abandon him. There is no loyalty in fear."

"And we are to wait and pray for your success?"

"Without his army, Demetrius will not be feared by other nations. You must wage a political war. Show the leaders of the world the brutality we have suffered. More importantly, show the citizens of the world. I will take his army. You must take his allies."

We speak for a few more minutes. Both of us aware of our absolute desperation, neither of us willing to name it. There is a finality in our conversation which makes our words feel pregnant with double meaning.

"You will not see me again unless we are successful," I say. "I will not allow myself to be captured and I pray you will refuse surrender."

He nods, wrestling with the implications of my mandate.

"Your people will follow you. Lead them with truth and conviction."

We leave the command room, heading for the launching bay, where my tiny transport vessel awaits.

"Will you say goodbye to Fiona?" he asks.

"No. She must rest and I must push her far from my mind if I'm to do what is necessary."

"When she wakes, I will make sure she understands," William says.

"It is better that way." There is much more to say, but I leave it at that. I suddenly feel like an elephant trying to walk a tightrope.

It takes me less than an hour to make it to the beach. Just before I crash into the sandbar, I surface the tiny boat and coast the rest of the way in. The sun isn't up yet, but I'm sure there are sentinels patrolling. I'm five kilometers north of where William's troops landed.

Other than a light, crisp wind, all is quiet. The clouds have cleared and the moon is bright enough to cast soft shadows across the beach. I quickly make it to the tree line and begin pressing south. If my assumptions are correct, there won't be any guards for another few kilometers. Castor has surprised me lately, so I move as silently as I can, listening for the slightest noise.

After a few minutes, I fall into a comfortable cadence of sprinting for about two hundred meters, then dropping down and scanning the expanse before me. I do this for about three kilometers when I notice all of the forest noises have silenced. Either there is a predator near, or one of Castor's patrols are in the vicinity.

I crouch behind the stump of a fallen tree and wait. Two minutes pass. Then five. I'm about to start back up when I catch a brief flash of moonlight reflected off the polished metal of a Celcean weapon. Once I've spotted the weapon, I trace it back to the soldier. He's sitting against a tree, looking in my direction. If he's spotted me, I can't tell.

In an instant, I have engaged my implant and the invisible field is snaking across the forest floor toward the soldier. Rather than killing him, I use the field as a sort of lasso around his legs. It silently circles his ankles, then cinches. In seconds, I have dragged him to my position. Before he can call out, I clench my hand over his mouth.

"If you make a noise, you will feel more pain than you ever imagined," I hiss.

His eyes are wild as he struggles uselessly against the energy field and my grasp.

"Do you recognize me?" I ask.

He gives me a quick, panicked nod.

"Then you know I'm not lying." I wait for him to calm. "Are you alone?"

Another nod.

"Are you part of a patrol?"

Yes.

"How many and what distance?" I slowly begin to take my hand from his mouth, "Anything more than a whisper and I rip your throat out before your vocal cords stop vibrating."

Through gasps, "Five of us. One thousand meters apart."

"How big is the unit you're guarding?"

"About one hundred."

"What is your name?" I ask.

"Lucien," he says, confused.

"Listen very carefully, Lucien," I say. "I will spare your life tonight. But you will watch the rest of your unit die. If you do anything to interfere, or if you run, I will kill you. Do you understand?"

He stares at me with an open mouth.

"Answer now, or I will kill you and offer the same thing to the next guard in line."

He nods, dumbly. "Yes."

I immediately strike him across the jaw, knocking him unconscious. Just then, I hear the next guard making his way toward us. Saving my strength to use the energy field later, I creep behind him and slit his throat. He falls silently, dead before his body lands.

I dispatch the other eight guards with similar ease. Lucien is still unconscious when we find the camp. I rouse him after I've tied his legs and hands with some vine and positioned him so he can watch what I'm about to do.

"Remember what I told you. I know what you're thinking. You could alert them. And they may stop me. But if you do, you will die." I can tell by the look on his face that he has chosen to live rather than warn them. It's all I can do to keep from killing him for his cowardice, but I've made a promise and I need this weakling's help if I'm going to be successful.

I position myself at the edge of the camp and observe the comings and goings for five minutes. It is an hour until sunrise, which means only the officers and cooks are beginning to stir. I move quickly, unleashing the energy field before I'm at the first tent. Men die mid-stride, mid-dream and mid-sentence. I'm halfway through camp when someone finally sounds an alarm, but it's too late.

The field and I are in perfect sync. When I need armor, I have it. When I need to cut a razor sharp path through a line of men, the slice is complete before the image is fully formed in my mind. It's as if there are two of me fighting side my side. The people who engage my left side fare no better. My precision with the spear and sword is perfect. With each death, my opponents grow more fearful and I gain more confidence.

All one hundred are dead just as the first rays of sun filter through the leaves. I'm covered in the blood of my enemies. For a moment, the lingering guilt of causing death outside of the Temple covers me. But I remember the beach. Then the tortured bodies of Aegeans on the burnt pods, and the feeling is gone.

I return to Lucien, rage filled and ready to take more lives. He's panic stricken and covered in vomit.

"Where is the rest of your cowardly army?"

"Most are at sea, but the command post has about three hundred. There's another unit like this to the south." He looks like an animal, caught in a snare.

I cut the vines from his hands and feet. "Go," I say. "Find them and tell them what you saw. Tell them that I'm coming for them."

He stands, shaking. Assuming I'm baiting him into a trap. His stupidity and weakness ignite me. I strike him with full force, likely shattering his cheek and collapsing his nose.

"Go," I yell. "And quickly. I'm on the move. If I catch up to you, I will kill you and deliver the news myself."

I watch as he crashes through the forest. He's dazed and wild with terror, which means I've got plenty of time before he makes it to Castor's camp. I turn my attention to the outpost I just destroyed. Tents are on fire, mangled bodies litter the forest floor and the ground looks like it was bombed by a squadron of drones. Anyone else would see this and assume the Celceans were overrun by a marauding army. I close my eyes and listen for any sounds of life. After a few seconds, I hear a weak groan coming from the center of camp.

It takes a few minutes of sifting through debris and dead bodies until I find a badly burnt man, lying face down under a pile of rubble. His breath is shallow and there is a perfectly cauterized hole through his stomach.

When I first turn him over, he is too dazed to register who I am, but after a few moments, he recognizes me. His breathing quickens and he holds a trembling hand out, as if to push me away.

"General," he pants, "please."

I pause. "Your voice," I say, "were you one of the Generals in training?"

"Yes," he says, wincing through the effort. "You helped me prepare for a Mid-Year match."

Even though I had prepared to face, and kill, the Generals I had helped train, I find myself unable to do what I must.

Sensing my struggle, he tries to sit up, but his wounds are too serious. He collapses back to the ground. "Just do it. Continue your treason against Demetrius." The fear in his face from a moment ago has been replaced with hatred.

"You blame me for this?" I say.

"Who else? You purposely lost to Aegea. Then defected. When Demetrius stood up to Marcail's demand for immediate surrender, you began the raids on Celcean outposts. You even murdered your own Mentor when he tried to stop you."

"Are these the lies being fed to you by Demetrius?" My voice shakes with anger. I can handle being called a traitor. I'm not even bothered that Demetrius blamed the initial skirmishes on me. But to use Tori's death as a rallying cry is inexcusable.

"They are the stories being told by a father, devastated by his son's treachery." I see his only good hand moving across the dirt, looking for any sort of weapon.

"I was once like you. A mindless tool of a devious madman. I remained loyal until the moment Demetrius had his attack dog take my arm and my Mentor's head."

His hand pauses as he looks at what remains of my arm, then back to my face. I watch as he wrestles with reconciling what he's been told with what he sees. This must have been what it was like for Marcail as she tried to help me understand.

"Think, child," I say. "Is there any logic in his story? If I wanted to truly hurt Demetrius, why would I align myself with a nation such as Aegea? Why wouldn't I just end him and take his place?"

"There is no logic in the actions of a madman," he says as he launches the tip of a severed spear toward me. It soars harmlessly past as he slumps back to the ground.

I kneel so our faces are only a meter apart. "You speak truth. There is no logic left in this world. Thanks to Demetrius, this world has been turned upside down. But we are complicit. He starved us, then dangled rancid meat in our faces. In our hunger, we were willing to accept his scraps and treat them as a feast."

His eyes grow dim as death begins its march across his body.

"Forgive me," I say. "If I had been smarter, he would not have grown so powerful. His lies would not have poisoned so many people. All this death is my fault."

The young soldier finally succumbs. His chest caves slightly as his lungs eject the last bit of air from his body.

I thought I had prepared myself for this. To kill my countrymen. But in those scenarios I saw these men equal to Demetrius in their greed. This is different. This is like punishing a blind man for his inability to describe the colors of a sunset. And yet, I can offer them no mercy. To let them live would be the same as allowing a contagious man to roam through a city unabated. Spreading disease and suffering with every unwitting breath.

Chapter 59

The blood of other men fills my pours. As soon as Lucien reached the Celcean command center, Castor sent all of his land forces on a hunting party, directly toward me. At the same time, he took Demetrius and a small, elite, unit of soldiers and set off for one of the other Aegean islands. Judging from the reports I've received from William, he's also commanded his Sea Forces to join him. It seems, if only briefly, William and the rest of the Aegeans are safe from the Celceans.

It's an hour past midnight and I've hunkered down in a small cave formed by the tangled roots of two giant trees. Today has been especially violent, and equally devastating for the Celceans. From what I can tell, only one quarter of the soldiers who awoke this morning are still breathing. I am weary from all the death.

I tilt my body, allowing the light of the moon to shine on the wound on my left leg. It's a deep gash, roughly fifteen centimeters long. Luckily, only the muscle has been damaged. No tendons or ligaments seem impaired. I diverted a small vein of the energy field to cauterize and cover it, but that was only after I'd lost a significant amount of blood. Right now, I need calories and rest. With the exception of a few roots and berries, the calories are scarce, and I cannot risk being discovered and killed while asleep. Every time I feel myself drifting, I force the image of Tori's face when Demetrius raked the blade across his throat. Hatred and revenge will serve as my fuel until this terrible business is over.

My Comm Link beeps once in my ear, then I hear William's voice. "It's official, they have stopped their search for us and are congregating on our Medical Island. Our latest estimate puts their numbers at three thousand."

I don't answer, unwilling to do anything to give my position away. William, not expecting a response, continues. "News of your skirmishes has circulated the globe. There is even some footage being hijacked from the Celcean drone feed. Most assume the Aegean Army has rallied and is seeing some success. You were right. As the Rulers see a weakness in Castor's Military, the rhetoric is changing slightly. Unfortunately, it remains only rhetoric. No Ruler is willing to offer any help."

They won't offer help until there is a final victor. If Demetrius wins, they will defer to his military might. If Aegea survives, I wonder how many vultures will circle the remnants, looking for bits and pieces to scavenge.

"Fiona is getting better. I was able to speak to her earlier." His voice trails off, either unsure or unwilling to share the rest of his thought.

"We're finding more survivors now. And we're making our way to a remote location in the South Seas where multiple currents converge. The citizens who stayed back should be there and if there are any stragglers, they are likely to end up there eventually. We'll be there in about three days. It's far enough out that unless Demetrius is able to get an entire fleet of deep sea vessels, we should be safe for the time being. If you survive, we'll come back for you."

There is movement to my right so I switch off William's voice. I tense my body, readying myself for a fast and severe strike. Rather than one of the Celcean Guard, a mid-sized boar nudges through the brush. It seems luck is with me. In spite of the devastation which has churned through the forest, this animal has remained. Just a quick sting from the energy field and I will have the fuel my body so desperately craves. Just as I'm about to release the field, I stop. There has been enough death for today, and there will be more tomorrow, and the day after that. I've played the predator too much already. The creature passes by me, either oblivious or uninterested in my presence. The mercy of my decision gives me more energy and clarity than I would have gained from consuming its flesh.

I allow myself a moment of peace as I watch it wander over the forest floor, rooting for an easy snack. These tiny seconds of peace are shattered when the boar screams out as an arrow strikes it in the back of its neck. A second arrow hits its hindquarters, then a third in the shoulder. I'm on my feet, scanning for the shooter, when a fourth arrow finally pierces its heart, ending the needless misery.

The archer drops from a tree, no more than twenty meters from me. In his excitement over killing the pig, he doesn't see me. My rage boils over. I disengage the energy field and charge the tiny soldier. Just before I crash into him, I realize he is no older than sixteen and those shots were likely the first he has ever fired at a living being. But I am too far gone to regulate myself. The next few seconds are savage. I rain down blow after punishing blow. Each designed to punish and torture, rather than kill. What could have been a fast death, I turn into a needlessly slow affair.

Just before I end him, I stop and whisper, "It didn't need to die. And even if it did, it should have died fast."

One second, his eyes are electric with pain, then I snap his neck and watch as they blink out. I sit back against the tree, breathing hard, tears in my eyes. This is what my world has become. Torturing and killing a child to prove to him that torturing and killing are wrong. In an effort to stop a marauding madman, I have become no better than his equal.

Next to the soldier's body, I notice a satchel. In it, I find three protein bars. They are tasteless, but they give my body the charge it needs. As the moon is covered by a coming rainstorm, I make my way to the now stiff boar and bury it. Just as the first raindrops make their way to the ground, I put the last of the dirt over its shallow grave.

What is left of the command center is in sight. It's surrounded by what appears to be three hundred well-armed, well-trained and confident soldiers. But I can see the subtle signs of fear and doubt bubbling just below the surface. I step out of the tree line and begin a slow walk toward them.

As soon as they spot me, I hear their commander, a tall and severe looking man, yelling, trying to realign their formation so they have as much firepower as possible. There's a low rumble as five of their war machines emerge from the left, splashing through the tiny surf. It doesn't take long before they've dialed in their guns and they unleash their arsenal.

Their missiles make easy targets for my energy field as I snake tendrils of pure power into the air, tearing the projectiles apart in bursts. They then switch to enormous bullets, emptying their chambers. There are too many of them and they're too fast for me to target individually, so I contract the field into a shield around myself. Even though the bullets don't penetrate my perfect armor, the impact of such powerful ballistics sends tremors of pain throughout my body and brings me to my knees. I hear the soldiers cheering as they see me falter. But as I rise, their cheers fade through pale lips. Not wanting to see what else the war machines have in their arsenal, I go on the attack. I focus on the field, making it as dense as possible, then I send it out with blinding speed. The front two war machines erupt from the force of the blow, sending shards of molten metal into the soldiers, killing many, but the bulk of the army remains in formation. I then whip the field, bringing it down as if it were an enormous cleaver on the third war machine. It crumbles under the blow. The fourth and fifth are incapacitated by precision strikes into their engines, turning them into nothing more than ominous piles of metal and composites.

I'm fifty meters from the army, just close enough to make out the orders of that same commander. In spite of what they just saw, they are preparing for a full assault against me.

"Stop!" I yell. At first, they don't hear me, so I repeat myself, holding my hands to my sides as I continue forward. Nothing. They continue to listen to and watch their leader. It's clear he will not stop until either I'm dead, or I've killed every last soldier. This needs to end.

When I'm within fifteen meters, I yell again. Finally, the commander stops and faces me.

"Your war machines could do nothing against me. Your hunting parties failed. Why keep fighting?" I yell.

He gestures around himself. "You may have forsaken our Father, but we will not. No matter how powerful your technology is, it can't overcome this army's dedication."

I shake my head. Just a few months ago, I could have easily said the same words on behalf of Demetrius.

"There is a difference between Demetrius and me," I yell. "If you lay down your weapons, I will let you return to your lives unharmed. Demetrius, on the contrary, would hunt you down and kill not only you, but everyone you care about. Which would you rather follow? A man who seeks to end this war with peace, or a man who would extend it with revenge?"

The commander laughs. "It's easy to promise mercy when mercy is what you're asking. No, as long as I stand, this army will hunt you and your bastard nation until there are none of you left."

"It is as I've feared, then," I yell. "But I wonder, if you're not standing, would these men feel the same?" Without pause, I reach out with the full might of my energy. It splits and grasps him at the ankles and at the shoulders, then lifts him so everyone can see. "I do not wish to inflict any more death than I have to. But if I'm forced, I will kill with more cruelty than you can imagine." I pause, letting the words sink in, then with a slight shrug, I send the two arms of the field in separate directions, ripping the commander in half. I release both sides of the corpse and let them fall with a sickening thud on the sand. "Your choice," I yell. "My mercy, or my wrath."

The only noise is the lapping waves and the burning war machines as I stand defiantly in front of them. After a few moments, a small man in the front row drops his spear and removes his armor. The person next to him does the same. Within seconds, the beach is awash in clanking metal.

A message of kindness made possible by sadistic violence.

After they have all forfeited their weapons, they continue to stand in front of me, unsure of the next move. "Go," I say, "return to your loved ones. Repent to your gods, atone for your wrongs and do no more harm while you live." I turn and begin my hike back to my small vessel. Castor and Demetrius are still at large and they will not remain docile much longer.

Chapter 60

I finally sleep while my vessel carries me toward the Medical Island. The last time I was there, I was consumed with recovering from the shark attack so I could represent Demetrius as his General. This time I will be equally single-minded in my campaign to end the devastation of his regime. The rest is fitful, interrupted by visions of the last few days as well as the wounds I've sustained. My leg is tender and in spite of my field dressing, looks to be in the early stages of infection.

After ten hours of sleep, my Comm Link breaks through.

"Trajan." William's voice.

"Prince," I say.

"News of your victory has set this world on fire," he says, with shortness of breath. "For the first time in memory, there is hope."

"Do not allow yourself to dream damaging dreams. The soldiers I beat were nothing more than well outfitted farmers. It was easy to turn them. The lion is as strong as ever."

"As is the thorn. And I think you've inserted yourself into its paw deeper than you think." He pauses, but when I don't respond, continues, "Rulers have begun turning from him. Already, some have imposed sanctions and are demanding an immediate retreat."

"Sanctions and demands," I say. "Fleas nibbling on concrete."

"It must start somewhere. Some are even calling for you to take over control of Celsus if Demetrius is beaten. We are winning the politics."

His optimism is as irritating as it is misplaced. "And what will happen if Demetrius wins? Those same politicians will bow to him and give him gifts, celebrating his resilience. I understand your desire to find encouragement. There has been precious little of it lately. But mistimed hope can do more damage than the sharpest enemy blade. Don't make the mistake of thinking this war is coming to an end."

There is a prolonged silence. "What is your plan? They will see you coming and the island is too small to easily hide."

"Destruction and fear. I'm made for nothing else." I switch off the Comm Link and settle back into the seat. My leg throbs and I can tell my strength is almost gone. One way or another, this will end soon. Eight more hours until I must face the best Celsus has to offer. I finish the last of the rations on the vessel and close my eyes. When I wake, I will face the man who both made and unmade me, and I will face the man who took my Mentor from me. They will have an army to shield themselves from me. But I will have my revenge. Before I rest again, I will hold Castor's head in my hand and Demetrius will beg for forgiveness.

The island juts out of the sea like a mosquito bite. I'm a kilometer away and, even from here, I can see the impossibility of my task. Every meter of the island is under surveillance. Castor has set teams of sentries in concentric circles, with less than twenty meters between each team. Even if I make it through the first circle, there's another, denser circle of soldiers waiting, and then another, and then another.

They will expect a covert attack. Likely at night. Before I decide, I circle the island, completely submerged, trying to find the weakest entry point. Finally, on the extreme eastern rim, I find a sheer cliff face. At least two hundred meters of smooth rock. There will be a sentry at the top, but Castor wouldn't have bothered to have the same density here than at the easier landing points.

I surface my vessel and program coordinates for the front of the island into the autopilot. As the vessel begins to make its way, I dive into the ocean and watch while it submerges, then surfaces every thirty meters. I'm still a mile out, but I figure that by the time the vessel is spotted on the other side of the island, I'll likely be at the cliffs. It's a simple plan, but I hope it will work. While everyone is watching and attacking the empty vessel, I'll be scaling the cliff and silently slipping into the heart of Castor's Army.

If not for the energy field, I would have been ground to a pulp by the surf. Even with it, I'm sustaining quite a bit of damage. Every time I think I have a solid grip on the rock face, I'm either ripped away by a retreating wave, or knocked off balance by a new one. After what feels like twenty attempts, I finally gain a hand hold.

The trick now is to figure out how to start climbing. Without a second arm, and with the field surrounding me, it's virtually impossible to progress. After a few chaotic moments, I redirect the energy into a thin hook and begin probing the cliff above me.

While the field is a warrior's dream weapon, it is a liability on these cliffs. It does not allow me to feel for the best hold, which means I'm basically just hooking it to a ledge and hoping it's caught something strong enough to hold my weight.

I'm halfway up the cliff when my gamble fails. The field hooks on a loose piece of shale and, as I begin to pull my body up, the shale gives way. One second, I'm secured to the cliff and the next, I'm in a free fall. Before I can envelop myself in the energy, my left side smashes against a sharp outcropping. As soon as I feel the impact, I know I've broken at least three ribs and sustained a significant gash. The pain takes my breath away. Just before I hit the water, the field covers me, saving me from the waves.

It takes another series of failed attempts until I'm back on the cliff, clinging against the sea. This time, instead of using the field to pull myself up, I focus it downward, which gives me the ability to see where I want it to grab. Once it's fixed on a secure portion of the rock, I use it to push myself up, where I can find footholds and a strong grip while I reposition the field. Within just a few minutes, I'm three quarters of the way up the cliff. The damage, however, has been done. I can feel the blood dripping down my side and every time I reach up or breathe, my chest ruptures with pain. My eagerness and stupidity have just made an already impossible task even more difficult.

When I'm five meters from the top, I pause, forcing my breathing to slow, listening for any sign of Celcean troops above me. I remain silent for at least five minutes and I hear nothing but the crashing waves far beneath me. Either Castor has left his back unguarded, or the sentries are asleep. Either way, my choice seems to be a sound one.

Slowly, I raise myself so I can peek over the ledge. Nothing. Only a clay and brush covered plateau. The forest line starts about fifteen meters inland. If there are guards, they will be shading themselves in the trees.

The second I am fully on the ridge, I restrict the field into a thick armor. Wasting no time, I crawl through the brush toward the forest. After five meters, the arrows start to glance off me. Judging from the amount of volleys, there's a cluster of six soldiers directly in front of me.

I stand and begin to rush toward them, wanting to take them out quickly, before they can communicate with the rest of the army. Three steps in, I'm struck by an explosive device straight in the chest. The impact sends me flying back and skidding toward the cliff's edge. Desperately, I dissolve the field from around me and dig it into the clay. As soon as I've stopped skidding, I contract the energy again and start rushing toward them. This

390

time I'm sure to vary my direction, speed and height, as I should have the first time. In less than thirty minutes, I have made two beginner mistakes. My reliance on the implant has made me reckless and stupid. Tori wouldn't even recognize me if he were still alive.

Another explosive projectile flies by my head, narrowly missing me, and then another. I'm five meters from the tree line and I can finally see the bunker, dug deep into the ground with an opening just big enough to fit their weapons through. The second I see it, I focus my energy, slicing down and through the opening. The barrage stops instantaneously.

I jump into the bunker and begin searching for a communication device. None. A good sign, but I'm sure the surrounding units heard the explosions and are making their way toward me. My chest is on fire, both from the broken ribs and from the impact of the explosion. I'm lightheaded and I can tell I'm not getting enough air. Likely a punctured lung.

Breaking twigs and rustling trees to my right alert me to a group of five Celceans, all of them armed with automatic rifles designed to shoot jagged chunks of iron faster than the speed of sound. As soon as they see me, they open fire. I'm hit by at least three of the rounds before the field can fully cover me. The impact is so fast that my wounds are cauterized as soon as they're created. One of the projectiles hits what's left of my right arm, shattering the bone and dislocating my shoulder. The other two leave gaping holes in my side and left thigh.

When their first salvo stops, I sweep the field out, decapitating all five in an instant. I drop to a knee as their lifeless bodies crumble to the ground. If this keeps up, I'll be dead well before I make it Castor. My element of surprise is gone and it's clear the Celcean Guard has been given orders to annihilate upon sight. There's no time for planning.

I hear more movement behind me, coming from the interior of the island. The second line of defense is moving toward me. I smile, this army acts just like Castor. Allowing their aggression to subvert their strategy. Let them come. As they move outward, they spread themselves thin, losing the advantage caused by their dense ranks. I pick up one of the rifles and nestle myself into the pile of corpses I just created.

Seconds later, a group of twenty soldiers come crashing through the trees. They stop, observing the carnage. Judging by the shift in their formation, they think I've either left, or am dead. Once all of their weapons have dropped I unload the near molten iron. They're grouped closely enough that one projectile is able to cut through at least three of them. They crumple, dead without ever even seeing me.

I jump up, dropping the empty weapon, and pick up one of the portable missile launchers, as well as a pack of explosive charges and make my way deeper into the island. I don't need to kill them all. I just need to cut a path through them, directly toward the heart of Castor.

There is little strategy to the next few hours. I keep moving; baiting Castor's forces to break rank in their excitement to find me. I kill in clusters, reap new weapons from the dead and re-engage. As I draw nearer to Castor and Demetrius, the quality of soldier increases. Their skill is greater, as is their unwillingness to be baited out of position. I also begin to recognize them. These are the same Hopefuls who used to train under me. It's as if I'm fighting ghosts of myself.

I've stopped using the energy field. The more exhausted I become, the more ineffectual the energy is. Better to save the power for when I face Castor.

The terrain has become familiar as well. As I reposition myself for a more powerful strike, or to better see the movement of a squadron, I recognize remnants of paths I walked with Tori, or nulls on which I sat with Fiona as my arm recovered. These scorched and disfigured spots in the forest scream at me for revenge.

Three hundred more meters and I'll have reached the hospital where Castor has established his base camp. Being this close, I'll need to contend with mines and traps in addition to the best of Castor's soldiers. As if thinking it manifested it, I see a spot of freshly dug soil. Beyond it is another, then hundreds more. In their haste, the Celceans weren't able to disguise the mines well enough. I begin to pick my way through the mines when I hear the unmistakable clicks and shuffles of weapons being prepared to fire.

To my right, a line of soldiers level their rifles at me. Before they can fire, I swing my pack off my shoulder and toss it, aiming for the mine, buried four meters in front of them. It lands perfectly. First there is the thud of the pack, then the terrible, hissing click of the pin dropping on the mine's detonator.

I'm already running, doing my best to avoid activating any more mines, but I know that once one is detonated, the rest will follow suit from the concussion. The first mine explodes sending a cloud of dirt and a spray of shrapnel through the air. I feel pinpricks of searing metal rip through my calves and I can only hope the soldiers have been cut completely down. At the very least, the explosion has obscured me. I feel the concussions of the rest of the mines more than I hear them. Each one draws closer, in spite of my dash to the edge of the field.

I crash into the cover of the forest and dive behind a rotted out tree stump as the last of the mines erupt. Clods of dirt and metal fall on me as I curl into a ball. The only noise I hear is the high pitched ringing of ruptured eardrums. If I could, I would remain here, if only to catch my breath and examine myself for wounds. But the mines have surely alerted the base camp of my proximity. Seconds from now, this section of the island will be crawling with Castor's strongest and most skilled.

If I'm where I think am, there is a small, obscured cave entrance not far from here. Fiona showed it to me on one of our walks. At the time, I was disinterested and irritated at what seemed to be a distraction to my healing. I rise to my knees and scan for the patch of ferns which signify the nearby stream. It takes a couple of seconds to focus my eyes, but as my vision clears, I see them, thirty meters to my right.

My hearing is still incapacitated, so I have no idea how close my enemies are. But I can't be hesitant anymore. I'm on my feet, crashing through the brush before I can consider the implications. Luckily, I make it to the ferns without being spotted. I drop to my stomach and crawl the rest of the way to the stream under the cover of the ferns. Once at the stream, I slide in. The icy bite of the water both invigorates and soothes me as the gentle current nudges my bloody and exhausted body over the smooth pebbles.

The stream bends left, then right, then straightens just before flowing over a gentle waterfall, maybe five meters high. Behind the waterfall is the cave. I slow myself against the bottom of the stream before the waterfall, then allow myself to be carried over. The splash at the bottom is louder than I'd like, but I immediately turn and fight the current until I'm behind the waterfall. Just like Fiona showed me, the small, black entrance awaits, three meters above.

It takes the last of my strength to pull myself through the mud and across the rocks. The inside feels like a tomb, carved perfectly for me. It's oil black, and I'm able to move my arms only a few centimeters before hitting the sides. If this is my tomb, at least Castor will spend the better part of a week trying to find my body. This is the last thought I have before I pass out.

Chapter 61

I'm in Celsus, training with Tori. My body is much smaller and slower than I'm used to. Tori looks at me through clear eyes and speaks through lips which haven't been wrinkled by age.

"You are lazy," he says, as he swings a shinai as hard as he can against my stomach. My wrists are tied together and attached to a chain above my head. The impact of the shinai stings and leaves a welt, but nothing more.

"But I won," I say through a pre-pubescent voice.

"There will be a time when merely winning is not good enough. You will face an adversary with more skills and strength than you. It is the way of life. Youth fades and strength wanes." Another strike, another welt.

"What's the point, then, Moto-San?"

Tori pauses his strike. "The point, General, is to know how you are shaped by the Battle."

Another strike. This one draws blood. I don't wince this time. Rather, I smile. The pain enters me, rather than dissipating. It's as if my body metabolizes it.

"Some are undone by violence. Some shrink with each blow. But there are those who are reborn through the pain. They grow stronger as they are punished. They feast on the abuse, using the punishment of their opponent as an unending spring."

He strikes, and strikes and strikes. Each blow opens fresh wounds and brings greater pain. And every time, my body consumes it. And no matter how much I devour, my craving grows.

These dreams of forgotten times continue while my body tries to recuperate its strength. Each vision is more violent than the next. I wake to the empty blackness of the tiny cave, unsure of how long I've been unconscious. Images of severed limbs, broken bones, deformed faces and lakes of blood continue to tease me while I struggle to regain my grasp on reality.

I try to listen beyond the falling water for Celcean troops, but I'm unable to filter out the current. It's not ideal, but if I want to know what's waiting for me outside, I'll have to leave the security of the cave. Before I start wriggling myself out, I engage the implant, hoping I've recuperated enough to use it effectively. I feel the familiar pulse of energy and heat at the back of my neck. A good sign.

This is it. There will be no more respites. The next time I sleep, it will either bring my death, or it will be after I have seen both Castor and Demetrius defeated. A Battle to end a truewar.

I land at the base of the waterfall with a thud, my legs buckling as my wounds scream their displeasure. The dream of Tori's post-Battle discipline pops into my head again. If I'm to win today, it will be because I'm able to consume the torment raging throughout my body and turn it into strength. He prepared me for this moment from the beginning and I will not allow his tutelage to return void.

The cloud-packed night sky obscures both the moon and stars, which adds to my disorientation. I can't tell if I'm an hour from dawn or an hour after dusk. Regardless, I take a deep breath and sink below the surface of the water, letting the current carry me from under the waterfall. The night is so dark that, even if soldiers were lining the banks, I would be able to slip by unnoticed. If memory serves, the stream will carry me to within fifty meters of Castor's headquarters. If this were any other time, I would revel in the peacefulness of floating down a gentle stream, through a silent forest as the island sleeps. But now, I clear my mind, preparing myself for the fury which is mere minutes away. I can only hope the Celcean Guard has given in to the tranquility of the night. It will make my terrible task much easier.

Tiny lights in the distance are the first indication of my target. Then I hear the voices of sentries, casually discussing the situation. These disembodied sentences float toward me, oblivious of the danger creeping toward them.

"He's dead. No one can live through an explosion like that."

"It doesn't make sense. Why would he come after us by himself?"

"I hear he can't die. The Aegeans gave him some strange serum and now he rejuvenates. Now that they know it works, they've given it to all of their citizens. We're facing an unbeatable force."

"Why does Demetrius want this nation so badly? I think he's going senile."

What I hear pleases me. My campaign of violence and fear is working. Even the most dedicated Celceans have started to question. Demetrius's weave of deception and fear has begun to unravel. All I must do is continue to pull at the frays.

There is a muddy bank up ahead which will turn into an animal trail. The trail runs within just a few meters of the back of the hospital. Along the back of the hospital is an old door, used by the nurses and physicians when they needed to take a moment to clear their minds. This will be my entry point. Even if there are guards, it will likely be the least secured.

I'm out of the water and on the trail in a matter of seconds. There are no signs of the Celcean Guard. In fact, it feels as if they have left this part of the island completely untouched. I push myself along the trail as fast as I can. The dense growth will allow me to surprise them regardless of stealth. As I round a bend on the path, I see signs of a sloppily placed trip-wire, which I easily avoid. A few more meters and I see another. I slip off the trail and follow it from five meters inside the brush, virtually ensuring I won't slip up and trigger one of the explosive devices.

The overgrowth slows me slightly, but not enough to make a significant difference. Three minutes after leaving the stream, I pause in front of the hospital. There is a lone, sleeping sentry at the door. Weak leaders beget weak followers. He dies in his sleep.

The interior of the hospital is exactly how I remember. Sterile and sparse. I encounter a few more Guards as I make my way to the center of the building. They all fall, silently, where they stand. In spite of my rest, I can tell my strength is incredibly low. Each time I reach out with the field, I feel my energy drain. So much, in fact, that I become lightheaded after using the field a third time. I disengage the implant, hoping to recover some strength by the time I find Castor.

As I pass one of the larger rooms, the stench of rotting bodies overwhelms me. Inside, stacked in a sloppy pile are countless bodies of the Aegean physicians who were here when the Celceans made landfall. My stomach turns. Somewhere in that mass of tortured and defiled flesh lay the bodies of Lilith and the countless physicians and nurses who nurtured me back to health. There was no reason for these people to die, just like there was no reason to hunt and dismember the Aegean survivors at sea. This is the fate of the entire nation of Aegea if I fail, and it is the fate of any other nation who chooses to oppose Demetrius ever again.

Just then, a sentry rounds the corner and stops. Shock and terror overtake his face. I rush him before he can draw his weapon or yell for help, sweeping his legs from under him and plunging a knife deep into his throat. There is a low gurgle as he dies. I don't stay to watch, nor do I clean the blood from the blade.

Chapter 62

Castor has turned the main recovery room into his command center. I expected it to be well guarded, but as I approach, I don't see any sentries. He must have ordered them all to join the hunt for me.

Inside the room, Castor and Demetrius huddle over a screen which displays the topography of the island.

"He's most likely hiding in the overgrowth near the minefield," Castor says. "We should just send one of our drones over that quadrant and drop its entire payload. Level everything in that area." There's an excitement in his voice.

"And what message would we be sending? We're so scared of a single man that we're willing to bomb the very piece of land on which we're situated?" Demetrius rebukes, "Remember, the world is watching. And after what happened to your army on the beach, we can't handle another show of weakness."

"What then? Just wait for him to begin assassinating us again? I say we remove any doubt as to his survival and deal with the dissenting nations accordingly. If he's dead, the tiny prince will surrender unconditionally. Trajan is the only hope they have," Castor says.

"You are correct. Our success begins and ends with Trajan. But we must have a body to parade. He's already proven mythical. Without a body, they will always hold on to their hope."

They are silent as they both go back to studying the map. This is my chance to end it all. I engage the implant and focus first on Castor. One fast, decisive strike of pure energy and this entire war will end. My strength is horribly low, but I have just enough left. I'm about to unleash it when, too late to react, I hear a shuffle behind me.

My back ignites as I feel a blade slip through my ribs on my right. I try to turn and face the attacker, but my legs buckle and I slump to the ground.

"Commander," yells the young man standing over me. Castor and Demetrius turn, ready to rebuke him for the interruption. Their faces go from agitation to elation as they see me lying in a pool of my own blood.

Castor steps toward me when Demetrius calls out, telling him to stop. My breath is shallow and I can feel my feet going numb.

"We can use this," he says, as my hearing begins to muffle. I try to focus on the two of them, but my vision begins to blur, then darkness starts to creep in from the sides. No matter how much I force myself to rise, my body cannot match the determination of my will. This is how I die. Not in Battle against a better opponent, but by the silent blade of an insignificant man. I have failed. Tori will not be avenged. Fiona will wake to a world of slavery and degradation. The will of our Ancestors thrown aside by a deceitful tyrant. All of it because I was too stupid and weak to prevent it.

The last thing I see before I black out is the boot of Castor swinging toward my face.

Chapter 63

"This is the man who would oppose me?" The voice of Demetrius rings through the darkness.

I open my eyes against the glaring sun. It takes me a moment to gain my bearings, but I finally see that I'm tied to a pole. Across from me, Castor stands with arrogant assurance while Demetrius paces back and forth. The remnant of the Celcean Army surrounds us.

"This broken, mangled, shadow of a General?" The army listens silently. Above the circle is a minidrone. From its movements, I can tell it has its cameras focused on Demetrius. Ever the showman, this speech is likely being broadcast to every nation.

So I am to be sacrificed as a warning to any Ruler who may think to question Demetrius.

"My heart breaks to see him this way. Clearly, the toll of treachery and deceit has torn him apart. A once mighty and proud General reduced to a skulking assassin serving a scheming nation.

"While Castor and I worked late into the night, trying to find a humane end to this terrible war, started by Aegean greed, this viper slithered into our camp, killing innocent members of my Royal Court. His sights firmly locked on me, he was cut down just in time by the brave actions of one of my personal guard."

The army cheers at the mention of one of their own.

"And what did we find, as we rushed to save Trajan's life? Unable to let him die in spite of his treason? This," he holds up the burnt out implant.

I am undone. Without the implant, there is no way I can weather what I know is to come.

"This technology of war. Designed solely to destroy and wreak havoc at an unprecedented level." He pauses as he spins toward me. "With this, he led an army of lynchmen against our volunteer peacekeepers on the Celcean coast where they terrorized and slaughtered every single one of my countrymen."

I tune him out. He has the upper hand and the world as his stage. He will build his case on lies. Detailing the actions of his own army, but attributing them to me. At the end of his tirade, he will cut me loose and turn Castor on me. My final Battle will serve as a graphic warning through my humiliation and execution.

Rather than listen to him, I study Castor. My pupil. On some level, I must claim this puppet as my creation. When he first came to the training center, he idolized me. Followed me around and tried to emulate everything I did. At first, he was no more than a buzzing fly. But as I saw his talent, annoyance turned to irritation. And when I saw his ambition, I began asserting my dominance in the hopes of crushing any desire for him to usurp me. In my desire to remain unchallenged, I treated him no better than a dog seeking my scraps.

You will face an adversary with more skills and strength than you. Youth fades and strength wanes. The embodiment of Tori's words stands across the makeshift Temple from me, ready to claim his right as successor. Ready to punish me for my arrogance toward him.

More skills than strength. Yes, he has both. But only physically. I think back to the videos of when Tori was champion. Where he would look when he was victorious. He didn't look to his Ruler. He looked to his wife, then his child, then his father. Never his Ruler. It was only when Demetrius took his family from him that Tori lost. And it was only when Marcail valued me for something other than my physical abilities that I questioned my dedication to Demetrius. What does Castor have? The same contingent love from a greedy Ruler.

"But I will not let this conflict be settled through war any longer. We have two champions. Aegea has chosen Trajan. I choose Castor." Demetrius says. "And since Trajan has proven to be the aggressor, I choose the terms. Hand to hand combat. To the death."

Chapter 64

The Celcean Soldiers scream their pleasure as they look to Castor. Across the circle, he hunches over, a raging bull barely able to contain his vengeance.

"To the victor, immortality. To the victor, the world," Demetrius yells. A soldier on the left pulls a knife and slices the ropes which holds me to the pole. Once the ropes are severed, I stumble into the circle, struggling to keep my balance. My foot catches on a root and I crash to the ground, landing on my severed and shattered right arm. In spite of everything Tori has taught me, I'm unable to hide the pain which radiates through me.

I roll to my left and push myself to an unsteady defense stance just before Castor crashes into me. The soldiers cheer again as I slide across the dusty ground. His hit was perfectly placed to exploit my broken ribs. If my lung wasn't already collapsed, it is now.

He stands above me with raised fists, soaking in the adoration of his makeshift Crowd. Where will he look at the end of this Battle? Demetrius will shower him with praise and give him every fleeting pleasure he desires, but there will come a time when Castor's hands are slower and his ability to recuperate will be less certain. There may even be a time when Demetrius turns jealous over how much the Crowd loves him. Who will he turn to then? As I look at this perfectly designed usurper, I fully embrace the truth. He is too powerful and my wounds are too extensive. I will lose this fight. But when I do, my last thought will be of the lessons Tori shared with me. The quiet confidence Marcail had in me. The tender, unselfish love of Fiona. When I die, it will be with a full understanding of the thing I missed out on as a General, and gratitude that I finally learned them, even as the world fell apart.

"Your cowardice is revealed by your weakness," Castor bellows. "Rise! At least give me the satisfaction of killing you while you're standing."

The noise of the tiny Crowd begins to die down as they try to hear Castor's taunts.

I push myself to my knees, "What then, Castor? Will my death finally vindicate you?"

He shifts his weight and lands a sloppy kick against the side of my head. There is no technique to the strike. My weakened state, in his opinion, does not call for precision or guardedness. Even still, the force of the blow sends me back into the dust.

"Will this victory make the Crowd love you more?" I ask as I rebound to a crouch.

Another kick. More powerful, less accurate. It's not enough to knock me off balance. His anger and greed have taken over. If I were at half strength, his sloppiness would be enough for me to win handily. As he steps back, gathering strength for another strike, I lift myself to full height. The strikes have ignited my adrenaline. In place of pain, I can feel a primeval strength rushing through me.

"What will it say about you when you lose to a lame, weakened, and dishonored General?" I rumble. If the soldiers are cheering, I do not hear them. There is only Castor and me on this island.

I strike with my left hand. Only a jab, but it serves to measure his distance and reflexes. Castor's head snaps back and a trickle of blood drips from a nostril. Another jab causes him to step back. This would be when I would follow up with a crushing right fist, but Castor took that from me.

Instead, I throw another quick jab, which Castor slaps away. But it served its purpose to focus his defenses higher. Before he realigns himself, I stomp with my left leg, focusing the full force of my weight into my heel as it thrusts into his knee. The blow hyperextends his joint, forcing it to bend backward. I hear a crack. Either shredded ligaments in his knee, or a broken bone.

Castor's face contorts briefly as he stumbles back, but he's able to regain composure quickly. Regardless, I can see by the way he stands that his leg is no longer useful. "Resorting to the tricks of a child," he says.

"Still fooled by the tricks of a child," I say.

He looks to his right and motions for one of the soldiers to throw him a weapon. A second later, he charges, thrusting and swinging a titanium tipped spear with vicious accuracy. Even with a hobbled leg, he is faster than me. Within seconds, he's opened a gash across my stomach, almost severed my right ear and impaled me through the right shoulder. I fall back with the spear still stuck in my joint, which rips the shaft from his hands.

No time for pain, I pull the tip from my body, causing a brief shower of blood, and refocus the tip at Castor. He's not able to pivot quickly on his injured leg and his momentum causes the spear to pierce him through his trapezius. Six centimeters to the left and I would have severed his jugular.

He steps back, releasing the spearhead from his flesh and pauses. I'm on my back in full guard, weapon leveled at him, leg cocked and ready to snap his other knee. Blood begins to seep through his shirt, dying the fabric in crimson rivers.

We stay in this stalemate for longer than either of us should, using the faceoff as an excuse to catch our breath. It's clear neither of us expected the fight to last this long. The initial rush of adrenaline is beginning to wear off. I struggle to keep the spear pointed at Castor. If he waits long enough, I will likely just bleed out in front of him.

He kicks his foot through the dust, blinding me with a grainy cloud of sand. I blink, trying to clear the particulates, but he pounces before my vision returns.

Grappling has always been a strong suit, but without one of my arms, and with so many shattered ribs, I'm quickly outmatched. He takes my back and secures a deep chokehold against my chin while simultaneously wrapping his legs around my ribcage and squeezing. My chest feels as if someone has injected each organ with acid. It's so intense that I don't realize how deep the chokehold actually is. Within moments, however, my vision begins to blur into boiling bursts of light.

It's a dirty trick, but my only recourse is to reach for the soft, tender flesh inside Castor's thighs, millimeters below his groin and, with my fingernails, pinch and twist the smallest portion I can grip. Castor arches his back in an attempt to overcome the animal instinct triggered by an attack on such a vulnerable area. Just before I lose consciousness completely, his instinct wins, causing him to relax both his arms and legs and squirm away.

As I gasp for breath and wait for the pain in my chest to subside, I can't help but smile. That pinch was the first thing Tori ever taught me. *No matter how strong a man grows, Child, his fear of losing his masculinity will always be stronger.*

This is likely my last chance to gain the upper hand. If I'm to win, I can't let him continue to be the aggressor. With my chest still screaming in agony, I grasp the spear and use it to stand. Castor's massive back is to me as he struggles to stand on his wounded leg.

My aim is true, but my strength is lacking. The spear pierces his flesh but catches on one of his ribs. If I were stronger, the thrust would have penetrated his heart and burst through the front of his chest. I pull back and aim for his right kidney. Without a ribcage to stop it, the spear plunges deeper. I feel the gentle opposition of the organ before it succumbs.

Castor arches his back and falls forward. It's not an immediate kill shot, but I've released a significant amount of waste into his body. Each tiny blow steals a bit of his might. A few more well placed shots and our strength will have evened out.

I back the spear out again and bring it down on his ankle with a scooping motion. The tip digs in behind the Achilles and, with a flick of my wrist, the giant tendon frays.

His right knee is blown and his left Achilles is severed. Another of Tori's lessons comes back to me. *If he can't stand, he can't fight.* Castor could stand at this point, but he won't be able to attack and he'll barely be able to defend. My adrenaline surges again as I see the improbable victory inch closer. I take aim for the tiny point where his skull meets his spine. One more shot and the Battle is over, along with Castor's bloody campaign. I plunge the spear and feel the gentle pop which signifies the rending of his spine. Castor is dead, unable to command this army any longer. Before I can pull the spear from his body, I feel a thud on my chest. Then another in my shoulder. A third hits my arm, knocking the weapon from my hand. I look to where the first thud struck to see a gaping hole with blood pouring from it. Another dull thud in my leg snaps the confusion from me. I'm not in the Temple and this isn't a Battle. I'm standing in the middle of a circle of my enemies and I've killed their commander. Demetrius was never going to let me win this Battle.

I look around, expecting to see every soldier with a weapon pointed at me, awaiting the death-dealing signal. Instead, I see confusion and rage. I also see the majority of them looking not at me, but in the direction of Demetrius. I follow their collective gaze to see him with a rifle leveled at me, the barrel oozing smoke.

Before he can fire another round, one of the soldiers closest to him reaches out and wrestles the weapon away. The same soldier then pushes Demetrius toward me. I'm too far away to hear his exact words, but the rest of the army begins yelling their agreement. If Demetrius will not honor the rules he set for his General, then he must become the General.

He raises his hands, calling for the soldiers to calm. After a few attempts, they begin to quiet. My wounds are so numerous, I can't tell where one ends and another begins. Just standing here takes every bit of my strength and focus.

"Please!" Demetrius yells. "Protectors of Celsus, give me your ears." His eyes are wide with fear, but I can tell that he gains confidence with each word.

I begin to inch toward him, knowing how important it is to strike before he's able to spin his words and win back the allegiance of these men.

"I understand your confusion," he implores, "but you must understand Trajan's treachery and talent the way I do. This is a man who has never been matched. Physically and mentally, he is a God among men. The only time he has been beaten was when his loyalty to something greater was questioned. When it came time for him to sacrifice himself for the sake of his nation, he chose himself. And in so doing, he invited a wolf into our pasture." The soldiers listen quietly, but they're not completely under his spell.

"You respect him because of his strength. How could you not? Even at a fraction of his true ability he has undone your commander. And you question my interruption of this impromptu Battle. As do I. Even as I leveled the rifle, it was as if I could hear our Ancestors calling to me. Pleading for me to allow the Battle to do its job." There are tears in his eyes as he mentions the Ancestors. "And yet, the Ancestors could have never planned for one as powerful as Trajan. They certainly never expected someone as dominant as him to turn against the Ruler he swore to represent. So I took drastic and decisive action. Maybe it was wrong. But maybe it was the lone act of desperation that will save this world from the continued ravages of war. I'm willing to submit myself to an inquisition. But I must live if there is to be an investigation. If you turn me over to this feral lion, he will never allow me to stand trial."

I've drawn to within ten meters of him. If I had any strength left, I would rush him and end his incessant talking one final time. As it is, I can barely stay upright.

"Enough," I roar. In spite of a severely damaged lung, the words travel with power, causing the soldiers to turn from him. "No more twisted speeches, peppered with half-truths and rotten pseudo-confessions." I spin around, making eye contact with as many soldiers as I can. "He makes the issue too complicated. This is not a question of my strength. It is a matter of principle. Our Ancestors gave us a simple way for nations to settle their differences. One man against another. Winner take all. For years, the stakes were high enough for Rulers to shy away from entering into Battle. But then Demetrius found me, and he saw an opportunity to exploit my abilities. I blindly followed him into Battle after Battle, confused by the implied tyranny of foreign Rulers, but convinced of his dedication to help the citizens of this world. And he was happy to work within the structure of the Ancestors while his reign crept across the planet.

"Then I lost. And his acceptance of the Ancestor's system crumbled. At his first opportunity, he declared the rules to be faulty. And he continues to do so. My only question, Demetrius," I turn and lock gazes with him, "why were the rules sound when I was winning? What was it about my loss which revealed such terrible error to justify immediate and lawless truewar?"

The soldiers are silent as they consider my question, as is Demetrius. I think about the drone, high above us, and pray Demetrius has left the feed open. Regardless of what happens on this island, I hope I'm giving William the argument he needs to rally the rest of the nations to his side.

"And you," I turn to the soldiers, "you are guilty of the same mindless obedience as me. If I had been brave enough to question Demetrius earlier, he would not have grown so powerful, or greedy. Our unwavering faith has given him unabated license to wreak destruction.

"I realized, after my Mentor was killed in front of me, and my arm was taken, my error. The only power Demetrius had when I was his General was the power I unwittingly granted him. And the only strength he has now lies with your naive obedience. Lay down your weapons and end this."

Demetrius's face contorts and he springs toward me, pulling a perfectly polished knife from the folds of his clothes. He aims the blade for my chest as he closes the gap between us faster than I can react. I can feel my body try to respond, but it's sluggish with fatigue and abuse. My left shoulder rolls back in an attempt to shield my heart from the metal. As I fall, I feel the blade enter at the perfect angle to miss my ribs and continue its destructive path through me. The knife plunges until the handle grinds against my flesh, then the weight of Demetrius is on me. We crumble to the ground as he dislodges the blade and thrusts again. What he lacks in accuracy, he makes up for in speed and power. Again and again the blade slices through me. He pauses briefly, straddling me with the blade poised above my face.

"Thus ends the mighty Trajan. I made you and now I unmake you." As the last word escapes his mouth, I see a hole open in his skull above his left eye. Then another above his right. His eyes fully dilate as his body goes limp. The knife slips from his hand, corkscrewing its way toward my face. The tip gashes into my cheek, then skids off the bone as Demetrius falls across me.

My fingers and toes begin to tingle, then go numb. There is simply not enough blood left to saturate my body. After my digits, my arms and legs feel as if they're dissolving from my body. It is fitting. I have seen Castor defeated and Demetrius killed. There is nothing left for me to accomplish. My only hope, as my vision blurs and my lungs fill with the last drops of my blood, is that this world will be able to recover from Demetrius's greed, Castor's jealousy and my weakness.

Chapter 65

Before anything else, I hear the surf crashing methodically against the sand, sending foamy waves higher onto the shore with every ripple. I notice the sun, blinding even through closed eyes. There is a slight breeze haphazardly lifting and dropping the excess fabric of my clothing. Then I hear murmuring voices, caught individually by the wind, then spun into an incomprehensible chant.

I'm alive. Incomprehensibly, I am alive.

I open my eyes against the sun and try to sit up. A strong yet gentle hand rests against my chest.

"I would advise against moving."

I can't see who restrains me and I can't tell from his voice whether he's addressing me as my physician, or captor.

"If I haven't died from my myriad wounds, I don't think I will die from sitting," I say, trying to shrug off his hand.

"You did die from your wounds. Three times, in fact. I'm not a physician. Just a field medic, but I know enough to assure you that any sort of movement requires more strength than even you possess."

"Three times?" I ask, closing my eyes again and lying back.

"Your heart had stopped when we pulled Demetrius off you. An hour later, your heart stopped again as I was pulling shrapnel out of you. And earlier this morning, you began convulsing before you flatlined."

"What is your name?"

"Augustus. I trained under you before all of this."

I smile. "Forgive me for not recognizing your voice. It appears that I will be in your debt for my next three lifetimes."

"Your biggest issue is your blood loss. Both initially and currently. If you're indebted to anyone, it is the soldiers whose blood flows in your veins."

I open my eyes again as Augusts shields them from the sun. There are multiple IVs inserted into my arms and thighs, each of them attached to a soldier. Behind each soldier is another, all waiting to give me a portion of their blood.

"You're still losing almost as much blood as you're getting. I'm just not skilled enough to sew up all of the internal and external wounds. If we can't find a more skilled physician, I fear this will only delay your death."

"How long since?" I'm unable to put a name to the fight between Castor, Demetrius and myself.

"Two days," Augustus says.

"Have you heard from anyone? The Aegeans?"

"No."

"Take me to the command room," I say. If the drone wasn't broadcasting the fight, then the world is unaware of the demise of Demetrius and Castor. I was hoping William would have seen what happened, but even if he did, he would have no way of knowing if it would be safe for him to come out of hiding. Even now, I don't know the answer to that question.

The trip to the command center is painful. We have to stop twice because of my IVs being ripped out while the soldiers attached to the other side try to match the pace of my cot being carried. I pass out once during the procession.

They place me next to the communication console. "Before I contact Prince William," I say, "who controls this army?"

Without hesitation, Augustus says, "You."

"Me?"

"You know better than me, General. Celcus is a nation of warriors. You defeated our commander and our Ruler, which makes you the new Ruler."

My stomach turns at the thought, but there are more pressing matters. "In that case, if I contact the Aegeans, I command the army to stand down. This war is over."

"Very good, Sir," he says.

I program William's frequency and wait for the connection. Within seconds, I hear William's voice.

"My prince," I say. "It is finished. Come quickly to your Healing Island. Bring as many physicians as you can. There will be no more bloodshed."

"It's over? What of Demetrius?"

My head begins to swim. The exertion of even this simple task is too much. "Just come." My hand slips, severing the link with William and I black out again.

Chapter 66

The next few days are spent the same. Waking briefly, trying to fight through my weakness, but succumbing every time. Each time I regain consciousness, Augustus is by my side. We cover as much as we can. He asks me if I have any orders for the soldiers. I do my best to help him keep order. If I'm not able to recover quickly, however, they will grow restless. I fear what they will do if I'm not able to regain my strength quickly.

"They are good men, General. Most of them learned under you. They are loyal and obedient." Augustus says.

"Loyalty and obedience are only virtuous if they individually possess a moral rudder. From what I've seen, these men would follow whatever current is strongest at the time."

He bows his head, either unable or unwilling to argue.

"Cut the rations by a quarter until we can establish a better system of hunting," I say. While my blood loss remains, Augustus and I have fallen into a comfortable rhythm. He is my mouthpiece and my ears. While I rest, he compiles the needs of the army and brings me the most pressing issues. Once I make a decision, he then ensures my orders are carried out. "If you find any soldier hoarding additional food, he is to be whipped and denied all nourishment, save water, for a week."

"It will be done, sir," Augustus says. "There is still the matter of ordnance disposal."

"The best way to get rid of them is to detonate them. But we must wait until the Aegeans arrive, so they don't think a war still wages. Continue to guard the stockpiles. Make a count twice a day, at varying times."

"The Aegeans?" William's voice echoes off the sparse walls. "You speak as if we are aliens." While his voice is light, I can tell by his walk that he is on edge. The Aegean Guards around him have their hands on their weapons and take stock of every person in the room.

I do my best to face him while still lying on my back. "My prince. You voice is a sweet melody," I say, then gesture toward Augustus, "may I present my second in command, Augustus. He will see you are taken care of and unharmed."

They nod to each other. Then Augustus says, "Have you brought a physician? The General's wounds are dire."

William's smile fades as he beckons Katrina, the same physician who tended Fiona after the beach skirmish.

She steps through the guards and smiles at me. "Good to see you're still alive."

"I guess this is the toll of doing something outlandish," I say.

Katrina blushes at the memory of how she rebuked me. "Next time, I should be a little more careful when giving pep talks."

Augustus clears his throat, "We keep giving him blood, but he keeps losing it. The best I can guess is that he has serious internal bleeding. Even some of the surface wounds are too severe for me to close completely."

She nods, "You did well with what you have. Is there a sterile room? This amount of damage will require quite a bit of surgery."

Augustus says, "Most of the operating rooms were converted to serve other purposes when Demetrius took over. I've been able to restore one." He gestures to a small door on the south side of the room.

I tune them out as they discuss what instruments they need. Instead, I glance to William, "Fiona?"

He smiles, "Recovering. Her first words upon waking were of you as well." He shifts his weight a bit, then continues, "Forgive me for turning to politics so quickly, but we have been in the dark since the feed of your Battle with Castor went dark halfway through."

Katrina injects a clear liquid into my IV. It tingles as it enters by blood. "You'd better answer quickly. You'll be out in less than a minute."

"Demetrius and Castor are dead," I say through slurred lips. "While either dead or unconscious, I was deemed Ruler of Celcus. Augustus has the recording of the rest." My eyes roll back and, as I slip into a drug induced blackness once again, I wonder if there will be a time when I will lay my head on a soft pillow and drift into a sleep brought about by peace, rather than necessity.

Epilogue

"Why did you pick such a difficult robe?" Fiona asks playfully. The scars across her face wrinkle as her smile bends them. She sighs as she tries to thread a button through the fabric on the right side of my robe. "It's amazing how difficult simple tasks become when you're missing two fingers."

I laugh, and hold up the stump of my right arm. "Want to trade?"

She shoves me, "Always have to one up me."

I watch as she crosses the room. Her walk is less fluid than before her injures. Where she used to flow through rooms, she's more mechanical now. But she is no less graceful.

"This couldn't have come at a worse time," I say. We are in the Temple, preparing to watch a series of the first exhibition Battles since The Celcean Rebellion. That's what the world has named Demetrius's War.

"Still worried about the rebellion?"

"The longer they're out there, the more ammunition the Celcean Senators have." A small group of Castor's Army is still at large. At last report, they were trying to establish a stronghold on a remote Aegean island.

"Augustus will find the soldiers. He hasn't let you down yet. And the Senators do nothing more than rattle their sabers. No one would think to challenge your leadership of Celsus. Especially after," her voice trails off.

After I recovered from my surgery on Medical Island, the first thing I did was to identify the soldiers who participated in the execution of Aegeans at sea. Once they were found, I whipped, then banished, each one to sea with only a week's provisions. This was all broadcast so the rest of the nations could see. When I was convinced I had dealt with all of the participants, I formally disbanded Castor's Army. The severity with which I handled the soldiers still bothers Fiona.

"I could leave no doubt," I say, then drop it. We have argued enough about matters of state. "These Battles feel forced. Haven't we had our fill of fighting?"

She turns and offers an embrace. It is still odd to so easily accept her affection, but it is equally delightful. "We must show the citizens that the principles of the Ancestors still hold. As backward as it seems, if we were to shy away from Battles in this Temple, we would be leaving the doors open for other, more vicious ways of solving our issues."

The last time I was in this Temple, I watched as Tori's head was sliced from his body. It is an image I can't remove and it seems to grow more powerful the longer I'm here. But Fiona is right. Of all of the people in this building, my absence would be the most conspicuous.

"Representatives from most of the nations I conquered as General have formally requested their independence," I say.

"That may not be a bad thing. It would go a long way in acknowledging the wrongs of Demetrius."

It would also be an admission of how Demetrius used me to fulfill his desires. I don't say this. Rather, I say, "Yes. I've been thinking about how I could help them as they transition into new leadership."

We discuss these things as if they are the things normal people consider as they prattle about their houses.

"Who would have thought," Fiona says as she pins her radiant hair in a twist that follows the perfect curve of her neck and across her shoulder, "as a General you conquered under the guise of peace, but as a Ruler you liberate under the truth of reconciliation."

Maybe this is the start of wisdom. Undoing the evils which were perpetrated through manipulation. If Tori were here, he'd likely rouse me from such mutterings with a perfectly placed strike. Let others ponder the wisdom in the actions of Rulers.

"Spring is coming. I've been thinking about asking William if we could spend the season on one of his farming colonies. It would be nice to feel dirt on my fingers and the sea underneath me again."

Made in the USA
Monee, IL
09 June 2023

35544627R00256